CITY

OF

DREAMS

CITY OF DREAMS

Suzanne Burkett

Second Edition

ISBN-979-8-9871346-2-7
Library of Congress Control Number: 2022922581

City of Dreams

Contact: PO Box 5656, Incline Village, NV 89450

Second Edition

For my son Eagle Star

Acknowledgements

This book was completed with the effort and support of the
following brilliant people:
My husband, Pete Burkett, thank you will never be enough for
your patience, persevering provision, and meticulous toil on the
cover design.
To my son, Dustin for your strength of spirit. And to the precious
young souls, and their mother, that you have brought into my
life.
With sincere thanks to, Elaine Greynald Van Fossen for always
being my first reader and a lifelong friend and companion along
the varied paths of life. Thanks for untangling my plot lines.
Thank you to Janell Balfour for your kinship and reading with a
kind and unbiased opinion. I am always happy to see you.
To all my family and friends living across the country and
around the world, you know who you are. Sharing the earth
with you has enriched my life more than you can ever know. My
appreciation is eternal.

Bishop, Morris. *The Middle Ages. American Heritage Inc.,* 1968, 1996.

Singman, Jeffrey L. *The Middle Ages: Everyday Life in Medieval Europe.* Sterling Publishing New York, 2013.

Calvino, Italo. *Invisible Cities.* Harcourt Inc., 1974.

Hudson, Ph.D., LL. D, Thomas J. *The Law of Psychic Phenomena: A Working Hypothesis for the Systematic Study of Hypnotism, Spiritism, Mental Therapeutics, Etc.* A. C. McClurg & CO, 1908.

Wikipedia. www.wikipedia.org.

TransCreative Software. *Wordbook Dictionary: English Dictionary & Thesaurus.* Available on the App Store for IOS devices. #127 in Reference.

My Dreams.

Whispers from the Earth.

Table of Contents

Prologue

She told him, "As you know, not all men will keep the oaths they make. Weakness it is etched upon their faces and reflected in the hollow beam of their eyes. You are not like those men. You are one of the few, the fierce, a rare creature who burns with inner fire."

"I am not special. I only desire a life of meaning."

"You must remain wary. Evil lurks at the crimson edges of this city's cobbled streets. Many turn from the path placed before them. Some seek their own way in the world, no matter the cost." The woman turned her back and stoked the already blazing fire. He closed his eyes hoping to find her gone when he opened them. The flames hissed and his eyes shot open. She shook her head. You came to talk about dreams. I hear many dreams. I have my own dreams. I can't remember every dream someone tells me."

He glanced down at the slanted, dirt floor and wondered how it could appear so clean. "But will you tell me what they mean? I don't know if I can understand for myself, the words; *Come and find me . . .come and find me . . . find me and take me with you.*"

She stared at him until a clammy shiver made his skin tighten. His whole body hurt. He struggled to stand, but she stopped him with a deflective flick of her hand. "It means there is still time for you and all that you want. I know you still remember the day that you came here as a young lad. Close your eyes again. What did you say?"

As he obediently closed his eyes, he wished he hadn't come, now or ever. He reached out, clawing the air for something to grasp onto. Incense wafted above him. His eyes refused to open now as if heavy silver coins had been placed upon the lids.

"Do you want my help or not?" she hissed.

I don't remember," he gasped. "So much has happened. I wanted to get out of here. I saw a cloaked figure in your crystal ball." His eyes ached. "You stopped me from seeing more."

"Tell me what you will do."

He fought against the words, but they spilled from his lips. "I'll go walk among the stones with their ancient memories and become one of those memories myself."

She said, "You are swirling beneath the waves of the sea. But it doesn't matter, you can breathe anyway." The coins fell away, and he woke up. Deep in the night the nightmare left him, and he pulled back the covers and slipped out of his bed. Wearing breeches, but shirtless, he struggled with the latch. The cold metal bruised his hand. Swearing, he yanked the heavy door open and flung himself into the consuming cold.

Outside the air choked him; the street was as dark as a charred log. He ran a few paces toward nothing. The sudden silence sidestepped him and quickly the voice in his dream returned. Someone wanted to be found. *What does it mean*, he wondered. *And who was that haughty woman who frequently invaded his dreams?* She was not anyone he would ever want to meet. As he walked, he imagined her eerie cottage and hesitated. What if he were to come upon it?

A deep stiffness had set into his muscles, and he felt that despite the rain his bones had dried up beyond repair. His tired steps lacked urgency, there was no chance of seeing anyone outside this late, he alone could not sleep.

Lately when he slept, he went far away into a world of images and encounters that made no sense in the waking world. The rain came down heavier as he tried to elucidate his recollection of dreams, but the world looked blurry from the rain, or maybe from the spirits.

With nowhere to go, he stopped, stood still, and waited for whatever may come. *Where do you go? I don't know. I drift from here to there.* He had no answers for himself. He ached for something but knew not what. Peering into darkness chilled his vacant soul.

He turned his somber face toward home. *Something follows me,* he thought. His own steps echoed behind him. I'm not the same and never will be. Up ahead he saw the candle waver in his window like a long overdue welcome. He saw swirling images, and felt the astounding energy of a hug, a never-ending embrace that began with a man and a woman walking side by side and beholding the beauty surrounding them. He saw a place where alone was no longer necessary, or even a choice. And as he did, he realized that his incessant heartache was dissipating, and a new but unfathomable feeling would replace it.

Chapter 1

Orange torches flickered above the tall grass leaving sparked trails against the black sky. A clamor of voices called her name, a name Lucas rarely heard until this darkest of nights. She was Linnea but he'd known her as Mama. In the wavering light, eerie faces drooped into misshapen monsters. Farmers wielding pitchforks and clanging shovels blocked his every turn. Fingers clawed his tattered shirt as he darted between them. And when they found her, they spoke to her as if she would respond. The entire village wanted to drag him away from the field, to prevent him from throwing himself down onto that spot where she died. He had lain there too, and now all he wanted to do was follow her to wherever she had gone. The women placed blankets over her, because she was cold, he knew, and he also knew the blankets could not warm her. If she was able to come back, he would have already made that happen. He ran and ran until the smoky flames reached his clothes and swallowed him into soundless screams. His mother lay dead beside him. Their flowers, yarrow stalks, lavender, and tansy crushed beneath her. In her last moments Lucas and his mother were reaching for each other, but their hands never touched.

He awoke and rolled to his side clawing at his throat where damp hair had roped around his neck. In daylight hours, Lucas couldn't remember what happened to his mother on that sunny afternoon. They were together. Some days he remembered her warm breath on his neck, but when he tried to dig into that memory his eyes ached, and his head throbbed. Ever since then when he lay himself down to sleep, he felt the presence of a shrouded figure lurking in the shadows at the edge of his bed. It beckoned as it held open the door to the hollow space through which his mother fell. And then the nightmare slipped in.

Lucas pushed himself up from the warmth of his feather bed and pressed his palms against his eyes to block the glaring daylight. It was the morning of his tenth anniversary at the boarding house. Mrs. Kempel had promised a special surprise. If her calculations were correct, he was in his twenty-third year of life. It was—he had told her on his first or second night at the Kempel Boarding House—three summers since the death of his mother. Making her assumption from that information and his height and disposition, among other things, she determined he would have been thirteen years old when she found him. Each year since then, they celebrated the day they had met: the 24th day of March 1660.

At first, he looked forward to her plans each year, now that he was older and still battling the nagging nightmares, he'd prefer to ignore the occasion. But he would not deprive her of her celebration. He remembered that night, ten years ago, when Mrs. Kempel decided to rescue him from the street and provide him with a home. He marveled even then how a solitary widow could maintain a prosperous business. Now she felt to Lucas like a substitute mother, but not a replacement. Lucas respected Mrs. Kempel the moment she stepped in and saved him. He admired her then and now, if he thought about it, he could say he loved her. But he didn't feel that inexplicable pull of instinct that recognizes the blood of a kindred soul. Yet, a warmth and ease encircled their relationship. He did all he could to protect and repay Mrs. Kempel for taking him in, and he intended to always do so.

His own mother of course lost in that field forever. His hands bunched into tight fists. As in the nightmare, on the day that she died, Lucas and his mother had filled their baskets with lavender, yellow tansy, wild pink thyme, and the white flowered yarrow. Upon awakening in that flower field, next to the breathless body of his mother, he clutched bunches of tansy between his fingers. Since then, the contentment he'd glimpsed for a moment as a child eluded his grasp. Swinging his feet to the cold wood floor, Lucas went to the window and gazed down to the street below crowded with people. Running his hand through his hair he swallowed and relaxed his face. Everyone wore these false faces; his fellow citizens also masked their struggles.

This knowledge allowed Lucas to enjoy the ease of his days and the allure of the evenings when he went to work lighting the lanterns throughout the city. He began his rounds when the evening church bells rang, and craftsmen, laborers, shopkeepers, artisans, and patrons made their way home. He observed the inhabitants as they hurried to their dwellings before dark. Once ensconced in the safety of their homes, with candles and oil lamps lit, their personal activities provided entertainment for Lucas. Dusk brought a hush to the normally bustling narrow city streets. Knowing the habits of the wealthy, from whence they came and went, had also provided profitable gain over the years.

In the sunlit room, he filled his washstand from the large water pitcher and mopped himself with a linen cloth. Fragments filtered through his mind. His mother's face appeared. He dropped the cloth and braced himself against the stand, squeezing his eyes shut to keep his last sight of her, young, beautiful, and alive. And then the dream came flooding back. They were carrying the woven baskets she'd made from twisting and bending willow branches. He'd wandered ahead and when he turned around to see if she was following, she reached out her hand to him. But as he darted back, leaping over lupine's and scrub brush she collapsed among the flowers. Droplets formed on his forehead, the back of his neck felt hot and his head began to throb as he realized, in this latest nightmare, she did something she could not have done that day. She whispered to him: *The lock is the key*.

A man shouted, and a dog barked in the street. The memory of the dream vanished like patchy mist. Lucas straightened and looked around the room as if seeing it for the first time. The furniture appeared larger and brighter. Sunlight sprayed the floor with a tiny leaf pattern from the budding willow — the reason he had chosen this bedroom — that swayed with a contented rustle outside his window. The air smelled earthy after last night's downpour. He felt keenly aware of his arms and legs, his hair drying quickly as it hung around his face felt soft and light. Lucas allowed a smile to emerge from within a place long forgotten and barely known. The essence of his long-lost mother held him in a gentle trance until the dog yipped again. His hand groped the air, but he could not hold the moment. Irritation returned as he circled the room picking up items of clothing strewn about the floor. He had dreamed about his mother often in the thirteen years since she died. But never before had she spoken to him. He grabbed a pair of stockings and breeches and pulled them on along with a loose-sleeved shirt.

An assortment of aromas arose from the kitchen: roast mutton, fresh baked sugar bread, and a variety of herbs. Lucas hoped Mrs. Kempel was alone, so he could tell her about the revealing nightmare. After all these years, a message had finally come from his mother. The only lock he remembered from his childhood secured his mother's trunk. But he had no idea where his mother's possessions went after she died. Of course, he was too young then to think of such things. Still, the thought that his mother had possibly hidden something for him warmed his vacant heart. And in all practicality, he hoped that if not an answer to how she died, that it was silver, gold, or jewels.

Mrs. Kempel bustled around the large kitchen. He could hardly see her among the shelves stuffed with copper pots and pans, metal food bins and colorful glass bottles of various shapes and sizes.

She peeked through a row of shelves, "Well there you are! You had me worried that you would sleep right through your special day. I've already been to market. We have cheese for our picnic. The bread is in the basket and the roast is cooling." She squeezed his face between her damp hands and planted a kiss on his cheek. "Let's open the door and help it along."

Lucas crossed the large parlour and opened the front door then returned to the kitchen and took a seat at the long plank table.

"Did you sleep well?" concern puckered her normally cheerful face.

"It didn't feel that way when I woke up." He accepted the cup of tea that Mrs. Kempel handed him.

"Ah, another nightmare. I hope you feel rested enough. We will have a nice long day together. Did you tell the lad to take your shift for you tonight? We don't want the city in darkness," she laughed and placed a plum pie in front of Lucas. "Anniversary blessings my boy," she said with tears rimming her eyes. She patted them with the edge of her apron and plopped down beside him.

Lucas gave Mrs. Kempel a gentle embrace. That night long ago, a jewelry merchant, along with the servant of a wealthy client had a fierce hold on Lucas' arms. They were dragging him to the constable under the accusation of stealing. Lucas squirmed, kicked, shouted, and cursed. Even in his struggle, he saw Mrs. Kempel bow her head and hurry past. But she hesitated and sneaked a peek at him. Later, she confessed his wild dirty hair and long-lashed wet eyes evoked compassion. She understood his anguish and chose to save him from an unscrupulous fate. She followed the men to the constable and fabricated a most eloquent lie to convince them that Lucas was the son of one of her boarders, and that they would tend to his punishment. It was that elaborate lie that made Lucas realize he could live with this woman.

"Let's enjoy this wonderful pie together," he said as he shoved a piece into his mouth.

"Are you well enough then?" she asked.

"Yes, ma'am. It's going to be a fine day," he said, pushing the memory of the nightmare from his mind. Mrs. Kempel had worked hard to make this anniversary special. He didn't want to ruin it by talking about his mother. Feeling much like the young boy she had taken in years ago, he said, "Will you tell me about the surprise now?"

Mrs. Kempel finished chewing her pie, gulped her tea, and grinned like a mischievous child. "Lucas, for the anniversary of the day I saved you from a life on the street, in prison, or worse, we are going to look into your future."

"The day you saved yourself from a life of lonely tedium caring for strangers," Lucas corrected with a chuckle.

"The day we saved each other from our fates," Mrs. Kempel interjected.

"Yes, dear woman, agreed. You have my gratitude and eternal loyalty. Now, please tell me what the surprise is."

"I'm taking you to see the fortuneteller, Madam Trousdale." Her eyes sparkled as she popped another bite of pie into her mouth.

"What?" Lucas barked. He started to stand but the bench wobbled, and Mrs. Kempel had to grip the table edge to stop herself from falling backward. "Excuse me," he grumbled as he steadied the bench, sat down, and poked at his pie. A fortuneteller was the last person he wanted to see. He knew where that lot lived and nothing good had ever come to him from the dark zone, a neighborhood at the edge of the city that as the lantern lighter, he had no requirement to visit. However, as a young boy, the one who Mrs. Kempel liberated, he had spent most of his time in that part of the city. He slept in ditches behind abandoned huts, and sometimes under the table in a dim lit tavern if nobody noticed him. He learned everything he knew about stealing in the dark zone. Gypsies and pickpockets had taught him lessons he had used to survive on his own, but he had no wish to revisit that part of his past even though those lessons still served him well today. His prospects had changed since then. His fingers drummed the table as he considered how to grapple with the unexpected announcement.

"I don't believe in crystal balls and such," he said quietly and patted her hand. Mrs. Kempel meant well; he did not want to hurt her feelings. Where did she come up with this notion of taking him to a soothsayer? In his three years as an orphan, running with that like, none of them proved trustworthy. Maybe some of those who still scrounged out a living in the dark zone remembered and resented him. Possibly even this fortuneteller.

"You appear ill. Is it the pie or Madam Trousdale?"

"I'm sorry Mrs. Kempel . . . I don't like the idea of a fortuneteller. I see my own future."

"No, you don't. You see the past. Madam Trousdale can see beyond all that."

Lucas picked at the remainder of his pie. He turned his gaze to the fire where a black iron pot simmered. Supper for the boarders that the maid Carissa would serve this afternoon.

"Ten years ago, both of our lives changed. You are a man now. Wouldn't you like to know what comes next?"

"I know what comes next. Tomorrow comes; I go out and light the lanterns as I do six out of seven nights." Lucas swayed from side to side and sipped his tea offering a half smile to Mrs. Kempel.

"Surely you cannot be satisfied lighting lanterns and rescuing senseless citizens from burning houses and other calamities. What about the rest of your life? You must want to know about something for yourself. You need something to look forward to."

"I know everything I need to know. Besides, it is noble work, Mrs. Kempel. You said so yourself when you recommended me to the city leaders. I know we will always need someone to walk out and illuminate the streets. People do thoughtless things, tis true. But I find it amusing and rewarding to offer my assistance and light their way."

"Tsk! Stumbling oafs!"

"Not all . . ."

"But your future, Lucas. Have you not thought about it? Surely, that is why you can't sleep at night. Is that not true?" She reached across the table and took his hand. "Who will take care of you when I am gone?"

Lucas shook his head and gazed at Mrs. Kempel. Her plump face had gone pale. He could not ruin this occasion for her. Who knew how many more years they would share together? She had provided him with a clean and comfortable home. And by his own hand, he had acquired a stash of treasures that would more than provide for the future. Along with his pilfered treasures there was a chest of gifts—bribes presented to him by citizens needing favors, such as their streetlamps lit early, or a secret encounter kept quiet, a lady escorted through a midnight alley back into her world of chandeliers and boredom. These gestures he made for the pleasure of offering his assistance. And with the immense amount of trade coming through the harbour his clandestine business had grown. For now, though, she didn't need to know this. He genuinely enjoyed walking the streets and lighting the way for the citizens of the city. They respected him, appreciated him. Early in life, so many unpleasant things had come his way. The idea of peering far into the future made him uneasy. His insight got him through. It was enough, especially if one is to have the courage to continue each day.

He finished his pie and gulped his tea. "Let's just go to the river and have our picnic. The hell with the ugly old fortuneteller."

"She is not ugly," Mrs. Kempel scolded. "And she is much younger than me."

Lucas sighed. "What is this really about Mrs. Kempel? Are you trying to marry me off to a witch?"

She laughed and pulled her pie plate closer. He waited while she finished every crumb, then cleared her throat. "I don't mean to intrude on you Lucas, but I know that you have been enduring those nightmares. And I know, even if you don't, that you need answers about your mother's death. Someday this boarding house will be yours. You can remain here for the rest of your life. But you should know who you are. Everyone wants to know that."

Lucas took a deep breath. He had spent years avoiding thoughts about things such as what would happen when Mrs. Kempel passed on, and what truly happened the day his mother died. There was no one in the dark zone who could explain that. If so, he would have known about that years ago, when he ran wild there and learned life's lessons firsthand. But he couldn't bear the sadness in her face. It was so long ago, who would remember him? He had completely changed from the frightened angry boy he had once been. As much as it unnerved him to think of life without Mrs. Kempel, he deeply appreciated her intentions to leave the boarding house to him. No greater gift could one give to another than that of a secure future. After everything she had done for him, he could do this at least for her. He smiled and squeezed her hand. "Of course, let's go see the soothsayer, or fortuneteller, whatever you call her. But answers about my mother are answers about the past."

"Ach, you like to pester me." She rolled her eyes and clutched his arm, peering into his eyes. "Resolve your past. Discover your future."

Lucas chuckled. "You speak like a fortuneteller yourself."

She curled her upper lip.

"All right then. She may just tell me something I need to know."

Mrs. Kempel clapped her pudgy hands and jumped up. "And afterward, we will sit by the river and have our picnic. I'm almost finished preparing the basket."

Lucas noticed the open basket sitting at the end of the table and thought of the willow flower baskets he and his mother had once used to gather flowers. He wondered where they went after her death. So many years gone by, how could he possibly find anything that belonged to his mother? He did not even know if there had been a funeral after she died. Mrs. Kempel quickly straightened up the kitchen. She took a small key from a chain around her neck and with a grunt bent over to unlock the low cupboard. "What shall it be to toast the day? Whisky or wine?"

"Whisky now and wine later," Lucas said rising to help Mrs. Kempel with the preparations. She handed him the jug and he poured a cup for each of them.

"To the future," they said simultaneously.

A figure appeared in the doorway. Mrs. Kempel jumped.

"Good Morning, excuse me," the man said. He wore a heavy purple cloak over crisp burgundy trousers and a black shirt. He directed his question to Lucas. "I was told this is a boarding house?"

Lucas gazed at the man who was nearly as tall as he was. "It is a boarding house, not a tavern. It is customary to use the doorknocker."

Mrs. Kempel intervened. "Yes, it is a boarding house. How may I help you?"

The man stepped forward and extended his hand to Mrs. Kempel, turning his back to Lucas. "The apothecary suggested I inquire here for a room."

At the mention of Mister Padgett, the apothecary, Lucas peeked at Mrs. Kempel who wore a calm expression. He trusted her judgement of the boarders. They never had a problem with any of them, so he stepped aside and sorted through the picnic basket—adding the jug of whisky—while Mrs. Kempel negotiated with her new boarder. The well-dressed man agreed to pay in advance. Coins clinked into Mrs. Kempel's purse. "Turn left up the stairs, it's the second door on the right," she said as she handed the newest boarder, Dugald, a key to his room and the front door.

Chapter 2

Out on the narrow, crowded street, Lucas managed the picnic basket on one arm while Mrs. Kempel held onto his other arm. He steered them around piles of horse droppings and the occasional household rubbish. Most citizens used waste pits, but some had yet to enjoy that convenience. Before midday, the gongfermour came along to clean up what the lazy and careless left behind. Most of the time, the sea breeze along with the aroma of fried bread and roasted meat dispersed the smells of livestock and humanity. Lucas absorbed the bustling energy along with Mrs. Kempel's infectious enthusiasm. The walk to the squat cottages where the gypsies gathered and made their homes in the dark zone was long and Lucas had to mind his pace to allow Mrs. Kempel to keep up. He amused himself by noticing everyone who came along. Suddenly, a small wooden wagon wheel spun past him narrowly missing his leg. A donkey had broken its leather harness sending a cart of manure rolling toward them. Scurrying Mrs. Kempel out of the way, Lucas grabbed the wobbly rail and halted the cart just before it ran into a child. The donkey, rearing and braying, kicked its way through the parting crowd. Lucas pushed the cart to a wide turn in the road and secured it there, its owner nowhere in sight. They continued at an even slower pace. The cumbersome picnic basket bumped against his thigh and bounced into a young woman weaving her way among ambling individuals. She wore a dark blue cloak and a black lace funeral veil.

"Watch out," she snapped as the veil slipped revealing long amber curls.

"Pardon me," Lucas reached out to steady her but once again bumped her hip with the basket.

"Get away!" she hissed without looking up.

Mrs. Kempel tried to pull Lucas away. "We must not be late for our appointment."

Lucas stood fast. "Are you all right, Miss?"

Her slender form wavered. He released Mrs. Kempel and extended his hand to the young woman. Swatting his hand away, she peered up at Lucas. His heart skipped and his breath caught in his throat. He had never seen such riveting green eyes. He grabbed for her wrist, but she took two nimble steps backward. Rapt in the beauty of her delicate face, he laughed. A sparkling ruby pendant nestled in her golden-skinned décolletage. Instinctively, Lucas reached for the jewel at her neck.

"Keep your filthy hands off." She shoved him and fumbled to maintain her cloak before it slipped from her shoulders.

"That ruby suits you more than your mouth does."

She bounded away then turned around. Their eyes riveted on each other before fear twisted her childlike face and she spun to disappear in the crowd. The breeze caught her veil. Before it fluttered to the ground, Mrs. Kempel snatched it up, and attempted to hand it to Lucas who stood rooted like one of the stone statues scattered throughout the city.

"You will be wanting this I suppose," Mrs. Kempel said stuffing the black veil into the picnic basket.

Lucas didn't respond as Mrs. Kempel looped her arm in his and pulled him along. He babbled "Who is that? Did you see her?" Feeling Mrs. Kempel's gaze on him, he blushed and adjusted the basket. "Extraordinary little nymph," he muttered.

They made their way through the winding streets, past the steep-peaked, half-timbered buildings to the outskirts where the cottages huddled. The neighborhood was crudely familiar to Lucas. Memories threatened him from every bend in the road. He had starved here, fought here, schemed here. A career he had not intended, but continued to benefit from, began among these cramped cottages. The inhabitants never intended to stay. But the peaceful sadness of the place distracts them. Their hope is nurtured by the cluster of trees that arch over the crouched village. When the tenants gaze upward, they cannot hold back their dreams.

"These poor cottages should be lit at night," Lucas remarked. "I shall discuss it with the officials. The City of Dreams is growing larger, the renovations to Saint Siempre brings us more boarders and some will stay."

"You're right, Lucas. But I fear for you walking alone. The night carries sinister spirits on its shaded wings." She trembled and pulled her shawl around her shoulders. "We must focus on your destiny."

Lucas scoffed. I believe I just met my destiny, he thought. A shiver went up Lucas' spine. He had just now seen this girl, but he felt as if he had known her since the beginning of time. He pulled up the collar of his cloak and peered about hoping nobody recognized him from long ago, especially in the company of Mrs. Kempel. She knew he'd survived on the streets, but the details should remain unspoken. She believed her words and prayers had reformed him in the first few months of taking him in. He couldn't explain to this pious woman how his longing for the night went beyond lighting the way for citizens. Even though he'd outgrown the petty crimes of the street, he enjoyed the satisfaction of stealing. And in the City of Dreams teeming with trade and citizens of wealth, stature, and vices, he'd had many opportunities to perfect his craft. Along with his friend, Nikolas that's exactly what they had done. Nikolas stationed at the harbour, greeting merchant ships, made their vocation as simple as a pleasant pastime. He would never give it up, whether he needed the money or not. He thought of the first time he stole, a pocket watch, it was, from a drunken nobleman sleeping off ale and the exhausting effects of a prostitute. When the man came to, just as Lucas pocketed the watch, he helped him to his feet and escorted the gentleman to the steps of his fine home.

They arrived at a lopsided, stone cottage with a drooping thatched roof squeezed between a cluster of bent and scraggly trees. Twisting arms of ivy covered a split roof beam. A dead branch twitched in the breeze like a cautioning finger. The splintered front door hung open like a forbidding welcome. The entrance to his old nightmare.

Blood roared painfully between his ears. He gulped for breath, then exclaimed with feigned glee. "It appears that she is expecting us. Please, Irene, don't tell me that you have come here by yourself."

Mrs. Kempel ignored his statement. "Just set the basket there on the weeds, out of the mud."

Lucas followed her instructions. "A bit of whisky?" He bent over and rummaged in the basket until he found the jug and swallowed two gulps while Mrs. Kempel clanged the iron bell hanging from a gnarled branch.

Madam Trousdale appeared in the doorway. The whisky made its way through his veins. Her hair was long and black, not white, as Lucas had expected. She gazed at Lucas with a penetrating, rude stare. He puffed out his chest. At least he had no memory of her from his days in the dark zone.

Lucas turned his back and whispered to Mrs. Kempel, "Let's not waste our money."

"She owes me," she whispered back, giving Lucas a little shove toward the cottage.

The woman's black velvet dress dragged on the ground, around her neck hung an assortment of medallions. Some sort of a claw, a flat stone with a lion head carved on its smooth black surface, and a tiny hourglass.

Lucas took a step forward at the insistence of Mrs. Kempel's hand on his back. The doorway was so small he would have to duck to get inside. The woman was not as tall as she originally appeared.

"Don't be frightened, Lucas," she said yanking the creaky door wide open for them to pass through.

In the center of the room sat a round table arranged with a triangle of three yellow candles and in the center a crystal ball. He'd never see one up close before and couldn't pull his eyes from the ethereal dreamlike images that could have been reflections but were not quite discernible. When he moved, the images moved too and when he stood still, holding his breath, the ball moved with a mind of its own. Mrs. Kempel and Madam Trousdale watched him watching the ball. Madam Trousdale suddenly stepped forward and tossed a purple cloth over the ball. "Don't stare into the ball, you may catch your own reflection and invoke spirits that can shatter your dreams."

"They're already shattered," Lucas scoffed, clenching his jaw and finally, peeling his eyes away from the shrouded sphere. He noticed the walls held tapestries depicting the woods, wild animals, and solitary silhouettes. A musty smell emanated from the damp dirt floor. The hair stood up on the back of Lucas' neck. He did not like this sorceress; he wanted to flee her unnerving abode. He sniggered, "This is absurd. Let's go."

Mrs. Kempel put a finger to her lips as she shook her head. Lucas cracked his knuckles and shook his head. But she was following Madam Trousdale to the table, purposely ignoring him. He clenched his fists and inched toward the door. A strong herbal aroma forced him to swallow rapidly. Mrs. Kempel had clearly lost her wits taking him here. He fiercely felt the need to run. Something he'd loved since he was a child, running through the flower fields with his mother and then, after, running away from farmers, shopkeepers, the constable, even tavern proprietors. He could stretch out his legs and fly from a situation faster than anyone. He loved the heart-racing exhilaration of escape. The room, cluttered with unfamiliar objects, closed in around him. He took a wide sideways step to the door, circumventing the witch and Mrs. Kempel. But something caught his eye. A gold box inlaid with jewels sparkled from the top of a tall wardrobe. It would fit easily into the palm of his hand. Before the women noticed the smile that spread across his face, he bit his bottom lip and sat down in the chair opposite Mrs. Kempel, who relaxed her scowl and patted his hand.

"Shall we begin?" Madam Trousdale sat between the two and held out a hand to each of them. Lucas crossed his arms over his chest. Mrs. Kempel grabbed his left hand; he had no choice but to give the fortuneteller his right. Her thin fingers felt cold but soft.

"Let's get on with it then. I'm hungry and I need fresh air," he grumbled, with a peek toward Madam Trousdale. She squeezed his hand and he instinctively tried to pull away, but she held tight. He noticed a glint of amusement in her sideways glance, so he relaxed his grip and when she closed her eyes, he focused his attention on the golden box.

As she began speaking in a low monotone, her black hair turned a deep watery blue. It seemed to glow. *Lucas, we gather here today in harmony with the earth, the sky, and the eternal life force. On behalf of your tired soul, we ask for assistance from spirits and beings seen and unseen to invoke the light and penetrate the dark. In the never-ending, always beginning passage of time. If it is your desire to find answers, release your visceral hostility. Tell us what you seek.*

She sat back in her chair but did not release her icy grip on Lucas' clammy hand. He looked at Mrs. Kempel who appeared completely relaxed with her eyelids fluttering as if she were dreaming a lovely dream. Beneath the charcoaled lids of Madam Trousdale, her eyeballs spun and twisted so rapidly that Lucas expected them to roll from their sockets. *What do you seek?* The voice seemed to float around her rather than come from her, as her lips had not moved. He swallowed the urge to jump up and grab the gold-jewelled box in answer to the question. Instead, he blurted, "More whisky."

Silence!

Shifting in his chair, he again tried to pull his hand away. When that didn't work, he leaned toward the door willing the whisky bottle to emerge from the picnic basket and stroll inside. A cottage full of magic, why not a walking whisky bottle, he mused. Could this silly woman be serious, invoking answers when he had asked for nothing from her and didn't even want to be here? Mrs. Kempel remained still with her eyes squeezed shut. Was she all right? Her hand felt hot in his, while Madam Trousdale's hand remained as cold as the river in winter. A breeze stirred the stifling room, from where it came, Lucas could not tell. The women didn't seem to notice that one of the candles blew and went out. No one responded to his plea for whisky. A thick silence hung over the three of them gathered at the table. Lucas tried to take a deep breath, but his mouth was dry, he only managed a ragged gasp. He felt sure the pathetic roof would fall on their heedless heads. The cloth slipped from the crystal. Inside the glowing ball, a small shadow grew larger and larger. Lucas squinted, it seemed like a figure, but its shape shifted and twisted, floated, then fell before rising again like a cloak covering a boneless body. A faceless face hovered inside the gaping hood. He felt like something crawled straight up his back. He jerked forward dropping the women's hands to slap at himself. The little hourglass hanging from the fortuneteller's neck emptied.

"Lucas, dear boy! What is the matter?" Mrs. Kempel leapt to her feet.

"Sit down," Madam Trousdale demanded, her hair still glowing blue.

"Don't you speak to her like that!" Lucas, on his feet also, reached for Mrs. Kempel, wrapped a protective arm around her.

Madam Trousdale tilted her head, shook her horsetail hair. "You have all the time in the world, Lucas. But we don't."

He glared at the empty hourglass pendant. "What in hell is going on here?"

"It's all right now," Mrs. Kempel patted his shoulder and brushed her hand across his back to prove nothing was there. She took her seat and indicated for Lucas to do the same. "Go on, Madam Trousdale."

"Did you see something in the ball?"

Lucas watched the crystal ball and frowned. "It's gone now."

"What was it?" Madam Trousdale extended her spidery hand toward him. "What did you see?"

He swiped his hand over his eyes, pushing his hair back. "I . . . I saw," he swallowed, "I saw a man who is not a man. A hollow man."

"Ugh!" Mrs. Kempel cast a terrified look at the ball and pushed herself away from the table.

Madam Trousdale placed a firm palm on his arm, pursed her lips and closed her eyes.

What are you seeking, Lucas?

He folded his arms across his chest and peered around the room. The golden box glistened. The embedded jewels sparkled.

Madam Trousdale delivered a well-timed statement. "You can have what you seek if you speak."

Mrs. Kempel gestured that he should say something.

Lucas slowly shook his head, covered his face with his hands, took a deep breath, and blurted, "I had a dream about my mother. She told me to find a lock."

Mrs. Kempel's eyes bulged. "What, when?"

"Last night." Lucas drummed his fingers on the table. "I started to tell you this morning but . . ."

Hush!

"That new boarder showed up." Mrs. Kempel explained with a tsk.

What you seek is already here.

"I think my mother had a lock on her wardrobe trunk." . . . his words low and muffled now, "but I don't know where that trunk went after she died. If there was a lock, I don't have the key." He gazed at each of the women, unable to ignore the mysterious fortuneteller. "Her exact words were . . . she didn't say find a lock, she actually said: *the lock is the key.*"

There are three trunks for you Lucas. One is in the country. The others are in water. The second candle blew out.

"It's the first time in all the nightmares that my mother has actually spoken to me."

Lucas gazed beyond them to an indiscernible past. A shudder brought him back. "On the farm, where we worked gathering flowers, my mother and I shared a small room in the barn. She had a trunk. One trunk. Could it still be there?"

The third candle blew out. Madam Trousdale opened her eyes wide, her earth-bound-black-haired-self again. "There are three trunks," she said. "We saw three."

He shook his head not bothering to ask what Madam Trousdale meant by *we.* "I only know of one," Lucas said, looking to Mrs. Kempel for confirmation although she could not know if there were any trunks at all.

Madam Trousdale rose and crossed to the fire pit where a pot of liquid steamed. Lucas thought it must be the source of the strange aroma, some kind of tea. She filled three cups with a wooden ladle.

"None for me thank you, Ma'am," Lucas said standing.

She pushed him back into his chair with strength beyond her appearance. "It will help in the days to come."

Lucas scoffed. "Drinking tea today will not help me tomorrow."

"When you find the first trunk come back and tell me what's inside."

He studied everything in the room, the hanging herbs, the stones and sticks, animal furs piled in the corner. And the gold-jewelled box. It was a trap. He didn't remember her, but she must remember him. "Why should I tell you? What business is it of yours? I think you want what is in the trunk. You know what's in it. That's what this is all about. You plan to gain possession of my mother's trunk. Or trunks . . . who are you anyway?" Lucas snatched at her hair expecting a wig to come off in his hand. Even as he did it, he felt there was something alarmingly familiar about her. Had he lain with this woman during his youthful, drunken carousing?

Madam Trousdale nimbly stepped away. She grabbed an iron poker and stoked the fire but kept her eyes on Lucas. "If you don't drink you cannot go."

"If I find them, I will not bring those trunks to you, or tell you what's inside. What do you really want from me?"

Mrs. Kempel drained her cup and pushed herself to her feet. She seemed to want to go as much as he did. Madam Trousdale swigged her tea and served herself another cup. He watched her for a moment waiting to see if she keeled over dead. She tapped her knuckles on the table and gestured for Lucas to drink. He jutted his chin, swirled the pale tea, and took a sip. Across the room, the glittering gold box caught his eye once again. He couldn't possibly walk out of here with it. What a shame to leave it behind. It was just the right thing to brighten his day. Another time, he thought as he drank the tea that tasted sweet and somewhat pleasant after all. Setting the cup on the table, he glared at the fortuneteller. She made no attempt to stop him as he held out his arm for Mrs. Kempel. "This is over," he said.

When Madam Trousdale smiled, the first time since their arrival, her face softened to that of a pretty woman. "You know where to find me." She went through the door ahead of them.

"Do not attempt to trick me," Lucas warned.

Turning—as if he were no longer there—to Mrs. Kempel who had retrieved coins from her cloth purse. "No payment is necessary at this time. We will speak soon, Irene."

Lucas grabbed the picnic basket, hoisted it on his shoulder, and strode away from the house, glancing back to see her shove the door shut. He heard the bolt slide into place and wondered if she could read his intentions for her golden-jewelled box. That door latch wouldn't stop him. He could burst right through the crumbling walls if he so desired.

Mrs. Kempel hurried alongside him. "I hope you're not angry with me, Lucas. I believe you got the answer that you were seeking."

"Irene." Lucas said. "Why does that woman address you in that manner? I don't even do that."

"You have the right to . . . I believe I would prefer it, Lucas, child."

Lucas cast a sidelong glance to Mrs. Kempel. "You have not called me child in many years."

"Of course, you are no longer a child . . . but still . . ." her voice faded as she gazed down the road.

"Perhaps I will address you as Irene from now on."

Her eyes watered, "I can't replace your true mother, but we are certainly more like relatives than acquaintances."

Lucas, having forgotten about the whisky, put his arm around her shoulders and they strolled quietly toward the river, each silently processing the words of the fortuneteller.

It was Mrs. Kempel's idea to visit the fortuneteller and she obviously knew what to expect, but did she give that woman information about Lucas to help with her insights? His inability to sleep perhaps, but she could not have known about the latest dream. Nobody but Lucas could know that. It had just happened last night. He refrained from asking her about it for now. She knew nothing about any trunks, of that he was sure. He wanted to get to the river and relax. The strange tasting tea had managed to improve his mood. At his side, Irene took a deep breath inhaling the blossom scented spring air. Lucas did the same, mimicking the behavior of the woman who had selflessly assumed the role of his mother. The sky above a soothing blue, he meandered along at Irene's pace, his mood light.

They sat beside the rushing river beneath the fragrant branches of a flowering tree. Lucas leaned back on his elbows. "That woman knows her medicine. She brews her tea from the flowers of this Linden tree. I noticed several of these trees in her yard. My mother used to make this tea for us after a long day picking and selling our flowers. It's soothing, makes one feel calm as Trousdale said."

"I've never heard of making tea from this tree. You are full of surprises today, Lucas."

"I am surprising myself. The dream last night has stirred the ashes. Suddenly, I am full of memories. In the spring and summer, these trees produce flowers known as lime flowers. The dried flowers make the tea."

While he spoke, Irene unpacked the picnic basket and arranged everything on a blue cloth. She placed the roast and a wedge of cheese on a wooden board, and then handed the bottle of wine and two pewter goblets to Lucas. "Madam Trousdale isn't a bad woman. In fact, she was my first boarder after my husband Clive passed on. We felt akin to each other having both suffered loss. She does know how to stir the passions. And she has the gift, Lucas. I trust her, and you can too. She knows well her craft." Irene tore off a piece of mutton. Lucas handed her some wine; they touched cups and drank.

"Where did these goblets come from?" he asked turning the cup in his hand.

She held hers up to the sunlight. "They were wedding gifts. I put them away when Clive died. But today is a special occasion. Silly to save things. What are we waiting for after all?"

He nodded. "What evidence have you that Madam Trousdale knows what she is doing?"

"For one thing, the tea from this glorious tree."

"Clever woman," Lucas chortled.

"She has lots of herbs and interesting things in that house," Irene said.

"Many interesting things indeed." He bit off a piece of greasy meat.

"What have you told her about me?" He gazed across the river where four men stood on a sagging pier rigging a sail next to a battered fishing boat.

Irene sipped her wine and nibbled on a piece of meat, taking her time to answer. "Only, that you are my only family and I am worried about your troubles sleeping. I hope you will consider what she has told you and perhaps go and talk to her again. She lived at the house for nearly a year. We kept each other company. She had little money, but once she recovered, she made her way to the cottages and began seeing clients again."

"Hmmm . . . so, she was not born in the dark zone."

"No, she came from some other place."

"What place?"

Irene tilted her head to the side. "I don't know. Somewhere exotic I imagine."

Lucas smiled, intrigued by the innocence of his adopted mother. If only he could see the world through her accepting eyes. "And in this unknown, exotic place she collected all her trinkets, talismans and treasures?"

"I believe she acquired some of those things here."

"That crystal ball would be heavy to lug around."

They both laughed, then Irene narrowed her eyes. "What did you see that startled you so?"

Lucas closed his eyes and sipped his wine. "A shadow tis all. Probably the terrifying reflection of myself!"

He drained his cup and leaned back on his elbows. "Perhaps this wondrous woman fell from the sky, pulled by the weight of her magical ball."

"You yourself are magical."

"So, I'm told."

"Yet you have doubts."

"I've heard the rumors about me. I can't help but overhear indoor conversations as I pass through the narrow streets and light the lanterns."

"Certainly," Irene puzzled. "But you do realize that you are different. That you have gifts and abilities that the rest of us don't possess."

Lucas sighed, reached for the wine bottle, and refilled their glasses. "I realize." He pulled up a few blades of long grass and tossed them in the air. "There *is* something I would like to know, Irene."

"Of course, there has to be. We all want to know what lies ahead."

"Well, what I want to know is buried in the past as everything else. I would like to know who my father was."

"Oh, you've never mentioned that. I thought you wanted to know more about your mother."

"I do, but I also know she died. And there is only so much more I can learn about her. If I knew who my father was, it may answer some more questions."

"It may indeed, Lucas. You should go back to Madam Trousdale. You can feel free to consult with her. She won't ask for anything in return."

Lucas expelled a long breath. "We will see, my dear, but for now, let's keep this conversation between us. Let's enjoy this marvelous picnic and worry no more today." He poured more wine and a splash of red splattered the cuff of his white shirt. Irene quickly wiped it for him like a doting mother.

"When do you want to go to the country?" she asked as if he had already agreed.

Lucas rolled his eyes. "It's too much to think about all at once."

"We have to go." She patted his hand. "Your dreams are changing, and your life is changing. There's no denying it. Once it's got a hold of you it doesn't give up."

Lucas brooded, peering with earnest into his wine.

"I'll hire a carriage. We can stay at the Inn." She refilled his cup.

"Which Inn?"

"There must be an Inn out there in the country. It will be a holiday of sorts."

"I don't remember any Inn. I don't remember much of anything."

"But you remember the road that leads to the farm where you and your mother lived and worked, don't you?"

"Yes," Lucas relented, "that is, I see it in my dreams . . . if it is . . . I don't know."

Irene ruffled his hair. "In three days, on your official day off, we shall go."

"Yes ma'am, Irene. If you insist. But if we go, we must come back. I live here now. This is my home." He got up, walked to the river's edge, and splashed the chilly water on his face, and the red wine splatter. Irene rose slowly to her feet and came to stand beside him. To the north, they watched the small boats come and go as they serviced the ships that sailed to and from ports all around the world. Everything in motion. It cannot and will not stop, Lucas thought. A cool wind agitated the surface of the fast-flowing water. Simultaneously they turned their backs as a strong gust pushed them toward the picnic basket. Lucas grabbed the wine goblets just before they tipped over.

"Best drink quickly," Irene said.

"Yes," The wind blew his hair back as he squinted against the swirling dust.

"To the future," Irene said. They tapped cups and as they did a piece of black cloth swirled up and out of the picnic basket. It spun in a taunting typhoon before colliding with Lucas' face.

He snatched it away and almost tossed it into the air before realizing what it was. He had forgotten all about the beautiful young woman he had run into on the way to Madame Trousdale's that morning. Lucas held the veil to his nose, it held her alluring scent. A broad smile lit his face. "It's hers." Giddy thoughts that felt like memories whispered in the whistling wind. Feelings he didn't know existed spun in the swirling Linden blossoms. An image of the amber-haired girl filled his mind. His whole body trembled. It had nothing to do with the wind or the wine. He saw her and nothing else.

Irene gazed at him for several seconds before she collected the remains of the picnic, placed them in the basket, and took Lucas by the hand. "Come along."

He looked around and apologized for not helping. "I'm sorry; it must be the tea catching up with me." Intent on not letting the wind have the veil he stuffed it inside his shirt, against his skin. Taking the basket from Irene, he offered his free arm. As they made their way home, he maintained a watchful eye for the owner of the black lace veil. He couldn't possible miss that amber hair.

By the time, they arrived back at the boarding house, Lucas staggered with the desire to sleep. The whisky, tea, and wine had put him in a languid mood, but his tired mind smoldered with thoughts of the girl. He had so many questions. What was her name, where did she come from, why had he never seen her before? He thought he knew, or was aware of, almost every citizen who walked about the city. Three times today, he had met a stranger. The arrogant new boarder, Madam Trousdale, and the girl. Too many changes for a single day; his head spun with confusion. Dusk, his favorite time of day, settled around them. He had much to think about, but not now. Gratefully, he followed Mrs. Kempel through the front door. He would find his mother's trunks. Now he had no choice. He realized the need to make sense of his mother's death, and perhaps understand why he was different than everyone else. And somehow, he would make that incredible girl part of his world. Maybe his life promised more than living with Irene, and walking the streets lighting lanterns. It could be time to come inside for a life of his own. That girl aroused a range of emotions that caused uncertainty, bordering on panic. He must find her before she disappeared. Many only passed through the City of Dreams never to return. Crossing through the spacious parlour, into the kitchen, he set the picnic basket down and hugged Irene. "It's been a most remarkable day. Thank you, dear woman for all you have done and continue to do for me."

She patted his back, "You're all I have to focus on. It is my pleasure to assist you." She held Lucas away from her and stared up into his eyes. "You will tell me if there is anything else, I can help you with."

"Of course," Lucas said. "And what about you. What can I help you with?"

"You can take me to the country," she answered quickly.

Lucas laughed and shook his head. "You are relentless. We will go in three days' time, but now I will go to my room and rest if you don't mind."

"Please do. I shall do the same. Carissa will serve the boarders their supper."

Lucas pushed open his door and went directly to his bed. He didn't remember straightening his linens and coverlet this morning. He had left a tumble of twisted linens when he rolled out of the confusion of his dream. He lay back on the bed thinking that Mrs. Kempel must have tidied his room for him before the outing. But when she had the time, he didn't know. It wasn't the regular cleaning day, but things were not in their usual places. Perhaps Carissa had come in, although her maid duties had never included his room before. His eyelids fluttered, the morning with the fortuneteller already seemed long ago, not mere hours. The vibrant girl he'd encountered on the street appeared and disappeared. Strands of dusk lingered at his window. The tower bells rung the hour. To block the last fingers of light, and discourage his mind from thinking, he pulled the coverlet over his face. The weight of it relaxed him and he felt safe as he slipped into a deep and peaceful sleep.

Chapter 3

Outside on the darkening street below, Dugald walked briskly away from the boarding house. He had barely shut the door behind him when Lucas and Mrs. Kempel turned the corner. If not for the lightness of their mood and a conveniently parked hay cart, they would have seen him lurking in the shadows at the edge of the building. He must be more diligent. It would be foolish to allow discovery. He could not afford any more mistakes. There was much to do. Before she sent him here, the woman warned: the city is not like the country with wide-spaced estates, city dwellings sit close and on top of each other with numerous windows that mask unknown peeping eyes. She failed to mention the cunning characters shrouded behind those eyes. Although, now he understood she had tried to tell him that very thing. But if she had specifically said, *don't trust anyone in the city*, would he have come here to do her bidding? He glowered. Of course, he would, he had new clothes, he had money in his pocket and, well, a bump on his head.

When the front door clicked closed behind them, he stomped his feet and peered up and down the street swearing an oath not to make any more mistakes. The apprentice lantern lighter, a lamp boy named Ikarus, who worked on Lucas' rest day, arrived at his starting point on time. This change in schedule Dugald learned from the house maid, Carissa. But once she admitted Lucas and Mrs. Kempel had left for the day, she grew wary and refused to speak of anything other than meal service and linen changes. Dugald waited at his vantage point until the lad walked a few meters ahead. A smoky aroma wafted from the amber glass lamp. Dugald suppressed a cough, spit silently, then stepped into the light of the pungent lamp. At least he could feel grateful that his timing had worked out so that Lucas was not lighting the lanterns on this night. If he was going to seize Lucas, he needed to memorize his routine. The boy took his time lazily plodding along, visiting with young women who loitered on street corners, and friends that gathered in front of alehouses and taverns. Dugald enjoyed watching the boy and remembered his own swift youth. But the brief elation those memories evoked, rapidly morphed into envy. Settling into the comfort of a gnawing grudge for the lad's fresh bloom, he ambled a few paces behind. His attempted flirtations with the pretty, young girls hurrying home from the weaving mill garnered giggles and groans. He pulled up his collar and straightened his shoulders. A rightful place in the world was all he ever wanted. He would have it. Someday soon he would have it! He'd worked the land his entire life as if it was his own; it should be his. She had handed over papers to prove that she intended to give him his fair share of the estate. If only he could read those papers or trust someone enough to have them read to him. Many years ago, a shy farm girl had sat with him at the end of the long workday and taught him how to sign his name. She promised to teach him how to write letters and how to read anything, even books. He'd kissed her with deep gratitude, and she clung to him. But in the morning the girl was gone. He waited, signed his name over and over to show her what a good student he was, but she never returned. The sting of her loss burned for months. All these years later he couldn't forget her abandonment.

The woman had warned him to remain alert and avoid distraction so that he could fulfill his task, but still he drank too much when he arrived in the City of Dreams. Foolish, but he couldn't turn the corner and change what he had done. He hadn't counted on meeting the men. They found him in the tavern. They too made promises and gave him official looking papers. And like the woman, they gave him money as well, much more. He had already stuffed the coins into his leather pouch when they threatened to hurt him, rip him to pieces with a sickle if he attempted to leave the city before helping them with just one task. A task, like the one ordered by the woman, he feared he couldn't complete.

'Give the harbour master these instructions for the delivery of two trunks. Complete this mission and you will have more money than you have ever seen,' Vasil Sutcliffe promised. 'Beware the lantern lighter,' Campbell Barrington had warned without further explanation. Why does this person intrigue everyone so, from here to Arcana? The men were rich, any fool could see that. Emboldened by his copious imbibing, Dugald questioned the men. Why couldn't they retrieve the trunks themselves if they were of such immense value? Do they contain dead bodies? They laughed so gleefully at him; he regretted his fearful imagination. But the one called; Vasil was quick to reassure him. He explained that they also enjoyed partaking of whisky and had done such reckless damage to a ship in port that they'd suffered permanent banishment from the harbour. Dugald realized they were most likely pillagers but kept his assumption to himself. He had their coins and fancied he would find a way to get more. If he couldn't get hold of the lantern lighter, he may be able to find a way to collect the sought-after trunks and at least earn more money.

The lamp boy made the first stage of his plan easy. What great fortune to have the chance to learn the route Lucas followed every night lighting the lanterns. Dugald would know when and where to expect the lantern lighter on at least six nights of the week. If Lucas was as powerful as the woman claimed, he planned to avoid him as much as possible, while observing him at the same time. Even this legendary man who watched over the citizens of the City of Dreams must have a weak spot. When Dugald discovered it, he would use it to his advantage. He followed along keeping a close pace behind the boy. Patting his pocket, he made sure the delivery orders were still there as well as the land deed. He must be sure to present the harbour master with the correct packet of papers. The letter from the men had a folded over corner.

The streets leading to the harbour were narrow and the cobblestones slippery. As they grew near, the air smelled like sea and fish. Dugald pulled a clean handkerchief from his pocket and held it over his nose. He gagged as he passed a close alleyway where garbage festered, and tramps crouched in the shadows. For a few dreadful moments, he lost track of the boy and found himself plunged into absolute darkness. He felt his way along the wall dirtying his hands and scuffing his polished shoes. The lazy boy had skipped several lanterns, most likely frightened to cross the slimy street, and ignite the oil. When he inched around a corner, the street widened to reveal harbour lights and tall ships. Bells clanged, and sails flapped in the breeze. Cargo moved to and from the ships on rafts managed by the calloused hands of swearing, sweating, and bickering men. On the long, wood-planked wharf, small fishing vessels listed restlessly as their crews prepared for departure before dawn. Dugald avoided decaying fish carcasses and the offers of gap-toothed women as he made his way to the merchant ship called *Le Peresi*.

Her cargo was stacking up on the dock. The tentative lamp boy had vanished into the mist. The harbour oversaw its own lighting in patchy patterns depending on who wanted to be seen and who did not. Dugald spied the harbour master shouting at a group of hooligans as they attempted to carry off a large steamer trunk. Foolish youngsters without the sense to choose an easier target, he mused. Dugald retrieved the letter from his deep pocket and checked the folded corner. Pulling himself tall and pretending he was a wealthy merchant, he cleared his throat and approached, "I have special orders from the Ingleena Court that all cargo with the surname of Sutcliffe, arriving at this port, shall be brought directly to this address."

The harbour master eyed Dugald up and down while spitting sideways from his twisted mouth. "You're lost, I suppose. This ain't Ingleena. Nothing goes out for delivery without inspection. There'll be no plague brought through my port!" He spat again, this time more voluminous than the first, and walked away without even glancing at the offered papers.

Dugald strode after him. "Plague ended years ago."

"So, you say." The man spat a third time, the glob of brown splatter landing close to Dugald's shoes.

He dodged to the side and back again in an awkward dance. Raising his voice, ignoring the man's smirk, he persisted, "These papers are stamped by not only the High Ingleenish Court, but by the harbour master in Ortsmuth on the date of shipment, as well as the captain of the cargo ship *Le Peresi* which set sail one month back. She sits right there!" He pointed with the papers and his hand shook, as his resolve diminished.

The harbour master, who had walked away again, hunched his shoulders, and quickened his step.

"I demand you listen to me!" Dugald shouted as the boys mimicked him. The man spun round to halt Dugald with his eyes.

"This is very important cargo and it will not be crawled over by these misbegotten wharf rats," Dugald nearly whispered.

The bald harbour master turned slowly raising himself up to the capacity of his full scant height, "*Le Peresi*, comes and goes frequently. I don't know where sits the cargo that you're after! Come back in the daylight and prove that you yourself are not a scoundrel. Only thieves and miscreants do business after nightfall." He passed his hand over the top of his head as if there were still hair there but came away with only a damp hand, which he wiped on the front of his stained coat. With that, he disappeared into a doorway that Dugald had not even seen.

This development Dugald had not anticipated in his careful planning. He lurched forward intending to pound on the door when two bulky men stepped into the torch light.

"Mr. Merson is done for the night, move along," one said as he poked at Dugald's arm and another stroked his purple cloak.

Dugald pulled away from the filthy men. Dread rose in his throat then plummeted in a nauseating spiral to his stomach. "Of course, gentleman, good night," he hurried off without a further word. The harbour boys trailed behind him.

As he walked up the small incline that led away from the harbour, Dugald realized they continued to follow him. Swallowing so rapidly that it hurt, he said, "Want to earn a coin?" All three strapping lads rushed forward. Dugald spoke quickly, "Sh-sh-show me where the most valuable cargo is stored before delivery." He held up one glinting coin.

The burliest of the three shoved his companions aside. They slunk away among a smattering of curses. The boy led him rapidly through winding corridors of complaining cats and white fish bones. Dugald gagged on his own vomit but within moments, they stood in front of a tower of empty crates that appeared to have glowing eyes. The jumble wavered and swayed as the tenants scattered revealing a tall, heavy wooden door braced by steel bands and secured by a huge iron lock.

"The harbour is full of warehouses. Most are known but some are for . . . well let's say private use. My mate keeps this one."

Dugald eyed the thick armed lad. "If your mate keeps this one, why show it to me?"

The lad flinched. "You have money. And he won't share. I let him take my girl for a walk, but he won't share whatever's in here. If you can get through this, you can have what you want." The boy raised his hand, caught the coin in midair and vanished.

Back tracking slowly, while hurrying at the same time, Dugald memorized the turns. When he reached the harbour path again, he breathed in relief. The air felt fresh in comparison. And since his head was still intact, Dugald decided to celebrate his progress. Night had fully settled on the city, and he had yet to have any supper.

In the city square, he found a tavern called The Duck. It was tidy with small wooden tables. He ordered wine and roast mutton. His first goblet of red wine tasted good enough to require another, which he gulped gleefully, the soothing liquid seeped into the hollows of his bones and helped the stringy meat slide down his throat. He must take care not to overindulge and fall prey to any more scoundrels. In his mind, he constructed a plan for acquiring the trunks. He must lure the wharf lads with money. Money, he had no intention to pay. He had enough coins to dangle before their eyes. That arrogant little harbour master would regret treating him like a common wharf rodent. And afterward, perhaps the lads could help him throw a net over Lucas and toss him in a wagon or some such thing. He wanted that land. Money and land. But first the cargo. The men, Sutcliffe and Barrington scared him. In the crowded room, nobody paid him any mind, nonetheless, he kept a wary eye. Familiar feelings of doubt crept across the scarred table and leapt into his lap causing his stomach to cartwheel. His skin felt itchy just thinking about passing time with the likes of these persons in this peculiar city. But if he wanted to win his prize, the bequest, he would have to play along with the common lot.

By the time he finished his meal, comforted, and more relaxed, his confidence returned. An attractive serving girl asked if he wanted anything else, he considered her offer knowing she would take him upstairs if he tossed her a few extra coins. As he drained another goblet of wine, a nagging feeling nibbled at his mind. His good mood faded again in the noise of the crowded room. His entire plan now depended on harbour hooligans. Lucas and the trunks, he could not get a hold of either without the help of scary strangers. Sutcliffe and Barrington expected delivery before tomorrow evening. He must explain the difficulty of the situation. But not tonight, he would return to the harbour in the morning and find the big lad. Surely, he could find a way to complete these tasks in time. Forgetting about his plans for the serving girl, he tossed insufficient coinage on the table and left.

He wove his way back to the boarding house taking a wrong turn that took him into a serpentine alley so narrow that his cloak snagged on the rough stone. Just as the woman had warned, the city was closing in around him. A cumbersome rat kept apace just ahead. Dugald peered around planning which way he would run if the rat turned on him. After what seemed like hours the alley ended, and he emerged in the square just a few blocks away from the boarding house. There was the apothecary shop that he had visited just the other day. He gulped realizing that the rat was gone.

When he unlocked the solid oak door, a simmering fire glowed in the front room. He bolted the door behind him and slumped into an upholstered chair. The large stone fireplace and mantel held shelves that bulged with books. Built around structural timbers the long shelves also held candlesticks, slivers of stacked kindling, oil lamps and rusty pots. Dugald examined the shelves with half closed eyes, then decided it would be best to conceal the harbour orders and land deed in the tarnished bronze pot. He didn't need the maid sniffing around in his things. And if he must meet with the wharf rats, he wanted in his pockets only enough coins to bribe them. And the key of course. Now that he knew which door it fit. Everyone was after the same thing it seemed. From what he could tell by his quick perusal of Lucas' room nobody kept valuables within reach of others. An inconvenient location for a pot; it obviously hadn't moved in years. Climbing onto the hearth, he balanced one wobbly foot on the first shelf, then the second and hoisted himself up to reach into the pot on the top shelf. He felt round best he could from the awkward angle, and once he touched the empty bottom of the pot, confirming that it was a good and secure place, he let go of the bundle of papers and the sack of coins. As he pulled back, something sharp pinched his hand. He jumped sideways, feeling for the floor with his foot, it was farther than expected, a sharp pain shot through his knee, but he managed to stay upright. Seeing no blood from whatever had scraped the soft pad of his palm, he removed his shoes and quietly climbed the stairs to his room.

* * *

The next morning Lucas lay sprawled on his side with one leg dangling from the bed. He opened his eyes to dappled light and chirping birds. Rolling over, he stretched his legs, and pushed aside the coverlet. Memories of the previous day—most of all the girl— slid through his mind as he splashed water on his face. When the chilly water hit his face, he realized with a shock that he had not dreamed at all. Feeling lightheaded he dressed in clean work clothes. The upcoming trip to the country worried him, but Irene would be there with him. And she looked so forward to it.

But the fact that the maddening Madam Trousdale had something to do with the journey to discover his roots created a queasy knot in his stomach and an all too familiar thudding pressure in his head. She behaved as if she knew everything about him. She and her lot didn't belong in his life anymore. He'd lost track of that sad troop of beggar children. In his early days at the boarding house, with the help of Irene's occasional dose of laudanum, he had buried many troublesome memories.

At the wide-sash window, Lucas gazed out over the city. Why the fortuneteller invited him to return to her house, he didn't know. He wouldn't return there. Yes, he would go to the country with Irene. Ikarus needed a night's wages more than Lucas did. And he was curious what he may find. He had questions about himself and his father that only his mother could answer. Reaching under his hair, he rubbed the back of his neck, a trunk that belonged to his beloved mother may help fill the void of his missing childhood. Irene's prodding had stirred forgotten longings. For years, he had tried to truly remember the events leading up to his mother's death and the days afterward. He had yearned for a sense of himself that lay buried in the past.

A promising spring breeze caressed his hands as they gripped the windowsill, the wavering branches of the willow tree, he used to climb out on, eased his tension. He inhaled. Thinking of the girl, he leaned out the window to search the street below. Their meeting felt like more than just an accident. If it wasn't so highly inappropriate, he would have seized her right there on the street and carried her to the cathedral. He felt sure that she had appeared in the City of Dreams specifically for him. Possibly, she wouldn't agree. Her distrust showed in her eyes and her actions. That ruby! What compelled his hand to grab for it? Habit of course. He couldn't blame himself for his natural impulses. Yet, the jewel didn't matter; he had several, in various shapes and sizes in the cellar. At that moment, suspended in the hypnotic hold of her eyes, nothing mattered but the breath of her magnificent life.

As he finished dressing, he decided to find her today. Lucas was free to dedicate the daylight hours to nothing more than that. She must be new to the city. Locating a striking young woman such as her, should not be too difficult. He strode out of his room with pleased determination. As he descended the stairs to the fragrant kitchen, he made a mental list of citizens he knew that he could count on to help him. Best to start where he had last seen her and interview the local shopkeepers who may be familiar with the young lady.

Irene served him his morning meal of coarse bread with warm butter and strong tea. "Our new boarder came in rather late last night."

Lucas' eyes widened. He shoved a large chunk of bread into his mouth and chewed. After a moment, he said, "I forgot about him. Who is he?"

"He calls himself, Dugald Tendrick,"

"Hmmm, the name is not familiar." Lucas pushed his hair off his forehead and pressed his thumbs against his temples. He had waited too long to eat. He gulped his tea and filled his plate with more bread.

Irene handed Lucas the guest registry and pointed to a grandiose signature.

Dugald Tendrick, Merchant

"Pretentious sort. Thought so from his clothes."

"Mister Padgett sent him," she cast an eye at his place setting at the far end of the table where the boarders took their meals. "I suppose he's still sleeping."

Lucas watched her flutter around the kitchen wiping down the large wood table three times. "Are you uneasy about him?"

She turned away, "I don't know. I'm growing old I suppose. I wish I didn't have to bother with boarders anymore. I so enjoyed our day yesterday. It would be lovely to go out whenever I want."

Lucas stroked his chin. "Tired of chores, I'm sure."

"Don't worry yourself about me. I will tend to the new boarder's room myself, and if there is something to discover then I will find it." She pointed to herself and winked.

Lucas rolled his eyes and laughed. "Women . . . how is it that you are all so clever?"

"We're just made that way in self-preservation, young man."

Lucas sat with his chin in his hand. He had no idea how to help her except to admit the wealth he had hidden deep in the cellar. Once she knew of it, he would have to stop. Neither he nor Nikolas were ready to do that. She may even request he return it all. That, of course, could not and would not occur. Soon, someday soon he would tell her. But first the girl. He would bring the black lace veil, under pretense of returning it. His hunger satisfied; he rose. "Remain watchful," Lucas said as he squeezed her hand affectionately. "I will see you this evening before work."

Rushing upstairs to retrieve the veil, he discovered Dugald lurking in the hallway. The man stood halfway between his own doorway and Lucas's door. Lucas approached silently. "Lost?"

"Oh! Good morning." Dugald flashed a wan smile and dropped his room key. Bending to retrieve the key, he fumbled with the cuffs on his frilled shirt, and tried to inch past Lucas who stood with his hands spread wide on his hips, filling the narrow hallway.

"Off to work already?" Dugald stammered.

Lucas remained silent, watching as Dugald concealed his arm behind his back. Then, in a deep voice he said, "Do I know you?"

"No, well . . . we met yesterday. I am Dugald." He started to offer his hand but pulled it back and hid it in the folds of his abundant shirt.

Lucas noticed the bandage and grasped his forearm. "I'm Lucas," he said, while he peered directly into Dugald's bloodshot eyes. He squeezed his arm to get a glimpse of his hand. The bandage was black and wound tight. For a second, he thought the man had stolen his lady's veil. Closer examination revealed it was black hose, it appeared stained and damp. He dropped Dugald's arm. "What's happened to you?"

Dugald concealed his hand, "It's nothing. You are the lantern lighter. I . . . I saw your things downstairs. The lighting stick, oil, candles," his voice drifted off.

"You saw those things through the locked cupboard door?"

"The cupboard, it wasn't locked when I came in late last night, I was hungry. I meant no harm." Dugald bowed and stepped away from Lucas, creeping toward the stairs. Lucas glared. Dugald held perfectly still like a trapped animal.

"Mrs. Kempel will show you the workings of the kitchen, and if you are prone to keeping late hours, she can set your evening meal aside for you."

Dugald nodded with a false grin before darting down the stairs. "Good advice. Thank you."

Lucas hurried to his room to fetch the black veil. To his great relief, it was under his pillow where he had placed it last night. He peeked over his shoulder, to make sure Dugald hadn't followed him to his door. The veil already meant so much to him.

When Lucas returned to the kitchen, Dugald was sitting at the boarders table along with six other huddled men wearing puzzled expressions. Mrs. Kempel perched alongside Dugald examining his swollen hand; it was three times the normal size.

"Good lord, you're an ignorant bloke. That's not nothing!"

"He's been bitten," Mrs. Kempel said. She rose from the table and went to her herb closet.

"By what?" Lucas kept his distance. "You best not touch him, Irene. It could be a flea bite." He took a step closer to make sure she understood his meaning. She stiffened her back and ignored him, but the men; masons and craftsmen who worked at the cathedral, understood, and murmured among themselves. Dugald flashed a vicious expression at Lucas.

Mrs. Kempel retrieved a jar of crushed basil leaves from a shelf stacked with clay jars. "I'll make a poultice to reduce the swelling."

"Dugald can apply it himself." Lucas said staring at the man who now refused to meet his gaze.

Irene approached Lucas from behind and whispered, "There have been no plague outbreaks in decades."

"Don't touch him." Lucas insisted.

"Maybe a spider," Dugald said weakly. "I was looking through the bookshelf last night."

"Why were you doing that?" Lucas snapped.

Mrs. Kempel turned an inquisitive eye toward Lucas.

"I hoped to find something to read," Dugald, said speaking directly to Mrs. Kempel.

"The library is available to everyone," she agreed.

"And what about our supply cupboard? Is that available to everyone as well?" He strode over to the cabinet and yanked the door open. "How did this get unlocked? You said you were searching for food last night and a book as well?"

Irene finished mashing the basil leaf poultice as the apothecary had taught her and placed the small stone bowl next to Dugald. "There is only one key and I have possession of it."

Dugald remained silent. The six men rose and left the house, mumbling a collective thank you for their bread.

Lucas sneered at Dugald while he perused the contents of the cabinet. Satisfied that everything was in its place, he fingered the metal lock. It showed no signs of force. He couldn't remember in his sleepy state, if he'd unlocked it for Ikarus yesterday afternoon. A thick stillness settled in the kitchen. The stew pot bubbled then hissed, boiled over into the fire. Lucas swung the iron arm away from the fire. As much as he wanted to get out the door into the bright and busy street, he took a seat at the end of the table. He would not make this easy on Dugald. Something was wrong with the man, and it went deeper than the insect bite.

Irene went to the basin where she scrubbed her hands before placing a thick slice of bread, this time with warm honey, in front of Lucas. He devoured it as if he hadn't just eaten half an hour earlier. Dugald hadn't touched his food, his eyelids drooped, and his face turned ashen. He mumbled something that neither Lucas nor Irene could understand. Irene stood closer to him despite Lucas' agitation.

"I deserve . . ." he sputtered, and his head dropped to the table.

"Go for the doctor." Irene said.

Lucas stood up so fast the bench clattered to the floor. "Do not touch him, Irene!" He pointed an insistent finger at her, and then rushed out the door.

The bustling street quickly elevated Lucas's mood. He exhaled and hurried through the throng, searching for the girl while rapidly weaving his way to the doctor's house. If this were plague, if this sick and sneaky man had brought the Black Death to his cherished city, Lucas would make him suffer more than the burning lumps of pus that would soon appear. His life was just beginning, he would not let anything stop him now. Soon the bleeding would start, the man would be a mess of oozing blood. Sickened by his own terrifying thoughts, Lucas began to run. He dodged down winding narrow lanes, loped across narrow bridges and through crowded plazas with the dexterity of a country fox; he did not stop until he reached the doctor.

* * *

As soon as Lucas left, Irene set a bowl of bone broth in front of Dugald and hurried up the back stairs to his room. Her heart raced more from the climb than fear of discovery. She carried fresh linens as a decoy. The bed, of course, was the first place to search since the wardrobe door hung open revealing only one shirt. She didn't know exactly what she was looking for but felt sure she would know when she found it. And sure, enough as soon as she removed the lumpy feather pillow, she found a key sitting in plain sight. It was so easy to find that she wondered if it was worth consideration. But it's size and weight intrigued her. It was thicker than any key she'd seen, and very heavy, made to last, forged from shiny steel with more than the usual ridges and indentations. She held it for a minute deciding whether it was possible to take it. He obviously intended to check on it regularly. An unusual key like this must have a significant purpose. At night, before going to sleep, he would slip his hand under the pillow to feel for it. But if it was so important why leave it? Why not carry it with him on a chain around his neck or sewn into a pocket or hem as most citizens. Everyone has something to hide. They think their secrets are safe, when the truth is everyone walks the streets under the constant scrutiny of others. They hide behind polite nods, cheery good mornings— and all are pondering: where are your valuables hidden? She changed the linens and replaced the key before searching under two pairs of boot hose, a stained travel shirt and inside the pockets of his purple cloak, all tossed on the floor. She stepped heavy testing the floorboards to see if he'd pried any loose. Gathering the sheets, she fluffed the thin feather pillow and picked up the key again. Footsteps, soft but evident shuffled down the hallway. Spinning, just as the door flew open, she dropped the bundle of sheets on the floor as she slipped the key into the pocket of her apron.

"What are you doing, Ma'am?"

Irene shook her head and twisted her mouth. "No wonder you travel alone. No decent woman would stand for this. I nearly stumbled and fell trying to change your bed linens. It is not wise to leave your clothing strewn about the floor. Meager as it is," she added."

Dugald stood in the doorway staring at Mrs. Kempel. "I didn't ask for my linens to be changed."

"In your condition, it's for the best. Tsk-tsk," she waved her arm. "Stand out of the way now."

Blushing, he slunk to the corner of the room, his eyes cloudy, face pale, and expression confused. "Is there anything else you want Mrs. Kempel?" He coughed and cleared his throat.

"No, I'm finished here. You best lie down. The doctor is coming." She gave him a once-over, winced, and then hurried from the room.

Halfway down the narrow back stairway, she realized Dugald was following her. She gripped the handrail. Her arm hairs stood on end. A hundred thoughts ran through her head. He already discovered the missing key. She must pretend to have accidently caught it up in the linens. Turning so quickly her hand slipped and her foot dropped unsteadily to the landing. "What do you think you're doing?"

"I want . . . I am not ill. I'd like to sit in the parlour."

"No!" she scolded, "Get back to your bed. You must not contaminate the household!"

But he followed her anyway, head hung low, flop-footing in his bare feet behind her like a kicked puppy, mumbling that he hadn't finished his broth. When they reached the kitchen, Carissa was on her hands and knees scrubbing the worn wood floor. "Oh, Ma'am could you wait a wee bit. I'm just finishing up here and if you go you might slip and fall."

Irene glared at Dugald who glanced over at his untouched bowl of broth and heaved a sigh. "I'm not hungry anyway."

"And you're too feverish to sit up front."

Turning on his heel he plodded back up to his room.

High stepping across the damp floor, Irene slumped down at the table. "I need a cup of tea."

Why had he followed her upstairs? Her heart raced. He could be searching for his key right now. Suddenly, not sure why she had even taken it, she pushed the tea aside.

"Is something wrong with it, Ma'am?"

Wasn't a man entitled to his privacy? She had no actual reason to suspect Dugald of anything—except carousing all night—but Lucas shared her distrust. Glancing at Carissa, she shook her head. "It's fine." She tapped her fingers on the table. This Dugald person made her want to get out of the house. Perhaps a walk will clear my head and help pass the time until Lucas returns. He'll know what to do about the key. She knew Lucas well enough to believe that for him to single out an individual who bothered him he must have strong reasons. Lucas knew how to manage this kind of thing. He went about the city glowing like a seraph, always acquiring what he wanted and making things go his way.

"What is the matter Ma'am?" Carissa bit her bottom lip glancing around the big kitchen to see what she had missed.

"It's not you, my dear . . ." taking the teacup, letting it warm her thick knuckled hands. Then setting it down without taking a sip. Yes, best to go out for a walk.

"Is there anything else?" Carissa was wiping down the table and removing the bowl of broth.

"Please take that broth upstairs to that man's room."

"Yes Ma'am."

"And come right back down and wash your hands. Doctor is coming."

* * *

Doctor Wilhelm, who Lucas never needed to see, listened with attentive consternation as Lucas described Dugald's symptoms. Lucas relayed his observations carefully, hesitating long enough to collect his thoughts and avoid exaggerating the severity of the first signs. Dugald had been sweating in the hallway, he had not yet vomited, did he have headache? How was Lucas to know? An hour ago, he didn't care if the man was sick or dying, but now it greatly mattered.

"So, you say the only swelling so far is the right hand?" the doctor spoke in a low, slow voice that didn't calm Lucas but instead increased his concern. The gray-haired doctor, while listening to Lucas, deliberately placed items into his black leather satchel.

Lucas paced, adding details then retracting them. "Please hurry," he finally demanded.

Dr. Wilhelm suppressed a smile. "You know it has been many years since our city has seen plague. Why are you so nervous, Lucas?"

"I'm not nervous." Lucas said taking a seat in a chair by the door, his leg pumping up and down, he rested his elbows on his knees and buried his face for a moment. "Have you seen a young woman new to the city? She has hair the color of a low burning oil lamp."

"Ah . . . I see you have caught something yourself, Lucas."

"I haven't caught her yet. I must find her first. She bumped into me in the street just outside the square. I have never seen her before."

"Nor will you again if you waste any more time here. I don't know who she is, but I will keep an eye out. Now go along. I can make my own way to Mrs. Kempel's house."

"No," Lucas said rising. "I will see you there."

* * *

As Irene walked away from the house, the wind whirled down the narrow street. Turning her back against it, she peered up to the third floor of her stone boarding house. A shadow, a flutter of the curtain, was that Dugald at his window . . . watching her? When Irene had donned her shawl, and was going out the front door, Carissa had come downstairs. She said he lay sprawled across his bed, sleeping. She had left the soup at his bedside. They both wondered if he had fainted or feigned sleep. If he awoke, Irene thought, he had no immediate reason to come back downstairs and bother Carissa. A fierce gust flung her shawl across her face. She staggered backward and nearly lost her footing on the cobblestone street. When she looked back, the shadow had vanished. Yesterday, her thoughts were all for the day ahead with Lucas. She hadn't taken her usual scrutiny of the man. If she had, she wouldn't haven't let him a room. Hurrying away from the house, she scolded herself for having rented to him. After all these years, she should know better. A bitter sadness stung her. If she still had her husband none of this would be happening. Her house would still be her home, their home, without strangers skulking around with secrets and agendas. It was just a matter of time before something like this happened. She hurried along the bustling streets searching for an answer, she walked right past the dress shop where she often stopped in to run her hand over the new fabrics. And not even the baker could distract her today. Finally arriving at the apothecary shop, she paused to settle herself. An elixir will do me good right now; pushing open the door she stepped inside.

"Good morning. Mrs. Kempel."

"Hello, Mister Padgett." She offered her hand and remembered then that Dugald had mentioned the apothecary had recommended her boarding house. "Can you recommend a potion for nerves?"

"Certainly." Mister Padgett went to a wall of tiny wooden drawers where he removed two small alabaster bottles. "Clary sage, lavender and chamomile. A little of each on a soft cloth, hold it to your nose whenever you feel nervous. And slip it under your pillow tonight so you may rest easy." Pulling a square of white cloth from another drawer, he added. "I will show you how."

"Thank you. Will you please put it on my account? I'm afraid I rushed out of the house without my coin purse."

Mister Padgett eyed Mrs. Kempel. "May I be so bold as to ask what troubles you madam?"

She looked around the shop avoiding his gaze.

Coming out from behind the counter, Mister Padgett approached. "Would you like to sit down for a moment?" He gestured toward a wooden chair placed against the wall.

"That would be fine."

Holding the cloth as he suggested, she leaned back and closed her eyes. Seemingly overnight her world had changed. Lucas met a woman, and although a few hours ago she felt joy and excitement for what she saw as a potential extension of her family, now she felt vacant and fearful. What if this young woman wants to take him away from the city? He will leave me; I am not his mother. I hope he finds the doctor. He seemed so worried. What if he gets sick also? I will be alone again—in a house filled with strangers. He should have a rest before going out to work tonight.

Mister Padgett gently touched her elbow. "A cup of tea, Mrs. Kempel?"

She shook her head surprised to hear his voice above her own stream of thoughts. With shaking hands, she accepted the small porcelain cup and saucer. "I do not feel at all myself today."

"Is everything well at your house? I sent a lodger in your direction."

"Yes!" She said sitting upright. "How do you know him? Where did he come from?"

"Ah, well, he came in through the front door. He complained of stomach cramps. Too much drinking in my opinion. I gave him some herbs and told him about your house. Is there something wrong with him?"

"I just don't know who he is."

"Neither do I Mrs. Kempel. I'm sorry. He said he had business for a few days. He had been travelling on a ship from Ingleena. Er . . . no, not that he was on a ship, but that he was expecting it. Baggage or goods, if I recall correctly. Said his name was . . ." Mr. Padgett squinted toward the window over her shoulder. "Hmm, what did he say his name was . . ."

"Dugald Tendrick." She held the teacup in her lap.

He raised an eyebrow. "I hope he is not causing you trouble. Surely your child of light is there to assist you."

"Yes, of course, Lucas is with me. Why wouldn't he be? He doesn't like this fellow either. He makes both of us uneasy and that was before he injured his hand."

Mister Padgett scowled, "His hand?"

Irene nodded. "I will confide in you Mister Padgett, if you can keep it to yourself. A spider bite, I suppose but Lucas has gone for Doctor Wilhelm just in case it's something else."

"Of course, Dr. Wilhelm can provide services that I cannot."

"Well, he is the doctor."

"Yes, he is the doctor and I am the apothecary."

Irene blew on her tea. "Perhaps you need a cup of tea as well."

"Don't worry about me Mrs. Kempel, I feel secure in the knowledge that we have Dr. Wilhelm and Lucas."

"As do I." Irene searched for somewhere to place her teacup.

Mister Padgett rushed on, "Lucas is wise beyond his years. He will not let any harm come to your house. I see him walking through the city, handsome and glowing in confidence. Quiet sort though, almost secretive one might say."

Mrs. Kempel wrapped her fingers around the cup feeling revived now that she had someone to talk to. Mister Padgett, although fidgety today, was an old friend who seemed to understand Lucas, to an extent. "His secrets are my secrets. And I would hope yours as well."

He straightened his shoulders. "Of course, Mrs. Kempel, but it's a shame that you have to ask. We have known each other for thirty years. Your husband Clive was my friend as you are. Have I not always stood by you and that shining child?"

She sighed. "That child is a man now."

Mr. Padgett squeezed her shoulder. "Ahh, that he is. I hope you will remember that I am always here for you."

Mrs. Kempel dribbled tea down the front of her muslin dress. "Of course," perspiration beaded on her forehead. What a confusing day. She rarely saw Mister Padgett other than when she ventured into the shop, perhaps last summer at the Faire, oh and then for the winter solstice celebration in the square. He had been standing beside her and she hadn't noticed until he said, hello. Flustered, she handed him the teacup and fanned herself with the herbal cloth. Wishing he would step away from the chair, she asked "Does Dugald come here often?"

"No, not at all. I have only met him the one time. I served him tea, as I have done for you as he seemed rattled as well."

"I am not rattled," She rose, pulling her shawl over her arms and clutching it at her throat. "Well, then I will leave you in peace, Mister Padgett."

"Mrs. Kempel, you haven't finished your tea."

His sad voice and woeful eyes interrupted her retreat. She hesitated, tempted to linger with this lonely man. But her thoughts had already jumped to Lucas. He and the doctor should be back at the house soon. "Good day, sir. Thank you for the tea."

By the time, she arrived back at the house, she had decided to keep the matter of Dugald's key to herself. She didn't want Lucas to know of her folly. Dugald, so ill, could lose the key anywhere. Best to keep quiet until she could make sense of things. Nothing could interfere with their trip to the country!

* * *

When Lucas left the doctor at the front door, Irene —although flushed and panting—assured him that all was well, and he should go about his plans for the day. She didn't mention the girl and Lucas wondered if she was aware of his plans to find her. He decided to retrace their steps from yesterday. As he walked, he calmed himself as he always did by intently observing his surroundings. The trees were showing off their spring splendor and the local merchants had adorned their window boxes with fresh flowing flowers in multitudes of color. He best keep his concerns about Dugald to himself. It was far too easy for rumors to run as rampant as the plague itself. There was no reason to create fear and incite panic. Lucas took a deep breath, brushed his hair back, and pushed his sleeves up as he strode along the sunny street. He smiled at a woman carrying a baby with a little boy clinging to her skirts. Something jolted in his heart, like a memory or a vision; he could not be sure which. The young mother shyly returned his smile and Lucas forgot all about Dugald. He loved nothing more than roaming the familiar streets. The aromas, the sights, and sounds of life never failed to awaken his spirit. Several citizens waved, pleased to see Lucas out in the bright light of day. I'm looking for a magical girl he declared to himself and when he did, she appeared. And then disappeared.

He rushed forward, the crowd parting like a school of darting fish. He heard a curse or two as he nudged some strollers aside, but when he rounded the corner, there was no sign of her. It was she. It had to be. None other had hair that color, unless that silly witch, Madam Trousdale had cast a spell upon him. But then, there she was buying flowers from the vendor. Lucas tried to inhale and when that failed, he attempted to exhale. He ended up yawning just as she turned around. His breath caught in his throat, still deciding if it was going in or out, he could not speak. She flashed a captivating smile, flipped her hair over her shoulder, and turned her back on Lucas. He stepped forward and seized her by the elbow. Her bouquet of baby's breath, yellow lily, and orchid tumbled to the ground.

He held her arm fast. "What is your name?" he demanded.

"Here you are again. None of your business. Clumsy oaf!" She gestured at the scatter of fallen flowers that passersby had already begun to crush beneath their feet. "Let go of me." She yanked her arm from his grasp.

"Forget about the flowers. You must tell me your name."

"I don't have to tell you anything," she said. "But *you* have to replace that bouquet." She turned back to the flower vendor who had already begun to prepare a new arrangement."

"Yes, yes," he rolled his head from side to side and laughed. "Excuse me miss. Please select all the flowers that you desire."

Bowing he stood back and admired her as she chose her pink, white and blue flowers while sneaking coy glances in his direction. Yes, I am watching, he thought, with one hand on his hip, the other rubbing his neck. His countenance wavering from serious to boyish glee. When the woman presented the bouquet, Lucas gestured to add more blossoms.

This went on for several minutes before the bouquet became too large for even the vendor to manage, and the girl, as fresh and alluring as the dewy flowers, turned to him. "That's good enough," she said.

Lucas handed over a fistful of coins and turned to the girl. "Please tell me your name now."

She held the flowers up to her nose. Her emerald eyes sparkled. "Thank you," she said. "Now, I need a tulip."

Lucas beamed; he could play her game all day long. "Now, the young lady would like a tulip," he told the flower lady.

"No tulips today. This is all I have." The woman gestured to her display. "Is the young lady not yet satisfied?"

"I dare say she is not, but I will see to it that she is." Lucas flashed a confident grin at the girl who hid her face behind the grand bouquet. He leaned over the baskets brimming with colorful fragrant flowers. A lush purple rose caught his eye. "That rose," he said, pointing to it. The woman carefully wrapped the thorny stem in paper. When he turned around with his ultimate prize, the girl and her magnificent bouquet had vanished.

For the first half hour of searching, Lucas felt confident that she could not have gotten far. But in the winding arched streets of intermittent doors, gates, and vacant plazas, it became apparent that she had slipped away once again.

The black veil started to itch inside his shirt. *She is engaging in tricks. She lures me with the joy and light of a child, yet she runs. What compels a woman to behave in this manner? Surely, we could enjoy ourselves more if we were to share a cup of wine or stroll along the river.* He had a strong image of her now, and although the flower lady said she had seen the girl before, she didn't know where she lived. He need only to station himself at the flower booth each day. Perhaps, a disguise was necessary to deter any further dalliance on her part. He enjoyed games, but in the case of this girl, Lucas wasn't willing to waste any time. So many thoughts raced through his mind that he could not keep up with himself. Lucas decided to go to the harbour and inquire of Nikolas. He took his favorite route, traversing high running canals stretched over planked foot bridges entwined with bright green burgeoning vines. Rushing water echoed among the rocks and the tall stone buildings. He encountered a woman carrying an empty basket heading to market and presented her with the purple rose. She blushed profusely as she placed the rose in her basket and murmured, "Thank you, Lucas."

Ships arrived at the harbour almost every day, and the harbour men, like Nikolas, who came and went at all hours, would certainly know if a beautiful young woman had just arrived in the city. Lucas found Nikolas sitting on the bulwark with his sandy hair swept back by the sea breeze, his long legs crossed at the ankles. He was eating fried fish wrapped in paper. At the sight of Lucas, he set his meal aside, wiped his hands on his trousers, and gestured for Lucas to sit. "Ahh, my friend, you appear poorly, what ails you?"

Lucas rocked on his feet. He didn't feel ill. He peeked at his hands and rubbed his face, thinking of Dugald's swollen hand. Irene and Carissa were alone with him at the boarding house right now. Not alone, Dr. Wilhelm and others were about, but if they needed him . . . "I feel fine. Do I seem unwell to you?"

"Of course not," Nikolas laughed and cupped Lucas on the chin, but you have something on your mind, I can see that well enough."

"Who's in?" Lucas asked as he sat beside his friend.

"Nobody now. *Le Peresi* just set sail," Nikolas said. "It's a quiet day. Some merchants inquiring of goods soon to arrive, but no impending cargo of interest to us." He offered the wrapped fish.

Lucas grimaced and waved it away. "I can't eat. I'm searching for a girl."

Nikolas swallowed fast. "A girl!" he repeated wiping his mouth with his sleeve. "I'm glad to hear it. Where is this girl?"

Lucas slouched. "If I knew that, I wouldn't be asking for your help. Have any ships arrived with immigrants, maids, serving girls or heiresses?"

Nikolas fluttered his eyelashes and shook his head. "No, certainly, nobody like that has come through. And I would know. I keep a keen eye out for that kind of arrival. Ever since last week with the brawl of the wealthy merchants, it has been quiet around here." Both men laughed. A fight had broken out between two merchants regarding confusion over a load of cargo. The men showed up so intoxicated they began throwing punches at the harbour boys. The harbour master ordered them thrown into carts, hauled off the wharf, and forbade their return.

Nikolas peered at Lucas whose eyes were dark as he clutched a hand to his stomach. "Are you telling me you have fallen for a girl and you can't tell if she is a servant or a Lady? What is this about Lucas?" He furrowed his brow imitating the concern he noticed reflected on Lucas' face. "How can I be of assistance?"

"Help me find out who she is." He gazed out to sea as he spoke. "I encountered a young woman on the street yesterday. Mrs. Kempel and I were out walking. This girl, she accosted me and fled. Then, she did pretty much the same thing this morning after I bought her flowers."

Nikolas threw back his head and laughed. "You make no sense. Have you been to the tavern?"

"No, not yet. Do you think she works there?" He leapt to his feet.

Nikolas squinted up at him. "Lucas. I meant that you seem as if you've been drinking. I have not seen a girl and you hardly appear to have been accosted twice by a young maid . . ."

Lucas threw up his hands.

"Maybe the tavern will help." Nikolas spoke with his mouth full. "Shall we go together? I can take an hour or two away from here."

Lucas ran his fingers through his hair, as he peered around the harbour. "Have you seen anything unusual around here lately?"

"Everything is unusual here. Teaming with thieves if you know what I mean."

"I am also seeking some trunks."

"Many trunks pass through here as you well know," Nikolas said gesturing with his fish cake.

"These trunks can't possibly be here. But the woman said they were in water . . . .. I have to get back." He raked his hand through his hair. "We have a new boarder and he's sick," Lucas whispered.

Nikolas raised an eyebrow, "A complicated morning for you my friend. Go and do what you must. You will keep me informed?"

"Of course. Mrs. Kempel believes it is only an insect bite. The doctor is there now."

"In the meantime, I will keep a lookout for your little lady." Nikolas winked. "Describe her for me."

"She is younger than I am, but not by much, I think that is so." Lucas closed his eyes and turned his face into the wind. Her hair is the color of a low burning oil lamp. She is light and airy like a gull feather . . .." He brushed his hair back and added, "she is though . . . hmmm . . . skittish." Lucas hesitated, shaking his head. "This girl, what is the legend of the Siren?"

"Ah ha, well," Nik scratched his stubbled chin. "The Siren's beckon sailors to their flowery shore."

"That's it." Lucas clutched his stomach.

"Their island is surrounded by cliffs and rocks, my friend. You've met a girl who makes you sick."

Lucas nodded. "More so than any other."

Nikolas slapped Lucas on the back. "I know she won't lure you out to sea. But take heed. You will certainly like it much more once you catch up with her. But there is no need to worry yourself, the feelings fade almost as fast as they come. It has happened to me more times than I can count. You know that." He picked up his greasy fish and took a large bite.

Lucas hurried back toward the house. Irene would be worried; several hours had passed. How thoughtless of him to think of himself when she surely needed him. She had made no comment about the girl since retrieving her veil yesterday. Of course, Dugald had upset the morning. If not for him, they would have had a pleasant morning meal together discussing the previous day, the fortuneteller, and the girl. Lucas enjoyed following Mrs. Kempel around the boarding house as she did her chores and pitching in when he could. He had taught himself basic carpentry skills. He wondered if it was enough. Mrs. Kempel looked tired, the kind of tired that settles into the face and doesn't go away. His stomach churned. The smell of fish always sickened him, which is why he avoided the harbour as much as possible. He rarely needed to go there; Nikolas took care of that end of things and Lucas dealt with matters on the streets. Some evenings, he and Nikolas met up after work at the Blue Gate Tavern, it was far enough away from the harbour and the smells that lingered there. The food came piled high on pewter plates. Lucas had never fallen sick after eating there.

Hurrying along the market street and through the square, Lucas realized it would have been proper to save some of those flowers for Irene. At least the purple rose. He should have thought of that. The excitement over the girl swept him along in a shimmering daze. Possibilities and desires he'd never imagined before filled his mind. But Irene was at the other end of her life. While the very future she'd just spoken of beckoned him, her most tender days sat behind her. In her eyes, he detected sparks of happiness for him, but clouds of sadness threatened as well. A dull ache crept up his spine and settled around his head.

* * *

On the outskirts of the city, three streets north of Madam Trousdale's' cottage, the girl sat at her dressing table brushing her hair. It took five vases to hold all the splendid colored flowers. She had intended to share them with her widowed neighbors as she had done since arriving in the City of Dreams a few weeks ago. Flowers warm the most vacant heart. But these, she could not yet part with, not even one of them. The tulip was a mere stalling tactic, she already knew there were no tulips today. Within moments of running from the man, she had returned to the flower vendor to speak with him. It wasn't until she had fled–distrusting all men now–that she realized who he was. He was the very man to help her. *Go to the City of Dreams. Find the man of amber light* is what the note said. She'd found it in her father's pocket the night he died. He had written it, she realized later, in case she didn't return home in time. If they had walked out together that evening, he would have told her in person. Having only just returned home from boarding school, her bath beckoned and then, rode weary, she'd fallen asleep. How could she rest when the household was in disarray upon her arrival? Her father promised it was only preparations for restoration work. They were to have a long walk and then a talk over dinner, a dinner they never shared. If only she'd skipped the bath, fought off the need to nap. But how could she have known their time was up? The state of the house and the note were proof that her father knew, and that he had intended to tell her what was wrong. In the note he explained how to save herself. But, if they had talked the hour before he died, she would have made sure they found a way to both save themselves.

The scents emanating from the flowers brought the lantern lighter into her room. She brushed her hair far longer than necessary marveling at his bold nature. First, he tried to grab her throat in the street and now he adorned her with flowers. The sound of his voice rang in her ears. How dare he demand to know her name. Those dark piercing eyes. A gentleman should request a proper introduction. Could she trust him? She hadn't expected him to be so young and appealing. She had imagined an older, politer, and more subdued man. She hadn't prepared for this. His presence and strength of will had startled her. She closed her eyes determined to bury the feelings that struggled to emerge from her crumpled heart. Now that she had found him, it felt trivial to ask him to help her fight for her inheritance. An inheritance she wasn't certain she deserved, even if it still existed. She wanted to talk to him though. Her father had told her to do so. Tears streamed down her cheeks and her heart thumped in slow painful beats. I don't want to be in this strange place seeking help from strangers. I should have thrown myself into the sea. If only I could ask father why he recommended this formidable man.

* * *

Lucas pushed open the front door to find Irene sewing in the parlour. Her eyes lit up and she set her mending aside. "There you are, dear boy." She patted the green velvet settee. "Join me."

He plopped down beside her, and she gave him a gentle hug. He rested his head on the pillowed cushion. As far back as he could remember, he had not been able to summon a memory of hugging his real mother. After so many years with Mrs. Kempel, she had become his true mother. "All is well," she said, picking up her mending again.

He stretched his legs out in front of him. "What did the doctor say?"

"It's only a spider bite." She patted his knee. "Dugald is upstairs resting."

"I don't like him," Lucas declared.

"I don't either, but we hardly know him."

"There's something about him that bothers me. I can't describe it."

"Let's wait and see when he recovers in a few days. He seems harmless now. I think he'll leave soon. Would you like some tea?"

"Yes, I would. I'll make it, you stay there."

She followed him into the kitchen, nonetheless. "Well?"

Lucas swung the iron pot from over the fire. It clattered against the stone hearth spilling the boiling water into the simmering flame. He felt a dull ringing in his ears until he swallowed several times and smiled gently at Irene. He knew he could have brought her some flowers, but she was none the wiser. He stirred honey into the tea. She waited patiently. He felt a distance between them that yesterday hadn't existed. Did he put it there or was she withdrawn? This is the cycle of life, he realized. All living things thrive in the sun but eventually begin to fade. He shivered, wondering if it would ever happen to him. It didn't matter. It was natural for a man to want to find a woman. It just never occurred to him that it would happen so abruptly. The sudden arrival of the girl amazed him. And from the look of Irene his feelings affected her also. He wanted to protect her, but from what he wasn't sure. The fishy harbour wasn't the only thing that upset his stomach. And as exciting as it was, at the same time, he could not relax into the feeling. A sense of urgency overpowered him. Staring at the wall, he imagined hurling the pot against it, the bricks crumbling into pebbles of confusion at his feet. Why did she run away? He turned to Irene; her expectant face eased his nerves.

"I went looking for the girl."

"Did you now?"

"It's foolish." They sat across the table from each other. Lucas returned her steady gaze, trying to hide his feelings from her. He gulped his tea. "I don't know anything about her."

"But you will."

"So, before I lose you completely, let's plan our trip to the country."

Lucas patted his shirt feeling for the comfort of the black veil. "Of course. Who will mind things here? Certainly, not little Carissa."

Irene scoffed, "Madam Trousdale has agreed to come and stay. She will take care of things here with the help of Carissa."

"No! Madam Trousdale in our house? That is not humorous at all."

"It's not a joke. She is a good woman. We can trust her. I told you she stayed here some years ago. She was helpful and trustworthy. A shrewd businesswoman she is. Many rely on her insights. A few weeks before I found you, she moved out to her cottage. I dreaded her leaving and she promised that I would not be alone." Irene reached across the table and stroked his hand. "You're cold Lucas, what is the matter? Why don't you like her?"

"She makes me uncomfortable. She must be after something. She behaves as if she knows more than she does."

"Well, she is a fortuneteller. It is her vocation to know."

"Some would say that she is a charlatan."

"Lucas, as one who abides by no laws, you know better than to say such a thing."

He wrinkled his nose, "I don't believe in these things. Pretending to know what will happen to a person for money," Rising he went to the basin and splashed water on his face.

"There are some who walk among us and help others simply because they can."

Lucas looked at Irene, his eyes softened. Crossing to where she sat, he leaned down and kissed the top of her head. "I have to go to work now."

He went to the cabinet to retrieve his lighting sticks, candles, oil, wicks, tall square lanterns, and short round ones. "It all seems to be intact," he muttered.

Irene shook her head and lifted an eyebrow. "I don't recall if I left the cabinet open yesterday . . . all the excitement about our day together."

"And Dugald showed up just as we were leaving," Lucas added.

Irene sighed. "Madam Trousdale will be here tomorrow. She will deal with Dugald. Nobody knows better than her if someone can be trusted or not."

"I do not trust *her*, Irene!"

Her eyes widened. "She will watch him while we are in the country."

Lucas grimaced.

"You can trust her, Lucas. She will make sure he touches nothing of ours."

Lucas nodded seeing the logic in the plan despite his disbelief in the woman. They had nothing for her to steal. Not as far as anyone could tell. She did seem to know things. "If you say so, I have no choice but to agree with you. As usual, you are most likely correct."

"As usual," her eyes sparkled.

"In the meantime, it appears that Dugald can't leave his bed. Can you see to it that he stays that way?"

Irene nodded. "A special tea from Madam Trousdale and a large dose of nutmeg will keep him faint and out of sorts."

They gazed at each other for several long moments, each knowing that nutmeg may indeed ward off plague as well. Neither dared say so and bring the cursed word into the household.

Lucas gathered his tools and turned to go. "That's the arrangement then. I can always count on you, Irene. We shall depart the day after tomorrow."

Chapter 4

Lucas left for his rounds and, as always, lit the lamps outside the front door first, then all the lanterns closest to the house so that Irene always had light surrounding her house. From there he continued along the twisting, crisscrossed streets. Once he completed his official route, he headed toward the old, two-story dwellings. They had once been desirable homes. As the city grew with the increase of harbour traffic, more fortunate citizens moved closer to the square along the Boulevard. Now, these two-story buildings housed mostly transient travellers. This was the last area to benefit from lantern light and it was minimal. Many houses had no set lanterns and the hand-lanterns he placed always disappeared. Only one oil lamp stood at the end of this street. Lucas doubted his lovely lady would tolerate such conditions. But since everyone is subject to misfortune at one time or another, he lit the lamp and from his bag retrieved several hand lanterns and set off down the smoky street.

The cool air and darkening sky welcomed him as he walked peering into curtain-less windows as he went. He took great delight in observing citizens emerge from their homes and step into the lamplight he created for them. He peeked through doors searching for the girl. Lucas travelled to the end of the street, lighting and placing hand lamps until he found himself near to the dark zone cottages at the end of his route. There beside a low wall stood the last oil lamp before the dark zone. Relieved and disappointed at the same time, he lit the lamp and crossed the street just as a door flew open in front of him. A hooded figure pitched out and collided with him. Lucas instinctively thrust his lighting stick, while his other hand reached for the dagger concealed in his waistband. A bundled bouquet framed with tiny white baby's breath fell at his feet. The draped figure fumbled for the flowers before becoming tangled in the cloak and tumbling to the ground. Lucas dropped his tools and extended a hand.

A pale face turned upward. "Oh! I didn't see you! I thought I tripped on the step."

"You did," he said in startled disbelief. Bending down he grabbed her wrists and pulled her to her feet. "You are more than just beautiful; you are clumsy as well!" he muttered, as he gathered the scattered flowers. He cupped her elbow in his hand and presented the mangled bouquet, his heart racing. "Once again I offer you flowers."

She glared at him with narrowed eyes. "Once again you have spilled my flowers."

"You don't think *I* made you trip, do you?"

"Why are you laughing? I go in and out of this door, every day. I have never tripped before."

"Seriously, I must say I doubt that. Your feet are bare, and your cloak is too long."

She bit her lip and lifted her skirts to examine her feet. Lucas admired her thin ankles and bare feet.

"The flowers are ruined. I cannot deliver them now."

"You sell flowers? I used to sell flowers myself."

She looked at him for a moment. "Don't mock me. I don't sell them. They were for a friend."

"With my mother, I sold flowers," Lucas said, releasing her arm.

"I see," she pursed her lips.

Wiping his oily hands on his sooty coat, Lucas began to speak but his mind went as blank as the slate sky. "Are these the flowers that I bought for you?"

She gazed openly at him but did not answer. He leaned forward. In her eyes, he saw the green fields of his childhood. "Where do you come from?"

She gazed past him.

"You are new to the City of Dreams? Yes, I see that you are. Welcome young lady." He held out his hand and waited several moments until she placed her warm hand in his. He could feel her pulse pound into his, filling him with fire. She stood silent, like a statue carved from the finest fluid marble. She bit her lip, pulled her hand away and turned her head to peer over her shoulder.

"Is someone inside?"

"I hope not," she whispered.

Collecting his tools, he offered his arm. "Shall I accompany you on your errand? Or would you like to get your shoes first?"

"No," she said but took his arm offering a half smile.

"Well then, shall we just stand about for a moment?"

She giggled.

His tools slipped from his hand with a clatter. He took her hands in his. "Are you all right?"

She breathed long and slow, staring at the ground.

He squeezed her hand. She squeezed back.

He pulled up the sleeve of his shirt and placed his wrist against hers, entwining his fingers in hers. When she peered from beneath her lashes, he noticed a glimmer of joy in her eyes before she started to pull her hand away and then didn't. This girl was more than he had even imagined. He gripped her hand tighter for fear she would disappear into the gloaming. His heart drummed so loudly in his ears that he could barely hear himself speak. "You should not venture out now."

Relaxing her hand in his, she spoke in a soft breathy voice, "I had only intended a quick errand around the corner." She turned her head and her hair tumbled down her back.

He couldn't decide on the color; it was like the dark just after dusk and the glow of his lantern as well. "I should hope it not too far since you travel without shoes, precious lady."

Taking a step away from the door, she said, "I was in a hurry. That bouquet was for an elderly woman I visit."

"She could not wait for you to put on shoes?"

"I suppose . . .but I like to feel the warm cobbles on my feet." she peered up and down the abandoned street, "And I wanted to surprise her." Glancing over her shoulder again she added, "Also, I wanted to be outdoors for a while."

They stood staring at each other in the fading light with clasped hands. Above them the sky filled with stars. The air grew cool. The world held its breath. And where their skin touched at the palms and wrists, their blood ran together.

Somewhere in the distance, a cat screeched. She shifted from one foot to another and kicked at a loose stone.

"Perhaps that is why you tripped."

Tilting her head, she fluttered her eyelids. "Perhaps . . ."

"Shall we sit a moment?" Fully aware of his thudding heart, he led her to the low wall beside the oil lamp across from the house.

He lifted his hand to caress a silken curl at her neckline. She caught his hand.

"I'm sorry, my hands are dirty," he said pulling away.

"You always grab at me."

"No... I . . . ah, the ruby pendant. You must accept my apologies. It's, well, shall we say . . ."

"An impulse?"

His shoulders slouched. But she reached for his hand and held it again. He felt her pulse merging with his once more. He took a silent breath and bowed his head, stroked the inside of her pale wrist, then placed both his palms atop hers. In a house nearby a lone musician played music from the lyre. The spring-scented breeze ruffled their hair. Nightfall swallowed the twilight. Since their first encounter, he'd practiced his inquisition. Now, his throat felt dry, his tongue thick, and his questions foolish. The entire world could go black if he could remain in the company of this girl who did not seem to want to let go of his hands. In the darkness, they focused on the light in each other's eyes.

A man's voice bellowed from inside her house, "Alina!"

"That's me," she whispered leaning into him with a finger to her lips. Inside the stucco, half-timbered house, lamp light suddenly beamed through the part open door. And something shattered inside. She yanked her hands from his and scurried toward the door.

"Trouble?" Lucas lurched after her.

"No. Don't!" her eyes wide with fear.

"Who's inside?" Lucas followed.

She bowed her head. "Not now. Come back." Pulling a sprig of crumpled baby's breath from the pocket of her apron, she opened his fingers and placed it in his palm. Then she spun into the house and slammed the door.

"Wait!" Lucas reached for the iron doorknocker, but let it fall without a sound. He pressed his ear against the door and hearing nothing grabbed the handle and shoved. It held fast. Who was in there with her? She could not possibly have a husband! He would not allow that to be true. Pacing, he waited for her to emerge again, his mind spinning with concern and anger. Three-quarters of an hour later, he was still there. Watching the windows in hopes of catching a glimpse of her. Finally, he did. Upstairs, in the front window to the left of the door, a small flicker of flame appeared. Then, to his immense delight, her small hand pressed against the glass for a fleeting moment before the candle went out. From the deep pocket of his supply bag, he took out the last hand lantern, lit it, and placed it in the arched nook next to the door. He lit fresh wax candles on all the window ledges and left some extras there because they burned longer than tallow. If she was watching, she could come down and retrieve them when it was safe to do so. Filled now with a warm hope that he didn't know existed in the world, Lucas stepped back from the house to stand by the wall where they had just sat. He looked up to her window and bowed. Retreating backwards, he watched the window and door hoping Alina would appear one more time, but his will failed to conjure her.

Carefully placing the crushed baby's breath into his pocket, he wandered the city where his lanterns still glowed. It seemed that tonight, the lamps shone brighter than ever before. Embraced by the comfort of his own light, he could think only of the girl, Alina. At least he learned her name, although by no effort of his own, so mesmerized by her. Her name floating like lyrics through his mind, he wondered how he could whisk her away from the sad, bleak house and the angry man inside. They could escape to the country where they would roam the grassy hillsides and dance among the flower fields. By the time, he reached the Blue Gate, his impatient ideas could only dissipate into a somber swig of whisky. Hours later he returned to Alina's house. It was completely dark. He imagined her lying on her side, amber hair spread across white linen sheets, her breath soft and slow as she dreamed of him, of them, he hoped.

* * *

Still in the throes of sleep Lucas heard a low growling followed by a yip and a shout that brought him fully awake. He recognized the voice of his ancient neighbor shouting at the dogs that breached his crumbling house. He rolled over feeling remarkably rested as he lay there and thought about what he needed to do before going to the country. He had to remember to get more oil for the lamps along the Boulevard and he wanted to take more hand lanterns to Alina's neighborhood and as many corners of the cottages and dark zone as possible. He needed to fill his supply bag with candles and wicks and instruct Ikarus to pay attention to the hand lanterns he wanted placed on the streets close to the dark zone. When he returned from the country, they must secure permanent lanterns with steel bolts in that area. Leaping from bed, he flung open the window sash, filled his lungs with fresh air and waved to his neighbor, Clancy who tossed scraps to three grateful dogs. In the morning light, he noticed just how smudged his hands were. The next time he saw Alina he must appear more presentable. Opening his door, he called into the empty hallway "I need hot water please!"

Irene appeared at the top of the stairs. She pressed her lips together and pretended to cover her eyes. "You need a towel as well, Lucas."

Lucas ducked behind the door. "Pardon Irene, I thought you were below in the kitchen."

"Now the entire street knows you want a morning bath. You're looking healthy, I dare say." She laughed and tossed her head to the side. "I'll put the pots on, but you must carry them yourself."

"Of course, I'll just be a moment." He closed his door and hurried to pull on his trousers.

In the kitchen, the fire glowed under the black iron pot. Irene fed logs to the fire. "If you recall I scrubbed you when you arrived here, just a scraggly villain."

He blushed and laughed poking a finger into the pot.

"I'd forgotten about the scar," she said.

Shirtless, Lucas scratched where a white scar crossed his breastbone.

"At first you told me that you got it climbing into the wagon that took you out of the country."

"I did say that."

"You knew then."

"I knew something."

"But not when it began."

Lucas set a log on the fire. "I only knew that my mother was dead and that I wasn't."

"Lucky, I found you when I did." she scolded.

"Fortuitous for you as well, Irene." Lucas wrapped an arm around her shoulders.

"Take the water before it's too hot," she said pinching his side.

Lucas languished in his tub that he had placed directly in the morning sunshine. He laughed and talked out loud to himself to the point that Irene knocked on the door to ask if he needed help. "I could do with a linen dear woman."

Irene entered the room carrying two large linen towels on her plump hips. "Lucas, you're like a lad again."

He sprawled in the hot bath. "I believe I shall bathe every day instead of once a week. It relaxes my muscles and frees my mind."

"Makes an extravagant poet out of you too," Irene, remarked.

Lucas swept a wave of water over the side of the tub dousing Irene's shoes. She darted from the room exclaiming, "You are possessed, Lucas!"

Having slept so late, by the time he finished his bath it was afternoon; Lucas prepared his clothing for the trip to the country. Ikarus arrived to go over the arrangements for the next few days. Lucas gave him extra hand lanterns and explained upon which streets to replace them if necessary. After a quick supper by himself—Irene was busying packing and unpacking her luggage—Lucas could barely hold himself in. He set out for Alina's house. Not knowing yet what he could do tonight about the man in the house, he reassured himself that at least, for now, light would surround her. How inconvenient now, the timing of the trip to the country. He intended to ask who the man was, and then decide if he needed to steal her straightaway.

After an hour of waiting outside her house, his head ached. Conflicted thoughts clamored for attention in the red glare of the sinking sun. Inside neighboring houses citizens already lit candles, closed shutters, and pulled curtains against the chilling entities that rode in on the breath of night. Although he spent much time alone, Lucas never felt the isolation that accompanied his route through the city. He felt welcome on every street as he provided light and safety. The City of Dreams was an enchanting place to call home. He feared nothing of the legends of evil spirits who rule the dark. The only evil he had seen in his life had come from the hands and minds of men.

As he paced, worry gnawed at the back of his skull. Who was the man? Father . . . grandfather, ungrateful brother perhaps . . . but certainly not her husband.

Glancing up and down the street, he sensed eyes upon him. Not knowing what he would say if the man answered, he decided to bang the door knocker. He banged again, tried the latch, banged repeatedly until pale fearful faces appeared at neighboring windows. The sun had vacated the sky. A single, silver star danced daintily overhead. He gazed upward whispering an oath. Undaunted by his longing, the distant star sparkled seductively, soon joined by more beacons twinkling despite the plight of men. As tempting as it was to kick the door down, he decided it best to continue with his work for the evening and return later.

He took backward steps away from her house. When the street veered left a gray cat bounded from an invisible launch and ambled beside him sharing the silence. Lucas ignited the last lantern he'd brought. He didn't have enough to take to the dark zone. But Alina's way shone like day. The cat sat on its haunches and licked one paw then the other, rubbed its face much like Lucas often did, then darted down the obscure lane that led toward the squat cottages in the dark zone. With no mind of the indistinguishable road, Lucas placed his last lantern at the crossroad. Whether the idea came from his mind, or that of the cat, it was an excellent time to spy on the inscrutable Madam Trousdale. Silver glimmers of worn cobblestones guided him.

Tiny cottages, with their shutters drawn tight hugged the narrow lane, most emitting a waxy smoke from their leaning chimneys.

In the distance, Lucas saw a tiny flicker of light haloed in the window of the fortuneteller's cottage. The cat traversed several paces ahead, occasionally luring Lucas with its yellow eyes. Sure-footed and as alert as his companion, he made his way through the dark. The dim light indicated the witch was at home, unless she set a candle on the sill before setting out on her nighttime rituals. He checked the depth of his cloak pocket and felt sure that the gold-jewelled box would slip in with ease. That decided, the presence of the cat began to annoy him. He kicked a stone toward it. Undeterred, the cat kept pace as if it intended to have the box for itself.

Outside the cottage, Lucas quietly set down his tools and waited motionless beside the largest Linden tree. Nothing stirred except the cat who circled, rubbing against his legs. After some time, he reached down and petted its warm, sleek body. A loud bang and the cat shot from his grasp.

Madam Trousdale appeared in her doorway holding a thin candle and the iron fire poker. The tiny hourglass glinted against her chest.

Lucas pressed himself against the tree.

"Hello," she said. "Lovely evening for a walk."

Hand on the dagger in his waistband, he returned her watchful gaze.

"I knew you'd come back. Come on in then." She motioned with the poker.

He could already feel the poker colliding with his skull. "No, thank you. I'm working."

"Not way out here you aren't," she taunted gripping the poker. Lucas retrieved his lighting supplies and walked away.

Madam Trousdale didn't call out, but he knew she watched, and it irritated him. Thoughts of Alina stopped him. If she really could tell the future, he would like to know what she saw for them. Swiping his palm across his forehead in anticipation of a headache, he turned around. "Well," his words came out as mist. "I did enjoy your tea the other day." And the gold box he thought to himself.

Her crooked door hung wide open. "You enjoy many things about me." She tossed the poker onto her bed. "I won't hurt you, Lucas. You need not be afraid of me."

"I am not the least bit afraid of you." Leaning his tools against the tree, he stepped into the scented cottage. The hourglass that appeared empty when he arrived, now appeared full. Whose time was it keeping, hers or his?

As she shut the door, Lucas located the glorious gold box shining above the confusion of the single room cottage. It sat in its place of regal disdain on top of the wardrobe, jewels twinkling at him. His fingers flexed; he could already feel the weight of it. Turning his eyes to her, a spontaneous lie spilled forth. "Mrs. Kempel wants to be sure that you will show up to mind the boarding house as promised. We have finalized our plans for the trip to the country."

Madam Trousdale stood staring at him for several long moments. Then she floated across the room to the stone hearth and pumped the bellows. Flames came up from the ashes. Her diaphanous skirt and thin shawl fluttered toward the flame. Lucas rushed over pulling her away from the sparking embers.

His arm hairs stood on end. He dropped her wrist and coughed. "Use caution."

Madam Trousdale straightened her shoulders. In the firelight, Lucas noticed she had removed her abundant makeup and the feathery accoutrements from her hair. This was not an old woman at all.

She plopped herself on the plump feather bed. "How old are you?" he demanded standing in the middle of the room taking it all in. The gold box, for the moment, was not the object of his attention. Her scattered possessions were more those of a young gypsy than an old, jaded, fortunetelling woman. She sat in the corner of the room, silently observing him. "This is trickery. You are not the same woman from the other day. Is it your mother then? Where is she?"

"It is I. It is only I." She rose from the bed and gazed unblinking at Lucas.

Her flawless, olive skin shimmered as the room brightened with firelight, the smooth black hair and dark blue eyes could not belong to the same woman who just the other day told him about his mother's trunks. When he stepped closer, she stood as tall as he remembered, and her eyes reflected the burning coals.

Lucas stood back and folded his arms across his chest. "What magic is this?"

"The magic is yours, Lucas. You have questions and I have answers."

"Do you now?" You have more than answers Lucas thought as he leaned against the center post sneaking a peek at the gold box. "What are your answers?"

"What are your questions?"

He slapped his hand against the post. "I know how the likes of you operate. I tell you what I need to know, and you fabricate an answer to a problem you didn't know of until I told you about it in the form of my question." He pushed his hair out of his eyes and glanced at the box again.

"You must go to the country and find the trunk."

"I'm going, Irene and I are going. But it has nothing to do with you or your trickery to get me to go. I am going, but . . ." — and contrary to his thoughts, because he wanted to know more about his mother and who his father was, and he wanted to know if he had a future with Alina— "not because of you or anything you have said. I don't believe in looking into the future. We all want to know what lies in wait for us, but nobody does. What do you want from . . . from us . . . from me? Tell me the truth. You seek the trunks for yourself. How many trunks are there?"

The hourglass drained. Anger flashed in her spectral eyes She shook her hands as if they were wet and mumbled under her breath. "I don't want anything, but you want everything, Lucas." She swung her arm around the room. "I know you and I know what you want." She retrieved the iron poker from the fireplace folding her hands over it as she resumed her seat on the edge of the bed.

"You don't know me at all." Even as he said it, he knew it probably wasn't true. He'd spent every night of his youth meandering through the cottages, drinking, carousing, stealing, and whatever else; he could no longer recall. Many a witless victim among these dark streets had fallen prey to his adept pick-pocketing skills. Quite possibly, she had been one of those victims. At the least, she knew about his past. Of that, he was sure. Now it was up to him to discover who she was and what *she* wanted. He didn't believe for a moment that her intentions were entirely good or that she intended to help him. Even though Irene believed in her . . . they could be in danger. And now he had Alina to think about too. But in case Madam Trousdale could actually read his mind, he pushed Alina as far from his thoughts as possible. He took the same seat at the table as before focusing on the boiling water. Whoever she was, she made excellent tea.

"Where are you from, Madam Trousdale?"

"Where are you from, Lucas?'

"For the love of God, stop with the exasperating mimicking. Have you not a thought of your own?"

"Do you?"

Lucas shook his head and laughed. Madam Trousdale laughed as well, placed a teacup in front of him and took her seat beside him at the table. "I'm an orphan too."

"Now we're getting somewhere," Lucas leaned forward, sipped his tea. "Have we met before the other day?"

"Not that I know of."

Lucas' pupils dilated. "What does that mean? Must you be so cryptic?"

"It means, I don't remember your face. Therefore, I suppose we have never met."

"Therefore, I suppose not," Lucas mocked. "Are you truly friends with Mrs. Kempel? She is like a mother to me and I won't have her hurt or upset by you, or anyone, or anything."

"We are devoted friends. She helped me long ago and we meet every few weeks to discuss things. She asked me to help you and that is all I want to do. Mostly." She drank her tea and leaned back in her wobbly wooden chair. "I won't interfere in your life if you don't interfere in mine. Unless . . ."

"Unless what?" Lucas's face burned assuming she referred to the gold-jewelled box. Where did she get it, he wanted to know but dared not ask. She wasn't confronting him so best to remain silent. "What things do you and Mrs. Kempel discuss?"

"Woman things. And you."

"I'm not getting specific answers from you."

"No, you're not. All you need to do is find the trunks."

"The trunks hold answers. There are three?"

"Correct."

"Which one holds the answers?"

"I didn't say they hold answers. The trunks contain what you need. That is all I can tell you right now. Find out for yourself."

"What about . . ." he wanted to ask about his past, if she knew anything about him, and he wanted to ask if she read anything about Alina in his future, but he noticed the crystal ball, hidden still under the cloth. He didn't want her to uncover it. He blurted, "What about Mrs. Kempel?"

"Irene loves you like the son she never had."

"I know. And I feel the same about Irene. She is a good woman."

"A very good woman, indeed." She brushed back her sheet of iridescent hair.

"So, all I need to do is find these trunks."

A slow nod. "Find them, Lucas. See where it takes you."

"It's intriguing."

"It is." She stretched her arms out in front of her with clasped hands.

"A truce then," Lucas murmured and sipped his tea.

She offered a languid smile.

"There is a new boarder at the house. His name is Dugald. He is ill from an insect bite or worse. I caution you to avoid direct contact with him. Also, I do not trust the man. Will you keep an eye on him?"

"I will, of course."

"I believe it is best to keep him subdued. He shouldn't be allowed to wander about until we know the exact nature of his illness."

"What did the doctor say?"

Lucas tugged his shirt away from his neckline. "He thinks it's a reaction to a spider bite."

"And you think . . ." she prompted.

"I think he should not be allowed out of his bed chamber." He shuddered at the thought of this strange, Dugald staggering about the City of Dreams spreading plague among the citizens. He must warn Alina tonight. He longed to take her to the country with them. Her safety could depend on it.

"I see." She gazed evenly at Lucas.

"Do you really see?" Lucas said drumming his fingers on the table.

"Yes, I do."

"Then see what this man is up to."

"Do you have any other orders?"

"That will do for now." Lucas extended his hand.

Her eyes flashed black, then blue; her hourglass full, she extended her hand offering a firm grip.

He rose and stepped away from the table taking one last bold look at the gold-jewelled box. When she opened the door chilly night air rushed in. With relief, Lucas stepped outside. He was halfway down the street before he wondered where the cat had gone. The impenetrable night gave no indication of the hour. He turned in a circle searching for his feline friend. Nothing moved or breathed except himself, at least as far as he could see. Up ahead the flickering, orange glow of his hand lantern cast looming shadows against the uneven walls of the ancient city. Stepping forward into them, he observed his overly tall form—familiar and strange at the same time. The old walls eked black water, drawing maps and misshaped images. As alarming as the images were, he felt drawn to their orphic mysteries. Never fearing the night, but craving its secrecy and potential, Lucas walked as always along the narrow lanes of the City of Dreams, where he overhears murmurs of conversation, and notices furtive glances that the weary residents fail to observe among their own companions. As the lantern lighter, he is accustomed to moving about unnoticed and keeping his observations to himself. His knowledge of the city and its residents is unsurpassed. Thus, the amazement that Alina had gone unnoticed.

Seeing no shadow of the cat, he hurried toward her house. There was much to discuss. But Alina's house was still and dark, even the lanterns had burned low and the candles were out. He re-lit everything while watching her window. Knowing better than to call out and put her in danger or bang on the door and alarm the neighbors, he quietly tried the latch that wouldn't budge. He sat down to wait.

The bell tower rung through two cycles before Lucas could force himself to leave. With a heavy mood, he walked toward the Blue Gate in hope of finding Nikolas. His friend's insight would be welcome. And Nikolas would certainly be happy to hear that he had found the girl. He would keep an eye on her while Lucas was away.

With the taste of warm whisky already on his tongue, Lucas rounded the corner. No light from the tavern welcomed him. He stood in front of the bolted door trying to discern if Nikolas had been there. His mind drifted from the present to some years ago, when he and Nikolas frequented the Blue Gate Tavern every night and met women who were more than willing to drink with them and invite them home to their rooms. One woman, who called herself, Lady Philomena had captured Lucas' attention for more than a few weeks. He could not determine what it was about her that intrigued and simultaneously annoyed him. He knew she was no lady, but he took comfort with her every night until she began to speak of marriage and babies. Embarrassed still by his behavior—he had fled in the middle of the night, leaving his shirt behind—Lucas smiled to himself. It seemed so long ago now, and since then he had refrained from consorting with women who lived in the city. For a year afterward, Lucas and Nikolas avoided their favorite drinking establishment and sought libations at the more obscure and less woman friendly taverns nearby to the harbour. Ultimately, on a warm spring morning Nikolas appeared at the boarding house to announce that he had just himself helped Lady Philomena board a ship to Ingleena. With great satisfaction and to Lucas' profound relief, he also reported she travelled only with her aunt, no babes in tow. To celebrate that day, they proceeded to the Blue Gate Tavern before the noon hour. How different he felt now. That woman could not hold a candle to Alina.

Lucas wandered away from the Blue Gate not ready to go home. He followed the streetlamps he'd lit earlier that evening. They would burn until daybreak. The City of Dreams suited him completely. Its very essence beat like a heart beside his. And now there was a heart he desired, Alina's . . . amber-haired Alina. He dreaded the trip to Arcana now, fearing she would vanish from the city while he was away. If not for the fact that he had her veil inside his shirt, and that Irene had seen her too, he would have thought she was merely a dream, a beautiful dream.

His agreement to travel to the country had come only from a desire to please Irene. But now, with the bothersome Madam Trousdale talking of trunks, he needed to go. The sudden changes of the past week were not all welcome—if only the past could rest—but he knew it wouldn't until he discovered who he was.

Where was Alina, why had she not come to the door or window this night? On the solitary walk toward home, he kept a keen eye, as he always did, in case someone, mostly Alina, needed help at this lonely hour. He dreaded the thought that she could be outside so late. But he could clearly see that nobody except himself was about. The inhabitants of the City of Dreams felt protected by Lucas for good reason. He had pulled them from burning buildings, broken up fights, carried lost children home, and shared bread with the hungry. Everyone is home safe he murmured to himself.

In his younger days, Lucas helped himself to various goods poorly guarded by transients. Now, he was much more selective. The gold-jewelled box which had appeared in his life like a gift fell into an altogether different category. What that category was Lucas still had some reckoning to do, but one thing he knew as he envisioned the precious box was that it already belonged to him, as did Alina.

At home, the parlour was empty and the fire banked. He dragged his feet silently up the stairs and fell asleep the moment his body came to rest in the snug comfort of his bed with the black lace veil warm against his chest.

* * *

Secured behind her bolted chamber door, and surrounded by the remaining bouquets, Alina felt the luminous presence of Lucas before she saw him walking toward her house. Her candle already extinguished as she prepared to lie down for the night, she knelt at the window peering down at him from behind the curtain. She would throw herself on the floor if he noticed her. Last night, Vasil had threatened to run him through with his sword. And she knew all too well that he would do it. Even though he snored in a drunken stupor by now, she could not take the chance. From her small window, she watched and vowed she would ask for the assistance of Lucas but nothing more. Another man would not die because of her.

When Lucas walked away, disappointment pierced the cloud of longing that encased her heart. She could not peel her eyes away from his angular frame as he glided toward the corner, the night wrapping itself around him like a comfortable cloak, through the darkness he still shone. He fears nothing, she thought shivering and turning gratefully to the meager comfort of her small bed. That's him, without any doubt. He is the one. With the covers pulled around her ears, she tried to ignore the longing that stirred within her upon seeing the lantern lighter roaming the deep night that so clearly belonged to him. This was his city, not hers. Her father had acquired the house to assist in the management of his trade business. Now, that she was here, she couldn't imagine him here. The presence of Vasil tainted the house. Father never intended for her to live in such a place and she would not stay. Clenching her fists to her heart, she squeezed her eyes shut and imagined the beauty of the tree-lined streets of Ingleena where she and her father used to walk in the evenings. She must find a way to return.

Chapter 5

Irene was already in the kitchen when Madam Trousdale pounded on the front door. "Your Lucas is suspicious," she blurted.

Irene glanced up the stairs and indicated that Madam Trousdale follow her into the kitchen where the boarders talked in boisterous voices while they ate. "What do you mean?"

Madam Trousdale explained how Lucas came to her cottage. "He has many questions. He thinks *I* want something from *him*!"

Irene's eyes widened. "He is most disturbed by you. I'm surprised he went to your cottage. What did he say?"

"He loitered outside for a while. When I opened the door, he walked away, but I made him come in. He likes my tea and the various things in my cottage seem to intrigue him."

"I would like some of those Linden flowers. Will you bring us some?"

"I already did." Madam Trousdale plopped her satchel onto the table.

Irene picked it up and began emptying the contents. "Thank you. I appreciate your helping out around here while we go to the country."

"He warned me about this boarder, Dugald, apparently a scallywag of sorts."

Irene rolled her eyes, "Yes, he has me worried."

Madam Trousdale placed her hand on Irene's shoulder, "Don't worry, I'll take care of it."

Irene scratched her forehead. "I don't know, he was sent to me by Mister Padgett, but he doesn't know why the man is in our city. To pick up something from the harbour perhaps. Now he is ill."

"Leave him to me," Trousdale said patting her satchel of herbs. I have rosemary and rue among others in here.

Irene leaned closer, "And there is more," she whispered in the same tone as the pot hissing over the fire. "He had a key hidden in his room. I took it." She opened her palm then quickly folded her fingers tight, slipping her hand into her pocket.

"Has he missed it yet?"

Turning, Irene peeked over her shoulder at the boarders who shoved food into their mouths and mumbled among themselves. "He is feverish." With a clammy hand, she clutched Madam Trousdale's arm, "But if he were to awaken and attempt to retrieve this key. . ."

Madam Trousdale rubbed her chin and held out her hand. "Leave it to me."

But Irene patted her pocket and turned toward the cupboard examining the food supplies. "Where has Carissa got off to? I must go over the meal plans with her one more time. Forgetful girl."

Madam Trousdale folded her arms across her chest, her face dour.

Lucas awoke to the sounds of a full house. A dream floated through his mind. In the first part, he was running over rocky ground, fleeing. A frequent dream for Lucas. Then he was peering through the window of Madam Trousdale's cottage and she was waving her iron poker over the top of the crystal ball that blazed beneath its purple cloth. Making no sense of it he stretched out on his back listening to the voices that rose from the kitchen. He thought he heard Irene's voice mixed with the animated voices of the six boarders, a stonemason, a blacksmith, a mortar maker and three laborers. Apparently, they had not yet left for their toil. Was that Madam Trousdale already? Lucas got up, washed his face, and dressed quickly. He didn't want to miss the excitement of the morning and the preparations for departure. And certainly, he could steal a few minutes to see Alina. He would not hesitate to open her door this morning, rip it from its hinges if necessary.

As he entered the kitchen, the boarders were leaving for the cathedral site. A companionable lot, several of them nodded at Lucas before exiting through the back door. "Can you manage those men while we are gone?" he asked Madam Trousdale. She laughed, as did Irene. Lucas sat and the three of them discussed the journey ahead.

"Two of the men who just left are from the country. They suggested locations for lodging, one a boarding house, the other a proper Inn. The Grande Inn. We will stay there, won't we Lucas?"

"We certainly will," he flushed with excitement.

Ikarus came through the back door and Irene placed bread, jam, and tea in front of him as he took a seat at the table.

"I'm going to give Carissa some last-minute instructions." Irene patted Lucas on the back and hurried from the room.

The two men discussed supplies and the extra lanterns, Lucas insisted the lad not forget, while Madam Trousdale pretended not to listen. Ikarus devoured his bread and gulped his tea. "I'll take care of everything, Lucas." He flinched when Madam

Trousdale removed his empty plate. "I best go now. The day ahead is long. Good journey."

Madam Trousdale appeared completely normal to Lucas this morning. No flashing colors in her eyes or hair. His imagination and dreams were running wild he thought. "Do you keep any cats?"

"How do you mean *keep*?"

Those annoying questions with questions again, he thought. "I noticed a gray cat outside your house last night. Do you feed it or something?"

She laughed. "I don't feed it or something."

"Have you seen it though?"

She smiled.

"I'll take that for yes."

"It likes to climb the Linden tree."

Reminded of the willow tree he so enjoyed outside his bedroom window, Lucas mused, "The trees are beginning to bloom after the long winter. I am off to discover my roots," he pushed away from the table.

Madam Trousdale stood as well and extended her hand. "I wish you a fruitful journey, Lucas."

They shared a laugh and clasped hands. Hers felt warm now. "Thank you, Madam Trousdale. Remember about Dugald. Send for Doctor Wilhelm if you need him again. Be watchful."

She nodded, "Irene arranged for the apothecary to come by this afternoon and I brought plenty of tea and herbs." She indicated her satchel perched at the end of the table.

"All is well then. I will just step outside until Irene comes down." As he turned toward the door, he took note of the hourglass. It was full.

Irene came down the stairs. "All is ready," she said. "Lucas will you retrieve the luggage?"

His heart skipped. A stately carriage and a stoic coachman waited outside the boarding house. Two sturdy horses, as black as the carriage itself, stamped their hooves impatiently. Lucas cast a fleeting look down the street. He wanted to bolt down the cobblestones; there would be no chance to visit Alina now. A headache hit him like a club. His stomach felt like it was rolling down a steep flight of stairs. Madam Trousdale had come outside to see them off. No excuses came to mind.

Irene waited for Lucas to offer his hand. "The horses . . ." she said.

"Are strong and dependable," he finished her sentence.

"I've never ridden in such a carriage," her eyes round and dewy.

"Nor I." She must have given over two months board he thought. He took her hand and placing his other hand on her waist hoisted her into the carriage. Irene giggled and plopped onto the seat. They settled themselves into the plush pink seats. He sat facing forward while Irene sat facing backward. Should he suggest a roundabout route past Alina's house? Irene leaned out the window and waved. She was content so he kept his thoughts to himself. He waved to Madam Trousdale as the carriage jerked forward and the horse's massive hooves clattered on the cobblestones. Surely, the days ahead held some unforeseen surprises. He swore a silent oath that Alina would be waiting for him upon his return.

At the edge of the city, they passed the cathedral where massive stone walls were growing taller. The new addition extended the nave forward and relocated the crossing and lady chapel farther away from the old monastery that sat behind the cathedral hidden in ivy. Several hundred years ago, the early monks created a moat for their protection and utilizing the river created a loch system for their ancient harbour. Those adroit monks masterminded such an ingenious scheme that it defied the ability of skilled craftsmen to halt the influx of water. So, the moat remained, unheeded by all except for Lucas who sometimes thought he could see a faint glow reflected in the murky water. Even still, he hadn't attempted to cross it. There was no reason to. It continued to protect the abandoned monastery where no one cared to tread. The cathedral site hummed with the sounds of hammers, chisels, saws, and men shouting to each other.

"It appears our boarders will be with us for a very long time," Irene said.

"I hope Trousdale doesn't scare them off."

"No need to worry, dear boy. She is more than capable of taking care of them."

"Without doubt," he murmured furrowing his brow. "But what if Dugald wakes up and wants to go out . . ."

"He won't be waking up. I can assure you of that."

"I hope it is sure." Lucas breathed out slowly.

"I can be sure because Madam Trousdale brewed the tea for Dugald. He will sleep."

Lucas nodded. At least Alina was safe from whatever ailed Dugald.

A warm breeze carried the scent of spring grasses and moist earth. Lucas took a deep breath, smiling at Irene.

"This is good," she said with shining eyes. They clasped hands.

"Thank you, Irene."

"You're most welcome." She released his hand and sat back. The carriage rolled on.

"Are you beginning to remember anything now that we are outside the confines of the city?"

Lucas gripped the ledge and leaned out the window. "The openness, the scents of the earth, the touch of the wind, the endless sky, I feel it all as if it is part of my existence. I've dreamed of it." He blushed and laughed.

Irene clapped her hands. "Excellent! That is exactly how you should feel, as young as you are."

"I don't feel young, but I do feel . . . I'm not sure."

"Vigorous?"

"Yes," Lucas agreed. "Can you feel the force of nature. . . I'm not sure what it is . . . life, plants, trees, creatures. It's a different sense of being than that of men and structures."

"In a way, I see what you describe, but I don't have your youth. I have forgotten the exuberance and joy of the natural world. The days rarely excite me, except in my observance of you. Life flows as forceful as the river from you, Lucas. As for me, I am a stagnant puddle at the edge." She shivered despite the warm sun that shone through the open carriage window.

He unfolded the lap robe and tucked it around Irene. "Don't give up on your life, Irene. You are still here after all. The time to stop living doesn't arrive until your eyes close for the last time and the dreams cease."

"While we are talking about youthful exuberance, what of the girl?" Her eyes sparkled before she narrowed them and playfully kicked Lucas.

"Ah," he beamed, lowering his eyes, the blood rising in his cheeks and throughout his body. With a flourish, he pulled the black lace veil from inside his shirt and waved it at Irene.

Laughing, she took it between her hands and examined it for several minutes. "This is no ordinary maiden, Lucas. This veil is of the finest lace. So . . ."

"Either I have fallen for an heiress or a thief."

Irene nodded handing him back the veil. He examined the pattern before tucking it inside his shirt. She overwhelms me. Let her stay safe until I return. But Lucas kept his thoughts to himself. Now was not the time to tell Irene he had met the girl.

"She must be missing that veil. Perhaps she is not aware that you have it. After all, it floated away from her."

"Thank you for catching it.

Irene's eyes sparkled. "Anything for you. When we return, I will help you find her. I will make inquiries, although I don't think it matters to you if she is wealthy or a simple maiden."

"She matches me, that I know," Lucas said.

"If she is anything like you then I will love her too and she can come live with us. Unless of course she invites us to join her in her grand manor."

"I like how you think, Irene." But Lucas knew it would not be that simple.

They sat in silence listening to the rhythmic clacking of the carriage wheels. Within moments, Irene's eyelids fluttered, and she began to snore lightly.

Men on horseback passed them going in both directions. Horse drawn carts laden with hay, fruit, wood, barrels, and sacks of grain formed a procession on the wide road until they were well away from the City of Dreams. He noticed everything especially the flower carts, that was one of the few things he vividly remembered. He arrived in the City of Dreams in the back of a flower cart.

Appreciating the fact that Irene had carefully avoided inquiring about any memories of his mother, or her trunks, he allowed his mind to drift while keenly watching the changing landscape. He didn't want to miss any memory or clue from his childhood that may linger on this road to his former home. He didn't know why he remembered so little about his life in Arcana. The only reason he could come up with was the shock of it all had been too much for a young boy. His memories left off with his mother alive, close, warm, and encouraging under a clear blue sky surrounded by flowers. Their bond as solid as the earth beneath them. But something went horribly wrong. She died. He pictured her dark hair always worn in a loose bun and how she rubbed her damp forehead with dirty hands sometimes smudging herself with bits of petals and leaves from the flowers they picked. She had cuts and splinters on her hands, her skin tanned from the sun, as was his. She always held his hand as they walked to the flower fields in the mornings. Lucas closed his eyes, for an instant feeling his mother's comforting hand in his. He remembered her standing beside him in silhouette, a halo of sun behind her. Although a lot of time has passed, I don't miss you any less.

The carriage swayed from side to side, but the ride was smooth enough on the damp spring road. Expansive fields layered in wildflowers rose up, down and far across the hills. Lucas didn't want to miss a moment, but his eyelids fluttered, and his head bobbed. He leaned against the coach panel and allowed sleep. In the fields, he walked toward his mother; she held out her hand . . . he ran toward her, but she sped ahead. He ran again, she vanished, only to appear on the horizon, over and over he ran toward her, tripping, crying, and finally reaching her and feeling the soft brush of her fingertips. *The key is within your grasp,* she said.

Lucas jerked awake. The road had changed, now they were in a grove of tall sparse trees. Tiny green buds poked from their slender branches. His mouth dry, he licked his lips. The picnic basket with water, wine and whisky was on top of the carriage along with the luggage. He tapped on the front of the carriage twice before the coachman slowed, leaned over in an acrobatic pose, and peered through the quarter light. "What is it, sir?"

"I need to stop for refreshment," Lucas said softly, glancing at Irene who didn't stir.

"Not safe here sir."

"What? Why not?"

"Highwaymen frequent these woods."

"Oh hogwash." Lucas said. "I must stop. This horse needs to water both ends."

"The carriage horses require water as well. I will stop when it is safe for all." He nodded toward Irene.

"Yes sir," Lucas said. "Hurry every chance you get."

In three quarters of an hour, the carriage pulled up outside a tiny alehouse covered in ivy. The wood timber supports sagged and grass grew from every nook and cranny in the crumbling stone structure. Irene still slept so Lucas leapt from the carriage. "Stay with the lady. I won't be long."

"I don't advise going inside this particular establishment alone, sir." The coachman jumped down from his perch going directly to the horses and inspecting them as he ran a wide hand over the harness pulling and tightening.

"It's an alehouse. Why not go in?"

"I travel this road often. They know me here. You're a stranger. They don't like strangers in this part of the woods." He mumbled to the horses and led them forward to the water trough.

Lucas followed, shook his head, and began to laugh. "You are an interesting man. But you brought me here. I'm sure it's safe to go inside."

"I always accompany my passengers inside to make the introductions," the coachman said in an ominous voice.

Lucas peeked at Irene resting peacefully. He examined the nearby woodland, and the distance from the carriage to the entrance of the dilapidated drinking establishment. He saw no sign of any other carriages or men on horseback. In the time, it would take for the coachman to walk Lucas inside, nobody could approach without notice. Leaning into the coach, he bent over Irene, concerned that she had possibly drunk some of the tea they had made for Dugald. A low rumble in her chest, like a purring cat, assured him she was all right. "Bring the picnic basket down and set it inside but don't disturb Mrs. Kempel. Stay here and guard the carriage," he said.

He adjusted Irene's blanket and turned around; the coachman stood directly in front of Lucas. "It is supremely stupid to enter this alehouse without accompaniment."

Lucas waggled his head. "They do serve ale?"

"Of course, a mighty potent one."

"Then, I'm going in."

The coachman pulled himself up to his full height, but he was still shorter than Lucas. He said, "I told you it is a stupid thing to do."

"Well, if you're going to do something stupid, you may as well be able to get a drink out of it."

Lucas strode up to the alehouse, stepped under the sign that read—*No Horses Allowed*—flung open the door and strolled in. A rusty chandelier hit him squarely in the forehead. Four men who leaned against the bar in the narrow room broke out in laughter. Lucas rubbed his head and his fingers came away smeared with blood. "My coachman told me to wait. I should have heeded his words."

One of the men came toward Lucas, a tankard in his hand. "Well stranger. In which direction are you going?" The chandelier, covered in cobwebs, swung between them.

Lucas gazed upward. The man was taller than he by two inches and carried quite a few extra pounds. Scowling, not accustomed to looking up to anyone, he said, "Where am I headed, you mean other than straight into the chandelier?" This time nobody laughed. Lucas swallowed wanting his ale and a quick exit. "We're headed to the farming village of Arcana. Won't be long here." He pulled coins from his waist pouch. "A pint of ale is all I'm after." The barkeep had already begun pouring from a tilting jug. Lucas stepped past the man to the bar.

"What's your business in Arcana?"

With his back to the giant, Lucas said, "I was born there." He took a long drink, and then smacked his lips together. "That's good ale," he said to the barkeep who ignored him now. The other men stared with empty eyes, either too drunk or too lazy to care about Lucas anymore.

"I was also born there," the giant said.

"Good for you," Lucas drained his cup and turned toward the door.

"What's your family name?" the giant demanded blocking Lucas' way.

For an imperceptible second Lucas hesitated. Others had inquired, but not in a long time. He had no family name. At home, in the City of Dreams, he was known as Lucas the Lantern

Lighter, but he did not intend to share that information with the giant who stood before him. He wanted to get out the door and make sure Irene was all right, after all what did he know about the odd coachman anyway. Heat rose quickly from Lucas' toes to the roots of his hair. He clenched his fists then turned to the barkeep. "Two more, for my driver and companion." He threw several coins on the bar, took the fresh pours, stepped past the giant, deftly ducked under the chandelier, and burst out the door. To his great relief the coach had not moved.

A prickling sensation crept up his back but a quick glance over his shoulder assured him the giant had not followed him outside. The coachman cocked one shoulder. "Brave move."

Lucas leered shoving the two cups of ale at the man. He stepped behind the carriage to refresh himself and entered from that side. Irene was awake and holding her ale. "You nearly got us killed for this?"

"Certainly not! I can take care of myself in a tavern. But please, Irene where did you find that coachman?" He flipped open the lid on the picnic basket.

"He came with the coach. He carries two pistols for our safety," she said and gulped her ale.

"Of course. Well done." Lucas laughed, squeezing her knee, happy that she was alert and cheerful. She mopped his forehead with her handkerchief dipped in the ale. Relaxing he allowed her to dote on him. "It's merely a scratch, it won't last long."

"Now it's a clean scratch."

They shared bread and dried meat as the carriage rolled closer and closer to Arcana. Wagons rattled past full of apple barrels and fresh flowers resting in willow baskets.

At twilight, in the hushed and golden glow of Lucas' favorite time of day, the carriage clattered across the stone bridge that marked the entrance to the village of Arcana. His breath—held captive by his swelling heart—escaped as slow and measured as the countless days since his departure. His skin tingled, his hands shook, his eyes absorbed the ineffable beauty of his long-lost home. As far as he knew, the place of his initial birth.

The moment the carriage stopped at the sprawling two-story Inn; Lucas sprang out the door. The soft earth welcomed his feet like old friends. The gentle breeze caressed his cheeks and toyed with his hair. The air smelled familiar, like home, a place one never forgets. He turned to Irene with shining eyes and held out his hand. "We are here at last."

Irene stepped from the carriage with a sigh of relief. "I'm surprised I can stand at all after that tiresome journey. Well then, Lucas, are you ready to discover who you are?"

"I am ready. You can't be tired. You snored most of the way." He lifted Irene off her feet and spun her around. The wide windows of the Grande Inn glittered with warm orange light. Lucas stamped his feet while the coachman untied the luggage and carried it inside. They paid him, and the carriage lurched away.

After settling into their second story rooms and changing from their travelling clothes, Lucas and Irene met downstairs in the rectangular dining room adjacent to the foyer, tables set with white tablecloths, yellow candles, and vases of fresh flowers awaited them. The evening meal consisted of roast beef, spring vegetables and red wine.

"The Innkeeper can arrange for a buggy to take us to the farmhouse in the morning," Irene said.

Lucas swallowed and sipped his wine. "Not too early, I hope. I am anxious to get started but after that long ride I would like to stretch out and rest."

"Of course, sleep as long as you like. We can go whenever you're ready. Do you remember anything new about your mother?"

"Yes," he said leaning forward. "I had a dream in the carriage. I was running to her as always. When I reached her, she said: *the key is within your grasp.*" He grazed his fingers over his palm remembering the feeling of his mother's fingertips in the dream.

"Incredible," Irene murmured fanning her pink cheeks and gazing keenly at Lucas. "Perhaps your mother will lead us directly to the trunks."

"Let's hope it will be that easy." They touched glasses above the candle; the flickering flame reflected in the deep red hue of the wine. After dinner, they strolled into the great room to digest their meal beside the oversized hearth. Tall black iron candle stands with channels to catch the dripping wax stood in the corners of the room like guardian angels. The childish enthusiasm and anticipation that had filled Lucas the moment he climbed into the carriage that morning remained. He admired the arrangements of the candles. They cast light exactly where it should go, so that the guests could openly gaze at each other without feeling threatened by dark shadows. There were a handful of guests seated about the room on loveseats and overstuffed wood framed chairs.

Accomplices, Lucas, and Irene caught each other's eye as they settled onto a loveseat and silently agreed for the moment to refrain from conversation about their mission in Arcana. They engaged in small talk about the weather, the comfort of carriages, the delightful dinner, and the fine furnishings at the Inn. The conversation lulled Lucas into a content stupor. All the other guests were older than he was by many years, their topics trite. His eyelids drooped, his bedchamber with the elevated feather bed called to him, but Irene sat upright and alert, engaging with the women, all of whom were close to her age and two widows as well who marveled at the fact that Irene maintained a well-established business in the City of Dreams.

A thin, elderly gentleman stared at Lucas, diverted his eyes then snuck another glance. The impeccably dressed woman beside him, his wife no doubt, openly gaped at Lucas but quickly turned her entire body away when he caught her eye. He noticed that she nudged her husband in the ribs; the man apparently couldn't help but stare again until Lucas returned his gaze with steady but bored interest.

Finally, the gentleman gestured to Lucas and said, "You seem familiar to me. You remind me of someone." He had wide eyes, gaunt cheeks, silver hair, and a cropped white beard. He did not appear the least bit familiar to Lucas, but when the man directly addressed him, the hair on Lucas' arms stood up and he felt a prickling sensation along his spine. Lucas wrapped a protective arm around Irene's shoulders. She leaned against him and patted his leg.

"You are mother and son," the man said. "I am mistaken then."

Irene's hands trembled; Lucas tightened his grip around her shoulders. He took her empty wine glass from her and set it on the marble-topped side table, while looking around the room for a serving girl. "Perhaps we can get a refill for the lady," he called out. The serving girl appeared allowing Lucas a moment to think. He didn't often reveal himself to strangers. His mind raced but he finally gave in to the easiest response. "Yes, we are family," Lucas said winking at Irene. She sat up straighter and peered proudly around the room at the other guests.

The man held out his wineglass for a refill, nodding at Lucas. "You resemble a young woman I once knew." This man reminded Lucas of the gray cat that had led him to Madam Trousdale's the night before. Was it the sudden intrusion or the penetrating glassy eyes? He could not comprehend the unlikely association, but they had met around the same time of night.

"How so, sir?"

The guests, scattered about the parlour, turned their attention to Lucas and the silver-haired man waiting for his explanation. "There was a young woman some years ago, we bought flowers from her. The similarities are striking. You could be her son."

Irene huffed and blurted, "Is she still alive?" She coughed, spitting wine down her dress. Lucas pulled a handkerchief from his coat pocket and handed it to her. He steadied her hand. "Have another small sip," he said softly. Turning his back to the man, he assisted Irene with her wine and whispered, "Don't fret, I can manage this."

She forced a smile and sipped her wine. He watched her as the wine took affect and her dismay dissipated. "Rather sudden, but this is why we came," he murmured.

Lucas held his wine glass up to catch the light of the fire in the delicate red liquid. Peering through that filter of hesitation, Lucas decided to seize the opportunity. Exhaling slowly, he felt Irene do the same. The fire crackled and sparked; tall flames sprang from blue to orange. A scorched log fell through the iron grate and hissed in protest of its abrupt descent. Immediately a lad appeared and added fuel to the fire. The candles, Lucas took note, still had an hour of burn time. Thick drapes covered the long windows except for one adjacent to the door that, by the glow of the lantern outside, allowed for a clear view of anyone approaching the front door of the Inn. On the windowless eastern wall, a faded tapestry depicting a fallow field, a dilapidated farmhouse and a tired horse attached to a rider less wagon hung beside a larger one that burst with the bright colors of a crowded village faire. Lucas gazed from one scene to the other wondering why anyone would choose the farm scene when given a choice between the two. Lucas gave Irene's shoulders a squeeze then removed his arm and straightened his back. "Please sir, do go on. I am sure we would all enjoy an interesting story tonight. What of this young woman and her son?"

The gentleman lowered his eyes, cleared his throat, and coughed as if his own comment regarding the appearance of Lucas now proved too much for him. His wife rose, and as she left the room without a word, Lucas noticed a silver medallion shimmering around her neck. Now, the man had no companion, no wife to hush him to polite silence.

"My wife is not much for conversation," he said with a sigh." And for several moments, the gentleman sat transfixed by the spiral design on the rug.

Just when Lucas decided the man had fallen asleep, the gentleman stirred, having pried open the door of an abandoned room in the corridors of his mind, he began to speak. "There was a woman who had a child. Nobody knew how she had come to be alone in the world without a husband, no father for the boy. But she was a good mother who never let her child out of her sight. The two of them lived on the Radzger's farm in a room beside the stables. She helped with the animals, and milking too, I suppose. Every day at mid-morning, when the dew had dissipated, she and her boy walked the flower fields for picking. They filled dozens of willow baskets with the brightest assortment of colorful blooms. They had a knack for picking the buds at just the right time so that they would last, never had one of theirs bend over at the neck or slump and turn brown before a week's time. And they never over picked. Those two, understood which flowers were ready, but they also had keen insight into how many would sell in a day. My wife, God rest her soul, loved having fresh flowers in the house and I often bought her a basketful just to watch the light sparkle in her eyes."

"Oh!" Irene exclaimed glancing up the wide staircase. "I thought that woman was your wife." Lucas chuckled at her boldness but remained silent.

"Yes, of course she is my wife now. But I was married before. My wife died in a carriage accident many years ago."

"How tragic, sir. Please excuse me." Irene blushed, peering at Lucas who offered a wink that only she could perceive.

"You were speaking about the flowers," Lucas reminded the man.

"Yes, and I must admit that I also bought them out of courtesy to the labors of this woman and her child. On Sundays, they waited outside the church, him kneeling in the dirt whispering to those flowers as if they could hear him and she stood by watching as if it was the most normal thing in the world to talk to a flower. Maybe he's convincing them to thrive, my wife used to say. She grew fond of the woman and her child, gave them loaves of bread and cheese from time to time."

Lucas leaned forward. "They spent time together. Your former wife and my . . . the woman?"

"Yes," the man said. "She asked about the boy's father, but the woman only said, he didn't come from around here."

"Oh no, and then she died." Irene rolled her eyes, patted her chest, and took a swallow of wine.

"My wife passed away a few weeks before the flower lady died."

"They both died." Irene fanned herself with Lucas' wine stained handkerchief.

"Flower lady," Lucas repeated.

"That's right," the man continued. "They were known as the flower lady and her mystical child. Whatever the reason they were here alone, those flowers were their family. That's what my wife used to say; *The flowers are their family.* And I do believe it, because when the flower lady died, she fell in that remote field where she and her boy had always picked. Anyway, they were brave to wander out there, or ignorant, some say. That earth, rich and fertile as it was because of all the blood it absorbed."

A woman seated on the edge of a pink brocade wing chair wheezed and clutched her throat. "Mind your words," her husband growled.

"What are you talking about?" Lucas asked through tight lips.

"Ah, excuse me ladies and gentlemen." The old man inclined his head. His voice growing quieter with each sentence. "I've lived here for so long that I forget there are some who do not know our history. Long, long ago there was a village there. So many died. Then the bungalows all burned to the ground in 1350. The old church too. Had to go. Black Death. Full of ghosts."

The woman and her husband excused themselves, rustling past Irene and Lucas–who still perched at the edge of the divan–the woman cast a pitiful glance upon them. Lucas' heart sank toward his roiling stomach, suddenly reminded of Dugald back at the boarding house, confined hopefully to his bed. The idea of plague had never left his mind. He took a deep breath and peeped at Irene who rolled her eyes. "Please sir, go on, Lucas said."

"That field where so many had died during the plague years had become a miracle of flowers. So, it was a good place for a farm. But when the woman died out there, the field and the three adjoining ones never grew so full and bright again." Averting his gaze and lowering his voice, he whispered, "The farm where the woman and boy lived eventually burned too." Stifling a sudden yawn, his shoulders sagged succumbing to weariness, or the weight of his own words. He took a breath and drained his wine glass. "The empty fields are still there, and remnants of the barn, but nothing left of the footprint of the old village, or the woman and her little boy."

"Why did you refer to her child in that manner?"

"Manner. . .? Ah yes, mystical. He was. Never acted like an ordinary boy. Wise as an old tree my wife said." Grimacing he added. "My wife. My first wife is who I'm referring to."

Lucas half smiled and slumped into the loveseat.

Irene squeezed Lucas' hand, but he did not feel her grip or even her presence so absorbed was he in the picture of the past that the man was painting. Pictures, he had seen before. This man had just described a part of Lucas' childhood. He heard a thundering of hooves followed by a persistent banging that seemed to come from the heavy mahogany door. Lucas jumped up, peered through the sidelights. He couldn't see anyone. When the banging continued, he pulled open the door. Nobody was there. A whip of pain split through the center of Lucas' head like an axe and reverberated through the polished wooden floorboards. A scrap of breath trapped inside the chest of a boy, long dead, screamed inside his head. Standing in front of the open door, he gripped his glass so tight, it shattered in his hand, crystal shards drifting downward in unison with the thick red wine hitting the floor in a splattering and delicate chime.

Through blurred eyes, he realized all eyes had turned to him. Suppressing the urge to scream, he gurgled instead. The front door banged shut behind him. Lucas turned toward the door then toward the parlour. Was it possible to ever recall all that he'd buried in the past and if so, would any of it explain the mystery of himself? He wanted to grab the man who had known him and his mother and squeeze every aspect of the memory from him. It was true, she had existed. He truly had a mother. The man's words loosened the sticky grasp of cobwebs from his mind. He hadn't felt this close to his mother since he lost her. "For the love of God where is the wine maid?" Lucas shouted.

As Irene struggled to rise from the plush cushions, the serving girl and lad went to Lucas. The lad took him by the elbow. "Let me assist you, sir." He led Lucas away from the mess on the floor while the girl suggested that Irene remain seated until she swept up the shards of glass. Beside the roaring fire where the lad left him, Lucas peered into the depths of the flames, keeping his back to the room, absorbing the smoky aroma of wood and peat. His hand bloodless. An ancient blaze burning through his veins.

The remaining guests shuffled from the room wearing masks of startled confusion. The old man came up behind Lucas, placed a translucent hand upon his shoulder. "If you'd like to see what's left of the Radzger farmhouse and barn, I can take you there tomorrow."

Together Irene and Lucas slowly climbed the stairs to their rooms. His attention turned now to seeing her safely to bed. He didn't know what to expect of this trip, but he felt it was already more than Irene had anticipated. It occurred to Lucas that for her, the idea of a holiday in the country had overpowered the hard truths that they had to uncover. Now, he remembered why he didn't want to come back here. "Take a good rest. We'll have a late morning repast and go forward into the day from there." He kissed her forehead and patted the quilt before blowing out the candle. She murmured a sleepy good night as he closed the door.

Lucas' bedchamber had a large four-poster bed made up in white linen sheets and piled in thick green, gold, and red patterned coverlets. Heavy curtains draped the large window that overlooked the front of the Inn. A low fire glowed in the small fireplace. His nightclothes waited in the wood armoire where he hung his coat, trousers, and shirt. He extinguished his candle and slipped under the covers, stretching his legs that surprisingly didn't hang over the edge of the long bed. He had never slept in such a soft enveloping bed like this before. I should like to sleep in a bed like this with Alina, he thought overcome by weariness and incapable of analyzing the story that the old man had told. His mother was real, so there must be a father. He realized the truth of it and that was enough for one night. Closing his eyes, his thoughts drifted into filmy images of flower fields. Although he felt aware of a looming presence at the edge of the field, the scent of lavender, from either his pillow or his memories, pulled him away from himself and the reality of this onerous day. Lucas slept as a child, blessed with warm and comforting dreams, surrounded by those who loved him and meant him no harm.

Chapter 6

Dugald awoke hot and wet with the bed sheets twisted around his swollen feet. He wiped his brow with a clammy, clenched claw. His bandaged hand lay numb at his side. The light seeping through the shuttered windows in louvered angles onto the bare floor gave no indication of the time of day. He rolled to one side and reached for the porcelain water pitcher beside his bed. The weight of it pulled his arm down and it slipped from his grasp. It didn't break but the precious contents spilled out leaving him with nothing but a splash across his face. He lay back, moaning as loudly as his dry throat would allow. Kicking away the sheets he managed to place both feet on the floor and stand; he took two steps then fell face first on the plank floor.

The bedroom door creaked open and a woman stepped inside. She cradled his head in her cool hands and wiped his brow with a white, linen cloth. She whispered words that he did not understand. She held a cup to his lips. He gulped the sweet, warm liquid and she helped him back to his bed where Carissa was just finishing the change of his soiled sheets. She refilled the pitcher and placed it in its stand. His head ached from the lumpy pillows propped under his head and shoulders. "I have a meeting. I must go," he croaked.

"Not today," the black-haired woman replied before gliding out of the room.

She left the room and Carissa pulled a stool beside the bed to feed him a vegetable broth. "What day is it?"

"I don't know, sir."

"You don't know? How can one not be aware of the day?"

She continued to push the wooden ladle at him. His stomach growled as he ate, how long had it been? Trying to recount the events since his arrival in the City of Dreams, he questioned the girl who simply shook her head and continued to feed him. When the pot she held was empty, Dugald asked for more. His strength was returning. Given some moments and a few more mouthfuls, he felt certain he could rise from the bed and make his way downstairs and outside. He had to meet Vasil and Campbell.

"That is all you're allowed for now, sir." Carissa tossed the ladle into the pot. "There's fresh water in the pitcher if you need it." She crossed the room and slipped out the door. In an instant, Dugald heard her turn the key in the lock. He was a prisoner. Anger rose so suddenly that his lumpy broth came up with it. He had to turn on his side to gag and swallow to avoid vomiting all over himself.

He lay back and began to shiver under the layers of blankets. He could do nothing but watch the yellow light of day, whatever day it was, turn to gold, then orange, then red and finally give in to gray and blackness. On the street below, a dog yelped, and a woman shrieked, young men shouted and laughed. He longed to join them and their female companions, to visit the taverns with careless gusto as a man his age should.

Even in the moonless night, his eyes refused to remain closed and ultimately adjusted to the dark. He tossed from side to side with a will to escape that gained no ground beyond the confines of the bed. The spider bite had apparently infiltrated his entire body. Who was the woman with Carissa? The room took on threatening shapes of tedious frustration, and dread. Suddenly, he hated the noise and smells of the city. The streets that went in every direction, crowded with vendors hawking their wares, leering at each other to glean what they could grab. I only want the life promised me, he thought, coughing from the cool air. Were the papers still concealed in the iron pot downstairs? They were his only hope of going home and living out his days in comfort.

In the corner of the room where wide strips of chair rail interrupted the blank wall, something stirred. Dugald pushed up on his elbows, peering through the grip of darkness. He sensed movement, felt the breath of another sentient being. The murky yellow eyes of the rat spat at him. He screeched, flung the covers over his head. It had followed him home after all. How long had it waited hidden in a secret corner known only to a creature that skulked through shadow to achieve its goals? A varmint, that with scurrying disregard, scorned the disgust of more worthwhile and profitable beings. Once again Dugald fought to hold down his soup knowing that the rat waited for the very opposite. He dared not open his mouth to scream again, lest the rodent should jump from a near vantage point and consume Dugald at its hideous, gray-toothed leisure. Now that the rat had revealed itself, it would fight for what it desired. Dugald's fingers walked across his waist and down his trouser leg searching for the tiny dagger he hoped he still possessed. A thud deep in his chest collided with the bile that rose in his stomach. When his fingers felt the hard object tucked into his stocking, his breath stuck then spilled in staccato waves as he worked the weapon free. Finally, grasping it firmly in the good hand, he allowed his body to relax just a little. Now, only to decide how best to kill the rat, or perhaps, if necessary, not right away but eventually, use it on the women. After a lifetime in the wide-open spaces of the countryside, he could not endure confinement. Clenching his teeth, he readied the dagger, intermittently opening the blanket just enough to take a quick breath, otherwise lying perfectly still, a clock ticking loud and slow inside his head while waiting for the impression of tiny feet on his leg. Perhaps the vile creature already nibbled at the edge of his woolen blanket.

* * *

Alina sat statuesque at the window long after the lanterns were lit. The appearance of a lad instead of Lucas this evening stole her resolve. To make matters worse, downstairs, Vasil entertained besotted guests. He called for her, but thankfully, hadn't bothered to climb the stairs to force her to join in the boisterous banter. Her plan to call to Lucas from her window for help had failed. Shivering, she prayed that Vasil hadn't already done something to Lucas. But if not, then where was he? All alone in the world, she should never have believed that Lucas could save her. As much as she loved her father and trusted his words, and still did, even after his horrible death, she deeply feared the need to depend on a man. *It is how the world works;* her father had often reminded her. Not for me, she thought. She must not lose her fortune to Vasil. He had already taken her father. The well-worn note–soft as cloth–with words faded into each other, told her that Lucas was the one who would help her. But Lucas had frightened her when he tried to snatch her ruby in the street. Was that what he was after, the ruby? She laid a delicate hand at the nape of her neck. Her cape had blown open and the dress she wore that day revealed more than is proper for a woman walking alone. She wanted to trust Lucas, and, in some ways, she did. They sat together. She felt safe sitting beside him, and more. The thought flushed her. But when she couldn't open the door the next day he hadn't bothered to come back. Her father's words, his choice for her was Lucas. But he couldn't have known for sure. After all he was dead now. She covered her face with trembling hands and wept.

The sounds of raucous laughter swept upstairs to her room. Perched by the window she grew cold. With a last look to the street below, at the lanterns lit by another, she patted her eyes with her palms and drew the curtains. If she didn't go down soon, Vasil would come after her and she didn't want him in her room. He frightened and disgusted her, but right now her only chance for survival was in his ugly, fat hands. She must let him believe she remained ignorant of his deeds. And if Lucas didn't or couldn't return to help her regain her inheritance, she decided as she dressed in her loose-fitting, worn out gown, she would find a way to go home. She lifted her chin. Someday soon she would return home. And for now, if nothing else, she would have a little supper.

She hadn't let Vasil know she was waiting for her trunks. Daria had said her father had sent them three days before his murder. If so, where were they? They should surely have arrived at the harbour by now. Could they have gone to another port? It was possible that Vasil had intercepted them, especially since he always seemed to be one step ahead of her. He could have hidden them to search through the last of her belongings. But it appeared he was waiting for them as well. Thankfully, she had taken care to sew her small collection of jewels inside the hem of her shift. The only jewel that she wore in public, the blood red, ruby pendant, she had been wearing the night her father died.

If not for her devoted maid, Daria who had rushed from the house and shrieked the alarm up and down the street, Alina may have died as well. And it was Daria who rushed Alina to the ship and helped her safely aboard. Her father had instructed them to go together to this safe house, his house in the City of Dreams, but Daria had hurried off to bid her family farewell and Alina never saw her again. She locked herself in her cabin for the entire journey. She ate only the bread Daria had packed and crept to the water barrels in the middle of the night. Her fears kept her company. Daria had little time to explain what she was to do. She had written the address of the house on a slip of paper. When the ship pulled into the harbour, Alina stayed in her cabin until the ship's men forced her to vacate. She walked for miles inquiring only of women to find the address scribbled in Daria's rushed hand. And then at last, just before dark, she found her father's house. To her delight the front door wasn't locked. She pushed it open only to find Vasil waiting for her. He claimed he too feared for his life and had to flee Ingleena. And apparently on the very same ship! If she had known what she was coming to, she would have flung herself overboard. But she kept quiet behind trembling lips and brimming eyes, grateful that he showed her to her own private room. Now, she had only the few dresses and personal belongings she had brought in her hand baggage. She missed Daria and worried every day where she could be. Meanwhile, she had no choice but to play along with Vasil's game.

She tiptoed downstairs and crossed the parlour full of flickering candles and bright oil lamps, a healthy fire blazed in the hearth. He entertains ghosts and greed burning light to an empty room, she thought. In the dining room adjacent to the kitchen, another fire blazed and candles dripped wax from their stands onto the table crowded with platters of food. She skirted past the entrance and slipped into the kitchen. She heard Vasil bragging. "This is just the beginning my friends. Soon I will be moving to a magnificent house." From the sideboard, she grabbed a plate and began to pile it up with food. She took a swig from the wine jug and stuffed bread into the pocket of her smock.

Clammy fingers slipped around her neck and a sinister voice whispered "Hello, Alina. . . don't you remember me?"

"Ach!" She spun and slapped away the hand of Campbell Barrington who grabbed her by the wrist and pulled her into the dining room.

"Alina, at last!" Vasil heaved himself up from his tight chair and waddled to her side. "This is my beautiful Alina. You see I have not exaggerated!"

Around the table four men and three women gaped as they stuffed handfuls of meat into their mouths with greasy hands. Two of the men stood and bowed. The others were too fat or too disinterested to do more than nod. The three women peered from eyelids heavy with coal makeup. They elbowed each other and whispered behind cupped palms.

"Don't get any ideas, the lot of you. Alina is exquisite, and I intend to keep her that way." He glared at not only the men, but the women as well, then added. "Until it suits me to collect her value that is."

Everyone broke out in laughter except Alina who, having lost her appetite, turned to flee back upstairs to her bedchamber, but Vasil pushed her into a chair and Barrington set her plate in front of her and took his seat beside her. "Pass the platters and wine,"

Vasil ordered. Pointing his index finger at her, he demanded, "Eat."

Alina picked at the vegetables and overcooked meat washing it down with small sips of wine from a silver goblet. She dared not lose control of her senses. Her bedroom had an iron lock on the door, but she had no doubt the hinges would give-way easily to anyone who seriously desired entry. Although he professed his loyal devotion, Alina didn't doubt that he would change his mind at any time and for the right price. Until she could retrieve what her father had sent in her trunks, she must pretend that she had no inkling that Vasil was the person responsible for the murder of her father, that he crouched in the hedge, lying in wait at the front door of their home.

Campbell Barrington passed her platter after platter of food and filled her wine glass when he thought she didn't notice. Alina took small bites and shoved the food around on her plate making little piles of this and that. Taking small sips of wine then holding her cup below the edge of the table, she poured the wine out onto the floor. He leaned forward and placed his hand over hers, whispering, "Let me say, it would be my great privilege to escort you around the city. There are romantic dining houses. I can assure you; I am a man of wealth and means as was your dear father."

"You are nothing like my father," she snapped. "Nobody here is."

He squeezed her hand until her knuckles cracked. "I will give you a few days in which to change your mind."

She pulled her hand away and replied in a loud voice so to be heard above the drunken din. "Vasil has forbidden me from stepping out with strange men."

A sudden silence consumed the table of mismatched merrymakers. Alina's face burned as everyone ogled her. Vasil's glare sliced her with a cold stab between her ribs. Her hand fluttered toward her heart then dropped to her lap. She fought to hold his stare hoping he would look away, so she could swallow.

Vasil shouted at Campbell Barrington, "What did I just say? Arrogant bastard!" He stood and slammed his fist on the table so hard that the plates jumped. "Alina, go to your room!"

But she was already gone.

Racing up the stairs she slammed her shin on the riser, bit her lip, and stumbled to her room. Bolting the door, she threw herself onto the bed. After several moments of staring in anger at the ceiling, she pulled her stockings down revealing a slim gash on her pale skin. Sitting up, she untied her shoes and kicked them across the room, then lay on her back to unlace her dress, all such a chore without Daria. The dress however, she carefully smoothed with one hand following the other, checking for spots of food or wine then hung it in the narrow musty wardrobe. It's only for a few more weeks; I will avenge my father and regain my trunks. 'That man, the lantern lighter helps the righteous,' Daria had told her as they rushed to the ship. 'He's practically a legend,' she said with breathless admiration. 'Your father said he is very handsome and the tallest man in the City of Dreams.' By now, Alina knew that Lucas was a striking man, but he had disappeared after their first meeting.

What would father think of the noble Lucas now? He would claw his way up from his grave if he knew she was living under the roof of the treacherous traitor and murderer, Vasil. But he would be proud of her and would warn her to use great caution. It would not be long before Vasil tired of her hostility and acquired what he wanted. Time was running out. Tomorrow evening if the boy appeared, she would follow him. The boy might be able to lead her to the man.

* * *

Dawn climbed the trellis of dark, green ivy that clutched the sooty, white wall of the boarding house. Dugald slipped the blanket away from his pasty face. He peeked around the room, sat up and tossed his covers up and down in a wave. After wrestling with tormented thoughts and the ponderous presence of the rat throughout most of the night, he ultimately fell into a deep sleep. Now, he felt well and rested. His hand no longer throbbed in pain. The pitcher of water on the bed stand showed no evidence of rodent intrusion. He drained it, grateful that it was tea after all. Surely, that would give him strength to climb out the window. It would be the first time he utilized shutters and window ledges as a stairway but surely, he could do it. Stretching, bending, and flexing allowed life to creep back into his limbs. He managed to retrieve the chamber pot from under the bed and relieve himself without soiling the sheets. Best to wait a little longer before attempting to stand. He need not draw attention to his plan by falling and creating a ruckus. The girl, Carissa, could not stop him, but the dark-haired ogress, he feared, could thwart his escape and more. What or who she was, he dared not think. He hoped she was merely a phantom of fever. Convinced that his roommate had found a hole in which to sleep out the day, he laid back down to do the same.

The next time he awoke, the room hummed with sounds of midday tangles rising from the street below, the shutters casting ladders of light across his bed. When he sat up, his head spun, and his eyes swam backward. Footsteps in the hall had awakened him; he lay down on his right-side feigning sleep with his forearm flung across his forehead. Blonde and airy, Carissa entered the room carrying a pot. Her delicate feet slipped across the floor like a ballerina on stage. Dugald was about to sit up and explain that he had a headache, that he needed water, not tea, and hopefully let her serve him some more of the delicious vegetable soup. But the dark head of the other woman bobbed over the threshold, a jungle of hair concealed her features. He held his breath, then let it out slowly, trying not to cough.

"He's still asleep," Carissa whispered.

"As he should be," the illusory woman replied. She motioned for the girl to empty the chamber pot. Dugald winced with embarrassment. He did not know who this ghastly woman was, but he hated her.

Her feet heavy now, he heard Carissa tromp down the hall to the narrow alcove, the pot hit the floor with a clunk, the window squeaked, she probably held her breath as she heaved the contents of the pot to the waste pit below. Dugald wondered who oversaw shoveling dirt into the pit, and hoped it was the job of Lucas. Even as he thought it, he knew it would not be Lucas' job. There were people for that kind of work, and they were not like Lucas. Lucas lit the lanterns; he did exactly what he wanted to do. Dugald snapped out of his musings and realized that the thin woman with hair as long as a cape stood beside his bed murmuring and moving her hands in slow but exact patterns above his head. No, he thought and swore to himself. He peeked below his elbow toward the doorway hoping for Carissa only to see her stop abruptly at the threshold, set the pan just inside the room, turn on her heel and slip silently away. His legs twitched, and his ankle popped revealing he was awake. The woman stopped speaking. She reached for the cup and forced it between his lips; the tea filled his mouth; he turned his head into the pillow and let it drain out then rolled onto his back to conceal the stain. "I need to sit up. Where is Mrs. Kempel?" he croaked.

The woman pressed a cool wet cloth against his forehead. "You are sickly. Be silent." Dugald fumbled beneath the scratchy sheet to extend a hand, grab the woman by the throat, slash her with the dagger, but he could not feel it. She stared at him, her eyes deep, black pits. Then amusement flickered across her face and he saw his dagger clutched between her long fingers. He flinched, but she whirled out of the room like a gust of air.

* * *

In the morning, Alina sat at her dressing table gazing into a scratched mirror, a wooden comb in her hand. Daria would normally be combing her hair; the tangles were tedious. Trying again from the ends she gathered handfuls until it finally shone. Creeping downstairs, she went out to the well, three trips to fill the barrel in the kitchen. She brought water to her room and rearranged the flowers, removing a few that had turned brown, but still her room held their abundant fragrance. With no more plans for the day except to find Lucas in the evening, she moped about the room putting off the need to eat. When she finally swallowed her revulsion, and headed to the kitchen, she peeked in on Vasil. He was snoring loudly, lying sideways across his bed. After nibbling some stale bread—the piggish revelers had eaten every morsel of the supper—she searched through the cupboards and drawers as she had done ever since her arrival. She even took the bold step of rummaging through Vasil's wardrobe. There must be some sort of evidence of her trunks. But, as before, she found nothing. A few dusty books in the bookshelf held no secrets either. There must be a hiding place outside the house. Of course, someone as shrewd and devious as Vasil would not risk her father's things showing up at this house.

He needed time to go through everything in her trunks. Where do people hide large objects? In barns, in cellars? The house had only a tiny root cellar, but perhaps one of his friends stored them. Now Alina wished she had paid better attention to the rude guests. They could all be in on it. Vasil, that clawing leach, could do nothing on his own. She tiptoed out of his room and pulled the door closed behind her.

She dressed in one of her better dresses and went out into the street hoping to find Campbell Barrington. She could certainly tease some information from him. Once outside, she could think of nothing but Lucas. His windblown hair and his dark eyes that stared at her as if he himself had created her and was admiring his masterpiece. Could she ever walk away from a man such as that? She found herself at the flower stand. The woman gestured. Alina stepped forward. "Good day Ma'am, the flowers are gorgeous today."

"Thank you, young lady. Are you in need of more already?" She fluttered her eyes at Alina.

Alina blushed; she had behaved like an ignorant vixen the other day. Lucas had a way of confusing her. "I do not have room for any more flowers at this time, thank you. But, the gentleman . . ." Alina's lip quivered, "Do you know where I can find the gentleman who purchased all those flowers for me?"

"Well, certainly you know who he is. He is Lucas the Lantern Lighter of the City of Dreams," the woman said with dramatic emphasis.

"Yes, I realize who he is." She tilted her head and frowned. "I do," she added wringing her hands. "Please, Ma'am can you tell me where he lives?"

"He lives in Mrs. Kempel's Boarding House. Everyone knows that!" Customers approached, and the flower vendor turned her attention to them.

Chapter 7

For the morning meal, the Inn served fresh fruit, buttery bread, and orange blossom tea on the sunny verandah with a view of the bright green hillsides. The color had returned to Irene's cheeks. Lucas, wearing only shirtsleeves and no coat, inhaled as he took in the expanse of land spread out before them.

"Did you dream last night?" she asked examining his face.

"Ah, no I did not. I slept deeply without moving."

"And you, Irene?"

She smiled, "I as well. No dreams thank goodness, after that story."

"Yes, I agree. It was not a pleasant story, but we have heard these kinds of stories before, haven't we?"

"We have, but not directly related to you!"

Just then, the storyteller appeared on the verandah. He made his way to their table. "Good morning, excuse me for not introducing myself last night . . . the wine and the memories, you understand."

"Of course." Lucas rose extending his hand. "I am Lucas, and this is Irene Kempel, proprietor of the Kempel House in the City of Dreams."

"My pleasure, to meet you both. I am Wentworth Bodden. The carriage awaits, if you are ready?" He bowed to Irene. She pushed aside her empty plate, nodding at Lucas who offered his arm. The wide expanse of his childhood greeted him in front of the Inn. This grand lodge, of course, did not exist when Lucas was a boy roaming the rolling hills wearing his soft handmade shoes. He inhaled the familiar but melancholy air, savoring the sense of solitude he always gleaned from the outdoors. The dirt road wound down in a snaky curve, crossed a little stone bridge, meandered past a row of ancient mortar and stone houses then climbed laboriously up the hill. Deep in a cup like hollow on the other side of the hill sat the farm and the flower fields of Lucas' birth. They left the carriage and walked along the rutted dirt road looking for the old barn. It sat sad and sagging in misplaced, mostly charred pieces, nearby to a gurgling stream, the sound of which jolted Lucas backward. Irene patted his forearm. "The valley is prettier than I remember," he whispered.

"The Radzger's lived here," said Wentworth standing inside a stone rectangular remnant of the farmhouse. "Over there was the bunkhouse, it was a grand farm in those days. And you and your mother lived there in the southwest corner of the barn. Right there." He pointed, indicating to Lucas as if he expected him to run to the spot. "It was you, wasn't it? You are Linnea's boy."

Irene gazed at Lucas who stared blankly but his chest rose and fell rapidly. He released himself from Irene's grasp and turned away from the collapsed structures. He walked toward the woods and entered the copse of maple and linden trees, taking a lost path, now only visible in his mind's eye.

He heard Irene and Wentworth murmuring and turned around to see Irene entering the barn; he wavered and lifted a hand, about to warn her that the dangling rafters may loosen from the ridge beam at any moment. But Wentworth hurried to her side and Lucas continued into the woods beside the stream to the cool pool where, as a child, he had bathed.

He removed his shoes and stockings, then his trousers and shirt laying them carefully on the same boulder that long ago held the clothes of a small boy and his mother. He could hear their lost laughter as he plunged into the milky blue depths. The world changed instantly. It had been many years since he'd swum here or anywhere. The deep pond swirled in a circular motion fed by an underground stream. He sometimes entered the river but never the sea where he had to fight the current, he disliked the feeling of an outside force pulling him where he didn't want to go. Exhaling, he blew bubbles into the water and remembered.

He was out in the field with his mother. The two were gathering their flowers. The basket he carried overflowed with blossoms. He held it high and called to her. She raised her hand and waved. *Well done son*, she called. Setting her basket on the ground, she held her arms out to him. Lucas placed his own basket on the ground, careful not to damage the blossoms, and ran to her. His fingertips just brushed hers before she fell among the flowers. He fell too. When he awoke, the bees buzzed, and butterflies flitted around a puddle of thick blood that seeped into the fertile ground and collected between them.

Lucas swam to the surface of the pool gulping for air. Water blurred his eyes. He rolled over on his back and floated with arms widespread. Could she see him now, after all this time? Did she attempt, still, to watch over him? His heart felt so heavy he felt sure it would drag him to the bottom of the pool. But he did not care.

Long into the dark cold hours of that excruciating day, possibly longer he didn't know, but he did remember not wanting to leave her side. Lucas lay in the field beside his silent mother waiting for her to wake up. The buzzing insects of a humid evening finally driving him from the field. Before leaving his beloved mother's side, he placed their overflowing flower baskets beside her, so she wouldn't be lonely. He lost his way twice, finally arriving just after sunset at the farm. The farmer noticed Lucas plodding along the road alone and rode his mule out to meet him. Dirty and sobbing Lucas described how his mother fell. Even then, his small hopeful heart expected her to rise again.

"We must take the wagon and fetch her right away, sir. Mamma will be frightened when she wakes up out there all alone."

The farmer and his wife stared blankly at Lucas for several agonizing moments before they gazed past him to the field and the darkening sky. He flung himself at the farmer. "Bring my mamma home, please!"

The farmer hitched up the wagon while his wife took Lucas inside. She showed him how to help her add meat and vegetables to a cast iron pot of simmering soup. "Will there be enough soup for mamma?" he asked.

"There is enough," she said, "but best to have yours now."

Lucas refused to eat without his mother and broke into a torrent of tears when the moon refused to show its face due to a thick green fog that had followed Lucas home. He sat outside huddled in a blanket until he heard the clomping of the old mule and wagon. A figure sat on the bench beside the farmer. Lucas dropped the blanket and ran toward them just as one of the young plow boys slid down and trotted toward the bunkhouse. The farmer shook his head. There was no choice but to wait until morning. They put together a makeshift bed for him beside the fire in the main house.

At dawn, the farmer, along with several helpers, set out to the flower field. By the time Lucas woke up, screaming and feverish, the hay cart had already taken his mother to the churchyard. He never saw her again. They convinced him to move into the corner of the kitchen. Sometimes the farmer's wife tried to feed him, other times it was the plow boy who offered a bowl when he awoke asking for his mother. For weeks, Lucas did little more than sleep, often shouting and moaning in the grip of devastating dreams. When he finally sat up and admitted he was hungry, the farmer's wife fed him and said, "Gather flowers and we will lay them upon your dear mother's grave."

"Where are the gathering baskets?" Lucas asked. "I left the baskets with my mother in the flower field."

Neither the farmer nor his wife gave an answer. They stared at the threshed floor, the pale mortar walls, the timber ceiling. Lucas noticed a spider carefully spinning his web on the window ledge, indifferent to the human emotion suspended in the sticky summer air. His head ached, and he could barely breathe, the sickening smell of soup permeated his tattered clothes. "I'll find them myself!" He made for the door.

The farmer stepped up blocking his way. "We found no baskets," he said.

"I don't believe you," Lucas shouted. "I left the baskets beside my mother." Tears sprung out of his eyes. He pounded his fists on the table so hard a plate spun off the edge and broke into splinters. The farmer dove for Lucas who dodged sideways around the table. He flung open the door hitting the farmer square in the face. Lucas returned to the field where his mother had taken her last breath. He found the grass stamped down and remnants of crushed flowers, but no woven gathering baskets. He threw himself on the ground hoping to die also.

Over the next several weeks, the farmer's wife went back and forth to the field where Lucas waited for his mother. Every time she brought him home, he ran away again. "It's time you stopped this foolish behavior," she growled, squeezing his wrist. "I can offer you a home, but I cannot bring your mother back. You can be my boy now, my child."

"She will come back for me." Sniveling, Lucas squirmed from her grasp and threw himself on his cot. In the morning he left before dawn to return to the field and plant himself cross-legged on the spot where he had last seen his mother. When the farmer's wife came with food, Lucas hid in the reeds until she gave up and left the bundles. He never showed himself again.

As Lucas sat in the sun beside the iridescent pool allowing the warm sun to absorb the droplets that shimmered on his olive skin, he had no concern that Irene or Wentworth would approach. They would leave him alone all day if necessary. But his stomach already rumbled with hunger and he knew Irene would be weary of standing around in the barn. They had not thought to bring a blanket for her to sit. Nor a picnic basket. But the memories he'd buried upon his arrival in the City of Dreams, so long ago, had surfaced and there was no stopping them.

The morning he left the flower field, he had a sack stuffed with loaves of bread, chunks of cheese and apples. He walked along the dirt road until he came upon a wagon filled with baskets of flowers. He slipped into the back believing that the gathering baskets were those he and his mother had made. By nightfall, Lucas found himself many miles from the farm. He settled down to sleep among the baskets, although by now he knew they were not his. He dreamed he followed his mother through tall swaying grass. He ran after her. But she did not stop and wait for him.

During his journey, he roamed the countryside stealing food and occasionally accepting the kindness, or meanness, of strangers. His heartache increased as the days dragged on. Without any personal knowledge of death or loss, he gradually came to the overwhelming conclusion that his mother could not find her way back to him. Sometimes he collapsed exhausted in unfamiliar fields or under a shade tree for days at a time, unnoticed by the passing villagers. The days morphed into months.

Lucas worked on farms and slept in barns, as he was accustomed. He encountered families who thought it a promising idea to take in a lad who could provide labor. But they beat him and withheld food when he couldn't perform all the demanding tasks. Lucas worked as hard as he could. In the end, it was never enough. There was a particularly brutal encounter with a farmer. At the end of the workday, Lucas and the farmer's daughter often frolicked in the barn. One day they had tossed aside their shoes and jumped from the loft. Just as her father arrived, the girl landed in the fresh hay; her dress sailed over her head. It was easy to misread the situation, but Lucas did not deserve the whipping he received. He left that very evening darting along the dark, deserted road agile and undeterred by nightfall. By morning, he'd taken up lodging wrapped in the burlap of a long cart carrying flowers. He spent that day hidden among the flowers. The driver wrapped in an oversized cloak never noticed him. Ultimately, the flower cart carried him into the heart of the City of Dreams.

And the City of Dreams drew him back now. Lucas rose from the warm grass and dressed. The calling birds covered the voices of Irene and Wentworth who had temporarily slipped from his mind. Alina appeared in his thoughts as abrupt as their first encounter in the street. He pulled the black veil from the pocket of his trousers and placed it back inside his shirt over his heart. His mother was gone. He understood all too well about death now. He gazed into the deep pool. Answers had come quickly. But he still had questions. There had been blood. It was not a weak heart but a, what? Not enough blood for an animal, not enough time for a wolf to leap from the bushes. Surely, he would have remembered something like that.

As he walked up the overgrown path to rejoin Irene and Wentworth, he thought of his first impression of the City of Dreams. He had arrived in the fading light of evening when a hush trembled through the cobbled streets. The stone walls shimmered like silver-tipped dragons welcoming the descending darkness. Smoke filled the alabaster sky, glinting gold specks from scattered torches, and an occasional candle flickering in the window of a house that hoped a loved one would return soon. Among the huts, cottages and fine homes, Lucas easily found daily labor. But as in the country, not everyone he encountered treated him well. Lucas learned to defend himself, realizing that stealing food was often safer than working for it. On occasion, he was caught by night watchmen or civilian guard, and locked up. But he always managed to escape. Lucas couldn't escape the memory of his mother. His despair became more familiar than her vanishing voice and warmed him more than the flea-bitten blanket he carried in his small bundle of belongings. He learned to fight like the dogs with which he slept. Within weeks he worked like an accomplished street urchin. He excelled at picking pockets and stealing food from vendor carts.

At the end of the path, he found Irene and Wentworth. They perched on the edge of a fallen beam in the corner of the barn diagonally opposite to the location of the room he and his mother had shared. Irene pushed herself up. "Thank goodness, at last." Her hair was loose from her bun and her hands and dress smudged with dirt. Wentworth was filthy, one knee of his trousers torn, a piece of his white linen shirt wrapped around his elbow oozing blood.

"What in heaven happened?" Lucas rushed to them. Irene staggered to Lucas. He wrapped his arms around her trembling shoulders. "Irene . . ." Lucas peered into her eyes clasping her dirty hands.

"We found the trunk," she blurted.

"We got most of it out but this last bit . . ." Wentworth indicated the large trunk half buried in the earth, the back corner wedged downward as if it were sinking, lodged under a split timber.

Immediately, Lucas recognized his mother's trunk and would have ripped the lid off right there except for a metal lock hanging from the clasp. He spun around searching for more pieces of his past, feeling the actual presence of his mother as he had not since the day she died. A stabbing pain seared up his backbone through his skull and stabbed his eyes. He fell. His face hit the dirt. Irene cried out and stumbled to her knees.

Lucas roused as Wentworth shouted, "Lucas! Madam, please get up. Mrs. Kempel . . . Lucas . . . Mrs. Kempel . . . Lucas!"

Lucas groaned and clutched his head. He blinked up at Wentworth. "Who?" He began to say, then realized where he was and clamored to his feet. "Irene!" he barked. She extended her hand and Lucas pulled her to her feet.

"What a pair we are. Lucas, are you alright?"

"I'm fine . . . it was one of those spiking headaches. It has already passed."

Irene peered at him. "You've remembered, and the pain knocked you down."

Lucas brushed himself off. "The surprises are overwhelming today."

"They certainly are." Wentworth agreed.

Lucas guided Irene to the trunk. "Can you sit here a little bit longer?" He took a lap around the old barn. "We need the carriage driver or someone to help us with the trunk. Can you two remain here for a little longer while I go and fetch somebody?"

"We sent him for water and bread an hour ago. He should be along. . ." Wentworth replied.

"I'm famished," Irene said.

They sat and listened to the birds. All of them too fatigued to speak.

"Ah, here he is now." The carriage driver clattered up the rock-strewn path, followed by another man driving a long open wagon.

Hands on his hips, Lucas gazed in confusion.

"You were gone for over three hours," Irene said.

"That's Oliver with the cart," Wentworth said. "He works for the Inn. I took it upon myself to make the arrangements to get the trunk out, since you weren't here," Wentworth said resting a hand on Lucas' shoulder.

"I'm sorry. I . . . it didn't . . . I had no idea." He brushed his hair away from his eyes and once again walked to the corner of the barn where he and his mother had lived. "Have you searched everywhere already?"

"We have." Wentworth said. "And the trunk is all we found. But from what I hear, it's what you've sought all this time."

"Yes." Lucas said shaking his head in disbelief.

Oliver came forward with a pick and a shovel, which he handed to Lucas. They set to work while Irene and Wentworth sat on the back of the wagon imbibing on the bread and water.

"There's wine!" Irene announced holding the jug up for Lucas to see. He strode over with the shovel in his hand and took a swig.

In less than an hour, the trunk was loaded onto the cart and concealed under burlap sacks. Irene rode in the carriage while Lucas and Wentworth positioned themselves alongside the trunk. On the way back to the Inn, Wentworth explained how he and his wife spent most of their time at the Inn to be around other people. "We have land, but we can no longer manage it. The two of us alone on an isolated farm is not a pleasant way to pass the time."

"The Grande Inn feels like a safe place," Lucas agreed. "One must be careful of whom he chooses to trust in this world."

"I agree," Wentworth said. "But you can rest easy that, I, and this man, Oliver, we can be trusted.

Lucas rested his arm on his mother's trunk. "I hope that is true."

As they rode in silence back to the Inn, the sun crept closer to the rim of the hill. He felt like a stranger in his childhood home. I loved it for a while, Lucas thought but these things they go away, like a hush when one gazes upon the splendid dawn that, with clarity, suddenly reveals the true nature of the day. He wanted to get back to the City of Dreams as soon as possible.

They passed the wine jug back and forth. Neither of the men asked Lucas what was inside the trunk. And for now, he didn't even want to know. Whatever his mother had possessed could keep a little bit longer. The memories from the pool were all he could manage for one day. After all this time without answers it was too much to think about. All that mattered now was a hot bath and a satisfying meal.

Just after dark, Oliver drove the wagon around to the back of the Inn. The lanterns were not yet lit. Lucas chuckled to himself. It couldn't be better if I planned it myself. Wentworth escorted Irene to her door. The trunk, still covered in burlap, carried easily between Lucas and Oliver up the back stairs. They set it on the far side of Lucas' bed. For now, the contents would remain a mystery. A candle flickered on the nightstand. The fire crackled bright orange flames. The bath was warm and ready. Lucas stripped off his soiled clothes and slipped into the steaming water. A wash of relief flooded his body and soothed his mind. He closed his eyes. When he opened them, the black lace veil floated on the surface of the water. He rested his head against the rim of the steel tub and imagined the girl beside him in the bath.

The black lace veil was too wet to slip inside his shirt as he dressed for dinner. He had nearly fallen asleep in the tub, but Irene, never one to allow him to skip a meal, tapped on his door and announced that she was on her way downstairs to wait for him.

In the dining room, Wentworth, and his wife Marion had joined her. They relished the dinner fare of roasted lamb and venison with vegetables and potatoes prepared in a delicious broth. The conversation around the table was minimal. Lucas had nothing to say, keeping his varied feelings to himself; he barely knew the others were there. But he noticed a flush in Irene's cheeks and realized that she had enjoyed being outside on this unusual day. At some point, before the pudding pie arrived, he decided he would wait until the light of day to open the trunk. He would have to break the lock. He had no key. Would he find out what his dream meant? *The lock is the key.* Lucas struggled to keep a cheerful light in his eyes for the sake of Irene. She patted his hand and offered the wine bottle which he passed along. His melancholy crept across the table and consumed the last of the day. Placing his hands on the white tablecloth he said, "Thank you. Greatly appreciated,"

Irene pouted for a second, then said, "I'm fine here."

Lucas rose and quietly left the room.

Chapter 8

Dugald lay on his back sweating and grinding his teeth. A devastating thought had roused him from troubled sleep. It seemed plausible that Lucas and Mrs. Kempel were wise to his plot to abscond with Lucas. Could they be whispering downstairs waiting for him to die? He imagined them at the kitchen table laughing, drinking, and celebrating every time they sent the spooky woman upstairs to torment him. He must escape. The room was growing darker, the hallway silent. It was time to go. With the determination of a prisoner focused on freedom, he forced himself to his feet. His mouth was dry, but he dared not drink from any containers in the room. His trousers slid up his pale sticky legs with ease, but his stockings felt overly tight. His shirt smelled like the harbour, but he donned it anyway, then clasped the purple cloak at his neck. He crept to the door and to his surprise found it unlocked. Holding his shoes in his hands, he opened the door a crack and peered down the hall. The candelabra, judging by the lack of wax on the alcove ledge, recently lit. He pushed a brave foot through the doorway, then another. Reaching behind his back, not daring to turn around for fear of changing his mind, he pulled the door closed behind him. An almost imperceptible thud combined with a crunch and a small squeal. Leaping aside, he stumbled against the wall, bumped his head but recovered without falling. He had to stifle a squeal of his own. The rat had tried to follow him out of the room. Its long gray body now crushed in the doorjamb.

Footfalls struck the stairs. Dugald shoved himself back into his bedchamber, kicking the rat aside with his stocking foot. He bolted toward the window, yanking the blanket from his bed on the way. A firm hand gripped his shoulder. He grabbed his injured arm with the other and swung them both, knocking her to the floor. His shoes slipped from his grasp. He dared not look at the woman, fearing her crushed like the rat. Swiftly setting his blanket on the window ledge, he shoved the shutter outward until it held the blanket. Glancing back, he caught a glimpse of bloody, blonde hair fanned across the floor. He grasped the end of the blanket and climbed out the window. His cloak swung wildly covering his face. His frantic foot found a wooden timber ledge, but when he applied weight, his knee buckled, and his stocking foot slipped. The blanket ripped but held in the window long enough to swing him into the side of the building, then it tore free and he plummeted to the cobblestone street. The blanket spiraled down over his face. A soft rain began to fall.

* * *

Alina approached the well-kept stone house and read the sign. *Kempel Boarding House.* Her heart fluttered. The iron doorknocker, a triangular rapper joined by a circular bolt to the head of a lion with eyes of perhaps bronze, gazed upon Alina as if it had been awaiting her arrival. A shiver ran up her spine as she scrutinized it and let the rapper fall upon the plate. Glancing around, she noticed along the side of the house a vagrant already curled under his blanket. Those who had no home to go to, often lay down where they were, having fallen from copious drinking, or from the daily exhaustion of a beggar's life. Whoever lay beneath the tattered blanket, alive or dead, didn't matter to her right now but she kept a wary eye lest the bundle should move. From behind the door, a sharp voice called out. Losing her nerve, Alina spun and fled so quickly that she tripped over the beggar catching herself with outstretched hands. Behind her the door creaked open. She flung her cloak over her head and pressed into the corner of the adjacent building, flattening herself against the wall. If only she could be so fortunate as to catch a glimpse of Lucas. But the figure that opened the door had long black hair that covered her face. Alina suppressed a laugh as the woman dressed in black and adorned in necklaces held a broom and a bucket like a sorceress. Without even glancing up, the woman tossed the contents of the bucket into the gutter where the beggar lay. He did not stir.

The woman closed the door, and Alina heard the lock slide into place. Clearly the flower lady had mistaken the name of the house in which Lucas lived. But the door opened again, and the lad came out carrying the lighting tools. She caught his eye. He bowed as he made a wide berth around the beggar. Allowing herself to breathe, she adjusted her cloak, then followed the boy. For several streets, she kept a careful distance behind the young lantern lighter who struggled with every lamp in the increasing rain. If he realized she followed him, he paid her no mind. It was not uncommon for someone caught out after shutting in to follow the lights home. Warm in her hooded woolen cloak, she remained several paces behind, not sure when or how she should approach to inquire of Lucas.

Rounding the next corner, she passed a dark lantern, rushing forward she admonished herself for venturing out at dusk in the strange City of Dreams. She passed another unlit lantern. Her heart raced as heat crept up her neck and around her throat. She removed her hood but soon the rain drizzled down her back. Where is the lamp boy? Up ahead at the entrance to a narrow alley she saw an amber glow and rushed toward it. Just past this lantern hung a weathered sign marking the entrance to the Duck Tavern. The faded dreary duck painted on the sign needed refreshment himself. Alina approached slowly peering around the edge of her hood. By the time, she reached the door, the rain had stopped, and steam rose from the cobblestones. Her cloak hung damp and heavy on her shoulders, but she didn't dare remove it. Just inside the door, the lamp boy leaned against the worn bar top clutching a pint of ale. Alina stepped inside.

Aghast, the boy mumbled, "I thought you found your way home already."

"I am not lost, but certainly I could be, what with you skipping half the lanterns! Whisky," she said turning to the barkeep.

The man raised his eyebrows. "Who's paying?"

"I am." Alina said shortly, "and for his ale as well. But serve him no more. He has a long way to walk yet tonight."

The lamp boy hung his head. "I do not like this job. I have no stomach for the dark."

"Well, that is the point, isn't it? It's up to you to create the light."

"Only Lucas can do that," the lad said.

Alina narrowed her eyes and patted his arm that rested upon the bar. "What's your name?"

"Ikarus, miss." He sipped his ale when clearly, he wanted to gulp it. With downcast eyes he added, "Please don't tell Lucas where you found me."

"I won't tell Lucas where I found you, if you tell me where to find Lucas." Her eyes shone. She drained her cup. Rain once again pelted the foggy windows. Outside the Duck Tavern, the cobbled street turned to rivulets of sludge.

"The rain is too heavy now. I'll not get those lanterns lit tonight." The boy clutched his forehead with one hand and his ale with the other.

"Go to work now before it is too late," Alina said pushing his empty cup toward the barman and shaking her head.

The boy turned toward the window with a forlorn face. "Yes miss," he said softly as he shuffled toward the door.

"Wait!" She grabbed his arm. "What about Lucas? Where can I find him?"

"Nowhere now. He is in Arcana with Mrs. Kempel."

Alina tilted her head.

"Proprietor of the Kempel Boarding house," the barman offered.

"Yes," Ikarus agreed. "Please miss, I do need this job. I am trying. I truly am. And on this terrible night, I'm supposed to set out extra lanterns. Promise me you won't tell him."

Alina accompanied the boy to the door. "If Lucas finds out about the missed lanterns it won't be from me. But I can't speak for the citizens who are struggling to make their way in the dark and rain right now."

The boy averted his gaze. "I'm meeting Lucas at the boarding house tomorrow evening." He opened the door and stepped through into the foggy rain.

Alina sat down to wait for the rain to subside. Immediately, she noticed all the men staring at her. She made for the door, but it opened and a man in a saturated cloak and tattered blanket stumbled in. His white face was sallow and sunken with purple-rimmed eyes gouged deep into his skull. He gestured like a street performer; his clothes reeked of urine. The group at the bar reeled left, then right. Staggering, he grabbed the bar as if he'd just surfaced from the swarmy depths of the sea. His bandaged hand clawed the air. Alina's unease diminished as she noticed the expressions on the faces of the other patrons. They appeared as startled and uncomfortable with the filthy man as she was. They had revulsion in common.

"Hail there, old mate, this is not the place for you," the barkeep scolded.

"Hot whisky," the man said waving his good hand. Nobody moved. He said it again, louder this time. "I want a whisky and some warm water from the kettle!"

"We don't care what you want. Clearly there's no coin in your soggy drawers," a short man with no teeth said grinning at his companions who laughed and spurred him on.

The man staggered away from the bar balancing himself on sideways feet. He paused and glowered at each person in turn, then with the bent and bandaged arm tucked against his abdomen he swung his good arm and grabbed Alina by the throat so swiftly that neither she nor any of the others saw it coming. "I'll break the lass's neck like a twig if I don't get my whisky!"

The crowd of drinkers and tired laborers rushed him. His clammy hand slipped from her neck as he tumbled to his knees. He swore and swiped his bad arm in the air as he crab-crawled out the door accompanied by kicks in the buttocks from the men.

"Better go whilst you can!" the barman shouted shoving a glass of whisky into Alina's hand. She gulped it, then fled through the door that banged behind her. Some men who had followed the beggar outside prodded at him. Never once looking back she followed the haphazard lantern lights down the rain-soaked street running all the way until complete darkness slowed her. She spun around, then peering ahead she made out a candle glow against a stone house. She ran toward it, but it was not the house, not her father's house, now Vasil's house. She had no home anymore she realized with a sharp ache in her heart. Her feet slipped on the cobbles as she ran one way then the other searching for the lantern trail.

* * *

Campbell Barrington approached the Duck Tavern for the third night in a row. Crumpled in a heap of rags outside the locked door he finally found Dugald. He would have stepped past him, but Dugald croaked his name.

"What's happened to you? You're a filthy wreck." Barrington didn't offer a hand. He placed his foot on Dugald's bandaged arm. "We gave you papers, coins, and a key and you disappeared with them." He delivered a swift kick to Dugald's abdomen. "Vasil is furious and so am I! Remember, we will always find you. There is no place in this city, or the country where you can hide." Barrington rolled Dugald over and rummaged through his clothes. "Have you found them. Which warehouse. What have you done with the key?"

"I can't," Dugald mumbled before he went unconscious.

Barrington waited until the wee hours for Vasil to arrive. They paid three aimless street boys to carry Dugald to Vasil's house.

Chapter 9

In the morning, birds sang outside his window. Lucas stretched and yawned, relishing the comfort of the lavish bed.

And then he remembered the trunk. His tranquil mood slipped into reluctant anticipation as he tossed aside the blankets and placed his bare feet on the sumptuous rug. He stared blankly at the trunk while fractured memories drifted through his mind. Remembering his mother's words from the dream, he felt he must preserve the lock, although in all likelihood, the contents of the trunk were the key.

Still, he needed a chisel or something to carefully pry the lock open. At the wash basin he scrubbed his face three times, then went to the window to search the tree for starlings.

Too distracted to dress right now, he flung his cape around him, silently opened his door, and slipped down the back staircase. The Inn was quiet and empty but passing through the kitchen he noticed sweet cakes set out to cool. Lucas helped himself, holding the cape around his waist. He rummaged through a bin of kitchen utensils and found a long knife-sharpening implement with a pointed tip. It made a perfect tool to pick the lock. At the top of the stairs, he turned left instead of right and ended up in the eastern wing of the Grande Inn. Approaching from the other end of the hall, to his surprise, was

Marion, Wentworth's wife. She gawped at Lucas as he stood half-dressed clutching the pointed tool. Throwing her arms out defensively she screeched and fled back the way she came. Lucas hesitated for barely a second before making a hasty retreat to his own room.

Sitting on the floor he examined the trunk. It felt so familiar he found it hard to believe it had been thirteen years since he last saw it. He rubbed his chin and wiped his eyes. This was his mother's trunk, freed from the earth. A piece of her, no longer buried. With a racing heart and trembling fingers, he inserted the pointed tool into the lock, twisted it in one direction then another, the same again and the lock sprung open, an easy feat for one as practiced as Lucas. He noticed nothing special or unusual about the lock itself and he didn't remember it, so he set it aside. In no hurry now, he got up, dropped his cloak, and pulled on his brown trousers and a beige shirt. Placing his palms on the top of the trunk, he took a deep breath and lifted the lid. His mother's scent rose from the layers of her clothes. His throat clenched; he squeezed his eyes shut awaiting the shooting daggers of pain to assault his head, but they did not come. With an inward sigh, he knelt before the trunk and gingerly retrieved the top article of clothing: his mother's nightgown. One by one, with shaky hands and deep breaths, Lucas set each piece of his mother's clothing on the bed. Her faded blue dress, his favorite that she mostly wore when picking flowers. Her threadbare dayshift. These articles brought her into the room with him. Shouldn't these pieces of personal clothing have dissipated when her soul did? He held them up to his face. They smelled more like the trunk than her, but a faint scent lingered, he thought. Below them he discovered items he hadn't seen before: a red and black dress, with a low square neckline, a beige shift, lacy and delicate like her. A heavy gray travelling gown with a matching burgundy cloak. Three shawls of various weight, summer, fall, and winter. Tears bit the corners of his eyes. At one point, he stopped to splash water from the basin onto his face that felt like it was on fire.

Halfway through the trunk he found a small packet, settling it in his lap he unwrapped the soft cloth. An arrow tip fell out onto the floor. He gasped and clutched the edge of the bed where he remained transfixed until the morning sun swept through the window. Lucas picked up the arrow tip and ran his finger along its sharp edges. Despite his shock and confusion, relief struck him. The clothes as lovely as they were to see—even jarred vivid memories—had little to say. But this, a broken arrow. Certainly, neither he nor his mother had used a bow and arrow. And nobody he could think of from his mostly forgotten childhood had used the bow. Narrowing his eyes, feeling the weight of it in his hand, he noticed a dark stain. Blood. Here at last, an answer. His beautiful mother, her life still blooming, then suddenly, abruptly ended. By this very arrow tip? Crying out, he flung it across the room. It bounced over the rug and slid over the polished wood floor to the corner below the window. Now, nausea and a throbbing headache struck him into blindness. Leaning forward, hanging his head between his knees, he took deep groaning breaths waiting for the daggers to diminish. An arrow shot her. Someone. . . a person . . .some person wanted her gone.

Stumbling to the window, shielding his eyes from the glaring sun, his lips trembled. He grabbed the arrow tip, glared at it in his open palm. It shuddered with lifeless truth. He squeezed it as tight as he could. A single hot tear fell upon the deadly object leaving a trail as the blood had. This mark, however, would not last. For a moment he wished it would launch itself into his chest even though it couldn't hurt him. Setting it on the sill, he unlatched the window to take a breath then latched it again fearing the fresh air might disrupt the aromatic vestige of his mother's possessions. Ignoring the arrow tip for now, he turned back to the trunk. His headache began to subside. Reaching inside he felt a small cylinder. His heart leapt, colliding with the tinny drum beating in his heart. The wooden cylinder was tied up in an oil skin and wound around with waxed jute. Shaking his head, he stretched out on the bed, leaned against the wooden headboard, and unwound the rope. Enclosed inside was a miniature painting. It was only the length of his forearm, a portrait of a young woman standing in a field of flowers. His mother! No. He turned toward the window light and squinted. The woman resembled his mother, but it was not her. This woman had a sharpness to her. The face of one who knew much. Far from the angelic countenance he remembered of his sweet mother. Someone was missing from the painting; it was sliced neatly in half. He turned it over but found no markings on the back. No matter how he scrutinized, he could not recognize the woman in the portrait. Placing the painting carefully beside him on the bed he rose and crossed to the window and opened it. No one could possibly see in, but he studied the grounds anyway. A carriage sat idly unhitched, its horse no doubt resting in the barn. The scene outside as still as a painting. With a clenched jaw he paced. The arrow tip and the mysterious painting were remarkable. Yet, he had hoped for a note from his mother explaining why she died and declaring her love for him. A childish dream. But still, one cannot prevent the heart from wanting what it wants. He spotted one last thing at the bottom of the trunk; a neatly folded yellow blanket. He recognized it as if she had just wrapped herself in it last night. Pulling it to him he cradled it like a baby, and then buried his face and wept in long wheezing sobs.

Outside in the courtyard, a spotted brown bird whistled a shrill and mournful accompaniment. It perched on a thin branch of a twisted gray tree. Odd that tree had yet to yield spring buds. It didn't appear dead. The blanket found its way around his shoulders, the folds settling in his lap. He closed his eyes, caressing it, inhaling her scent, phantom or true. Lucas sunk into the bed and slept.

When he awoke, he noticed that the bird had flown off, but the tree was bathed in sunlight and budding tiny bursts of iridescent green. Lucas spread out the blanket on one side of the bed. The contents of the trunk were all now fully revealed. He refolded the blanket, but before placing it back in the trunk felt around for anything else. Nothing more. His stomach growled, and he knew that Irene would be waiting impatiently for him to enter the dining room. He wrapped the arrow tip in its cloth. There was a bloodstain and he knew it was his mother's. But how did it get inside the trunk?

The verandah was awash in sunlight and fresh cut flowers. "This lifestyle I could get used to," Lucas said as he took a seat across from Irene.

"As could I," she exclaimed, her eyes shining. "Now, tell me what you found in your beloved mother's trunk."

Wishing he didn't have to speak about it, but knowing Irene would not let the matter rest, he leaned forward, and whispered. Lucas described the carefully folded clothing, the yellow blanket, and the woman in the torn painting. Then in clipped words dripping with anger he described the bloody arrow tip. Irene patted his hand, dabbed her eyes with a handkerchief when his voice faltered and finally with a sigh murmured, "Where do we go from here?"

He thought about the girl, Alina, back in the City of Dreams and a surge of panic flooded his senses. What if she were only passing through? It was entirely possible that he would never see her again.

"Perhaps you should go back upstairs and lie down again," Irene said. "you're pale as a sheet. That arrow tip. It makes me shudder."

"No, well yes. But I just thought of . . ."

"The young lady," Irene finished his sentence. "You should destroy it."

Lucas recoiled.

"Destroy the arrow tip and then we'll go home and find your girl."

"You know me too well," he smiled and sipped his tea, "but for now I will hold onto that particular object." The serving maid placed a platter of food in the center of the table.

"I ordered everything since I suppose this is our last day," Irene said, as she cast a fond gaze about the room.

Lucas took Irene's hand and squeezed it. "I'll serve," he said. "I'd like to forget everything and live here, walking in the countryside in the mornings, dining on robust meals, drinking fine wine, gazing blankly into the evening hearth." He piled her plate high and then his own as well.

"But there's the girl," she said.

He cocked his head. "The girl, yes, but please don't worry about the girl, Irene."

Her eyes watered. "I'm not worried . . . not too much . . . at least not yet."

Lucas nodded his mouth full of food. He was worried too and wished he had been honest about meeting Alina. He did want to get back to the City of Dreams. But first he must try to find his mother's killer.

"You have so much life ahead of you. I have fewer thresholds to pass through," Irene said averting her gaze. "Have you ever noticed how everything happens at once? Days follow each other for weeks, months . . . years. Then suddenly the sameness ends in a moment. It's as if one day you're scrubbing the floor and when you stand up nothing is as it was. Sometimes I wish I could step into a cupboard and close the door behind me."

Lucas swallowed hard and gulped his tea. "I suppose I do understand about the sameness. The days pass acceptably well, stable, and predictable, and then change hits like a sack of flour in the face of a distracted baker's boy. Certainly, Irene, stepping into the cupboard . . . where would that lead?"

Irene pouted, picked up her fork and shoved her food from one side of the plate to the other. Lucas chewed carefully but didn't take his eyes off her. He thought about his mother's trunk and all the mysteries of late. More trunks somewhere–Trousdale had said–and the girl, Alina who had him so shaken. It all did happen quickly, unexpected like a muddy splash from a carriage wheel: clothing and perspective must change.

He deeply desired to return to the City of Dreams today. He had already checked with the carriage driver to be sure they could carry the trunk. Best to get it safely home in the light of day. Then Alina. He had to see her again.

Irene's appetite had gotten the better of her melancholy mood, her plate now empty; she sat back, relaxing into the chair. He hadn't spent time walking with her in the countryside as they had imagined. No picnic with wine and lighthearted conversation. He remembered it was just a few days ago that he had nothing to think about except lantern lighting. Simple, yet instantly gratifying. "How long can one hold on to the ease of ordinary days?"

"A moment at a time," Irene said softly.

"Shall we stay one more night?" he said surprised to hear his voice say the words she wanted to hear, especially when his thoughts were the opposite. Of course, he'd love to remain here and forget about lanterns, trunks, the boarding house, Trousdale, and Dugald. He laughed to indicate his joke, but Irene's eyes were alight and her smile grand. The girl is expecting me to call on her, he wanted to say. She is the future. The mystery of my mother is buried so far in the past. I'm afraid to stir that dust. His lips moved but his voice was silent. He set down his fork. The grandfather clock chimed nine a.m. Its golden pendulum shimmering in the morning light. It caught his eye, as gold always did, and he remembered Madam Trousdale's gold-jewelled box. His heart leapt. Had she left it sitting in plain sight on the wardrobe in her simple cottage? An opportunity had fallen into his hands and he never thought of it until now. It would have been possible to approach her cottage before leaving the City of Dreams, why had he not considered it. He would have passed her on the road as she went to the boarding house that morning, but Madam Trousdale would never have seen him, he was like the cat, only visible when he wanted to be. Surely, he had too many thoughts skittering through his head. Alina . . .

Irene squeezed his hand. "Where did you go, Lucas? I was saying; yes, let's stay another night. We could both use the rest. All of this news about your mother, it must be devastating."

The painting and the arrow tip, too much to understand. Lucas tilted his chair back, "Of course, we shall stay." He motioned for the serving maid. "Brandy for our tea please." And to Irene, "then a stroll in the lovely garden." His mother's trunk of course would remain in his room and he would try not to think of the contents. But he would ask questions. Another day in the country might provide some answers. What a relief it would to be to return to the City of Dreams unburdened by the past.

He only hoped Madam Trousdale had had the sense to conceal the golden box, or better yet bring it with her. He entertained a happy thought of it, at this moment, concealed somewhere in the boarding house. Most of all, he implored the heavens to keep Alina safe until his return.

"You are pleased," Irene said. "I'm glad we decided to take our ease today."

"So am I," Lucas said with sincerity. He did so need a rest. Ikarus, he hoped, would continue lighting lanterns when Lucas didn't show up this evening to discuss supplies and any new developments in the routine. Sunlight streamed across the table. They set their gold-rimmed porcelain cups on their respective saucers and rose simultaneously.

Irene looped her arm in his. "The garden will be brilliant at this hour."

Warmth greeted them as they stepped under a fragrant arch into the bountiful landscape. The expansive earth, the sweet-smelling blossoms, Alina would appreciate this, he felt sure. There was so much to learn about her. One thing he already knew was her love for flowers. They had this in common, as if she was chosen especially for him. He laughed inwardly, soothed by an innate awareness that his life and hers were just beginning.

He and Irene strolled until they came upon a well-placed bench. There they enjoyed the fluttering of delicate white pear blossoms budding against a deep blue sky. Accompanied by the hum of bees, Lucas answered Irene's questions about everything he had found in his mother's trunk. She always wanted details and his description at breakfast had skimmed only the surface. Irene wanted to know how it all appeared from the moment he opened the lid. Not only that, she wanted to know how each item made him feel. Not just the arrow, but everything. Lucas understood that Irene would not let him build a wall around his feelings, lest his pain turn into rage. As he spoke, the anguish lessened. His mother's carefully folded clothing evoked much emotion, was he nearby when she placed them there? For a few moments he allowed himself to remember how it felt to be a child. Hot tears slid down his cheeks, over the strong curve of his jaw, and landed in the crook of his neck. Irene wrapped her plush arms around him.

Once the tears had dried and his breath came easy again, Lucas told Irene about his encounter with Alina. He wanted no secrets. His mother was gone, murdered and he couldn't imagine why. His desire to find the murderer a mission that would require the assistance of his most trusted person. He must tell her his true feelings. "Irene, this girl Alina, she is already a part of our life. I feel it somehow."

"As do I," Irene said, patting him where the lace veil rested against his chest. "We should go home as planned."

"Let's make inquiries first. The arrow tip must be the murder weapon; therefore, my mother could not have placed it in her trunk. Someone went to significant effort to leave that clue for me. What they didn't know is that it would take me thirteen years to find it. Now, only that person and the two of us know it's there. I want to know who would want to kill my sweet mother and why," Lucas stood and offered his arm. Just then, Wentworth entered the garden.

"Ah, there you two are. I'm running late this morning and feared I'd missed you. Marion is not feeling well today."

"What ails her?" Irene asked.

"She's had a terrible fright. Apparently, a man accosted her in the hallway this morning."

"That's horrible!" Irene exclaimed with a hand to her throat.

Lucas frowned. "At the Grande Inn? I find that difficult to believe. "I've kept a keen eye. There are no thieves or highwaymen residing here. Surely your wife has overreacted."

Wentworth and Irene gazed at Lucas but neither spoke. Realizing the rudeness of his comments, Lucas thought for a moment. Then he said, "Perhaps you're right after all. I suggest we speak to the Innkeeper. Apparently, the countryside is not as placid as it appears. My mother was murdered here thirteen years ago."

"How do you know that?" Wentworth's face went gray.

"Apparently, this delightful country hamlet harbors secrets and discord."

Wentworth's eyes darted left to right. "As I mentioned yesterday, I've always felt safe here at the Inn. Safer than I do at home."

"Is isolation the only reason?" Lucas asked.

"My wife," Wentworth cleared his throat. "It is true, she is the nervous sort. Our farmhouse is off the trodden path. We cannot see a neighbor's light."

"So, you always stay at the Inn?"

"Yes, I go out and check on the land. As does Bernard. Marion wants to sell or trade the property. But it's my family land, and my first wife died there," he added in a whisper.

"You told us your first wife died in a carriage accident," Lucas said.

Wentworth nodded. "It is true. But the carriage was our own. It rolled over her in front of our house."

"How awful!" Irene shuddered.

"Unfortunate," Lucas said.

"Quite so," Wentworth agreed as he retreated across the threshold.

The rosy hue that had returned to Irene's face drained into the soil, along with any hope of the two of them enjoying a lazy day in the bountiful color of eager spring flowers. Lucas peered at her with concern. She tightened her grip on his arm. "We need answers. It's why we came after all," she murmured so that Wentworth, who was already several paces ahead, couldn't hear.

As they walked to the reception room, Lucas thought about his early morning encounter with Marion in the hallway. She could not have possibly mistaken Lucas for a stranger. He did not lay hands on her. She knew him. He saw the recognition in her eyes.

"When I found the arrow tip, I knew the answers we sought would lead to more questions. I need to find out what happened back then. It's unusual that Marion and Wentworth live here at the Inn, don't you think? And now Marion claims she was attacked."

Irene shook her head. Her eyes clouded with worry.

"I'm so sorry, Irene. You haven't rested. This is more than you expected."

"I'm fine." She sniffed.

"Then at least take a seat in the parlour. I will ask the innkeeper about the longtime residents here in Arcana. Someone around here must have knowledge of past events."

"Wentworth seems agitated this morning," Irene said.

"Indeed, I agree." Lucas noticed Wentworth standing at the end of the hall staring at them. "Rest a moment Irene. I will send the maid with tea."

After alerting the kitchen to tend to Irene, Lucas took the back stairs two at a time. His bedroom door was still securely locked. Upon entering he found the trunk as he left it, as well as his personal belongings arranged in a specific manner. Nobody had entered his room.

Voices outside startled him. In the courtyard, Wentworth and Marion argued with a tall man who waved his arms in anger. Leaning against the window sash, Lucas studied the scene. Something about the man was familiar. He leaned out and his movement caught Marion's eye. The others followed her upward gaze. The man standing next to her was the man from the tavern, the giant, the one who had questioned him. Lucas secured the lock on his chamber door and hurried back downstairs to the parlour. Irene sat where he'd left her, sipping tea, and chatting with one of the widows from last night. He caught her attention and pointed outside. She gave a relaxed wave.

As Lucas approached, the group stopped murmuring. "So, we meet again," Lucas said.

Marion's hand fluttered to her chest. With a furtive look at the giant she stepped in front of him.

Wentworth said, "Ah Lucas, where did you get off to? Allow me to introduce you to Bernard, my stepson."

A smile flickered across Bernard's face. He extended his hand. "How's the head?"

Lucas felt for the scratch on his forehead. "I'd forgotten about it."

"The gash is gone," Bernard remarked.

"Where have you met before?" Marion squeaked.

"At a tavern in the woods," Lucas turned toward her in time to notice an expression of shock on her pinched face. "On the way here," he added.

"At the *No Horses Tavern,*" Bernard said.

Wentworth laughed. "Wonderful! I enjoy coincidence. Now, let's step inside and speak with the Innkeeper about Marion's attack this morning."

"What attack?" Bernard narrowed his eyes at his mother.

"It was more of an encounter," she murmured avoiding the penetrating eyes of not only Bernard but Lucas as well. Wentworth headed toward the front door as did Bernard, but Lucas waited for Marion to take a step, and when she did, she shot a sidelong glance his way.

"What is this about?" he demanded.

"I was frightened. You had a weapon." She walked on to catch up with the others.

Lucas came up alongside her and took her elbow. "A polite woman does not tell lies."

Marion pulled away. "You and Mrs. Kempel should leave at once. There are no answers for you here. Get back to the City of Dreams where you belong," she hissed.

Bernard stood at the top of the steps holding the door open. Inside, Wentworth had arranged for the lobby boy to bring the ladder-back chairs from the dining room into the Innkeepers office. Judging by the expression on the Innkeeper's face, he did not appreciate the intrusion into his small space that was already overcome by a massive carved wood desk, and floor to ceiling bookshelves full of leather-bound books. Brass oil lamps accented the dark paneled walls. A large, green desk lamp glowed with candlelight in the middle of the day.

"Let's keep Mrs. Kempel out of this," Lucas said glancing toward the parlour at the end of the hall where she still chatted with the woman. He remained in the doorway to keep an eye on her, and to avoid having to climb over chairs to sit in one. He resisted the urge to suggest that in the event of fire, with all these lamps lit, the Innkeeper should take a dive out of the large draped window behind his desk. He pulled loose the laces of his shirt and leaned against the door jam.

Once the others were all seated, Wentworth asked Marion to describe what had happened to her in the upstairs hallway earlier that morning.

"Let's forget it," she said merrily. "I was mistaken, it was nothing . . . nobody."

Bernard rolled his eyes and Wentworth grimaced. "Were you attacked or not?" Mr. Hartwinn, the innkeeper asked.

"I think it was a shadow. I arose too early and after the wine last night . . ." she let her voice drift.

The Innkeeper picked at the cuffs of his sleeves. "Are you certain Mrs. Bodden? Surely you didn't send for your son to find a shadow."

"I didn't send for him," she miffed. "I need to get outside. This room is too crowded." Marion rose stiffly but was trapped among the chairs. Lucas, who had remained standing inside the doorway with his arms folded across his chest, glared at her but didn't move.

"After all, the best marksman in all of Arcana rarely graces us with his presence here at the Grande Inn" Mr. Hartwinn said.

"Tis true" Wentworth agreed, "and we spend most of our time here."

"I prefer the farmhouse," Bernard said.

"Who is the best marksman?" Lucas said. Turning his full attention to those gathered in the Innkeepers office.

"Why Bernard of course," Mr. Hartwinn said. "Most of our meat comes from him. He can shoot the bow and arrow like no one else!

Lucas' eyes widened. His head buzzed, and his throat constricted. He began to cough, needed a place to spit and resorted to his handkerchief. Their mouths moved but he could no longer hear their words. The noise of his own clamoring thoughts roaring in his ears. Bernard was on his feet extending the water pitcher. From afar, Lucas watched his hand take the pitcher, felt the cool release in his mouth, then the water found its way down his throat. "You shoot? For how long?" he demanded.

"My whole life," Bernard said.

"He shot his first rabbit on the farm, at only five years." Wentworth said. "Isn't that what you told me, Marion?"

Auspicious occurrence, Lucas thought taking notice of Marion's white face. Her puffy eyes darted from him to Bernard, who ignored her. Marion is crumbling so rapidly on the inside it's showing on the outside. Why does she so desperately want me gone. I won't allow this wretched woman to run me off. The blood burned through his veins bombarding his brain. A creeping, cold sweat climbed upward from his feet like a cat ascending a tree, prickling his soaked skin, seeking his neck then settling there with a stifling stranglehold. All eyes cast toward him. No one moved, standing frozen as in a picture, moments marked in timeless time, suspended with no will to go forward.

A gap opened in the fabric of his former life and Lucas slid through. His head pounded, a deafening waterfall of awareness. Someone in this tiny room had quite possibly murdered his mother. They are country folk; they stick together. Marion is protecting Bernard. Or, Lucas thought, as a cold finger of blame stroked his cheek, she's wondering if he will protect her.

"Sir, you're ashen, as if you've seen a ghost." Mr. Hartwinn leaned forward and placed his palms on the edge of his heavy wooden desk. "Steady the man, Wentworth!"

"Lucas, lad . . . take a seat." Wentworth rose gesturing toward his chair, taking the water pitcher from Lucas' trembling hand, giving it back to Bernard who straddled one of the chairs to get out of the way, then shoved it at Lucas hitting him in the back of the knees. Lucas wavered but remained upright. "Hurry have the maid bring more water," Wentworth barked to Bernard.

Bernard made for the door, but Lucas moved in front of him and stood solid as stone. His frame filled the doorway. His heartbeat discernible in his throat.

"Give way now fellow, we're trying to help you," Bernard said giving Lucas a shove.

His eyes as black as the night he so cherishes, Lucas grabbed Bernard by the throat. "How old are you–where is your quiver– who was your teacher?"

Marion's nostrils flared; her breath rasped. Wentworth who had rushed toward Lucas and Bernard changed direction darting toward her, upsetting a chair, and tumbling into another pulling Marion down on top of him.

"Good heavens, what is going on here?" Mrs. Kempel stood wide-eyed and white-faced in the hallway.

Lucas released Bernard, who said, "Easy soldier." He straightened his coat but made no move to assist his mother and Wentworth. He peered at Lucas with a wry smile.

Returning to his senses, Lucas glared at Bernard then turned to Mrs. Kempel. "Are you all right?"

"Me . . . I am . . . was quite well. But what about you? What is going on in here?"

"What is going on indeed?" Mr. Hartwinn demanded gesturing for Lucas and Bernard to help sort out the chairs. "I will not have this kind of behavior at The Grande Inn!"

Mrs. Kempel said, "He is upset of course. Lucas has just discovered that his mother was shot with an arrow!"

Lucas rapidly shook his head, but it was too late. Once again, everyone stared at him. Marion flopped into the chair uprighted by Mr. Hartwinn. Wentworth muttered incoherently. Red-faced Marion mopped her brow with a handkerchief, then fanned herself. "I must get out of this tiny room!"

With a grunt, Bernard swooped his mother into his arms and carried her from the room swearing as he went. Mrs. Kempel took Lucas by the hand rubbing it between her warm pudgy palms. "You need a whisky, I think."

"Brilliant woman," Mr. Hartwinn agreed and withdrew a bottle and four glasses from behind a small door in his desk. They downed their drinks and the Innkeeper poured again.

Bernard returned. "Don't leave me out. She'll be fine. The maids have her on the divan."

"This is all most unusual," Mr. Hartwinn said swigging his whisky.

By the third pour, the tension lifted from the stuffy room and their faces reflected ease. "You may as well begin the explanation," the Innkeeper said to Lucas.

Lucas sat silent and motionless. Since arriving in Arcana, the sense of foreboding had been lurking, but Lucas had thought it merely agitation from searching the mind of a child he barely remembered being. He felt Irene's fingers massaging the back of his neck. His breath came out less ragged as the whisky coursed through his blood.

"Let's clear this up and go home," she said.

Lucas grunted and continued to stare blankly.

"Let's get the trunk home," Mrs. Kempel said.

Lucas flicked his eyes in agreement but remained silent, spinning the last of the whisky in his glass.

"The girl will be waiting, won't she?" Mrs. Kempel whispered directly in his ear.

He sat up. "Fine." Clearing his throat, "To begin with, Marion and I encountered each other in the hallway this morning. I had retrieved a knife sharpener from the kitchen with which to pry open the lock on my mother's trunk. I wore a cloak. Perhaps she mistook me for an intruder."

"Ye gods!" Wentworth said. "It was you?"

"It was I but let me assure you there was no contact made. She stood her ground at the one end of the hall and I at mine, then we both retreated to our rooms. Quite simply nothing to it."

Bernard laughed. Wentworth held out a shaky hand for more whisky. "That sounds like Marion," Bernard said. "Fabricating stories to get attention."

"Hush," Wentworth snapped.

"Tis easy to become confused in the early hours," Mrs. Kempel said.

"Bernard, please check on your mother," Wentworth said. "If she is able to speak now, ask her if it could have been Lucas whom she saw this morning."

Bernard rolled his eyes. "Can you not ask yourself? She's your wife."

"And she is your mother. Show the required respect."

Lucas and Irene glanced at each other. This cross side of Wentworth they had not yet seen. Bernard shrugged as he was accustomed to doing and strode down the hall, his footsteps echoing on the polished wood floor.

"Well then," the Innkeeper said exasperated. "It is all settled then?"

"Not quite," Lucas said. Setting his glass on the desk and standing. There is still the matter of my mother's murder. I need to make inquiries. To begin with, Bernard, how many years has he?"

"Why . . . him? He is not much older than you." Wentworth said sitting upright in his chair.

"It's just a question," Mrs. Kempel said.

"He is twenty-five. And you?"

"I see." Lucas said. "He has only two years on me. Excuse me Wentworth. I don't mean to accuse Bernard but . . ."

"But we have come for answers," Irene said, patting Lucas' hand. "This journey has been difficult . . . shocking. It's time to put this matter to rest. Lucas needs to move forward with his life."

"You believe your mother was killed with the bow and arrow? Therefore, you suspect Bernard, I suppose. I can assure you everyone in Arcana shoots the bow and arrow." Wentworth said.

"At each other?" Lucas once again felt the heat rise in his body.

"Bernard was barely older than you were when your mother died!"

"He would have been twelve. At the age of twelve I was making my way in the City of Dreams. There was little I wouldn't do to survive." Lucas turned to Bernard who now stood in the doorway and had not taken his eyes from Lucas since returning to the Innkeeper's office. "Bernard, why do you say nothing?"

Bernard gave his half smile. "I prefer to listen. We all seek answers. Is that not so?"

"It is quite so. Have you any answers for me, Bernard?"

"I can assure you that I did not murder your mother. I remember her and you as well." Bernard scrutinized Lucas. "I watched you suffer after her death."

"How is that?" Lucas rose, began shoving chairs out of the way. He carried Marion's vacant one into the hallway and his too, waving his arm in dismissal. The Innkeeper pulled the woven cord beside his desk and the lobby boy showed up to carry the chairs away.

"Speak up please, Bernard!" Mrs. Kempel insisted.

Bernard turned toward Wentworth who swiped his hand across his damp brow, then gestured, "Go ahead. We have nothing to hide. I will excuse myself and check on Marion."

"Let me accompany you," Mr. Hartwinn followed Wentworth from the room closing the door behind them.

Bernard poured another whisky. Lucas took a seat. "You and your mother were the lights of the valley. Every morning you walked together to the flower fields. Your baskets were always full of the brightest and best blossoms."

Lucas nodded. Mrs. Kempel sat quietly sipping her whisky.

"Your kind mother brought herbs and berries to the bunkhouse. She made pies and shared them with the farm hands. You walked with her as if in a dream. The two of you radiated peace and tranquility. None of us knew where you came from." His voice grew softer as he spoke. "Your mother had no husband. No father for you, Lucas." Gazing openly into Lucas' eyes he said, "Perhaps for the best," he added, "in my opinion anyway." Bernard put his palms on his knees and pushed himself up. Sunlight poured in the open window from the garden. "To all of the boys in the bunkhouse, it was quite natural. As if the two of you had sprung from the earth like the beautiful flowers you shared with the world."

Through blurry eyes, Lucas imagined the picture that Bernard painted. "Are you saying I was torn from the center of a flower? A flower bloomed and out popped me? Ha! It is nonsense."

"You seemed to float when you walked. You rarely spoke. You never fell sick with the winter fever. Your mother gathered flowers and herbs for healing the rest of us, but she didn't need to use them on you."

Lucas sat back in his chair enjoying the words of Bernard. The unruly giant had keen instincts and his deep mesmerizing voice laid smooth mortar among the jumbled bricks of Lucas' fragmented childhood. The words invoked images real and unreal at the same time, as in an intricately woven tapestry, recreating a memory one begs to be true. He wanted nothing more than to stay in those images of the past, to allow them to absorb him, return him to who he once was, who he may have been if he'd had more time with his mother. The life that once lay at his feet, had, in a sudden whir of wind, disappeared. A safe silence settled in the room. A bond forming between two of similar age, born on the same soil. Lucas noticed Irene sitting with eyes closed clutching her empty glass. He wasn't sure if she had fallen asleep. Bernard seemed as if he would say more, so Lucas waited until the ticking of the clock hanging over his head thoroughly vexed him. "Those flower-filled days with my mother were wonderful days, tis true. But they are gone and will not return. I want to know who killed her. Someone put the arrow tip in her trunk before it was packed away. It is a message, purposely placed. Who could have done that?"

The blood drained from Bernard's face. "There are unexplained events here as everywhere. Just ask Wentworth, his first wife was run over by a carriage."

"That is a terrible death, surely the driver was intoxicated or an idiot."

"Neither, there was no driver. At the house where Wentworth no longer cares to live. It just rolled forward on flat ground."

"Carriages don't usually roll on their own." Lucas said his gaze fixed.

"Not without a push from behind," Bernard stated.

"Who would do such a thing?" Irene huffed.

Bernard cast his eyes down, "Again, I do not know. I must go now, Lucas." He offered his hand, a firm grip. "I am pleased to see you again and wish you good fortune in discovering who killed your mother." To Irene, "Lovely to meet you ma'am. I'm glad for the two of you." He looked away and as he turned to leave the room, mumbled, "a tragedy it was."

"Bernard!" Lucas started after him.

Mrs. Kempel said, "Let him go, Lucas. There will be no answers today." The arched timber door of the Grande Inn closed with a definitive thud.

"I'll never resolve my mother's death."

"Shall we stay, or shall we go home?" Mrs. Kempel pushed herself up from the chair.

"My memories are stirred now. Bernard's recollections have illuminated more of the mystery of my past. It was not a dream."

"He has given life to your memories."

"Yes. We haven't seen the last of him."

"We'll stay then, and I shall enjoy a nap this afternoon."

Lucas clasped her hands, "Very well, Irene. We will walk the garden again in the gloaming."

The maid met them in the lobby, carrying a tray with tea and spice cake for Irene; she escorted her upstairs. Lucas stood at the bottom of the stairs and watched them go up. So far, the day hadn't gone in any direction that he hoped. Bernard's words banged around in his head like a bat in a box. He enjoyed the luxury of the Grande Inn with its shiny wood banisters and warm tapestries, but the rush of events marred its beauty. And not only that, he felt a nagging urge to hurry back to the City of Dreams despite his need to remain.

Dugald lay ailing in the boarding house. Why had he allowed that man to stay? It could be plague! What was he thinking leaving Madam Trousdale in charge? And how could he leave the city without notifying Alina? He should have broken down her door and insisted she accompany him to the country and forever more. He wandered into the parlour–empty now but for a blazing fire–and sat on the low hearth feeling the warmth of the flames on his back.

The lobby boy appeared immediately. "Do you require anything, sir?"

"A whisky, if you please."

"Not so fast," said a voice.

Lucas looked up to see Bernard standing there with his hands on his hips.

"I have horses ready. You must accompany me now. You need to see for yourself."

Lucas stood, returned Bernard's gaze. "See . . ."

"The flower field where your mother fell." Bernard wrung his hands. "We should go before daylight fades."

The lad returned holding a tray with two glasses of whisky. Lucas snatched them both, then remembering himself realized one was for Bernard. He offered it; they drained their glasses simultaneously.

"Why should I trust you?" Lucas wrinkled his nose at his empty glass.

Bernard took a step back cocking his head sideways. "Why shouldn't you trust me? You have nothing I want."

"Don't I?" Lucas chuckled and walked to the window pushing the heavy drape aside to examine the sky. "We have a few hours." He dropped the drape and strode to the door.

Outside, Oliver held the reins of two, tall black steeds, one was shoving the other sideways and pawing at the dirt. "That one's mine," Bernard said. "He doesn't like to wait."

The men mounted; Lucas turned his horse in to trot behind Bernard. Once away from the Inn, they broke into a gallop. The mane tickled Lucas' hands, the wind felt cool on his face, dancing through his hair. He had not ridden since he was a boy, having no need himself for a horse in the City of Dreams. The rush of remembered youth filled him as he streamed past Bernard. His shoulders and back relaxed as he fell into rhythm with the powerful horse, trees blurred past, sure-footed hooves glided over the uneven ground. Lucas forgot where he was going in the intoxicating exultation of movement. His frustration dissipated. He could ride all day; he could ride to the edge of the earth and jump off. What did it matter? The horse stretched out his legs as if he could read Lucas' mind.

In a little more than a quarter hour they pulled up their horses at the edge of what had once been Lucas and Linnea's flower field. Spring warmth had no effect now, mud puddles and sparse grass, no flowers greeted them. Lucas allowed his horse to canter in circular strides and catch its breath. Bernard had already dismounted and tied his horse to a tree. After a few rounds surveying the field, Lucas did the same.

"Different." He stomped past Bernard out into the middle of the field with his head down as he examined the ground, breathing deep to slow his hammering heart. He crossed to one side of the desolate field then the other and back again. Finally, he knelt before the broken trunk of a fallen tree. His mouth quivered, lips trembled . . . he tried to take a deep breath, but it left him, and he fell forward bracing his open palms on the earth and then his forehead upon the ground.

The sun moved low across the sky warming his back. Sitting back on his haunches he wiped his eyes with the back of his hands. In the angled afternoon light, shadows crept toward him from the far end of the field. He saw himself and his mother walking side by side. His head ached; his stomach knotted as he struggled again to catch his breath. Coughing and spitting, his throat constricted. Bernard handed over his flask. Lucas gulped; the warm whisky pulsed through his veins. He raised a hand and Bernard pulled him to his feet.

"This is the spot," Lucas said.

"It is."

"How do you know, Bernard?"

Bernard gazed unblinking into Lucas' eyes for several moments. "Well . . . what I know is . . ." He shuddered and looked away into the distance as if he could retrieve the past.

"Go on. Speak to me of what you know," Lucas said clutching Bernard's shoulder.

Bernard pulled away, walked in a circle around the area. "In the evening of the day, neither of you returned to the farm."

"I did, at dusk," Lucas said. "I stayed with my mother until dusk."

"No," Bernard said. "That is not what happened, and it would not have made sense anyway. If you had seen your mother fallen, you would have run for help!"

"Well, I held her. I remember that . . . and I know that it was full dark by the time I reached the farm."

"That is true. The farmer tried to feed you, calm you with tea. But you kept saying, *there's no time for that*. Do you not remember me, Lucas? I am the plow boy. You and your mother brought food to me in the bunkhouse. Sometimes I ran into you in the main house when I was helping with chores and you brought the flowers in."

"You . . . the little plow boy? Not possible, he was so small."

"As were you," Bernard said laughing gently.

Lucas narrowed his eyes, taking stock of Bernard. "I don't see it. I can't place you as him." He shook his head. "Are you not Marion's son, with a farm of your own? Why would you stay in the bunkhouse?"

Bernard clenched his jaw, "The day after you two didn't return I came out here."

"What do you mean the day after?" Lucas pushed his hair away from his face, groaning, his eyes squeezed shut. "What are you talking about?"

"You were here. You and your mother, lying side by side."

"Sleeping? Had I fallen asleep? Was my mother already gone?"

"You both were. You were dead. Neither of you had a pulse. The arrow went straight through her heart and into yours. You were dead right here on this spot, Lucas. You were gone too, no breath, no heartbeat, just blood."

"No, I wasn't. I'm alive, here . . . now." Lucas slapped Bernard on the back. "Can you not see me?"

"You were as dead as the ancient kings. I was terrified. I ran. I . . . I ran and hid in the forest. When I returned to the farm under cover of night there you were, crying and pleading for your mother. The two of you had died the day before. Then you, and only you, had sprung up like a flower after winter . . . brighter, stronger, and more striking than before . . . but in the broad light of day, I had seen you lying here, dead."

"That's impossible," Lucas said with a dazed expression. "Bernard, what are you talking about? You are causing me much distress right now."

"You aren't like the rest of us Lucas. You came from nowhere. Your mother was here in the valley for years and one day she suddenly had you with her."

"Must I explain where babies come from, Bernard? Lucas grinned. "Too much day drinking . . ." but the expression on Bernard's face made Lucas stop talking and his grin faded.

"They wanted you and they got me."

"Who did?"

"Marion and Darnell. You don't remember Marion. She is the farmer's wife!"

"The farmer's wife, from the farm on which my mother and I lived? Mrs. Radzger, then? How can that be?"

"When Radzger died she married Wentworth. He was a widower by then and a farmer but much wealthier. Now she is Marion Bodden. Radzger may or may not have been my father. I think not. It would explain why I was shoved off into the bunkhouse."

Lucas turned in a circle and sat down on a patch of dry grass. "Spill it all, my friend." Brushing his hand over the ground picking up tiny pebbles examining them and tossing them aside. "What happened here?"

Bernard flumped down beside him. "We all knew there was something unusual about you. The way you appeared without a man in your mother's life. She gathered here for several years, then she disappeared from Arcana for many months. And when she returned, she carried you along with her flowers."

"Had she shown signs of pregnancy?"

"Some said yes, others said no. I remember your mother described as skinnier than a beggar's candlestick."

"Was there sickness or fainting? Perhaps, her apron and gown covered . . ."

Bernard shook his head. "Once you appeared, many of the village gossips pried, skittered about asking Linnea who the father was."

Lucas sat up placing his hand on Bernard's forearm. "And her answer?"

"Time will tell."

"That's it?"

"Yes, and as everyone has told me—I was only two and a half years when you showed up, don't forget—there were a few accused, but you are similar to nobody from around here and all denied your paternity."

"That doesn't mean . . . I don't know . . . mean what? I came from somewhere. My poor mother, some villain must have accosted her."

"I think not."

Lucas laughed. "So, I am the son of a spectre."

"In all likelihood! There was a cloaked entity that roamed the fields at dusk. When your mother died, nobody ever saw it again."

Lucas shivered thinking about his shadow nightmare. Shaking it off, he said, "You speak of hearthside gossip. There had to be a man involved. Babes aren't born from faeries." He swished his hand around in the air and smirked, hoping Bernard would withdraw his words.

"It wasn't a man. It was a cloaked thing, ethereal, that wavered in the wind . . . like a tall . . . um plant, I suppose you could say." He waved an arm toward the woods. "Like a tree struggling against the wind. I think you are born of the earth and that's why you didn't die. Your skill for finding flowers that for others didn't grow. The tenacity in which you accompanied your mother, walking when still so small. Your strength and keen awareness for one so young. If you cut yourself, it healed right away! Even now, you shine like a lantern on a pitch-black night. And now even, there was a gash on your head from the chandelier at the *No Horses*, where is that gash, Lucas?"

Lucas felt his forehead even though he knew he had no gash and had completely forgotten about it. He reached inside his shirt and scratched his scar. The black lace veil sat nestled in its usual place over his heart. "Who would want us dead?"

"It could have been an accident." Bernard gazed off into the distance, swept his arm out. "As Wentworth said, everyone in Arcana shoots the bow and arrow."

"A foolish mistake?"

Bernard gathered a handful of dirt, let it sift through his fingers.

Lucas glowered, "I don't believe that and neither do you!"

Bernard swallowed, "Well, I thought sometimes that, Darnell, Mr. Radzger, would have killed your mother to appease Marion. She was desperately jealous of your mother. As young as I was, I could see that Marion wanted you for her own child. Especially as you grew. They tried to keep you afterward. . . but you got away. She finally gave in and accepted me as her son. But what boy could love a mother when he has already felt her rejection? They were the worst of people. I hope Darnell Radzger is not my father, but I will never know. And he is long dead, so . . ." he clutched his stomach. "He beat her. Sometimes she made him sick with her cooking."

Lucas scowled. "On purpose?"

"I believe so. She enjoyed her freedom when he took to his bed." Bernard laughed. "Women and their wiles, we will never understand. I don't know how Wentworth abides with her. Her own brother left her behind. Went to the City of Dreams when the barn burned down."

Lucas' eyes grew wide, "Marion has a brother in the City of Dreams!"

"Oh, not anymore. Marion adored her older brother, but he never sent word or returned. She went there looking for him and came back with a notice of death stating that he walked into a canal and drowned, so that's that. She was terribly angry that he left her behind. I think she drove him away with her ordering him about." Bernard rubbed his hands together. "I don't even remember him."

Lucas leaned back on his elbows and studied the sky. Bernard's words annoyed him; the complications were too many. These Arcana dwellers made no sense to him, he realized. He cast an inquisitive look at Bernard, indicating he wanted to hear more.

"Once you disappeared Darnell and Marion allowed me to move into the farmhouse. And later with the marriage of Marion to Wentworth, the richest farmer in the valley, he is generous as well, I became wealthy too. Now I can live as I wish. Others farm his acres and they pay well for use of that land." He slapped Lucas on the knee. "But I have wondered all these years when you would come back. I knew you could not have died."

"Marion is your mother?"

"Yes, such as she is."

"Put you aside in the bunkhouse. Why?"

Bernard tilted his head from side to side. "She preferred Linnea's baby to her own. She intended to raise you instead of me. Darnell confessed on a drunken night."

"You remember that?"

"How could I forget? But Wentworth is a good stepfather. And she pretends now to care for me as her son."

"You live as a hunter now," Lucas said.

"Yes."

"Alone most of the time."

"That is true."

"No wife for you, Bernard?"

"I prefer it that way."

"Except when you entertain yourself at the *No Horses Tavern.*"

Bernard threw his head back and laughed. "You begin to know me, but trust me, no wife will appear in that establishment!"

Lucas laughed with him.

"And you, Lucas? You will have a wife someday, won't you?"

"Yes, I intend to."

A flock of black birds soared overhead. The essence of his old home filled in the empty spaces around him. "I remember the birdsong."

Bernard stretched his legs out; he squinted at the birds then turned directly to Lucas. "One day you walked into the bunkhouse with your mother, both carrying bread for us. The other boys teased you, said you clung to your mamma's skirts. Maybe you had four or five years by then, you said: *we are losing the knowledge of our elders. Who is wise enough to pay attention, to seek and understand the wisdom of times ago?*

Lucas laughed and lay back on the earth, it felt cooler than he expected. He sat up and spread his cloak on the ground. He wanted to lie where he had with his mother. He realized now why lying on the ground always soothed him.

"Why do you laugh, Lucas? I never forgot those words. From that day on, the other boys shut their mouths and left you alone."

Lucas sat up, "Spectre speak, I suppose." He smirked at Bernard, "What I said is truer now than then."

"Yes, it is. You are not like us. You are as no one else has ever been."

For a long time, Lucas sat silently scratching shapes in the dirt with his fingertip. For a moment, he remembered how it felt as a child here. He could feel the purple lupinus standing taller than he. The dark soil bursting with colorful flowers, pungent with life. He tossed some dried grass into the air letting it fall on his trousers.

"Do you remember?"

"I'm starting to. And now I begin to remember you too, Bernard. You were the only one who didn't pester me."

"You intrigued me. I could see that you lived in your mind. Always watching, rarely speaking, but missing nothing."

"One must keep alert to be safe."

Bernard swallowed and pulled a stained piece of cloth from his pocket. "When you appeared at the farm two days after your mother's death, I came back out here and watched them put her in the wagon. And when they rolled away, I found something."

"What did you find?"

"The arrow tip."

Lucas' eyes turned a thundering black. "*You* found the weapon!? The arrow tip that now is in my mother's trunk?"

"I . . . I suppose that is the one, yes," Bernard said. "Forgive me Lucas. When I met you at the *No Horses Tavern*, I knew who you were. And I knew you came for the trunk. I buried it there for you long before the barn burned down."

"Why did you bury my mother's trunk?"

"To keep it safe from Marion. I knew you'd come back."

"Did you put the arrow tip in the trunk?"

"No!" Bernard shook his head furiously, "No. I picked it up that day with this cloth and took it back to the farm."

"And then what happened to it?"

"I don't know."

"Did you see a painting inside my mother's trunk?"

"I didn't see anything in it. I only buried the trunk for you."

"If you had that cloth why is it not with the arrow tip? Why are these things not together?"

"I kept this cloth. You know because of the bloodstains. . . your blood is on here. Then you disappeared."

"Hunh?" Lucas croaked. "I disappeared and so did the arrow tip? I ran away, Bernard."

"I know that now. I figured it out after a while."

"Why did you keep a bloody cloth for thirteen years?"

"Because you were born of the earth . . . you know, sprung up like one of your flowers as I've been telling you . . ." He stuck a blade of brown grass in his mouth.

"Stop saying that. I'm sick of hearing it," Lucas hissed. And when he saw the abashed expression on Bernard's face added, "Is that truly what you believed?"

"We all did." Bernard peered at Lucas.

"And now to see you, I still do. What do you believe, Lucas?"

"I believe what I know to be true. Not believing means not knowing. You must believe in your own life to understand it and truly live. But I also believe every living thing comes from another living thing."

Bernard tilted his massive head. "I've missed you here. Your presence breathes life into the rest of us." He wrapped his heavy arm around Lucas' shoulders in a fierce embrace.

"When did you last see the arrow tip? And how did the object that killed my mother get inside her trunk?" Lucas barked shaking Bernard off. "Who shot us with the bow and arrow, Bernard!?"

"I don't know . . ."

"Marion, or Darnell?"

Bernard dug his heels into the ground. "Possibly."

"Aagh, why don't you know? For hell's sake, someone must know! How did Darnell die?"

"A fire. The farm burned. He paced at night with his lantern, drinking and cursing his lot in life."

"His choices," Lucas corrected "Cursing his choices, which became his fate. Marion got away with hers it seems. It must have been her." Lucas got up and moved toward his horse. "Is Marion a threat to Irene?"

Bernard jumped up, "I don't think so. She pursues wealth and ease nowadays. She doesn't care about Irene, or you, now that you're a man. After all what can she do, force you to come home and live with her like a little boy?"

"You would know better than I, if she is dangerous."

"I can see that she is startled by your presence here in Arcana; you are grown, tall and strong. She must finally see that she can never possess you. I think she is afraid of you now that she sees you again. Will you confront her, Lucas?"

"Did Marion shoot my mother with the bow and arrow?"

Bernard's face turned white, he kicked at the ground. "I can't say. I don't know. She doesn't seem capable of shooting the bow."

Lucas stared until Bernard lifted his head and returned his gaze. "You can't say, or you don't know?"

"No, I do not know."

"But you say someone shot my mother and me with the bow and arrow."

"And you died."

"And I'm alive."

"Yes, you certainly are."

"Why?"

"We all want to know that."

"You country folks have little to do but spin ideas of enchantment."

Bernard shrugged, "Magic is everywhere. Good and bad."

"Tis true, Bernard," Lucas said as he went over to his horse and retrieved the waterskin, gulped and poured a splash over his head. "I doubt that senseless woman can shoot the bow. Excuse me, I meant, Marion. She is your mother after all."

"Barely."

"Are you sure my mother only had one trunk, Bernard?"

"I am quite sure of it, Lucas. Neither of you had many possessions. That's all I found."

"Then there are two more trunks somewhere. That crazy woman may be right. There are more worlds to explore." He reached out and they shook hands. "Thank you for speaking truthfully, Bernard. I will leave your mother to her self-imposed torment for now. Shall we return to the Inn? Irene will be waking up from her nap and I am hungry."

"Yes, let's away. The roads are not safe after dark. Many strangers pass through Arcana nowadays."

"They pass through the City of Dreams as well. We thrive in trade, but I wonder if it will be the death of us all."

"Not you," Bernard said, then added, "We survived plague but who knows what comes next. Go ahead Lucas, I know these woods best now. I will have your back."

"And I will see that the road ahead is clear for you," he declared, but the word plague worried him. He invoked an oath to protect his city and those that dwell there. Especially one astonishing girl. He rode back as he had ridden out, leaning forward over the powerful horse's withers, its mane fanning out, his own long hair flying, his dark blue riding cloak billowing behind, lifting him even taller, and Bernard close on his heels laughing and shouting encouragement. The light faded from a pale blue, cloud dappled sky into an orange horizon. Moments ago, his heart overflowed with anguish at the closeness of his mother's precious memory in the flower field that once belonged to them. Now, soaring on horseback over this land of his youth, he felt his strength renewed, his resolve solidly in place. To believe Bernard, he had escaped death already. It made sense, his healing. Ever since he could remember he had never had a cut or wound for more than a circle of the clock. Bernard's words answered questions Lucas hadn't known whom to ask. But those answers created new questions. How far could he go into the world and still maintain his ability to heal? Did this peculiar characteristic of his extend beyond Arcana and the City of Dreams? Perhaps that is why he never had the desire to board a ship. Most of all, why didn't his mother heal? The answer must lie within his father. What kind of man could create such a child? He rode faster than the wind, faster than any arrow, nothing could tame him.

He would take his mother's trunk home to the City of Dreams, maybe someday he would find out who the woman in the little painting was. The arrow tip . . . well he would keep it for now: the last thing that touched her, after all. He would persist until he found out for certain who shot that arrow. And if that person still lived . . . he would show them the same fate.

Through the trees, he noticed the lights of the Grande Inn. Tonight, he would enjoy it like an aristocrat, his mission in Arcana fulfilled for now. So far, there was only one trunk. He must remember to dangle that information in the obstinate face of Madam Trousdale. Her spooky behavior and implied secrets were vexing. He would find a way to make her reveal any knowledge she held back from him. If two more trunks existed, they were not in the country, and not at the bottom of his old swimming pond.

But now, Oliver waited in the courtyard and the horses skidded, neighing in the gravel, their fun finished for the day. Bernard slapped Lucas on the back. "Well done, brother."

Lucas smiled broadly. "I had forgotten the joy of riding!"

Leaving Bernard with Oliver, Lucas hurried to his room where he checked the trunk and a tiny wedge of wood jammed into the lock as he'd left it. After refreshing himself and changing his clothes, Lucas knocked on Irene's door and announced himself.

"Everything is well?" she asked her face cheerful and relaxed.

"It is, madam." He offered his arm and they descended the stairs to the hall that led outside. The garden now lit by dozens of candles placed along the path, atop the stone benches, and in the nooks of the garden walls. The tiny lights twinkled like stars guiding them along their way. Irene exclaimed with delight. "I am so happy we were delayed; it would have been a pity to miss this! How is it we did not notice this beautiful display last night, Lucas?"

"Perhaps we were so consumed by our thoughts that we failed to perceive our surroundings."

"I don't want to miss anything." She squeezed his arm and he leaned over to give her a hug.

Some of the trees that framed the garden paths were in their first bright green blooms while others had only hesitant buds; in those bare branches, candles nestled in the twisting limbs. They strolled along the winding paths scented by heady night-scented gillyflower. Content in each other's company, both knew well enough there was no urgent need to discuss the afternoon in the flower field. When a rumbling in Lucas's stomach broke the silence, they turned back toward the dining room.

Bernard and Wentworth sat at a table set for four. As they entered, both men rose. "Join us," Wentworth said. "Marion is feeling ill again. She won't be coming down this evening."

"That's unfortunate," Irene said as she settled into the chair that Wentworth offered.

"Quite so," Bernard mumbled. Lucas smiled to himself and took his seat.

The serving girl brought wine and heaping plates of food. Lucas and Bernard had second helpings of the roast and root vegetables. Irene and Wentworth discussed the beauty of the garden lights, Wentworth explaining that the tradition had begun one Yuletide and carried over for the joy of seeing the trees and flowers at night. In the winter when nothing bloomed, and all but a few small pine trees were skeletons, the lights offered welcoming comfort to the guests who enjoyed a walk outside before or after their meal. As they finished the last of their wine, Irene and Lucas answered Wentworth's questions about life in the City of Dreams. Wentworth suggested that he and Marion may travel out for a visit someday and Irene was quick to offer a room at the boarding house. Lucas and Bernard kept their discussion in the flower field to themselves. They moved into the parlour, each relaxing into chairs beside the fire. A few guests played cards at a round table beneath the tall candelabra. Lucas and his companions sat contentedly staring into the blue flames, sipping brandy, and sampling sweetmeats offered by the parlour maid. The conversation soon turned to their plans for departure in the early morning. Lucas relaxed when Irene didn't protest or ask for another day. His desire to return to Alina burned as hot as the flames in front of him, so urgent and persistent that Lucas feared another of his headaches, but he inhaled the soothing aroma of wood smoke and, with the brandy, managed to ease his yearning.

"We are not early risers, so I am afraid this will be our goodbye then," Wentworth said getting up from his chair.

Irene said, "We look forward to your visit in the near future, don't we, Lucas?"

Lucas stood up to shake Wentworth's hand. He watched Wentworth shuffle away and wondered what heaviness haunted the man's heart. His shoulders bowed under the load of burdens specifically designed for him.

The comfort of The Grande Inn mollified the memories of the past. As much as Lucas wanted to follow Wentworth upstairs and choke answers from Marion, he knew that life furnished its own punishment. Someday, once he had Alina by his side, the most important thing now, he would return and unravel the mystery of his mother's death. Also, he suspected that Wentworth deserved a fair portion of peace.

"And you?" Lucas gazed warmly at Bernard. "When will we meet again?"

"Maybe someday. Maybe never." Shifting from one foot to the other and glancing toward the door, "We know where to find each other. Fare thee well, Lucas." He grabbed Lucas pulling him into his thick chest in a suffocating embrace.

"Hmm," Irene said tilting her head to one side. "You have come to admire each other."

"We have," Lucas choked, muffled in the man's arms.

Bernard whispered, "We share a solemn secret. We are brethren now."

Freeing himself, Lucas gazed up at the giant. The two men locked eyes. "Thank you."

"I wish I could do more," Bernard said. Turning to Mrs. Kempel, "I'm glad you found him out there, wandering in the world. Goodbye Ma'am."

With a nod, instead of a shrug now, Bernard turned and strode toward the door closing it firmly behind him.

Chapter 10

Two hours before dawn, Alina darted from the cover of a dilapidated hut where she had crouched and shivered for most of the night. She finally found her way home coaxed by the light of a hand lantern that sat in the nook of the stone wall. Ikarus had done his job after all—returning to relight lanterns that the rain had washed out. The house offered grim comfort as she scurried up to her room and undressed in the dark, too exhausted to light a single candle. She slipped under her bedcovers warmed by her heavy nightgown. But trembling still, she envisioned the leering face of the man who'd grabbed her at the tavern. She would never forget his face, nor he hers, she fretted.

Loud voices crept through her slumber, awakening her in early morning light. For a few coverlet-clutching moments she didn't recognize her surroundings. Then, the recollection of her father's death and her pitiful situation crashed in on a wave of panic. She sat up, straining to make out the words. Vasil spoke in brisk bursts, then after a beat, Campbell Barrington, his pretentious voice raised to a screech. Then another voice, low, whining, mumbling . . . gagging . . . someone was having difficulty speaking. She tiptoed to the door and pressed her ear against it.

"Argh. . . stop . . . that hurts."

"Tell us what you found."

"In a warehouse at the harbour."

"Of course, but where, you fool!"

"Stone walls, thick like the cathedral . . . iron door . . . tall as two men . . . bolts . . . massive lock, owww. . . key gone."

"What do you mean gone?"

Alina heard a sharp slap. On several occasions she had seen Vasil clench his fist and feared he would strike her. She cupped her hand to her cheek as if she could already feel the sting of his lethal hand.

"The rest of the money. I need it . . . please . . . give me . . ." A muffled cry and a thud, something hitting the floor.

Vasil growled, "Search him for the key. I told you not to give it to him, dolt."

"You're the one who said, give him the key because we can't show our faces at the harbour," Barrington shouted. "We only avoided the cell by promising to stay away from there. I already told you he carries no key now. He carries nothing but disease!"

"You have also failed me, Barrington. Keep searching, try inside his trousers."

Barrington arguing, "I'm not putting my hand inside his trousers."

Vasil's voice louder now, closer. "No more time to waste. Maybe Alina has an additional key to the warehouse. Probably had it all along. That shrewd little wench has been lurking around here waiting for us to find the trunks for her! And the lantern lighter has been skulking around outside. I wonder how much she offered to pay for his help."

Footfalls pounded the stairs. Alina frantically yanked off her nightgown, threw it aside and pulled her shift over her head.

"I refuse to search him again," Campbell Barrington shouted up the stairs.

"Alina . . . a word dear?" Vasil's voice just outside her door.

Too late to dress. She dashed to the window lifted the handle and leaned out calculating the fall to the street below. A sharp crack as her door resisted Vasil's weight. With one arm in her sleeve, and one out, she slid under the bed. The door latch held until the third shove, then Vasil burst into the room. She held her breath.

"Alina!"

His black boots alongside the bed. The coverlet tossed to the floor blocked his view. Bumping into the bed, he knocked it sideways. Her face pressed to the floor, hands covering her head, she squeezed her eyes shut. The wardrobe creaked open. She peeked out as several of her garments fell in an airy whisper to the floor. The window shutter banged, a thud as her head bumped the wooden bed frame. Vasil expelled a succession of curses and stomped out of the room bellowing, "Wait, Barrington! She's gone. There's no key up here!"

Barrington from below. "I've already told you that, obstinate drunkard. I searched her room the other day. What do we do with this wreck of a man?"

Vasil thudded fat-footed down the stairs. "Leave the dolt there. He's useless to us."

An abrupt silence ensued in which she waited until the sun reached a certain split in the floorboards. When stillness assured her she was alone, Alina crawled out from under her bed, grabbed her muslin dress from the pile on the floor, slipped it on then gathered the rest of her things and stuffed them into two cloth satchels. What key. I have no key. That man said . . . an iron door at the harbour. Could this be the location of my trunks?

Panting, her blood racing through her veins, she packed her bags as full as possible. I'm fleeing again she thought, with a stab of anguish for Daria whom she would probably never see again. Did Vasil kill her too? How naïve she once was to believe her life with father was safe from the outside world. Studies, walking in the garden, writing poetry, drawing, and riding over the moor on her beloved horses, all gone now. Checking the small pouch of jewelry tucked inside the secret pocket of her shift, she took another look around the room which was a mess now. The once lovely bouquets broken, petals scattered across the floor. Her ruby pendant, safely tucked under her shawl, felt warm against her skin as she quickly descended the stairs.

There at the bottom lay the body of a man. Trembling, she stepped over him and to her utter horror recognized the man from the Duck Tavern. The wretched creature didn't move. Swallowing hard, choking on a scream, she shuddered. What was he doing here? Had he been following her? What a horrible place this city. I need enough money for ship's passage. Dashing around the room she snatched up the silver candlesticks, a silver cup, eight goblets, six small pewter plates, and crammed them into a satchel she found in Vasil's bedroom.

Tiptoeing past the bundle of rags, she shoved open the door, and peered up and down the street. The body twitched; she lurched away in revulsion but didn't feel his flaccid fingertips brush her ankle. Skirting down the lane hugging the walls, Alina made her way toward the home of the widow Keats. They shared an afternoon together just a few days earlier. Her friend appreciated the flowers even though they had wilted a bit from the encounter with Lucas. A tremor passed through her body before settling in her stomach like a stone. She hammered the doorknocker while simultaneously yanking on the door handle. "Mrs. Keats! It is I! It is Alina, please let me in!"

Her efforts produced nothing but an echoing silence. She leaned her forehead against the door, "Help me please . . . someone."

Pulling her hood over her head she ventured back out into the street which was now getting crowded. Among the market stalls, Alina deftly snatched an ugly shawl from a vendor's supply bin and slipped it over her hood and across her face. Better to appear like a peasant than a confused outsider. The luggage weighed heavy on her shoulders, but her arms were full of the satchel of treasures. Hungry and thirsty, she shoved her way through the alleys of the beggars, who leered and made revolting suggestions. Running from the chilling route, she burst out onto the street and stumbled into a young woman holding a babe in arms with two clutching her skirts. The treasure bag tumbled from her grasp, its contents clattering, skidding, and spinning across the cobbled street. The woman muttered and hurried on, the barefoot children wailing behind her. Dashing from one side of the busy street to the other, Alina retrieved what she could before it got kicked aside, or snatched by dirty, ragged hands connected to bruised and boney arms. In the shade of a dress shop, she attempted to sort herself out; tears streaked down her cheeks. A young lady gave her a pitiful glimpse and glided inside on the arm of a gentleman. Watching the passersby, a feeling of wretched despair gripped her. How witless was she to believe that a man like Lucas, who possessed all the confidence of an army of men, could find her worth his time? He must have a hundred women stashed about the city, willing and waiting for him on any given night. After all, she knew little about him. If she didn't so desperately need his help she would flee now. But even if she could board a ship, she would not leave without her trunks. It sounded like they were, actually at the harbour. Had Lucas promised to come back to her door, or had she misread their encounter? Did he return yet to the City of Dreams? If he had, and made no effort to find her, then seeking him out at his dwelling would be the worst course of action. The witch with the bucket and broom could be his maid or mistress, perhaps both. If only she could find him lighting the lanterns as he usually did. Nobody else could protect her from Vasil and his henchman. A lady and her maid whispered and giggled as they entered the elegant shop. Alina scurried from her refuge, balancing her baggage, and staggering like a vagrant. Walking in the direction of the boarding house, she hoped she could muster the courage to knock. If only Lucas would open the door and not the witch.

A golden sphere burst from behind the old cathedral steeple dousing her in sunlight, just as it had on the day that she first met Lucas. On that day he had a picnic basket, perhaps he was headed toward the river. He could be there now, refreshing himself after his journey. Surely, he would remember her in the light of day. Relieved to have thought of an excuse not to go to the boarding house, she turned around.

Her thoughts turned to her dear father. How disappointed and angry he would be if he knew his wonderful lantern lighter had already abandoned her. Father never intended to leave her alone and heartbroken. Only his horrific death prevented him from being at her side. He promised to always take care of her, keep her safe, but all he had managed was to purchase the small house in the City of Dreams that Vasil had discovered anyway. They were to remain in their grand house in Ingleena until her schooling was complete. Then, when the timing was right, her father promised to introduce her to society, and together, he had said, they would choose for her a suitable husband. This would not happen now that she had fallen into a trap in the City of Dreams. Her future nothing but a nightmare unfolding before her. Alina stumbled toward the river.

* * *

In the yellow fog of dawn, Lucas dragged himself from the feather bed. The promise of Alina, the one thing that could pull him from its enveloping warmth. He dressed in his travelling clothes. As he dragged the trunk toward the door, Oliver knocked. "Good morning, sir, your carriage awaits."

The two men lifted the trunk and carried it down the stairs. The pantry maid held the front door open following them to the carriage where she placed a basket of food on the seat. Lucas turned to go back inside intending to take his leave of the Grande Inn, and to fetch Irene, but she appeared in the doorway. Lucas rushed up the steps to her. The lobby boy brought out her valise and tied it next to the trunk.

"Ready?" she asked.

"I'll just check on things."

Lucas passed through the lobby into the parlour where the tapestries of the farm scene and the village faire hung like choices. Placing his hands on his hips, he thought about his mother who had never seen a place like this. He knew more about her now, but he would never understand how she was as a girl, a maiden who somehow had a child alone in a landscape that offered only hard labor. Still, she found a way to fill his life with beauty and love. A log splintered, it fell into the deep ash sending up a puff of smoke, a curl of blue rimmed flame, then nothing. He grabbed the poker and stoked the fire. Just above him, reclining in her warm bed with her wealthy husband by her side, slept Marion. Quite possibly that woman was the one who had caused his life to take such a fateful turn. He let the poker fall with a clatter onto the stone hearth. How could he take revenge if he wasn't certain? Grabbing the banister, swinging himself up three stairs at a time, Lucas strode to her door. The latch gave way with no protest. He glided into the room and gazed at the woman, safe in her cozy dreams. Impulsively, his hand went for her neck, surprised by the warmth, in comparison to his cold fingers, he drew back. Nobody moved. In an instant, he was out of the room with Marion's silver necklace clutched in his hand. Downstairs, he examined his prize in the light of the fire. The charm depicted wheat in a basket–the symbol for self-sacrifice. He took a deep breath and shrugged a tribute to Bernard. Turning to leave at last, he ran his hands over the plush fabric chairs as he made his way to the front door. Mr. Hartwinn stood quietly watching him by the front door. He held a willow basket full of dried herbs and flowers. "Here young man, take this with you."

Lucas stared but made no move to accept the basket.

"Something to remember us by," he said, holding it out to Lucas.

It was like the old baskets he and his mother had once carried. He carried it out the door as if it had belonged to him all along, finally leaving the country with his basket of flowers. Does comfort come from a place, or from within? Now that he had some answers, he realized they solved little. He felt his joy and appreciation for the country breaking apart, his memories of the green hills, abundant trees, and the vibrant flower fields nothing more than the scorched logs of a stolen childhood. Outside, the fog was pierced by spears of sunlight shooting down from billowy chariots of white and gray. Lucas climbed into the carriage and set his prize beside the picnic basket.

"Pretty," Irene murmured.

Smiling like a child, he settled in with Irene, the little painting secured inside his coat, the arrow tip tied tightly in a leather pouch in his pocket, and the pendant in the opposite pocket. Never leave empty-handed. He slapped the arched roof. As they rode away, he turned in time to see the door to the Grande Inn slowly close; the lamp lit entrance no longer visible.

Thumping hooves and birdsong brought the dawn into day. Irene sighed, swaying in rhythm with the rocking coach. In the between light, Lucas couldn't tell if she was asleep or unusually quiet. He need not ask. It didn't matter. The past fell farther behind as the horses trotted forward. When they passed the *No Horses Tavern*, Lucas leaned out the window. It was only then that he noticed Bernard following them. He must have been there all along. Reining his mount up alongside the coach he waved his pistol in the air and raced a circle around them. "All is well for you from here on!" he shouted, then turned back toward his watering hole.

Flooded with a sense of kinship and belonging, Lucas shouted, "I owe you a pint!"

He closed his eyes until, Irene woke up and reached for the picnic basket. Lucas signaled the coachman to stop at the crest of the next hill. There, with an unfiltered view in all directions, they spread a blanket and took their time to enjoy their final repast prepared by the cooks at the Grande Inn.

"Are you satisfied now, Lucas?"

"With the food or the trip?"

"Both."

"Yes, I am. There are more questions, but I enjoyed the Grande Inn immensely and meeting Bernard is like finding my only living relative . . . how about you Irene? You appear refreshed."

"I am refreshed and reassured," she said. "You have answers now and tangible objects to finally lay your mother to rest. Perhaps your nightmares will turn into peaceful dreams."

Lucas offered a thin smile. "I hope so. Last night I didn't dream at all." They walked out across the hillside, arm in arm enjoying each other's company and the fresh air.

When they finally meandered back to the coach, she offered her hand and he helped her inside. Late afternoon sun shimmered along the twitching flanks of the four-horse team in a blue-black iridescence. Lucas recalled his afternoon ride to the flower field. He must have Nikolas round up a horse for him. He could see himself galloping with Alina's arms tight around his waist, her amber hair flying like leaves in the wind. Even though the bountiful colors of Arcana were resplendent only in his mind now—replaced by a newer memory of the barren field—fresh hope coursed through him. The moment he met Alina; his thoughts had turned to a life he had never imagined for himself. A shared life, a life that included her. In the conversation with Bernard he announced his intention to marry someday. A week ago, he would never have said such a thing, yet it felt natural to confide his wish to Bernard, a man he'd only just met, who knew much about his early life, and had even thought about him over the years. Lucas felt at ease with someone he hadn't known existed before returning to Arcana. Some of Bernard's notions perturbed him: survived death, shot by an arrow, sprung from the earth. He wouldn't believe it, if not for his ability to heal, and the scar. He scratched it and felt for the veil resting in its place there. He leaned his head back thinking of burly Bernard, tame as a farmer's favorite lamb, but valiant too. It took audacity for him to show Lucas the exact spot where his mother died, she and apparently himself. His lack of memories had left him with no expectation, except a childlike hope that his mother was somehow still alive. Everything in Arcana felt familiar yet new. The pictures in his mind larger and brighter than the actual scenery. The scents of home had flooded back at the farm, the pond and even at the Inn. But they were most prominent while sitting in the field with Bernard, his brother. Lucas wished it could have lasted longer. He felt an affinity between them, even at their first encounter at the *No Horses*. For what more is a brother than one who shares the hollow secrets of an unbearable past?

Chapter 11

The clinking of iron against stone woke Lucas. The carriage rattled over the planked bridge that spanned the loch leading from the cathedral and monastery to the river. From there the river followed around the point to the harbour where Nikolas would be . . . what would Nik be doing? Lucas didn't know if a ship was in for Nik or not. He felt like he'd been gone for months, not mere days. It was past dark, but somewhere in the caverns of the cathedral site a lone mason chiseled out a last detail by lantern light. Lucas counted five circular glows as the horses trotted onto the echoing cobbles. Beyond there, toward the abandoned monastery he detected only its dark silhouette. The monks that once occupied it had lived in tune with the sun and the moon. Now citizens in the city struggled against the night. Irene sat up and smoothed her hair. The coach rattled down the hill. On the horizon, the City of Dreams.

"Home," she said.

"Yes!" Lucas leaned out the window drawing in the familiar scents of his city, salt air and wood smoke–combined with roasted meat and baked bread settling in with the pungency of people and livestock. Dark smoke swirling from narrow chimneys hovered like silent spectres waiting for their companions. A murky breeze pushed past the harbour, creeping low along the slippery streets, leaving salty white trails from the opaque ocean of unknown measure. The tall harbour torches glowed in expectation of a cargo ship. The city, poised and receptive, reflecting pale white and dark orange lights that flickered like fireflies hither and yon.

The driver turned down the last street before the boarding house. The lanterns were all lit. Lucas crouched beside the door, ready to leap out and run alongside the coach. Irene chuckled, "You're as wild as Bernard's horse! See me inside first, then off you go to find your girl."

The driver reined the horses to a clattering stop directly in front of the boarding house. There were white candles burning on every nook and stone ledge, and a glow emanating from every room in the house.

"Madam Trousdale must be entertaining guests," Lucas exclaimed as he flung open the door and leapt to the ground. Then he turned to wait for Irene to unwrap herself from the lap robe and straighten her legs that crackled in resistance.

The front door opened, and Lucas turned to see Nikolas standing in the doorway. "Blessed heaven where have you been? I thought you were lost or injured!"

"Nikolas!" Lucas exclaimed, "what are you doing here? And so late . . ."

"Where is Madam Trousdale?" Irene interrupted brushing past Nikolas.

The coachman followed with the luggage. "Excuse me gentleman, I need assistance with that trunk."

"Of course," Lucas and Nikolas spoke simultaneously. Irene called for Carissa and Madam Trousdale.

"A successful trip it appears," Nikolas grunted as they set the trunk down in the parlour.

"Yes, I will tell you."

Irene emerged from the kitchen with furrowed brows and a downturned mouth. "What is going on here, Nikolas?"

Nikolas shook his head, hesitated then took a breath. "I'm sorry for delivering distressing news directly upon your return. But Madam Trousdale is upstairs attending to Carissa. The boarders are working late or are out drinking now. I've reduced their fee for a few days since there is nothing but odd soup for supper."

"What are you talking about?" Lucas began to follow Irene up the stairs, then turned back, "Let's get my mother's trunk up to my room now."

"Old soup. How old could it be?" Irene questioned over her shoulder.

"Odd."

Lucas quipped, "To be expected with Trousdale doing the cooking."

"She's rather intriguing." Nikolas lifted the back end of the trunk and hurried to explain. "Dugald attacked Carissa and escaped. Carissa took a nasty blow to the head, but Doctor Wilhelm says she'll be fine in a few days."

"Damn that man. Forgive me, Nik, we stayed on. So many unexpected events. And now this. Is Carissa truly all right?"

"She is. Will be."

"And Trousdale is fine you say. Spooky as ever?"

"Madam Trousdale is fine. She is expediting Carissa's recovery with her potions," Nikolas said with a glint in his eye.

Setting the trunk in the hallway, the two men entered Dugald's room, the bed askew, the sheets removed. The small room smelled sickly even though they'd propped the window wide open. There was a jumble of wire stretched across it and jagged metal and broken glass piled beneath it.

"What is this?" Lucas demanded, standing in the middle of the room with his hands on his hips and a deep furrow in his brow.

"A trap. Madam Trousdale and I put it together in case he tried to climb back in."

"Interesting idea, my friend."

"Yes, we felt fairly proud of ourselves at the time."

As they turned to leave, a dead creature startled Lucas: a rat, its head crushed. It lay on its side a step from the door. "Hmmm, he doesn't appear to have fallen victim to the convoluted trap."

"Ach! didn't notice that." Nikolas grabbed a sliver of metal, hooked the rat, and shoved it through the wired window. No sound indicated its final resting place.

From the doorway of Carissa's room, they watched Mrs. Kempel and Madam Trousdale bustling around the girl's bed. Nikolas put a hand on Lucas' arm. "There is more, my friend. Ikarus came to find me at the harbour because of all this, but also to tell me that a girl has been asking for you. She appears troubled, he said."

The black veil, in its resting place, scorched Lucas' chest. He grabbed Nikolas by the shoulders. "Is it Alina?"

Nodding, Nikolas gazed at Lucas. "I believe so . . . amber hair, is what Ik said. I've walked out and through the city. Don't know where to find her . . . or who I'm even looking for. Lucas, I'm sorry to deliver such shocking news upon your return."

"Ahh . . ." Lucas rubbed his eyes, shoved his hands through his hair. "Not your fault. I appreciate your staying here. I never expected that one more day . . . it was so. . . well, now that's over."

"Who *is* this Dugald character?"

"The boarder that I mentioned was sick, the other day at the harbour. He isn't right. He went through my supplies." Lucas headed for his room and found the door securely locked. He frowned at Nikolas.

"No one has been in there since I've been here. Mrs. Kempel's room either."

Retrieving the key from the secure pocket that also held the arrow tip, he opened the door. They hauled the trunk inside, then Lucas examined his possessions and slapped Nik on the back. "Thank you." He plopped down on the edge of his bed. It seemed like a long time, more than three days, since he'd left it. He pulled off his boots, then stood and peeled off his shirt. Nikolas stood sentry in the doorway, averting his eyes while Lucas stripped off his trousers. He emptied his pockets, carefully set the picture, and the arrow tip back inside the trunk. He weighed the necklace in his hand—peeked at Nikolas who pursed his lips—then slipped it inside the trunk "Who can mind the women while we search for Alina? Have you been to her house?"

"I don't know where she lives. Neither did you last time we talked. Ikarus said she followed him to the Duck Tavern."

"It's on the way to her house, we'll start there." Lucas marched down the hall to Carissa's room. She was sleeping. Irene and Trousdale had gone downstairs. In the kitchen, the odd soup Nikolas described simmered in an herby froth. "What's in it?"

"Ale, among other things," Madam Trousdale said with a flicker of glee in her eyes. She crossed her arms. The hourglass at her neck was just emptying itself.

He clicked his tongue and turned away. "We have to go out, we will find Ikarus and send him back here to sit with you women until our return."

"That isn't necessary," Irene said with a wooden mixing bowl in her arms, already preparing to bake loaves of bread for them and the boarders.

"Yes, it is," Lucas replied in a tone that stopped her from further discussion.

"Dugald tricked us, spit out his tea and threw up his soup," Madam Trousdale grumbled.

Lucas rubbed the back of his neck. "I don't blame you. We stayed away too long."

The corners of her mouth turned up and the hourglass flipped and filled.

At the Duck Tavern, they found the barkeep willing to talk about the young woman who accompanied the lamp boy, Ikarus, and paid for his ale. Lucas and Nikolas exchanged glances, neither familiar enough with Alina to understand why she would be roaming around buying ale for strangers.

"She was a sweet thing which I suppose is why she caught the attention of the vagabond who stumbled in after them. She asked about you, Lucas. Wanted to know where to find you. Was very insistent with the lad, who feared he was in trouble, which I suppose he is now that I've told you he was drinking on the job . . . and missed a few lanterns . . . I'm sorry, gentleman . . . I should have stopped the girl from dashing out of here."

"What vagabond?" Lucas interrupted.

"A man wearing fancy, but filthy clothes. Must have gotten in some sort of struggle, his hand injured, covered in an oozing bandage, recent it appeared. Feverish sort. No shoes! Smelled like he'd rolled in the gutter, blood spiders in his eyes, hair sticking . . ."

"Where did he go?" Lucas demanded, pounding his fist on the bar to stop the man's babbling.

Nikolas grabbed Lucas by the elbow.

"He . . . I shoved him out the door," the barkeep bit his lip, "he wore a filthy purple cloak," he added as if that explained everything. Which it did.

"It's Dugald, sounds like," Lucas said to Nikolas.

"On the house." The barkeep slid two cups of whisky across the bar. "Warms the gullet," he was saying as they downed their drinks and left.

They found Ikarus at the corner of the street that turned left toward the dark zone, propped against a wall. His tools were in his lap, a hand lantern at his feet; his head bobbed. Lucas shook him awake. "Get up sleepy boy!"

"Oh Lucas! You've returned! I feared you lost . . . I lit the entire city so that you may find your way home."

"Hush, all is well now. Make haste to the boarding house. Guard the women there. Run!"

Ikarus fumbled for his tools, but Nikolas was already retrieving them. "We will take care of these. Get to the house. Have Madam Trousdale give you a sobering beverage."

"Have you seen the girl?" Lucas shouted after him.

"Not since the Duck!" Ikarus lurched into the dark mist, slipping, and sliding on the damp cobbles.

At Alina's house, they found the door unlocked. It swung open with a creak and stopped with a thump. Something was in the way. They leaned into it and pushed. There the heap of Dugald—lying in his own vomit. Lucas stepped over him, then turned and gave him a kick. He shrugged thinking of Bernard for a fleeting second.

"Dead?" Nikolas asked.

"Hope so." Lucas rushed through the house calling for Alina. He ran upstairs where he discovered her room. Poised in the entrance, stunned by the simplicity of her little corner, he noticed the once beautiful bouquets scattered around the room. She'd fled in a hurry. He went to her bed and gathered the bedclothes to inhale her delicate scent. She couldn't have been gone awfully long. He lifted the straw mattress but found nothing hidden underneath. Her wardrobe was empty, but for a long, white shift.

Downstairs, Nikolas had dragged Dugald outside. "What shall we do with him?"

"Dead or not?"

Nikolas pushed his hair out of his eyes. "Not quite."

"Damn nuisance." Lucas bent down, and with a candlestick poked around his neck and throat. He placed a tentative hand on Dugald's chest. Then he pawed through his clothing, searching his pockets. "Nothing here. Let's stuff him in the root cellar for now. Doesn't look like plague, but still a good place for him, I believe."

Nikolas grabbed Dugald's feet while Lucas tossed the tattered cloak over his face and lifted under the shoulders, carefully avoiding the swollen hand. They carried him around to the back of the cottage. Lucas swung his lantern inside the small stone cavern, then gave Nikolas a nod. They tossed him in. Together, they rolled a rusty wagon wheel against the door.

Back inside, Lucas searched the room of the man. He found a coat, two cloaks, one velvet in mahogany brown, and the other a soft black wool, trousers, and shirts all tailored for a short pudgy man. There were no papers or letters to indicate his name or station. The style and abundance of clothing indicated an older person. Nothing youthful in his choice of attire. Father, uncle, brother, cousin . . . Lucas let the man's garments tumble to the floor.

"Where now?" Nikolas asked.

"Through the dark zone and every street and every alleyway from here to the harbour."

"Taverns too, eh? Seems the lass likes to drink." Nikolas flashed a smile.

"Let's hope she does, and that we find her safely besotted beside a warm tavern hearth."

After collecting their lighting tools and hand lanterns they walked into the dark zone placing hand lanterns and lighting candles, setting them on narrow ledges of squat dwellings along the shadowy, close streets. Lucas and Nikolas turned every corner until they returned to the square and from there walked through each alleyway, peered beyond arched doorways, and behind barrels, crates, wagons, and walls. They came across, and escorted home, two terrified young ladies who had wandered too far from their guest house and had been walking in circles. Lucas and Nikolas encountered merchants, who waved them away and red-eyed whisky guzzlers who jabbered incoherently. None that answered had seen Alina. With every step, Lucas' eyes got darker, his chin set in determination. As the night settled deeper, they kept silent and held each other's gaze only long enough to communicate nothing, or nobody here. One extra day in the country, was it worth it? Digging in the past buries the future.

At the harbour, Nikolas approached laborers and sailors even the thieving wharf rats. Lucas stood beside a ship taking on cargo for a dawn departure. It slapped rhythmically against the pier, water splashed over his feet, but he didn't move away. Young men with eager faces went back and forth from the ship to shore; the older seasoned sailors loitered, allowing the youths to do their share of the work. Once at sea, it would be the men's turn to teach and protect the newcomers. They stared at Lucas staring at them, neither envying the other's station in life but all of them curious enough. When their ship sailed, Lucas knew those men would not sit in longing for someone left behind. They enjoyed the salty sea air, the endless horizon, whisky at night in their berths and new women in various ports of call. That kind of freedom didn't appeal to Lucas. He liked the feel of the earth beneath his feet. He intended to remain in the City of Dreams with the woman of his dreams. Nikolas approached white-faced and clammy.

"What is it?" Lucas grabbed him by the shoulders.

"It's not about her, but Mr. Merson, the harbour master, informed me that a man dressed in fancy clothing was here the other night searching for a load of cargo. He sent him away but found out later one of these wharf rats showed him where they store the prepaid cargo."

"What cargo was he after?"

"Mr. Merson wouldn't say, other than high-value."

"Where did he go from here?"

"Merson doesn't know."

"All right, let's get the lad who helped him and find out."

"Merson doesn't know which one."

"Tsk. Of course not. And they'll all deny it."

"Mr. Merson did say this man was pompous and arrogant, waving papers around, threatening. He was pale and wore a purple cloak . . ."

"And how many pale, pompous fools wearing purple cloaks wander this city?"

"The only one I know of is locked in a root cellar."

"And there he will stay for now," Lucas said. A familiar pain splintered up his spine; it clutched the back of his neck before pushing upward into his skull, a vision-darkening ache settled behind his eyes. But he held his head high as he turned his back to the rolling sea. The one time he had snuck aboard a cargo ship he came away empty handed, the rocking, even in port, so sickened him. That was many years past and he still broke into a sweat at the memory of it. Realizing then that he hadn't eaten since lunch on the sunny hillside with Irene, he declared, "I must have food. Let's go to the Blue Gate Tavern."

Nikolas hesitated, examining Lucas' face. "We best bring food and drink to Dugald as well. We should go back for him straightaway. Who knows when he last ate or drank."

Lucas kept walking. "If Alina is at a public house at this late hour, it will be the Blue Gate, other than the Duck, it's the only one open . . . officially that is. She won't stumble into one of the secret houses where strumpets serve libations."

"Among other things," Nikolas added falling in stride with Lucas.

"Trousdale took care of Dugald, if she intended for him to die, he is gone by now." Lucas quickened his step when the blue glow of the tavern appeared at the end of the long, narrow street.

Through steamed windows, they could see a throng of revelers. Lucas pushed open the door with heartfelt anticipation, but right away he could tell that she wasn't there. The room smelled of sweat, ale, roasted meat, and fresh baked bread. He sighed, long and weary, perusing the room with heavy lidded eyes. He knew full well, if she were there, he would feel her presence instantly.

Even Nikolas, who had yet to meet her, slouched as he squeezed past tankard wielding men, with half-dressed women draped over their arms, to a tiny cloth-draped table. Lucas acknowledged familiar faces but couldn't bother conversing with anyone now. He gulped wine, while Nikolas chugged ale. They had three hefty servings of meat pie between them. Lucas rested his chin in his cupped hands, the pain in his neck and shoulders still searing. "I have no strength for Dugald now. If he knew where Alina was, he wouldn't have been lying on her floor. Let's leave him til morning."

"Ah yes, go home my friend," Nikolas said. "To me the night is just beginning. I will drop off food at the root cellar."

Lucas shook his friend's hand, "He has some answering to do. Let's hope he doesn't die before hand. Thank you . . . and you'll keep searching . . ."

"I will. And bring her to the boarding house if I find her."

Rising, collecting the lighting tools, Lucas smiled. "I shall dream of that very thing."

Lucas found Irene sprawled across the sofa. The crackling fire cast a youthful glow on her plump cheeks. Ikarus, wrapped in thick blankets, lay curled on the floor beside her. For the first time since their return, Lucas relaxed. The lad had made a commendable effort and proved helpful to Lucas after all. Sitting in the chair next to the sofa, he removed his boots and placed them where Irene would see them upon awakening. In the kitchen, a pottage simmered over the banked fire, waiting for him. No sign of the odd soup. Swinging the iron arm outward, he removed the heavy pot taking care not to spill any and entice varmints. Once he secured it in the food locker, he stowed his tools, placed the tallow candles in their box and returned to the front room where he bolted the door and leaning over Ikarus, tucked in Irene's blanket before climbing the stairs to the sanctuary of his room.

The door to Dugald's room was ajar. Lucas softened his tread, crept silently to the doorway, and peered inside. It smelled clean now, the straw mattress gone, just the wooden bedframe remained. The trap of glass and metal was cleared away and the window securely latched. Lucas thought of Trousdale and wondered where she was right now, sleeping in one of the rooms, sitting with Carissa, or back home in her mysterious lair? He hoped wherever she was that she protected the gold-jewelled box.

The orange glow of the fire welcomed him into his bedchamber. Clean white linens and fresh blankets covered his bed. He removed his trousers before sitting down. A vase of yellow cowslip sat on one nightstand and a cool pewter jug of fresh water on the other. Placing his clothes neatly over the carved chair, he slipped into bed grateful for its warmth and that of the fire. Sinking deep into the embrace of his feather mattress, he told himself that Alina was safe in the home of a friend. He fell asleep before his weary mind could conjure any more worries.

Lying flat on his back with his arms at his sides, he drifted down through deep layers. Lucas dreamed of walking along the riverbank: a lady of graceful beauty walked beside him, her silent presence a comfort to his resting self. When he turned to face her, she moved behind him; he reached for her, but his fingers only brushed her velvet dress. The dream began to dissipate, and Lucas struggled to remain asleep. *I will see you by the river*, she said just before fading away. He opened his eyes to find himself twisted up in his mother's yellow blanket. The fire nothing more than a thin red line. Turning over he fell back into a fitful sleep. This time in his dream he recognized Alina. She was running toward him, her silken locks streaming behind her like a flag in a stiff wind. Her eyes were watery and fearful. He called to her, but the wind blew his words away. Although he stood directly in front of her, she did not see him. He shouted and reached for her to no avail. His own shouts woke him. Throwing aside the heavy covers, Lucas swung his feet onto the floor. The fire was out now and for a moment he thought the wind had blown down the chimney but realized it was only windy in his dream.

Dressing quickly, he silently descended the stairs, heard the steady rumble of Irene snoring, noted Ikarus sleeping in the stillness of youth, the fire burning low and well enough. Taking care to lock the door quietly behind him, Lucas stepped into the darkness before dawn. Plumes of gray smoke from near dead fires reached aimlessly above the cottages along the road to Alina's house. Nary a creature squeaked. He knew that she would not be there, but he couldn't ignore the need to check anyway. He glided through the house of empty rooms. Nobody had returned except perhaps Nikolas who would leave no trace. Outside in the root cellar, Dugald slept fitfully, wrapped in a wool blanket, and tied to a timber with ship line. Next to him was a half full jug of ale and an empty tin plate.

Lucas laughed to himself admiring Nikolas's efficiency. He closed the door and replaced the wagon wheel not knowing or caring what they would do with Dugald come daylight. As he turned to go, a cat—the gray cat—sat in front of him licking its paw. Lucas took a step; it came forward greeting him, wrapping itself around his ankles, arching against his calves. Abruptly, it darted off in the direction of the river. Lucas followed, pleased, and intrigued by the unexpected company.

The first yellow and blue glow of dawn cracked the sky. Reflected in the timid ripples of the gray river, the world began to wake. The cat pranced ahead of Lucas as if this was their normal morning routine. He sat down in his usual place on the sandy riverbank. The cat hunched into hunting form and crept off into the tall reeds. Shouts of men working along the wharf echoed down the river channel. Water lapped the soil, a pile of straw floated toward shore then away into the flow, some kind of green cloth snagged in the midst of it. Lucas jumped to his feet. Was that hair tangled in the cloth? A lady's dress. He plunged into the river. Swift moving water swept him along. He stumbled on the stony bottom and went under.

Gurgling and spitting he swam frantically through the murky liquid, surfacing in the center of the mangled straw and sticks. The dress swirled away toward the middle of the fast-flowing river. He dove and swam with long strokes until he got a hold of the dress, then floating on his back dragged it toward shore. His heart racing, his hands icy and stiff, he flopped onto the bank and pulled until the fabric fully revealed itself. No body attached, not even a dress. And the hair only a mess of fish net, nothing more. Probably a bolt of fabric dropped from a transport cart as it rattled over one of the bridges. Letting go he dragged himself to the grass and flopped on his back. The sun rose like a huge ball and steamed his clothes. The cat, who had watched the whole thing, made itself comfortable in the middle of his chest; her eyes more blue than yellow now she squeezed them shut, kneading, and purring then settling atop the black veil that Lucas didn't even remember putting inside his shirt but thankfully hadn't lost. They slept.

Scattered raindrops dotted his face. He sat up. The cat gone now. How long he slept, this time without dreaming, he couldn't tell, but from the sounds of the city buzzing beyond the river, the day felt well under way. Leaping to his feet and pulling his muddy cloak over him, Lucas made his way back to Alina's house. Not caring about Dugald, yet aware of him, he went around the back to see the wheel still in place. Again, he strode through her empty house wondering where the man of the house had gone. Crossing the street, Lucas began knocking on doors, oblivious to his wild wet hair and muddy clock. His front side felt mostly dry while his back felt uncomfortably wet. He knew of five widows who lived near Alina's house. The first, just across the street, knew of her and an older man, not the man who had originally purchased the house, that man she hadn't seen lately. Alina had arrived some weeks ago, by which means the widow did not know, but the man had come and gone from the cottage for the past year. He enjoyed the night, threw parties with sinister, snide men and loose ladies. "Then the girl appeared," the widow said. "Tsk, not a happy bride, I dare say. The first week, I heard crying behind her window. Now, she steps out from time to time, but she walks in sadness."

All of this observed from the widow's half-shuttered window. Lucas thanked her and introduced himself without need.

"I know who you are." The widow said with a sly grin. "And I know why you've started lighting lanterns out here. Don't forget us once you get your girl away from here!"

Lucas nodded grimly, if Alina was a bride it would be more difficult to abscond with her. "I will return with a permanent lantern for your house, dear lady and you will let me know if you see her again."

He knocked on two more doors with no response. Then, around the southernmost corner, on a wide street of sand, he knocked on the sagging door of a thatch-roofed hut. The place appeared abandoned except for fresh flowers blooming in the window boxes. The door creaked open by the effort of a woman with puffy clouds of hair; she stood half his height. "What do you want?"

"Excuse me for intruding Ma'am, I am looking for someone."

The old woman waited, shifting her weight to a cane that she held in the folds of her skirt.

"A girl with amber hair. She lives, of late, around the corner . . ." He ducked his head and peeked inside the small dark interior, trying to make out images of furniture or anything, but the room was so dark he couldn't see more than shadows. Then a sliver of light, a curtain moved away from a window. "Someone is inside?"

"Yes, someone is."

"May I come in?"

"No, this house is too small for you."

A large bouquet of flowers sat on the windowsill. Lucas pursed his lips and stepped inside.

She raised her cane like a shield and pushed against his ribs.

"It's all right, Madam Van Dessen. It's him!"

The woman grimaced and jabbed him in the chest with a bony finger. "You're the lantern lighter, I suppose."

"Yes, Ma'am I am. I am Lucas."

"I wouldn't know. I live in the dark here."

"I see that Ma'am. Please forgive me . . ." He gazed past her where a slender silhouette wavered. Alina stepped in front of the drape holding a thin candle.

"Tsk . . . had a swim before you came around here, did you?" the old woman clutched her cane and continued to block his way.

Lucas could not constrain himself. He lifted the tiny woman and set her to the side like a fragile vase. She swatted his leg with her cane. Patting the woman on her sponge of hair, he went to Alina.

"Lucas," Alina murmured.

Forgetting about his damp clothes, he took the candle from her hand and pulled her into him with one arm. "I am beyond relief to find you!"

She whimpered and stiffened, "You left."

"I stood outside your door. I tried to tell you."

She exhaled a ragged breath and placed her hand upon his chest. They stood silently holding each other. Lucas clutched her so tightly she winced, but he barely loosened his grip. She sighed and peering up at him rested her head upon his chest. She smelled like lavender. Lucas stroked her hair. He clutched a curl, it wrapped itself around his fingers. A thousand thoughts spun through his mind, but he said nothing, only held her. He could stand this way all day, enjoying how it felt to have her in his arms. The old woman shuffled outside and busied herself at the windowsill garden.

The rain had stopped, and sunshine slanted through the open doorway. Lucas took notice of the room, two cots in opposite corners, a table with a vase of flowers and a small fireplace made from cobblestones the chinking missing and cracked, the ashes black.

Lucas placed his hands at Alina's hips and lifted her off her feet. "Come with me now."

She pushed her palms against his chest and leaned back. "No! You vanished. I wondered if you forgot about me, or possibly died . . . I've been sleeping here, hiding out from my evil uncle. I think he wants to kill me!"

"You're uncle!" Lucas set her down on the cot. "Here?" he asked knowing by the bed that it was where she slept. She nodded, and they sat, knees together, holding hands. "That man in the house?"

"Yes, that is . . . was my father's house."

Lucas took a deep breath, "Alina, we have only just met, but never fear that I will forget about you or die. Now, why would your uncle want to kill you?"

"Money . . . of course. My father's money," she added. "Why are you all wet?"

He ran his hands through his grubby hair and rolled his eyes. "I had a brief swim in the river. I thought a nightmare had come true; I suppose. Anyway, the water cleared my mind and now I have found you, and you are well."

Her eyes sparkled. "I am now."

Gazing into her eyes, he said, "I returned late from the country. I thought I would see you before I left to tell you I was leaving. I went to your house, but you weren't there."

"I couldn't come out," she pouted.

"Your uncle?"

"Yes," she swallowed. He saw us that night and threatened to kill you."

"Ha! Not possible, my darling. So much has happened since we met, I feel like you've been with me all along, I kept your veil," he added patting his chest.

Alina tilted her head.

"You can't take it back. It comforts me."

Smiling she lifted her skirt to show a stained hem. "I nearly got swept into the river yesterday morning. The river is powerful. How did you escape?"

"I am powerful as well, my lady!" Running his finger along the side of her cheek, "You went to the river, but yesterday." His instincts were lagging, he thought. "What were you doing at the river? And standing too close it seems."

"I wished to rinse my hands and face. I felt dirty after fleeing the house." She tilted her chin and closed her eyes. "And . . ." she bit her lip, "I was looking for you."

"Bless you," he murmured as he cradled the back of her head. He ran his fingers along her cheek, pushed her hair out of the way, leaned down and kissed her with pent up ferocity. He felt her shiver, but she allowed him to taste her moist lips and opened her mouth to kiss him back. His tension melted away as he pulled her onto his lap and kissed her over and over, down her neck and up her ears across her forehead ending on the top of her head. Breathlessly, he said, "Come home with me this instant. We can bring your friend as well."

"I don't know what to do," she said gazing around the room, then back at him with a mixture of relief and confusion.

He kissed each cheek. "You must come with me to be safe. Let's gather your things."

"I have trunks, my personal belongings. My father had them packed before he was mur. . . before he died. My inheritance, treasures, should all be in the trunks. I'm not sure what exactly." She got up and paced, raking her hands through her hair. "I was forced to flee without them."

"You have trunks. How many? Who are you and from where did you flee, Alina?"

Alina took a moment to gather her hair in her hands, twisted it up then let it fall down her back. She pulled her shawl around her shoulders. "We . . . I am from Ingleena. I was born there, went to school there, was studying to be a teacher. My mother died when I was born. My father was a merchant, Louis Sutcliffe. He was murdered outside our home. Vasil thought I wasn't home from boarding school yet, but I was in the house. My uncle is malicious in every way. He killed his own brother, my father. That horrible night. . ." She paced faster, shaking her hands as if she could drop the memory. Her voice hollow now, she stood still, "My. . . my maid Daria and I hid in the house. We heard the shouts, but she is the one who knows what happened. From the window, she saw him attack Father. Then we hid until Vasil walked through the house. He didn't find us. We hid behind flour sacks in the pantry. We fled that very night. On the way to the harbour, she told me that Father knew something was terribly wrong, that's why he had written a note for me. We ran out of time," she sobbed.

"I understand." Lucas stroked her back, his face pale and jaw set, "take your time."

 Daria missed the boat and so far, she has not shown up." Tears sprung from her eyes. "I've heard Uncle Vasil talking late at night when he thinks I'm asleep." Her eyes grew large and ghostly. "He boasts about how he outwitted and killed my father." Alina covered her face with her shawl and wept.

Lucas stroked her hand. The man is wicked, but he is only her uncle. I can do away with him. He kissed the top of her head.

The square of sun moved across the floor. The old woman poked her head inside the cottage. Lucas bobbed his head in reassurance. She took a cloak from the stand and went back outside following the swiftly moving sun.

Alina dabbed her eyes with her shawl. "I'm sorry, Lucas, I didn't mean to tell you all my problems today."

"Is your uncle forcing you to do anything you don't want to do, Alina?"

"What do you mean? Oh no, that's not what he's after. Besides," she sniffed. "I have a dagger." Pursing her lips, she lifted her skirt and proudly displayed the dagger strapped to her leg.

"Good girl!" Lucas reached for it brushing his fingertips along her thigh. She giggled and slapped his hand away, threw her skirt over her legs. Staring at him, wide-eyed, and suddenly shy.

"Tell me about your trunks. Do you know where they are?"

"Yes, I think so! I heard the man at Uncle's house mention iron bolts and a tall door and a missing key . . ." she wrung her hands and shook her head. "It's difficult to remember. Uncle thinks I might have the key. If I do, I don't know where it is. He scares me. I can't remember what else was said."

"Which man was at your uncle's house?"

"There's a dead man on the floor in Uncle Vasil's house!"

"Ah yes, but he's gone now. Not dead." He stood and took her hand. "We must get you to a safer place. You say, you have two trunks."

"I did. I should, if they made it onto the ship, or any ship." she sniffled pulling her hand away to twist her fingers together.

Lucas kicked at the dirt floor, "My dear lady Alina, I am so deeply sorry for all of your troubles. Come with me now, and I will share your burdens."

In the distance, church bells tolled. She knitted her brows gazing around the cottage.

"What shall we take with us?" Lucas nudged.

Alina busied herself smoothing the folds of her dress. Glancing up at him, she dabbed the corners of her eyes with a trembling hand.

"I realize you're frightened," Lucas stated reaching for her again. "But you shouldn't be on your own. Please allow me to help you. I could never forgive myself if something happened to you out here."

Alina shook her head. "I always believed myself to be strong, but the loss of my father has shaken me dreadfully much." She looked up at Lucas, then off into a faraway distance.

"The world is a dangerous and unpredictable place," Lucas said taking her hands in his.

"I feel like I already know you. But I didn't know you at first," she trembled.

"Understood and agreed. Now, from here on, we go forth together. We will get to know all about each other."

A flash of joy washed over her face; her expression melted into one of childish anticipation. It was up to him now to make sure that she never lost that trust which she bestowed upon him. "Now, if you will please accompany me to the Kempel Boarding House, you will meet my dear friend Irene. We will take care of you. Rest assured, you will have your privacy and comforts."

Hope lit her green eyes that shone like the sea on a summer morning. "I have my personal items and some other things," Alina said pointing to her satchels. As he bent to retrieve the satchels, a silver candlestick tumbled to the dirt floor.

"What's this?" He picked it up, measured the weight in his hand and held it toward the light.

"I stole some things from my uncle to aid in my escape."

"Excellent," Lucas said smiling. He planted a kiss on her mouth. "I will give you a moment to collect yourself lest my eagerness overpower the situation." He shouldered her satchels and strode outside where the widow waited, clutching her shawl.

"Madam Van Dessen, please excuse my intrusion. Would you like to come and stay with us?'

Amused, the tiny woman extended her hand. "No thank you, young man. But I would appreciate if you brought me some artificial light now that you are taking Alina away."

"Indeed," Lucas said. I will see to it that the officials of The City of Dreams add these streets to the lighted way. We will send out additional lamp boys, whatever is necessary to make you feel safe. Shall I light the fire for you before we depart?"

"I can do it myself." The widow pointed to a stack of wood she'd piled beside the door.

Alina emerged from the hut in a dark blue herringbone dress with a low square neckline trimmed with white lace. Her ruby pendant sparkled in the sunlight, but she quickly flung her shawl over her shoulders leaving Lucas staring in startled admiration. She bent down and hugged her friend. "I left for you the silver candlesticks and five candles."

Lucas carried her satchels on one arm while keeping his other arm tightly around her shoulders. It made for awkward walking, but they soon fell into harmonious step. As they drew closer to her house, Alina slowed her pace. "What of Uncle Vasil . . . and that man?"

"Yes, what of them? There is much to discuss. We found Dugald Tendrick inside your house at the bottom of the stairs, he had been staying at the boarding house. He must have followed you from the Duck Tavern."

"I don't know why that man at the bottom of the stairs showed up at the Duck Tavern, but he can't have followed me home. I wanted to find you . . . I followed the lamp boy. When I ran from the tavern, the rain fell like a curtain and the wind blew me in the wrong direction. I didn't make it back to the house until near morning." Her lips quivered, she pulled the shawl around her shoulders, shuddered, and gazed toward the sea.

Lucas ran a finger along her cheekbone, wiped away a tear. Squeezing her small hand in his, he led her to the low wall beside the oil lamp across from the house.

He gestured for her to sit on the stone bench concealed by the lamp and the wall. From there they could observe her Uncle's house, without detection by passersby.

"It seems my decision to stay overlong in the country did not bode well back here. Dugald was a tenant in our boarding house." He explained about Dugald's injury, his trip to the country with Irene while Madam Trousdale minded the boarding house, and then Dugald's escape. "He must be associated with your Uncle. We have to find your trunks before they do."

Alina dipped her head. "You will find them, won't you?"

"Yes, I will, my beauty!" Lucas kissed her forehead and her cheek. "Let's begin with you. Tell me everything about you."

"All right then," she agreed as she focused on the ground. Lucas cupped her cheek in his palm and gazed into her eyes which suddenly turned from watery green to black. Are we safe here?" She peered up and down the street as she spoke.

"If your uncle shows up, I'll drop him where he stands," Lucas said with a flick of his wrist. "After he confesses of course."

Her eyes shimmered and she went on. "He believes I have a key. So, it must be about my trunks. Daria said my father sent them here. Somehow Vasil has discovered that, it's not surprising since he discovered that my father kept this house here for his merchant trade. Uncle has taken over my father's life. As if he never existed!" she exclaimed. "I've been feigning ignorance of his involvement ever since I came here. Aagh, I cannot bare this." She clenched her fists. "If I were a man, I would have choked him to death by now." She thought for a moment. "You're right, the man on the floor, Dugald, he must have been assisting him along with that disgusting Campbell Barrington."

Lucas studied her face, enjoying the expressions she made, and the inflection in her voice. Everything about her was new, charming, and heart wrenching. The situation was complicated, but he had no concern that he couldn't fix it all for her. What bothered him the most was that Alina had gone undetected by him for weeks. And devious events had occurred in the city without his notice. Had he truly been in a such a disconnected mindset? Irene was right about him needing the trip to the country. He felt like he was awakening from a fog and stepping into a new and, he hoped, exciting awakening.

"Campbell Barrington," he said. "I've heard that name before." Lucas frowned and shook his head. "He receives shipments at the harbour. At least he used to until a recent incident. Perhaps involving your uncle. I haven't suspected his cargo shipments to contain anything of immense value." He stroked his chin wondering what else he may have missed.

"Campbell Barrington is a pompous slob who is in collusion with Uncle Vasil, and he has the nerve to think he could court me!"

Lucas straightened his back, glared with narrow eyes. "I'll get rid of him."

She gazed at Lucas without protest. "He has been conspiring with Uncle Vasil. They've known each other for a long time. Uncle killed my father with his own horrible hands. But now Barrington dances for him like a puppet. He must have helped plan to mur . . . murder my father . . ." again, she broke down in sobs.

He held her close feeling her heart thud against his chest, her face wet on his collarbone, wisps of soft hair tickled his jaw. Blinking through welling pools, he noticed several iridescent starlings sitting in the branches of a Linden tree, whirring and whistling. Alina sniffed and peered up. "The birds are listening."

"They share your grief," he murmured.

"Do you believe that?"

"I do." He squeezed her hand.

She wiped her cheeks with her palms. "I'm making the birds sad. Yet, they must be happy enough to live in this fragrant tree."

"Yes, I know someone who makes the most relaxing linden tea." Lucas nodded toward the satchels, then peered into her eyes. "Do you want to go inside and retrieve anything else?'

"No, there is nothing left to steal."

"You left a shift in your wardrobe."

"I don't remember . . ."

"It's linen, quite lovely. Don't you want it?"

"I do," she glared at the house, shaking her head, "but I can't go back in there."

"And I can't leave you here alone . . ." He examined her profile, the slight wrinkle in her brow as she perused the house that was for a brief time her home. She folded her arms across her chest clutching one corner of the shawl. Just as he was about to suggest he come back for it later during his rounds, a man approached. The sun was at his back. Lucas shielded his eyes and recognized the gait of Nikolas.

Lucas stood up and pulled Alina to her feet. "Uh, yes Nik. This is Alina!"

"Alina, allow me to present my loyal friend, Nikolas."

"Lucas at last . . . you found her!" Nikolas slapped him on the back. Turning to Alina, he bowed, took her hand, and kissed it. She curtsied and giggled.

"The business is taken care of," Nikolas said. "Are you going to the boarding house? I'll accompany you. I've had nothing to eat yet today."

"We are," Lucas looked at Alina.

"Yes, please let's get away from here."

"The shift?" Lucas pointed his chin toward the house. "Upstairs, Nik, if you will, please retrieve the lady's undergarment from her wardrobe."

"With pleasure," Nikolas turned on his heel and hurried over to the house.

They waited, holding hands, and stealing glances at each other. Lucas still in disbelief that he found her, that she wasn't just a vision from one of his vivid dreams, could think of nothing to say. He rubbed her palms between his and kissed her fingertips. She fluttered her long eyelashes, bowed her head, and occupied herself by examining his leather boots, so much so that Lucas began shifting from one foot to the other. It was highly unusual that she would accompany him home so soon, but the circumstances allowed no other option. He had many plans for their future, but after his bold greeting in the widow's hut, he had finally regained his composure and feared frightening her. Finally, he said, "You sought me when you came to the City of Dreams?"

"Yes, well actually no . . . I was distraught when I came here! But I'd heard about you before. My father told me that you saved his life and that someday you would save mine."

"Aha, is that so!? How did your father know of me?" Lucas raised an eyebrow.

"You're a mess, Lucas. You could use a change of clothes yourself," Nikolas said coming up behind them.

Lucas swiped a palm over his chest, laughing at his muddy clothes.

Nikolas stood between the two. "What am I interrupting? Well . . . other than destiny."

"Your father, Alina?" Lucas repeated glancing at Nikolas, who stood holding the shift dangling from his arm.

"Yes," she sniffed, and spoke softly. "My father was a merchant, he travelled through the City of Dreams for the past eight years. A long time ago, he said, *there was a boy who walked in amber light. He lit the city at night and kept the citizens safe.*"

Nikolas whistled low and slow.

Lucas rested a palm on his chest. "Meaning me?"

Alina peered at Lucas as if seeing him from a distance. "Just six months ago he came here," her voice wavered, "on his final journey—to arrange the transfer of a shipment of rare spices. A group of men accosted him. Now, I know it was Uncle Vasil's henchmen. My father said, *the lantern lighter, no longer a boy, a tall man with eyes like night and long hair that loves the wind, he intervened and led me safely to my ship.* That was you, no? And the boy of amber light?"

Lucas' eyes sparkled. "I remember a noble gentleman. Dressed in the finest clothes I've ever seen. He'd lost his way on a blustery night. Robbed of his purse and parcels. I accompanied him back to the harbour. Could he have been your father!?"

"If you gave him coin from your own pocket, then yes, he was my father! Alive then and gone now." A solitary tear slid down Alina's cheek.

Lucas retrieved the veil from inside his shirt and wiped her cheeks. "We shook hands, my darling. Your father and I shook hands." Gently, he kissed the top of her head. In the distance he could hear sounds of ship bells clanging in the harbour, recalling his twilight walk with her father, remembering he'd said he had a home in Ingleena but feared it was no longer safe. His heart ached for Alina and her departed father.

She sniffed and wiped her nose with the veil, then snatched it from him. "My veil!"

Lucas felt himself blush for the first time in years. "Oh. . . yes, it is . . . I mentioned I had it, didn't I?"

"I couldn't understand what you were talking about." She examined the veil, then with a giggle stuffed it back inside Lucas' shirt.

He placed his hand over his heart, "I am terribly sorry about your father, Alina. I should have liked to know him."

"He told my maid, Daria, that when you walked toward him you were glowing."

Lucas scratched his chin. "I was probably carrying a lantern."

"Hmmm, maybe." Her shoulders sagged. "He left a note that said you would help me now."

"This is all rather unusual," Nikolas said with a wink for Lucas.

"Indeed, but not surprising the way things have been going lately." He took Alina's hand, raised it to his lips and kissed it, "I will honor your father's wishes and his memory. I promise to take care of you from this moment forward. And I will avenge his death for you!" He brushed her hair aside and kissed each flushed cheek.

Nikolas spoke to the shift, hanging from his arm, "Shall we go?" Everyone laughed like old friends. The two men made a show of carefully folding Alina's shift and placing it inside her satchel. She clapped her hands then looped her arms with each of theirs. As the three strolled away from Vasil's house, Lucas and Nikolas exchanged a look over Alina's head. Lucas understood that his friend had moved Dugald, most likely to the harbour where hidden stone cells could swallow a man for years. While Nikolas chatted to Alina, pointing out the tearoom, and shops that women frequented, along with safe taverns and sights and views of interest along their route, Lucas thought about her Uncle and Campbell Barrington conspiring to murder her father. The lowest of the wicked lie in wait to kill anyone, most of all their own kin. Now they were hiding out in his city. It was intolerable. And the trunks. Alina said she had two trunks. Were those what Trousdale referred to? If so, it wasn't good news. She'd said two of the trunks are in the water.

On the way to the boarding house, Alina gave them more details about how Vasil murdered her father to steal his business and the house in the City of Dreams. Realizing she needed to settle herself before meeting even more new people at the boarding house, Lucas suggested that they stop at an ale house and quench their thirst. Once inside seated at a table, she loosened her shawl to reveal her ruby pendant. Lucas blushed remembering how he nearly swiped it from her delicate neck the first time he saw her.

Flashing a tantalizing smile toward, Lucas, Alina said, "This was the last thing my father ever gave me. It hasn't been easy keeping it safe from the clutches of Uncle Vasil, and others I might add."

Nikolas laughed aloud. "You have no idea how lucky you are to still be in possession of that, young lady."

Lucas smirked and swigged his ale, all the while keeping Alina's hand tucked in his. Nikolas revealed that Dugald was now indeed jailed in a cell at the harbour. "We will question him and find out exactly what he knows of your uncle and your possessions."

"Yes, we will, but first we'll make sure that you're safely settled in the house with the help of Irene and Carissa." Lucas said. "And Ikarus, he will have to help with the lanterns again. Tonight, we will light the city like a cathedral and flush out the villains."

Lucas knew Irene would have concerns, he'd left before dawn and she never saw him return home last night. Even as he escorted Alina to the boarding house, he wished he could introduce the two of them under better circumstances. He and Irene had barely spoken since their incredible journey to the country and now he would shock her again with the appearance of Alina. He could do nothing about it, so he shoved open the batten and plank oak door and stepped into the inviting parlour which was empty, but the chair pillows were fluffed and the fire blazing. The aroma of spiced bread filled the room. Everything in place as always. The two men set Alina's satchels down at the bottom of the staircase. Lucas took a deep breath and gestured around the room. "This is where we gather, although the boarders mostly stay in the sitting room at the back end of the kitchen, which is through there. So then . . ."

Nikolas spoke up. "Why don't Alina and I warm ourselves by the fire while you find Mrs. Kempel."

Lucas flashed an expression of appreciation. Heart racing, moisture settling inside his mud-smudged clothes, Lucas watched Alina's face. She looked pleased, relaxed maybe from the ale. He'd never entertained such a woman; she came from a world completely foreign to him. Torn between gratitude that she was in his grasp, and confusion as to the proper decorum, he fought an impulse to run upstairs to bathe and change clothes. He offered his arm and led Alina to the sofa. Nikolas plopped down beside her making a shooing motion to Lucas as if he were an errant child.

In the kitchen, he found Irene bustling around the cooking pots. The ladle slid from her hand and splashed into the pot. She rushed over to him. Reaching up on tiptoes, she pulled him to her in a stew-scented embrace. "Should I hug you or slap you? Where have you been?"

Madam Trousdale sat at the table beside Carissa who had a bandage wrapped around her head. Other than that, the maid appeared well enough as she sipped what smelled like linden tea. Lucas relaxed, grateful even to see Madam Trousdale. "Please excuse me, Irene" — turning to each of them in turn— "and everyone" — he gazed at Trousdale and Carissa, then focused on Irene. "Nikolas and I have been sorting out the Dugald situation and at the same time . . ." a glint of light from the open window caught the silver frame of Madam Trousdale's hourglass, it was full, but draining swiftly.

Turning his gaze back to Irene and pressing his palms together he announced. "I found the girl."

"Hunh?"

Stepping closer, he took her hands and said quietly, "I found Alina."

Irene's eyes grew as large and buttery as sweet rolls. "Where is she!?"

Lucas placed his hand upon his chest as if the others knew he'd carried her veil next to his heart all this time. "Sitting by the fire."

Irene wiped her hands on her apron, frowned at the stains, pulled it over her head and flung it toward the table. Brushing her hair back, she swept past him knocking him sideways. Madam Trousdale's chair clattered to the floor as she followed Irene. Lucas gaped at Carissa for a second then hurried after the women.

Irene rushed into the room and snatched Alina up like a favorite doll, hugged her to her doughy self then held her at arm's length and examined her from head to toe, clicking her tongue and bobbing her head. Lucas half expected her to say, *this one will do*, as she did when selecting items at the market. Alina, who had downed a full pint on her own, beamed with glassy-eyed amazement. She peeked at Lucas every few seconds which made his heart race and his stomach simmer with a rolling wave of contentment that he had never experienced before. Madam Trousdale stood off to the side with a serene, statuesque gaze. Her hourglass halted. Nikolas, who Lucas hadn't realized left the room, returned with Carissa on one arm, limping ever so slightly, and a magnum of red wine. Carissa gathered the feasting glasses from the sideboard and began to fill them.

"Irene, this is Alina. I was lucky enough to find her at a friendly widow's home," he added giving Irene as many details to satisfy her curiosity as he could right now.

Alina made a subtle curtsey. "How do you do Ma'am? It is a pleasure to meet you."

"And, uh . . ." Lucas wasn't sure if he should introduce Madam Trousdale or Carissa first. "This is Madam Trousdale, our friend.

She stepped forward with a full hourglass and offered her long-fingered hand. "Here you are," she said.

"And Carissa, our maid, and friend," Lucas added. He swigged the wine Carissa handed him. Noticing that all their expectant eyes were on him, he scratched his neck. Nikolas chuckled from the corner where he now stood, and they all waited for the toast. Taking his place in front of the fire beside Alina, who appeared sprightly and demure at the same time, they touched cups. An awkward silence filled the room. He shot Nik an exasperated frown. Nik bowed and made a flourish with his arm. Lucas didn't enjoy the stage, but standing tall and swallowing several times, he gazed at everyone in turn. Nikolas laughing, Irene's eyes brimming with joy and relief. Carissa starry-eyed, and Madam Trousdale smug, as if she were responsible for Alina being there. He held his cup high, feeling the warmth of the fire on his back. "Welcome, Alina, to the City of Dreams, to our home." with a slight bow to Irene, "we invite you to make it your own, and promise you a dwelling of peaceful repose."

They all drained their cups. Alina gazed at Lucas in such a way that he could barely breathe. Carissa refilled the cups. Irene indicated for Alina to sit, then began to ply her with questions.

Now that he'd declared her part of the household, he needed to make it so. Lucas approached Carissa, "You have recovered well after your ordeal."

"I can thank Madam Trousdale for that. Her tea eases the aches, and the bruises are healing quickly."

Turning toward Madam Trousdale he said, "I appreciate your assistance these past few days." The hourglass flipped and filled.

He scratched the stubble on his cheek. "I need to choose a suitable room for Alina."

"Just this afternoon, we put a new boarder, a silk merchant in the room Dugald had occupied. And we don't want her in there anyway. So, the corner room next to yours is available." Carissa said.

Lucas's eyes lit up. "That suits me. Carissa why don't you rest by the fire with the ladies. Madam Trousdale and Nikolas will assist me."

Lucas caught Alina's eye as he gathered her belongings and mounted the stairs. She blinked and took a sip of her wine. Hesitating, he couldn't help but stare at her with dark-eyed intention, their connection unmistakable and incomprehensibly real. She returned his gaze then blushed and turned her attention back to Irene who was stroking her hand like a doting aunt. He hoped Alina felt the same as he did, even as sudden as it was. For him, their souls recognized each other; he felt poetically sure of it. With her satchels and their cups, Lucas and Nikolas climbed the stairs. Madam Trousdale went to the kitchen to retrieve fresh linens from the supply closet. It took several trips up and down the stairs for Lucas to collect everything he wanted to add to her cozy corner room. An oil lamp, a porcelain water pitcher and wash basin for the dressing table, several fat candles with drip holders to set on the nightstand, a thick rug, logs for the small stone fireplace, and a brass bell he'd acquired from his night travels. The last touch was the basket of flowers from the proprietor of the Grande Inn. He would have liked to freshen up in his own room, but the day grew short and darkness loitered at the edge of the sky. After pulling the curtain across the small window, he lit the lamp, built the fire in the low arched fireplace, and checked the lock on her door several times, keeping one key for himself.

Downstairs, Irene finished explaining to Alina the workings of the boarding house, the times the boarders took their meals and when they, the family, took theirs. "There are new rules as well," she said. "As of yesterday, we only accept boarders that come with written recommendation from their employer or a well-established citizen or merchant. We have only had one nefarious guest in all these years."

Lucas waited, listening at the top of the stairs. Mrs. Kempel ran her boarding house well. She would never allow distraction to intrude upon the arrival of a boarder again. It reassured him to hear her speak with competency. "This is an esteemed house and it will remain so."

Lucas descended then to let Alina know her room was ready. Surely, she would enjoy a few moments to herself after such an exhausting ordeal the past few days. "Alina, if you will accompany me upstairs, I'll show you to your room." Nikolas and Madam Trousdale were sitting together talking. Carissa rested in an oversized chair, but kept attempting to get up and serve wine, bread, and cheese. Despite their nonchalant behavior, he and Alina were the center of everyone's attention. He reached for her hand, ignoring the scrutiny of the others. Let them have their fun, nothing could disrupt his happiness. Just as they approached the stairs, something hit the front door with a thud. Carissa yelped, and Trousdale's hourglass emptied with a whoosh. Nikolas jumped up and grabbed the wood cutting board which he passed to Lucas who realized he had forgotten his dagger upstairs, but his friend had his in the palm of his hand. Lucas pushed Alina behind him, "Go up!" He noticed her hand go to her skirt where she kept her own dagger hidden. Irene stood up, but Madam Trousdale held her back with one arm. Carissa wielded an empty wine bottle like a club.

Leaping to the landing Lucas grabbed the edge of the door ready to slam it in the face of the intruder.

As it inched open, the thin shape of a pale faced Ikarus slipped inside. A sudden silence held the startled group in suspension until Lucas broke out in laughter. "Good evening Ik, charming to see you!"

"What . . . is it?"

"We weren't expecting you."

"I hope not with a greeting like that," Ikarus said. He held a crate of candles in his arms. "I tried to knock but had to kick."

Lucas took the crate from him. "Why don't you collect the tools and bring some of these extra candles and lanterns as well."

"I'll go out with you tonight," Nikolas offered following Ikarus into the kitchen.

"It will go quicker that way," Lucas agreed setting the crate of candles beside the supply closet. "Give me a few minutes."

Alina waited at the top of the stairs. Lucas went up, put his arm around her shoulders and led her down the hall. "Just Ikarus, you met, didn't you? I guess we're all a bit on edge." He handed Alina the key to her door and let her unlock it herself. Her hand shook slightly, but her eyes lit up when the door swung open.

"Will it do, Mademoiselle?" Stepping inside, Lucas made a grand gesture of welcome.

"Yes, It's wonderful!" She ran her hand over the thick stone wall and peeked behind the curtain to the small barred window.

"Irene's husband used to hide his money in this room. Now, she trusts it to the banker." Lucas said, with a brief thought to his secret stash hidden in the cellar.

"It feels safe." She turned to him with warm, grateful eyes. "Like home," examining the room with a sigh of relief, she flounced onto the bed. Lucas beamed with pleasure but resisted the urge to join her.

"I'm sure this doesn't compare to your Ingleena estate, but I do hope you will feel at home here. You can rest easy now. I will be in the room right next door to you tonight."

Flashing her eyes at him she began to unwrap her shawl.

"I . . . I'm afraid I have to go out for a bit and light the lanterns, but with three of us it will go quickly."

She nodded. Lucas stood in the doorway gazing at her, hardly able to believe his good fortune. Finally, he strode over, grasped her by the shoulders and kissed her softly on the mouth. Her touch light as she stroked his forearm and pulled him down beside her. He felt heat from her fingers course straight up his arm to his heart. "Shall I help you unpack your belongings?" he indicated her satchels sitting on the floor in front of the wardrobe.

"I can manage it. Thank you," she murmured looking contentedly around the room.

A clatter of voices from downstairs. "The boarders are being served their supper now. When I return the rest of us will dine together and celebrate your arrival!"

She smiled sleepily.

"I imagine this is a lot to take in, but for now have a lie down. I promise, you need not worry anymore." He kissed the top of her head and rubbed her back for reassurance—his own as well as hers. He held her hand, kissed her fingertips before dragging himself off the bed over to the door, where he held her gaze until he slowly closed the door and locked it with his key. She likes me, he mused.

* * *

Alina sat on the edge of the bed, all her frustration and fear gone now. The worries and wild imaginings of how her life would be—living with the widow Van Dessen—or on the streets. Just yesterday, she feared days of huddling in the alleyways of the City of Dreams trying to avoid Vasil and Campbell Barrington, and who knew what else. But just as her beloved father promised, Lucas had saved her! She went to the door and unlocked it, peeked out into the long narrow hallway—empty— but cheerful voices rose from downstairs. A warmth that began in her stomach rose to her heart, exhaling a staccato breath, she closed and locked the door again. Unlacing her dress, she slipped out of it and laid it at the foot of the bed, smoothing the fabric. She went to the basin and washed her hands and face, ran her fingers through her hair, grateful there was no evidence of mites from sleeping on the straw mattress in the widow's hut. She couldn't possibly bear any more disappointment. With a quick peek out the window, she guessed there were a couple of hours before Lucas and the men returned. The linen sheets felt crisp and clean; the coverlet warm. When she closed her eyes, the crackling fire reminded her of her bedroom in their ancestral estate back in Ingleena. The anguish of her loss struck anew. If only I had one of my fine gowns to wear to dinner. I hate Uncle Vasil. He ruined my life! Once I had everything I could possibly imagine, and now it's gone. My father, my friends, my maid and confidant, our household lost to the greed of one ugly little man. She reached down and felt the seam of her shift to be sure her pouch of jewelry was still there. At least she had saved this much. Her father would be proud of that. Even after his death he had managed to care for her. But she wondered if she would ever see her trunks again. Vasil and Barrington had quite possibly already made their escape with them. It broke her heart. And what of her dream to get out of this city as soon as possible, her dream of a life like the one she lost. But without her father, how would it be? She closed her eyes and pictured her father's kind face. What would he tell her to do now? Lucas and his clan were good to her so far. Before her father mentioned it to her, she had never even heard of the City of Dreams. Now, here she was with a room of her own, in a house in which she felt safe. It was almost as if he knew she would end up here someday. But she would not stay. Ingleena was her home. Once I find my trunks I will return. Father had keen foresight to send me here. If my trunks are here, Lucas will find them. Lucas . . . he takes my breath away. When he enters the room everything else disappears. Grateful that Lucas had met her father, if even for a moment, she pictured the two of them shaking hands and drifted off to sleep.

* * *

Before taking his leave, Lucas went to the kitchen and repeated the rules of the house to the Master Mason and his men as well as the silk merchant. They would keep to their four-man bunk rooms, or the ample dining and sitting area off the kitchen. Even as he spoke, he knew the lecture was unnecessary. They were all of a good sort and he could reprimand none other than himself for having allowed Dugald, a man he should have disliked on sight to stay even one hour in the house. Madam Trousdale lingered—in her custom—off to the side but within ear shot and when she turned toward him, Lucas noticed the hourglass was still full. As peculiar as that bauble was, it reassured him now. Irene walked him to the door, promising to take care of Alina. They shuffled past Carissa who sat in front of the fire with a glazed look on her face, her wine glass tilted sideways in her hand.

"She doesn't take wine often," Irene said, before giving Lucas a hug as he stepped out into the twilight where Nikolas and Ikarus waited.

Lucas gazed up at the inky sky crowded with stars. He offered a reassuring nod to his companions before reaching into his supply bag to pull out candles and lanterns while discussing who went to which street. Once they sorted and decided, Lucas said, "I will take care of those widow's homes," he held up an additional sack of lanterns. "We will meet back at the uncle's house, so save that neighborhood for last. Once there, remain in the shadows," he said to Ikarus who chewed his bottom lip. Gripping Ik's shoulder he added, "The constable is alerted. Those men won't walk freely in the city. And afterward, once all is secured," this time a glance directed at Nikolas, "you will check on our guest at the harbour?" Nikolas gave a vigorous nod and Lucas continued, "Then we will return home for supper. You will join us, Ik."

Nikolas was already walking away with a lighting stick and sack, when Lucas said, "Light up the city like a festival, and hurry every chance you get. Merriments await!"

Lucas, knowing his way through the winding passages of the City of Dreams better than anyone found himself back at Vasil's house first. He took the time to examine the root cellar and make sure that no trace of Dugald remained. He trusted Nikolas completely, but both men knew four eyes perceived more than two and had long ago acquired a habit of checking on each other. It had saved them from more than a few drunken scuffles, possible arrests, and run-ins with an assortment of adversaries over the years. He closed the cellar door, leaving it slightly ajar, as he and Nikolas had found it, and decided to light a lantern and enter the house. Although he had entered before, it surprised him that the main room was quite a bit larger than he remembered. Now it had the hollow grandness of unoccupied space. On the far wall was a large fireplace with a stone hearth and a thick log mantle. Next to that, a tall cabinet with hazy glass doors—mostly empty but on closer inspection he noticed several bottles. Helping himself to a bottle of whiskey, he took another tour of the place searching in cupboards, under chair cushions and behind the drawers of bureaus. Understanding he would not find the missing key, he searched anyway. Whatever he was meant to discover, he would know it when he found it. Upstairs, Lucas stepped into Alina's room, his gaze went first to the bed where his beautiful woman had rested each night since her arrival. Her small wood frame bed half covered with a luxurious burgundy coverlet brightened the tiny dark room. An assortment of handmade pillows that had decorated her sleeping chamber lay scattered on the floor. He took his time to understand her by the observance of the room which he hadn't done on his first urgent inspection of the house. Quite used to going through other people's things, he searched her room for anything else she may have left behind in her hasty departure and noticed a lack of books. She brought none to the boarding house so she must have had to leave them behind in Ingleena. Someday they would find time to enjoy the bookshelves at the boarding house and read the poets together. Setting the lantern in the corner, he gathered her coverlet into a bulky parcel; obviously, her personal comforter she would want it with her, and as he did so he imagined it spread out on their wedding bed someday soon. As he made his way downstairs, he heard a scurrying, a shuffle, and a thump. Instantly he extinguished the lantern and dropped the bundle. He knew neither Nikolas nor Ikarus would enter without whistling their arrival. The glow of a single candle and another thud came from the uncle's room. Inching his way down the gloomy hallway, stealthy and sure-footed in the dark, he reached for his dagger.

From a dark corner, a shadow spread across the ceiling. A man leapt forward sword in hand. "Halt thief!"

Lucas dove forward knocking the sword to the floor with a swift swipe of his forearm, his dagger glinted against the man's throat, lit by the glow of a lantern emanating from behind Lucas. He heard a familiar low whistle and stepped aside allowing the light to fall full on a pasty unshaven face. He kept a firm grasp on the man's wrist. But like a slippery worm, the creature slid to the floor and wriggled free. Swearing, crawling, and scrambling up on his stocking feet, he ran back toward the room from whence he had come. Lucas and Nikolas met in the doorway, bouncing off each other, in time to witness the terrified weasel leap, then slip and hit his chin on the windowsill. A flash of gray, and a flayed paw reached in from outside and raked its claws across the man's face. Four rivers of blood appeared on his plump cheek. The man yelled in horror before flinging himself over the sill and out the window with his stubby feet running in midair. Lucas and Nikolas right behind him, reached the window in time to see a tall man, wearing an elegant coat, stumble from a waiting coach. He grabbed the stout fellow and stuffed him inside the coach. Both men swearing, arms and legs flailing as the horse reared up, gathered its footing on the cobbles and galloped off with the door swinging wildly, aided by a protruding foot.

Nik and Lucas chuckled. "Uncle Vasil, I suppose," Nikolas said.

"Came for a change of clothing it appears," Lucas picked up a shirt from the bed, dropped it next to a bunch of boot hose. He kicked at a pair of small boots. "He'll be missing these."

"Not many with feet so small," Nikolas agreed. Back in the hallway, Ikarus, ghostly and shivering waited in the eerie glow of the lantern, sword in hand. Lucas took the sword from him examined it, felt its weight then handed it to Ikarus, clapped him on the back. "You've found yourself a trophy."

"More than a change of clothes," Nikolas said, lifting a leg of boot hose that clinked with several coins that he spilled into his palm and pocketed.

"He probably won't return," Lucas said. Going back into the room to close and lock the window, he leaned out to search for the cat.

"Let's get out of here." Ikarus wrapped the sword in the corner of his cloak.

On the way out, Lucas grabbed the bottle of whisky, which he handed to Nikolas. Gathering the bundle of Alina's bedding they went out the front door. They gathered their lighting tools from the bench across the way and passed the bottle around until it was empty. Nikolas sent Ikarus out front with a lantern while he explained to Lucas the events of his trip to the harbour. "Dugald is quite sick. Whatever bit him, well . . . it meant it. Best to go first thing in the morning, he is willing to talk and is babbling about an evil witch terrorizing the citizens."

Lucas walked on, eyes straight ahead. "Fine, we will go and pry every bit of information out of him."

"And the witch?" Nikolas chortled.

Lucas' eyes shone with amusement. "We'll see. But I believe she has done all she can for him already." He took a final look back at the house and thought, but couldn't be sure in the blackness, that he saw the gray cat sitting on the cobbles below Alina's window licking its paw with a yellow-eyed blink. "I'll let the constable know this property is vacant. Alina doesn't need to worry about it right now."

When the boarding house came into view, Lucas quickened his pace. As he pushed open the door, Nikolas commented, "The witch, do you think she is aware of her nickname?"

"I'm sure she is, and proud of it," Lucas said with an easy laugh.

Irene met them at the door. The fire blazed, lighting the room with orange warmth. Madam Trousdale sat glassy eyed with wine in hand. Her eyes flashed through all their colors when Lucas gazed at her, but then turned an indifferent blue. The hourglass, that for an instant appeared empty, flipped and filled. Lucas squinted, and caught the self-satisfied stare of Trousdale. "Where's Alina?" He carried the coverlet to the back of the kitchen for washing before presenting it to her.

"Carissa is up with Alina, helping her into her new dress," Irene said.

Lucas paused, "A new dress? Where did that come from?"

"A gift," Irene said shushing him. "Hurry, Lucas."

Nikolas and Ikarus went directly to the sidebar and poured themselves wine.

As Lucas climbed the stairs, Irene said, "There is thick stew for supper, warm bread, butter and honey and there is more wine to help us celebrate!"

"I should like to wash first."

"Take your time, but the wine may not last."

"I've had a wee bit of a head start."

"That may explain your soggy state."

Bubbles of laughter followed Lucas as he took the stairs two at a time, heart racing with anticipation. Stopping for a moment outside Alina's room, he placed his hand upon the door inclined his head, heard her soft voice, still new to him. She and Carissa were discussing something about hair up or down, or perhaps the new dress. He rapped lightly. "I've returned." Silence, then a flurry of giggles. "See you downstairs momentarily," then he added, "take your time."

"We will," Carissa said in an unusually high voice. Lucas realized they would have taken their cups to the boudoir—as he thought of it now.

In his room, he peeled off his oily shirt, stepped out of his pants and into the warm tub. Irene somehow always knew when he would come home and wish to bathe, or was it even she who had prepared the tub? He detected the scent of lavender and grew suspicious that Trousdale had prepared it for him. Of course, at the request of Irene. He had to admit he was glad she was still here. Her and her jumpy little hourglass. What about her spooky little cottage, who was guarding the golden jewelled box? That was his only real concern. Irene was fond of Madam Trousdale, obviously enjoyed her company, and she was a help, there could be no doubt about that. He lay back allowing the water to cascade over his shoulders and swirl like massaging fingers around his neck. His mind refused to settle though, it spun so fast his head felt like it was full of sand in a windstorm. Sitting up, pouring water over his back with cupped hands, he thought about Alina dressing in the next room. She smelled like new soap, even after staying at the widow's hut. He didn't know how she managed it. Her arrival created a special occasion. And she had a new dress. Never in his life had he felt so much like celebrating. The past few days had brought him several gifts, even Madam Trousdale who intrigued him—the unexpectedly enlightening trip to the country, his new friend—almost brother–– Bernard, who he hoped would come for a visit soon, a new understanding between himself and Irene, and Alina. Most of all Alina!

The door burst open and Nikolas stepped in grabbing hold of the door before it banged against the wall. Going for the washstand he said, "Apologies but I need a wash up as well." He splashed water on his face then wiped it on a small linen. "The boarding house is full tonight. Ikarus is cleaning up in the kitchen. We could both do with fresh shirts, if you don't mind."

Lucas pointed to the armoire. "Help yourself, no not that one . . . all right then," flicking water toward Nikolas, "those, they're clean enough for the two of you!"

"Get moving. I'm starving," Nikolas replied.

Lucas gripped the sides of the tub and pushed himself up. Nik turned and fled. "Save the theatre for your lady!"

Dressed in a dark blue velvet coat, with a black belt and charcoal grey breeches, Lucas made his appearance downstairs. Irene handed him his cup of wine and he sat down in front of the fire keeping his eyes on the staircase. "From whom did she get a new dress?"

Irene and Trousdale shook their heads. Themselves transformed in their own elegant gowns, Trousdale in browns and tans of the earth, and Irene in the blue of the sea as it shimmered just before sunset. Nikolas and Ikarus stood at the sidebar with their wine, chewing chunks of bread and slices of cheese. Lucas rose and joined them, helping himself to a large piece of bread and several pieces of cheese, his stomach gurgling its gratitude. When at last he heard footsteps on the stairs, he swallowed a large gulp of wine. All turned to watch as Carissa came down first, no longer wearing the bandage, a light of pride in her eyes and behind her, Alina, dressed in a glimmering green taffeta gown with a low-cut black velvet bodice. Her hair piled on top of her head with long curled tendrils reaching down along the elegant arch of her neck. Her ruby pendant shining in the curve of her cleavage. The candles flickered as she swept past them into the center of the room, with a sanguine blush climbing up her delicate throat to her high cheekbones. Lucas bounded forward and offered his hand. Pulling her toward him he brushed his cheek against her hair. "Welcome home Alina, welcome!" Wrapping a protective arm around her waist, he gazed with pride around the room, then poured her a full glass of the fine red wine that Irene had set out. Everyone raised their cups. He traced a finger along the edge of the gown. The style unusual, old fashioned, he mused.

Once they were all seated at the long board table, Carissa and Madam Trousdale started serving the hearty stew. Across the table, in the waxy haze between two fat candles, Lucas noticed Irene moping. He gestured Nikolas who got up and changed seats with Irene, so she could sit across from Lucas as they usually did. She cheered up immediately. And when Alina reached across the table and squeezed Irene's hand murmuring her gratitude, Irene dabbed her eyes.

With his arm around Alina's shoulders he leaned in and whispered, "The widow's houses are well lit tonight. And I can assure you it will continue to be." She peered up from under her brows with shining eyes that warmed him better than the wine. He didn't mention that the only house he'd left in the dark was that of her uncle.

While they devoured their food, no one spoke, but once the stew bowls were empty, Lucas rose to help Carissa serve the sweet cakes. She had made a great recovery since her encounter with Dugald, but with the excitement of Alina's arrival, and consuming most likely more wine than she ever did, a dark-eyed hollowness showed in her face. Nikolas engaged Alina in conversation regarding the business of ships coming and going from the harbour and the best days to purchase items when the ships with fresh wares arrived in port. As he spoke, Lucas watched Alina's reaction to Nikolas and could see that ships arriving in port appeared to be of keen interest to her. She was thinking about her trunks of course. And Lucas understood, as Alina did, that Nikolas spoke about everyday things to keep the conversation and mood light. There was no need to create unease or concern while enjoying the evening meal. The mind, like any other tool, should go idle at the end of the day.

A lazy, well-fed fatigue showed on all their faces. Ikarus, after finishing two servings of cake, accepted one to carry away and made his departure. With a marked gaze toward both Lucas and Nikolas he said, "I'll see you then."

Irene was telling Alina, "Sleep as late as you want. The workmen take early bread and most everyone is gone for the rest of the day. If you take your time coming down, you will never even notice that the boarders have had their meal and gone off to work. Lucas, rarely sees the boarders . . . do you my dear?"

Lucas' eyes sparkled, "Well . . .I can't say that I do, and for the most part I am satisfied with that." He gave Irene a warm embrace. "Thank you for a marvelous feast."

"It's my pleasure. All is well, now . . . yes?" She turned bright eyes from Lucas to Alina.

"Yes," Lucas said, releasing Irene, and going to Alina to offer her his hand as she rose from the table. "Shall we retire to the front room for a nightcap by the fire?"

"I must take my leave," Nikolas said, then added, "I'm seeing Madam Trousdale safely home."

Lucas blanched. "What?"

"I'll see her home. It's on my way, more or less."

Lucas shook his head. His eyes shot to the hourglass, half full, or half empty, it didn't seem to be moving, he narrowed his eyes and took a step forward to take a closer look, but stopped short as Alina leaned into him, peering up at his face. Nikolas had a bland expression. Lucas, mind spinning, wondered what he had been doing when this arrangement occurred. "Yes, fine. Quite thoughtful of you, Nik. Best to be sure everything is secure in the home of our friend, Madam Trousdale." He caught her eye, not difficult to do since she seemed to always have her gaze centered on him. "We are grateful for your help these past few days," he told her.

An inconspicuous tension evaporated from the room. The hourglass flowed. Get her home before that hourglass runs out, Lucas thought. As far as he knew, Nikolas had no knowledge of the golden jewelled box. But if he set foot in the fortuneteller's cottage, he would certainly notice it. When the door closed behind them, Irene and Carissa bid Lucas and Alina good night and went up together. Their haste to leave them alone amusingly awkward as they stumbled over each other to get up the stairs.

Alone at last, Lucas escorted Alina to a seat beside the fire. She offered a gracious smile and took her seat beside him, but her exhaustion showed. Since it wasn't possible to invite her to his bedchamber, Lucas took her hand in his. "Is everything to your liking in your room?"

"It's wonderful," she clasped her hands in front of her. "And warm too. I believe I will sleep soundly here in this house."

Lucas leaned forward, pressed his forehead gently against hers and caressed the back of her neck. "I am happy to hear that."

She sighed and snuggled her cheek against his neck.

"Do you awaken early or late?" he asked.

"I prefer late," she said with a yawn.

"As do I," he stroked her hair, twirled a curled lock in his hand. "In the morning, there is a business matter I must tend to. Will you be comfortable here, with Irene and Carissa, until I return?"

"I will." She sat up and her green eyes shone. "Does this matter have to do with me?"

Lucas gazed into her eyes and brushed his lips across each cheek. "From now on, everything has to do with you."

* * *

At her window overlooking the street, Irene watched Nikolas and Madam Trousdale dissipate in the amber haze. Perhaps Lucas would soften up to her more now that his friend showed an interest. The evening had gone very well. She found herself more pleased about the presence of Alina than she had imagined she would when the time came that Lucas brought a woman home. The young lady possessed a kind and sincere heart. With a shiver of bittersweet acceptance, she pulled her flannel sleep gown over her head and climbed into bed. Lying back with a staggered breath she snuggled into the serene warmth. But they were not yet safe. There was the matter of Dugald. She knew full well that the three men had been on more than a streetlamp lighting mission this evening. She must find a moment to speak with Lucas alone and insist he fill her in. It was beyond time to let him know about the key she took from Dugald's room. The one that she had slipped into her pocket the morning of their departure to Arcana. Which now, inexplicably, had disappeared. If only she had given it over to Madam Trousdale! She heard the soft footsteps of Lucas and Alina on the stairs. Their voices so low she couldn't discern a single word. She heard the click of the lock when Alina's door closed, and Lucas' door opened then closed. With everyone in their place, her dread dissipated. Lucas would resolve the key issue. She rolled over and fell asleep.

Chapter 12

Lucas slept soundly until a small red bird landed on the windowsill and pecked against the wood frame. He'd left the window partly open last night and the bird poked its head in, titled it left then right, watching with one eye at a time as Lucas got up and dressed in his work clothes. He remembered a dream about walking to the river with Alina's hand in his, her hair shining gloriously in the sunlight. Now that he had Alina with him his nightmares were over, he felt certain of it. His mother's trunk sat against the wall. He anticipated going through the contents once again, this time with Alina at his side. Before going downstairs, he slipped the necklace he'd taken from Marion at the Grande Inn into his pocket. It could be handy today and he wanted to rid himself of it as soon as possible.

The kitchen was empty except for a fresh platter with bread, honey, and cheese in the center of the long table. Carissa had managed to rise in time to perform her chores but was not about now. Perhaps she had returned to bed with a muddled head after the feasting and heavy wine consumption. Lucas poured a cup of strong tea from the cast iron kettle and enjoyed a few slices of bread with soft cheese. Before leaving the house, he sat down at Irene's writing desk, took a quill and inkpot from the drawer, and wrote the initial *L* on a slip of parchment. Silently unlocking Alina's door, he placed it on the bed table where she would see it upon opening her eyes. He longed to stroke her silken hair but feared awakening her from her pouty-cheeked slumber, her lips pursed like a child, her breath even and tender. Watching her with astonished pleasure, his breathing soon matched hers, soothing him to the point that his knees wobbled, he yearned to lie down beside her. Without even touching her, he could feel the pulse of her heart, could taste her ambrosial skin. Gazing at her threw him back to his childhood and the fleeting, contented peace that once filled his heart. Giving in to the desire to gently brush his fingers across her cheek, he whispered an oath to protect her beyond the end of time, and then silently backed out of the room.

As he walked to the harbour, his mind turned to the business of Alina's trunks. He fancied finding and returning them this very day. He pictured the pleasure on her face when she threw open the lids and rediscovered her treasured possessions. Once she had her belongings, the time would be ripe for his proposal of marriage. The sooner she moved into his bedchamber the more to his liking.

* * *

In a tiny room crammed with barrels and crates, Dugald fumbled in the dim light for the jug of water. He gulped, swallowed, and gulped again spitting some back into the jug. He cried out for help, as he had been doing since he'd regained his voice. Twice he'd heard a guttural shout for silence and once an angry banging on the door, but nobody had come inside. And then the door flew open and a boy walked in carrying a basket of bread and another jug of water. "Ah, at last . . . help . . .where am I?" Dugald wheezed.

"The harbour. Can't you hear the clanging of the ships bells?" The boy squinted and pinched his nose. "You need to bathe."

"Yes, I do, please . . ." Dugald pulled himself up with the help of one of the crates. A shadow filled the door and muttered something to the boy who scurried from the room. The door slammed shut, and the key turned in the lock. Dugald fell back on the bunched straw that was his bed, his skull aflame with pain, his thoughts gnawing through his resolve. The rat, he realized had made a valiant escape. If only I could be so brave to slam my head in the door and break my own neck. Vasil and Barrington won't find me here, if they even bother to come. They must think me dead. And soon I will be. I should never have come here. Barrington and Vasil, are wealthy trade merchants? I don't believe it. They trade in only lies and deceit! Leaning forward he splashed handfuls of water on his face. He stretched his legs and groaned. I will surely perish if I don't walk free soon.

At least, no one will ever notice my papers hidden at the Kempel House. Unless the place burns down, they're safe where I left then. If I get free, I will find someone to read them to me. I will not bring Lucas back to Arcana for her. I will kill him for treating me this way. He and his people will regret these things they've done to me. He hung his head, wiped his slimy face on the sleeve of his filthy shirt. His hand now wrapped in a clean bandage. He held it up: when did this happen, who did this for me? I who own nothing. My clothes aren't even mine. I was ignorant to believe she truly intended to reward me for bringing Lucas back. He is not so special. A legend she called him. Phhhttt. I don't remember him, or if he is that boy whose mother dropped dead in the flower fields. Who cares. I hate him and the cavalier, privileged life he leads. I believe we hated each other at first sight and that is good. Buoyed by his emotion, Dugald pushed the tattered blanket aside and struggled onto his knees. It's time to find a way out of here, he decided. Concerned that rats loitered nearby in the cluster of cargo, he searched for a weapon. There was a collection of barrels, one lay on its side with a band hanging loose. Crawling over to it, he rolled the heavy barrel, and the ring simply popped off the end, sheared somehow, only half of it remaining, a sharp half circle of steel. Good to kill rats or men. He shoved it behind him and devoured the bread before anything else could get to it.

When the bread was gone, his stomach still growled, struggling to his feet, he stumbled to the door and beat on it with his good hand, pressed his ear against the rough wood . . . silence, no footsteps, no shouting, no bells, not even a whisper of wind. When I get out, if . . . I will have my revenge on everyone in this city! He moaned and banged his forehead against the door until his ears rang and a trickle of blood slid down his cheek and dissolved in his tears.

* * *

Upon arriving at the harbour, Lucas went directly to the flats where Nikolas had a room. Normally he let himself in but remembering with a start that Nikolas and Trousdale had walked away together last night, he banged on the door.

"Go away."

Lucas flinched. His stomach churned with the uncomfortable prospect that Madam Trousdale had spent the night in there with Nikolas. He scratched his chin, paced up and down the narrow alley. Just as he started to walk away the door opened. Nikolas stood dressed and ready to go. Eyeing Lucas he said, "You brought me no bread?"

"Ahh, forgive me." Lucas chuckled. "I had other things on my mind this morning."

"I'm sure you did," Nikolas murmured. "How was the remainder of your evening?"

"Fine, all went well." Then noticing the mischief in Nikolas's eyes added with a scowl. "Alina is a lady, don't forget that."

"A lady indeed. I don't know how you missed that upon your first encounter."

Lucas chuckled. "I was blinded and dumbstruck."

When Nikolas stepped outside Lucas leaned in and perused the empty room.

"Is there something you need?"

"No." Lucas wiggled his eyebrows. "How goes it with the witch?"

Nikolas laughed out loud, slapped Lucas on the back. "I walked her home." His dark eyes flashing delight at Lucas' dismay. "Escorted her to her humble abode, nothing more." He motioned toward the warehouses. "He's over there."

"Did you notice anything in particular in her hut?"

Nikolas frowned, shook his head. "Typical eccentric woman things, hanging herbs . . .."

"Nothing else?"

"Nothing of interest if that's what you mean."

"It is what I mean. You saw nothing of value?" Lucas slowed his pace for Nik to lead since he didn't know where Dugald was among the rows of locked doors.

Nik turned a corner. "Nothing of value. Not that it would matter to us." He gazed at Lucas, "I took a good look. You've been there, you should know. This one." He stopped in front of a narrow iron door. Lowering his voice. "Dugald is in here. I had one of the girls clean up his hand when we brought him in, so he should still be alive."

"That's a good thing. I want to know why he was in Alina's house." Lucas' expression hardened.

Two burly, bearded, bald men came up the alleyway behind them. "Ah, Ragbone and Igmus," Nik remarked. The men stood on either side of Lucas and Nikolas who produced a full ring of keys from his belt and unlocked the door. It screeched slowly open. Nikolas stepped aside allowing Lucas to enter first.

Dugald was slumped on the floor his legs splayed out in front of him, the bandaged hand propped on a small crate, his head tilted sideways, his eyes closed, but he flinched, and Lucas knew he was alert and aware of their presence. "It will go easier if you just tell us everything you know. Who are you and why are you here? Don't bother to lie." Lucas stood over him, boots touching Dugald's extended leg. Nikolas stood beside him and the shipmen, solid as statues, behind them. The men stared down at Dugald.

He glared up at them with livid eyes washed in the glare of sunlight that had followed them in the door. "You have no right to hold me," he sneered.

The two friends grinned at each other. Lucas kicked at the dirt floor. "On the contrary, we have every right to do whatever we want with you."

"It's true," Nikolas said. "But we are growing tired of dragging your ratty ass around the city, so better for you to tell us why you are here in the City of Dreams."

"Why you came to my boarding house." Lucas with his hands on his hips stared down at Dugald who avoided his gaze. "And most of all why you followed . . . Al . . . the young lady! You laid your hideous hands on her!" Lucas shot a glare toward Nikolas as a warning, and with white knuckled fists grabbed Dugald by the front of the shirt and pulled him to his feet. Igmus and Ragbone stepped forward in unison with Nikolas, the three braced themselves like a wall behind Lucas, so when he cried out in pain and staggered backward, dropping Dugald in a heap, the three caught him. Blood spurted from a gash on his leg. Dugald scrambled to cover the metal band, but his bandaged hand got in the way and it tumbled to the ground. Ragbone swept it up and clobbered Dugald over the back of the head as he tried to crawl away. His face flumped to the floor.

"Bloody bastard!" Nikolas shouted and spat at Dugald before dropping to his knees to inspect Lucas' leg. "Lean on me." He put his shoulder under Lucas' shoulder. "Lock him up again," he said to his comrades pointing to the motionless Dugald. Nikolas shook his head. "It looks bad, my friend. Let's get you to the doctor."

Lucas, pale-faced and sweating stared at the gash that had torn through his trousers. "We don't have time for the doctor. Wake up the cur. We need answers!"

"The lout could use a doctor himself," Igmus said indicating a trickle of blood seeping through Dugald's dirty brown hair.

"I didn't mean to kill him," Ragbone said through tight lips.

Nikolas grabbed Dugald's good wrist. "He's not dead. This fellow has fortitude, I'll say that."

"Finish him. . . or what?" Ragbone stood over Dugald slapping the iron bar in his palm.

Everyone turned toward Lucas. "We have to wait for him to wake up. Let's take him to Trousdale's," he said to Nikolas.

"All right. We should disguise him in those flour sacks."

Ragbone tossed Dugald over his shoulder and strolled behind Lucas and Nikolas with Igmus jabbering about how much he enjoyed an excursion away from the harbour. "Let's stop for a moment, surely we are thirsty now."

"We can go by the doctor on the way as well," Nikolas said quietly to Lucas.

"I don't need a doctor."

"What about him? We need him alive, don't we?"

"It's too far. We can't pass through the city unnoticed."

"A drink then?" Igmus implored pointing. "There's an alehouse up ahead."

"Not carrying this bundle of ill begotten humanity," Lucas said. The ensemble continued but as they drew closer to the ale house, Lucas asked. "Do they serve whisky?"

"All day long," Igmus announced and stepped forward to open the hidden door.

Ragbone set his parcel down in an abandoned cart and followed them inside. The cart began to roll, nearly tipped on the cobbles. Dugald sat up, "Halt!" he called out in a raspy, spittle-filled voice. The four men turned in unison to gape at Dugald, his hair greasy spikes, his face smeared with dirt and blood, his eyes bubbling with tears. Each jaw dropped to hear him speak when they thought him knocked out.

"For the love of God, I am a human being! Don't leave me here waiting for slaughter like a banquet pig!"

Lucas and Nik stared at each other with stunned amusement. Igmus said to Lucas, "Spare a coin and I will buy the bottle."

Lucas tossed him a coin and said to Dugald, "Give us answers swine and I will elevate your position." He narrowed his eyes, looked Dugald up and down as if he were that dinner delicacy.

Dugald's red-rimmed eyes had dark gray hollows beneath them, his skin a dull yellow hinging on blue around his fingernails, lips cracked and white with threads of black. Lucas recoiled. Nothing about him resembled the vibrant and arrogant man who had appeared at the boarding house a few days ago. Glancing back at his companions, he saw Igmus come out of the ale house with a bottle in his hand. "Go back inside and get him a cup," Lucas ordered. Dugald could die, his fresh bandage was already beginning to seep. He didn't want to kill this man, not today. "Let's go, take that cart," he told Ragbone who, seeing the expression on Lucas' face immediately lifted the yoke. Lucas took a full cup from Igmus and held it to Dugald's mouth. He downed it in one gulp.

The men ran along the cobblestones, Dugald rattling in his perch like overthrown royalty, his purple cloak stained and torn—all following behind Lucas who led them through twisting narrow shortcuts toward Madam Trousdale's cottage. Twice he stopped and had Igmus refill Dugald's cup, the color rising in his cheeks from the whisky or exertion but not a drop spilled. Lucas stayed several paces ahead after that, making clear the roadway, and looking back to confirm that all followed, and Ragbone hadn't let the cart tip over. He turned, ran, and turned again, and then again, to be certain of what he saw; a huge rat was running alongside, keeping pace at the back of the pack. When the cottage was in sight, Lucas stopped, grabbed the nearly empty whisky bottle from Igmus, and took a long swig. The rat, sitting on its haunches, was nibbling scraps of garbage. Lucas shouted and pushed past them waving his arms at the rat. High above, poised on a stone wall twice as tall as Lucas, the gray cat leapt down and landed silently on its white paws. The rat darted away so fast that Lucas thought he had imagined it. "Did you see that?" he remarked to Nikolas.

"I've seen that cat before." Nikolas said.

"Me too. But that's the biggest rat I've ever seen!"

"I didn't see a rat," Nikolas patted Lucas on the back. "Let's get our prisoner, or patient as he may be, inside shall we?"

Lucas noticed that Igmus and Ragbone each had a firm hand on the whisky bottle, both more transfixed by the last drops than the creatures who shadowed them. But Dugald's eyes were as wide as supper plates and his entire body shook. Madam Trousdale swept like a wave out her door in a tangle of colorful hair and skirts. Nikolas greeted her warmly, momentarily clasping her hand. She glanced at Lucas then to Dugald, so Lucas said. "We need him alive, for all reasons but also to explain why he is here and following Alina. He may know of the two trunks."

Madam Trousdale gathered her skirts and ushered the men to the side of the cottage where a small angular structure made of tree limbs and furs stood. "Unload him here."

Surprised again, Lucas hesitated, having not noticed the lean-to on his previous visits. Shaking his head, he left them to situate Dugald and went back to the cottage seeking the comfort of the gold-jewelled box. It was not in its place. His shoulders fell, he peered around the cramped room. He wasn't surprised to find it missing since the day had gone in complete disorder. When he turned, Nikolas and Madam Trousdale were standing side by side staring at him. Lucas avoided their eyes.

"Let me see your leg," Madam Trousdale said coming toward him with a small knife in her hand.

"Never mind me. There's no time for that. We must save Dugald."

"Your men are bandaging his head wound and the hand. I'll bring him tea and herbs, along with meat–I can see that you haven't thought of that lately–but I'd rather touch you before I touch him."

"He had stew the other night," Nik said. "I got it from the Duck."

"With meat?"

"Maybe, it was chunky."

"Is he contagious?" Lucas asked.

Nikolas stood alongside her pumping his head up and down, pointing to Lucas' left leg. "Go on show her."

"If he was contagious, we'd all be ill or dead now," she said reaching for his leg.

Lucas harrumphed and pulled his pant leg up. A thin red line of dried blood marked his calf. He sat back. Madam Trousdale knelt in front of him, dabbed at the gash with a cloth. The blood flaked off, barely leaving a mark where the wound had been.

"How can that be!" Nikolas rushed over and grabbed Lucas' leg. "He had a gaping gash from a strip of metal!" Fumbling for Lucas' other leg and yanking the pant up, Nikolas stared at Lucas, then turned to Trousdale in shocked disbelief. Lucas sat back in his chair and beamed.

Madam Trousdale gazed evenly at Lucas, pursed her lips, wiped her hands together. "All right then, it seems all is well here."

Lucas couldn't help but wonder what she had done with the gold-jewelled box. The hourglass, empty since he'd arrived at the cottage, filled itself with a flip. Lucas closed his eyes, leaned his head back. "May I please have some of your marvelous tea before you tend to Dugald?"

Nikolas sauntered over to the table and sat down next to Lucas. Madam Trousdale scooped ladles of Linden tea into cups that she set in front of the two men. "No need to worry," she said.

"You're not going to explain how that gash disappeared?" Nikolas asked gulping his tea.

Lucas raised his palms, "I would explain if I knew . . . it happens . . . I don't know why."

"We've been friends for many years. I've never witnessed this about you!"

"That's because there is nothing to witness. I heal myself."

"All the time?" Nikolas knitted his brows leaned forward and took hold of Lucas' leg again. Satisfied with that one, he scrutinized the other.

Lucas pushed his hand away. "I appreciate the attention, but I think I will save the caressing for Alina."

Nikolas folded his hands in his lap. "Come now, Lucas, I should like to know this trick. Tell me how you manage to heal from gaping wounds all the time."

"Well," Lucas drained his cup, "it doesn't happen all the time, that I have a gushing gash. In fact, I rarely get injured. You would have noticed by now if I did. This is only the second time that I have sustained such a deep wound, and it has healed as the first." His eyes glazed over as he peered into the distance. "The everyday scrapes and bruises fade before my eyes. I had never given it much thought until Bernard explained to me how he found me dead in the flower field next to my mother. And then I showed up at the farm."

"Ah yes, the giant man who lives with the woman who didn't like your mother, maybe killed her . . . Marion. Found you dead in the flower field he said? It appears you have left out the most important detail of your trip to Arcana."

Trousdale stood beside the fire, arms crossed over the hourglass, the lion pendant snarling and her eyes flickering like flames.

"There hasn't been time, Nik. But here, I have this in payment." He pulled Marion's silver pendant from his pocket. "The woman, I barely noticed her as a child, but apparently, she had a fondness for me and wanted me for her own, even going so far as to rejecting her own child and delegating him to the bunkhouse for several years. There is something wrong about her. I can feel it."

"And you've paid yourself," Nikolas applauded, "I wish you would teach me how to patch myself up after a brawl, or murder even, so it seems . . ." he drummed his fingers on the table.

Lucas twisted his lips, rolled his eyes, and smirked.

"Why are you laughing?"

"I think you just have to embrace the folly of mortality. If I had answers, I would not be sitting here. I would be dallying with Alina on the riverbank."

Nik laughed, shook his head, turned his palms out. "Not one word of wisdom for an old friend?"

"Maybe it's a force of will." He leaned close to Nik and whispered, "I believe, possibly triggered by my mother's sudden death, I refused to succumb. In that last flash of beauty and innocent life, I must have been able to choose, and I chose to return."

Nikolas knitted his brows.

"Make the choice to live, and once you have done that, you can walk through the chaos. Let it drain like rain from your cloak. Eventually, nothing matters. I intended to save my mother. But I could not."

A pensive smile turned up the corners of Nikolas' mouth. "Hmmm . . ."

At the door, the sound of water pouring into the collection barrel outside the door. Ragbone peeked in. Madam Trousdale swept outside to order Ragbone and Igmus to haul more water from the nearby well.

"He's ready to talk to you now," she announced from the doorway.

Both men rose and headed to the door. As they followed Madam Trousdale to the lean-to, her hair spiraling like a wind ravaged tree changed from black to blue and back to black again. She turned, the hourglass empty, and spoke in an ominous voice, "Don't lose your head!"

"What?" Nikolas stopped and stared.

Lucas pressed his lips together and pushed past her. She grabbed his forearm. "I'm talking to you. Don't lose your head. That is a wound that cannot heal."

Lucas gaped and recoiled. "My God, woman, what a thing to say!" He reddened in a flush of nerves, looked to Nik. But a gray fear had frozen his friend's face. Lucas' stomach churned, and his blood pounded in his ears, his head aching for the first time since he'd found Alina. Trousdale was squeezing his arm and he thought the rushing blood was the result of her iron grip. But in a moment her hair settled down in a black sheen and her eyes were steady and calm. The hourglass flipped three times before it sat full and unmoving.

Sitting up on a makeshift bed layered with blankets, Dugald with a fresh bandage on his hand and one around his head, slurped a meaty broth. The midday meal, it reminded Lucas of the late hour, he must get back to Alina as soon as possible.

"If you want to live, tell us why you are here," he demanded.

Dugald swallowed and gulped, then said with eyes diverted. "I came to the City of Dreams to find someone . . . so that I may acquire lands that are due me."

"Find who? Land where?" Lucas stood at Dugald's side glaring down at him.

"In the country, in Arcana." Dugald's gaze flickered toward Lucas.

Lucas froze for a single beat, then insisted. "Exactly where in Arcana?"

"The farm of Marion and Wentworth Bodden."

Silence sucked the air from the makeshift hut.

"Are you their offspring?" Why didn't Bernard mention this Dugald? Lucas pressed two fingers between his brows. Bernard mentioned Marion had a brother, but this couldn't be him.

"Marion is my aunt. Her brother was my father."

"And your mother?"

Dugald reddened with anger or embarrassment, Lucas couldn't discern.

"Your father failed to marry her?"

"Yes, he refused to marry her. But nonetheless I am the rightful heir. My mother died in childbirth."

"With you."

Dugald stared at his bandaged hand, "Yes, with me."

"So, you never met her."

Dugald shook his head.

"Hmmm, good for her," Nikolas said, coming to stand next to Lucas. "Why did you choose to stay at the Kempel Boarding House?"

"And why did you pursue the young lady?" Lucas growled.

"Listen gentlemen, there are many decisions that I regret, now." Dugald rolled his eyes backward, swiped his good hand across his forehead that beaded with moisture.

Lucas glared at him, glanced around at his colleagues, scratching his chin. "It is the nature of life to swallow regret as we go. Spit it out, you'll feel better."

Nikolas and Trousdale stood shoulder to shoulder. Trousdale had replaced her bored expression with one of encouragement. "What do you know of the girl?" Madam Trousdale asked flashing a settling look at Lucas.

Dugald coughed into his hands, checked his bandage for spittle, but it remained clean. He swallowed several times then began to speak in a resigned tone. "Her uncle and his colleague duped me. I encountered them at the Duck Tavern on my first night here." He gazed at them with imploring eyes. "They talked me into helping them, for a price, to retrieve some property that had been misplaced. Two trunks, in a harbour locker. I needed the extra money. I'm tired of being poor when everyone around me enjoys more. They offered a generous sum." He opened and closed his eyes awaiting comment from his audience, but receiving none, continued. "After imbibing me with much whisky and ale . . . I agreed."

"Whisky and ale together?" Lucas scoffed.

"One of those regrettable decisions," Dugald said.

"Why didn't they just retrieve the trunks themselves? What did they need you for?"

"They can't show their faces at the harbour, it seems. They gave me papers to present to the harbour master."

Lucas and Nik gazed at each other.

Dugald patted his bandaged hand. He coughed uncontrollably for several seconds. His color drained and Madam Trousdale stepped forward with a fresh cup of aromatic tea.

"What do the papers say?" Lucas asked.

Dugald took a long, slow sip. "I don't know. I can't read," he whimpered, spilling the tea.

"You haven't said how you came to stay at the boarding house," Nikolas argued.

"After meeting Vasil and Barrington at the Duck Tavern, I thought it best to change lodging. I didn't want them to know where to find me. The apothecary suggested the Kempel Boarding House," he peeked at Lucas before averting his eyes to the far left of the room as if something was approaching from there. "If they couldn't retrieve their own property, I doubted I could either. And sure enough, the harbour master refused to allow access to the trunks. Vasil and Barrington will come after me again. They have given me a portion of the payment. How did you find me? Do they know I'm alive?"

"They left you for dead. But that's not why you came to the City of Dreams. Who did you come here to find, your father?"

"Nobody . . ."

Lucas sneered. "You just said you came here to find someone!"

"Oh . . . yes . . . ah, um . . . I came to find a wife."

"Ha!" Lucas guffawed, and the others chuckled. Dugald sniffled and hung his head.

Lucas gestured to Trousdale to take his cup away. "Tell us the truth or perish by your own stubbornness. Fortunate, you don't have plague. Spider bite I suppose after all."

Nikolas and Madam Trousdale both had their arms crossed as they glowered at Dugald. Igmus and Ragbone continued to block the door, even though Dugald wouldn't be trying to escape any time soon.

"You certainly were not offered land to come here and find a wife. Are you looking for your father?"

"Yes, my father."

"What's his name?"

"Er . . . his name is Dugald Tendrick."

"The same as you, then."

"Yes, sure. That's right."

"You lie," Madam Trousdale hissed.

Lucas clenched his jaw and kicked the pile of straw and furs where Dugald huddled. "I will find out who you came to my city to find. Now, what else can you tell us about the young lady's uncle and her trunks?"

"I saw her roaming the streets alone and thought she might be of help in getting my due. I swear I wouldn't have hurt her. I only wanted to plead for my money and get out of here alive. Vasil is a vicious, evil man. He will take her possessions and kill her like he did her father. There is something of immense value in her trunks."

"How do you know this?"

"They spoke freely the night we first met, when I was drunk, thinking I could understand naught. I got away for several days. But Barrington found me at the Duck, and they dragged me to Vasil's house." Dugald sighed casting plaintive eyes at his current captors. "That's all I remember. I just want to go home."

"You know where these trunks are." Lucas stated.

Dugald let his head fall back on the lumpy straw pillow. "Will you help me regain my own property if I tell you?"

"No, we will not promise you anything. You have only the choice to tell us," Lucas put his hands on his hips, "and hurry up about it. The day grows old!"

Dugald raised his bandaged hand, let it fall to his lap. "Something for the pain?"

All eyes turned to Madam Trousdale. She pulled a pouch of herbs from the waistband of her layered skirt and held it in front of Dugald, dangling it just out of his reach. "This will dull the pain and help you sleep. But first you must tell these gentlemen what they want to know."

Lucas took his place beside Madam Trousdale. "Make it easy on yourself."

Dugald rolled his head from one side to the other and eyed Lucas warily. "Will you let me go? I am an innocent soul. I meant no harm . . ." he coughed, "to anyone, please. I no longer desire to find anyone in this place. Let me go. I only want to get away from here."

"Yes, yes. Do tell us Dugald. Of course, we will let you go. We have no use for you other than discovering the trunks. As soon as you recover, I, and Nikolas, will personally escort you out of the City of Dreams." He flashed an encouraging smile. The pungent packet of herbs filled the room with an invigorating aroma. Eucalyptus and something more, Lucas couldn't be sure, but he enjoyed the feeling it gave him and wondered why he had so quickly misjudged Madam Trousdale upon their first meeting. As if she could read his thoughts, she squeezed his forearm, flashing a face that was familiar and encouraging. She poured a circle of herbs into a wooden bowl and crushed them with her long fingers.

Lucas pulled a three-legged stool alongside Dugald's bed. "Your remedy awaits your confession."

"Those men will hurt me and all of you. They will do anything to get those trunks. But I am the only one who knows where they are."

"Leave them to us," Igmus said with a fist to his palm and a menacing sneer.

Trousdale handed Dugald a small cup. He gulped and held it out for more.

"Speak now," Lucas said intercepting the cup.

Nikolas paced, then stepped outside to stand in the doorway. Lucas knew that Nikolas, like himself, didn't enjoy confined spaces. The lean-to was cramped and the roof was low. Not only that, he wanted to get the information out of Dugald and get back to the boarding house. He had no idea what Alina must be thinking or doing right now. Of course, Irene would take loving care of her. But he had just found her, he loathed to let her out of his sight for awfully long. "Speak!"

Dugald trembled. "The harbour," a glance to Nikolas. "Not far from where you put me. There are a series of very narrow passages that lead to a tall iron door. Those young hoodlums know about it. The cargo from the ship *Le Peresi* is in there. That is where you will find her trunks. But you must get past that Mr. Merson first. He wouldn't speak to me."

Lucas pursed his lips and narrowed his eyes toward Nikolas who gave a slight nod. Stepping closer to Dugald, with his forearm bent across his mouth and nose, Lucas scrutinized, "How do you know? Are you certain?"

"Yes, I'm more certain than Vasil and Barrington are. I saw that door with my own eyes. And your harbour master is a nasty villain!" he barked at Nikolas who burst out laughing.

"I know that," he derided as he followed Lucas out the door.

"Wait! What about me?"

Ignoring Dugald now, they strode in long determined strides toward the harbour. Igmus and Ragbone stumbled heavy-footed behind them, all surging through the shaded gray streets occasionally stabbed by slanting sunlight that sizzled foggy puddles from the concave cobblestones.

"You know where this door is," Lucas said to Nik as the sails of a tall ship came into view.

"There are many such doors. Mr. Merson will show us the one."

Lucas cocked his head and raised an eyebrow.

"One way or the other," Nik said.

Madam Trousdale came running up behind them, her voice preceding her, hair streaming behind as if she were riding an invisible horse. "He says, he had a key. It was hidden in his room at the boarding house, but it disappeared."

"He has a key!"

"For the warehouse door. He had it. But it's gone."

"Gone where?"

"He doesn't know but . . .."

"Very well." Lucas turned on his heel walking even faster now. When Nik didn't follow, he turned to see the two of them with their heads together, whispering. He gave her shoulder a squeeze then hurried to catch up with Lucas. When his friend came up beside him, Lucas fluttered his eyelids. "No time for romance, Nik."

Nikolas put his hand on the back of Lucas' neck as they walked. "She thinks she knows where the key is."

"Where?"

"She won't say but she's gone to fetch it."

"Is that so?" Lucas shook his head. "What's she going to do, pull it out of her bubbling cauldron?"

At the harbour, they went directly to Mr. Merson's office. His shiny head bobbed behind a tall desk. "Busy, go away," he grumbled when the door creaked open. Nikolas demanded he take them to the storage locker for the ship *Le Peresi*. The man laughed and waved them off. "You know better than that, Nik," he admonished.

Lucas stepped forward and leaned over the desk. He pulled Marion's silver pendant from his pocket and dangled it over the desk. The harbour master's eyes sparkled as his legs gathered under him.

Although he knew the city well, Lucas spent little time at the harbour other than to seek out Nikolas. The smell of fish and filthy men combined with the rolling of the waves that slapped over the soggy wharf boards, often wetting his boots, sickened him. He preferred the river, securely surrounded by its banks of rich dark land. He kept his eyes on Nik who strolled along behind Mr. Merson with his hands in his pockets. He stole a look at Lucas from time to time, assuring him that he recognized the route, that it was familiar to him. Igmus and Ragbone lumbered behind complaining about hunger, thirst, and payment for their time. Lucas silently agreed, this was not how he wanted to spend his day. But he imagined the joy on Alina's lovely face when she received her trunks. Key or not, he would get through that door. The path grew narrower as the warehouse walls grew thicker. Nik came alongside him and explained. "This is part of the old harbour where the wealthiest merchants store their goods. These stone walls are thick as six men!"

They stood in front of a stack of broken crates that poorly hid a tall wooden door with massive steel bands, huge hinges, and a lock almost as large as a fisherman's anchor. It glimmered in the sunshine that poured directly down on the top of their heads. Lucas tossed his cloak back and loosened his shirt laces. "How do we open it?"

"That's your problem to solve," Mr. Merson said, holding out his hand. Lucas pulled Marion's pendant from his pocket and dropped it in the egg-shaped man's outstretched hand. He clutched it with white knuckles, then squealed in gap-toothed delight before darting back the way they came.

Lucas swiped his hands together. Nikolas patted him on the back, "Well done. Now let's get this lock off here."

Ragbone stepped forward. He was still carrying the iron band that had cut Lucas' leg. He swung it over his head then down on the lock. Sparks shot out, but the lock scarcely noticed the blow. Lucas groaned, his shoulders slumped, he ran his fingers through his hair and swore. Ragbone swung again and again. Igmus stepped up, pulling a thick axe from beneath several layers of cloth hanging from his leather belt. Lucas stepped out of the way. Nikolas scratched at three days of stubble and shook his head doubtfully. A low whistling sound resonated between the blows. After several minutes, Lucas walked away to find something else to aid them in destroying the lock. He heard the whistle tone again and this time realized it was Ikarus. Lucas looked back toward Nik who had heard as well, the two headed in the direction of the whistle. Behind them, the reverberations of the axe and iron bar as Igmus and Ragbone took their turns on the lock.

Just past the third turn, Ikarus came into sight. He was pale and panting, pointing behind him toward something. The men rushed forward to see Irene and Madam Trousdale picking their path through the warehouse rows. Irene's eyes were wide, she held her cloak firmly over her nose and mouth. Lucas ran, his heart thudding in his ears. Why would they come? Alina. Something must have happened to Alina! There was no other explanation. Trousdale knew better than to bring Irene to such a place. Sweat beaded on his forehead, at the back of his neck and under his hair. His throat constricted; his head pierced with pain.

He grabbed Irene by the shoulders. Before he could speak, she blurted. "I'm sorry Lucas. I should have told you sooner." She wiped her nose with the back of her hand.

"What? Told me what?"

She wrung her hands together and stuttered, then tears sprung from her eyes.

Lucas turned to Ikarus who explained, "She said she had to find you. Alina and Carissa are safe inside," he added as if he could read Lucas' mind. "And we encountered Madam Trousdale who told us you were at the harbour."

Lucas took Irene by the elbow and walked her away from the others. "What is the matter, my dear Irene?"

She leaned forward and whispered, "The key. I have the key . . ." hanging her head she whimpered.

"You have the key to this lock?" His eyes lit up. He tossed his head back and brushed his matted hair off his neck while keeping one arm around her.

"I believe so," she whispered.

"Good for you! How did you acquire it? It doesn't matter! Come follow me." He pulled her toward the warehouse.

She held fast to her spot on the uneven street. "I don't have it with me."

"Oh, for heaven's sake. Say now dear woman, why did you come all this way and not bring the key?" He scowled at Trousdale as if this were all her fault.

"I . . . I had the key. But I lost it," Irene muttered.

Nikolas groaned. Ikarus hung his head and looked away. He began to edge away from the group having done his duty by finding Lucas for them. But a scowl from Lucas stopped him.

Irene tried to pull away from Lucas. "You are angry with me now."

He let go of her shoulder. "I'm not angry, Irene. Please just tell me what happened to the key."

She winced, keeping her eyes on the ground. "I snuck into Dugald's room before the trip to Arcana and found a key hidden under his pillow. So, I took it." She twisted her mouth. "I was going to show you but . . . now I don't know where it is. I think I left it at the Grande Inn. That's where I last had it. I had placed some items in the little chest of drawers in my room. My hose and corset, my hairbrush . . ."

"All right then. We will discuss later the danger of going through Dugald's room. But I'm certain it wasn't the first time you've done a thing like that," he gave Irene a reassuring hug. "Let's go. I will show you the lock and you can tell us if you think the key you found will fit into it."

He took Irene by the hand and headed back to the huge locked door escorted by the clanging tones of Igmus and Ragbone's attempts at destruction. Lucas said, "The entire harbour will come running if they keep that up."

Nikolas flashed Lucas an exasperated expression and hurried after him. Trousdale followed Nik. "Hmmph, that woman is so strange. Is she actually in pursuit of my friend?"

"Appears so," Irene mused.

Lucas hurried practically pulling Irene over the cobbles. "Carissa is with Alina?"

"Yes, Carissa is. She's fine. She was still sleeping but I left a lovely meal of my delicious jam, bread, and tea. Don't worry, Lucas. Carissa swept out the courtyard. She set out a stack of books for the two of them to enjoy together. Yesterday, Alina mentioned she enjoys poetry."

"Is that so?" Relieved yet annoyed, Lucas tried to slow his pace as Irene struggled to keep up with him.

The pounding had already stopped when they got there. Madam Trousdale sauntered behind Nikolas, then stood off to the side combing her long black hair with the claw that she wore around her neck. The hourglass was half full and moving at what appeared to be a relaxed pace. Warmed by the sight of it, like the presence of an old friend, Lucas led Irene to the giant door. "Examine the lock where the key fits in. Take your time."

Igmus and Ragbone stood back and pouted, they had made no progress but enjoyed attacking the lock. They threw shifty-eyed looks at Lucas who retrieved a handful of coins from his pocket and dumped some into each of their calloused hands. In a muffled voice he stated, "I better not hear any word around the city about the events of today."

"No sir, no. We have forgotten this day already." They bounced off each other as they scrambled off.

Turning to Madam Trousdale, he growled, "And you, what are you still doing here? Who is guarding Dugald?"

"The tribe," she snipped. "I went to fetch Irene and the key but Ikarus was already bringing her. I didn't realize she'd lost it."

"You're helpful. I see that." Lucas knitted his brows, knowing that, 'the tribe' meant those who occupied the misshapen cottages. A band of thieves, liars, scoundrels, and miscreants. Yet loyal, with great ferocity, to their neighbors.

"What do you think, Irene? Will that key fit?"

"It's a spring barb. The wrong key inserted in there will not come out. If it's the wrong key, this lock will never come off this door." Nikolas announced in a dour voice. Madam Trousdale edged nearer him. Lucas studied his friend's face, but it revealed nothing. Lucas however suppressed a snicker.

Irene took the bronze, oval-shaped lock in both her hands, it bore the engraved snarling face of an unknown creature. The shackle was nearly as thick as her hand.

Irene let the lock go with a resounding ring. "I think so. But how can I be sure?" She wrung her hands then reached for Lucas. "Firstly, we have to find the key and . . ." she bit her lower lip. "well, then we can see how lock and key fit together."

"Agreed," Lucas said. "But beforehand we must place a guard at this door." As he began tossing the crates into a tall heap, he continued. "I will ride to the Grande Inn tonight. I need a strong steed, Nik. In fact, I need two. Alina will accompany me. Ikarus, stay right here for now. Madam Trousdale go home and get two of your tribe. Send them back here to relieve Ikarus and do so immediately." He shot a worried glance at Ikarus, then retrieved the iron band that Igmus had abandoned and handed it to him. "It will only be a short while."

Nikolas and Trousdale clasped hands and turning together dashed into the harbour maze. "Horses and guards!" Lucas shouted after them.

Ikarus shuffled from one foot to another. Rolling his eyes sheepishly at Lucas he moaned, "How long will it take for Madam Trousdale's guards to come back?"

"Tsk." Lucas shook his head. "Within the hour at most. Be strong Ik." he squeezed his shoulder. "No one will come here without a key. And I'm fairly sure we have the only one."

"Had." Irene muttered.

"Let's go back to the boarding house. This is too much for you to be involved with, Irene." He cupped her elbow in his palm and glancing back at pale-faced Ikarus said, "Stand your ground, boy. That's how you become a man." Ikarus rolled his eyes and hung his head. Lucas reached into his pocket, pulled out a few coins that he tossed to him. "For the tavern when your duty is done."

Lucas could barely walk slowly enough to accommodate Irene. When the boarding house finally came into view, he let go of her arm and bounded ahead, flung open the door, and called for Carissa. He expected she would dash straight out the door and help Irene, but she didn't appear at all, so Lucas rushed back to Irene and swept her up in his arms and carried her, braced against his chest even though she panted and shouted that he set her down. Carissa came through as they crossed the threshold. "Tea, please," Lucas said, "where is Alina?"

"I am here."

And there, in the center of the parlour, stood Alina, regal and stunning in a high-waisted blue dress with a long yellow bow along her left side. Her amber hair hanging loose. Her pale neck adorned by her ruby pendant. Deftly dodging a footstool, Lucas rushed forward grasped both her hands and peered into her wide green eyes. "Pardon my absence, dear Alina. How did you spend your morning?"

She giggled and held out her skirts. "I slept. And then Carissa and I read books and after that we played like children trying on clothes. I have few to offer, but she was kind enough to share." He pulled her toward him and to his delight she wrapped her arms around his waist and leaned her head against his chest.

Carissa chuckled. "Yes, we had such fun, we barely missed you! The stew is ready. Shall we?" She scurried to the kitchen with Irene close behind her exclaiming how famished she was.

Lucas didn't move until Alina untangled herself from their embrace. In answer to the hopeful question in her eyes he said, "We know the location of your trunks. They are quite secure."

"Ah!" she gazed up at him with such an expression of trust that Lucas felt his face flush.

"They are so secure now, that we cannot yet retrieve them. But neither can anyone else. I believe there is only one key." Placing a kiss upon her cheek, he added, "And we will recover it right away. You will have your possessions back very soon."

"That's wonderful news! Thank you, Lucas," she beamed.

He brushed her cheek with his lips, hoping his words were true. Offering his arm, he felt that no time at all had passed since he left the boarding house that morning. As they joined the others in the kitchen, he wished this day, and every day, could just end here in the company of these three light-hearted women, a satisfying meal, and a rest by the fire.

Chapter 13

They sat at one end of the long table and enjoyed a stew of onions, potatoes, carrots, green beans, and sweet peas. Carissa passed the wine jug and Lucas filled their cups without a thought of riding out to Arcana on the horses that Nik should be bringing over any minute, or Alina's inaccessible trunks, or Dugald flailing in his sickbed in Madam Trousdale's lean-to. He held Alina's left hand in his right and still managed to eat with gusto. She leaned into him every time she took a sip of wine, so once her cup was empty, he filled it again. Irene held out her cup as well, smiling with shining contented eyes. Her worries diminished now that she had revealed her secret regarding Dugald's key. None of these things mattered in the glow of the tallow candles that always burned in the dark low-beamed corners of the meticulously organized kitchen. The women as relaxed together as sisters, spoke softly about nothing more important than the contents of the incredibly delicious stew. For now, the world could wait. A pleasant indifference captivated them. Outside the open window beyond the garden wall, a flute player had planted himself. Soft lyrical notes drifted around them. Flame shadows illuminated the hearth, the stew pot bubbled and splattered onto hissing logs. Once his hunger abated, Lucas leaned back, stretched his arm over Alina's shoulders, letting his fingers dance along the curve of her cool neck. Her hair cascaded down the length of his forearm. The women continued to sip wine and nibble crisp bread. These moments could last a lifetime. Their hushed corner of obscurity blurred them from outside intrusion until a clattering of hooves on cobbles banished the moment. Lucas groaned as he squeezed Alina's shoulder and got up. "There is business to settle, lovely. We shall travel to the country together. Would you like that?"

"Yes. I would like that. I love the country," she marveled.

Lucas smiled and leaned down to kiss her cheek. "There is much we have to learn about each other."

"And plenty of time to do so," Irene said pushing herself up from the table. "Nik will be hungry."

"I am hungry as well," Ikarus said entering the kitchen first.

"Of course." Irene headed for the hearth, wooden ladle in hand.

Nikolas peered around the cozy kitchen. "What have I missed?" He reached for the wine jug and plopped down on the other side of Alina. Ikarus sat across and reached for the bread basket.

"How went it all?" Lucas asked.

"Well, all went very well. Dugald is passed out . . . er, I mean resting comfortably." He observed the women, but none seemed to mind his words. "Brigit has sent three of her most accomplished guards to the door."

"More like Viking warriors," Ik mumbled.

"What?" Lucas inclined his head.

"More like giant Vikings, all hairy and fierce, no teeth, but lots of muscles and scars." Ik said with true fear in his voice. "They make Igmus and Ragbone look like pixies."

"Nothing and nobody can get to those trunks," Nik agreed, giving Alina a quick squeeze around the waist, and catching Lucas' eye with a teasing sparkle.

"Good. Well done, my friends. But what I want to know is, who is Brigit?" Now Lucas returned the same teasing gaze to Nik.

Irene harrumphed but remained silent as she cast pleased glances between Lucas and Nikolas. The table silently awaited Nik's response. Blushing, and taking a long draught from his goblet, he spoke with the cup to his mouth. "Brigit is the given name of Madam Trousdale."

"Ha!" Lucas slapped the table and Alina jumped. He patted her hand. "Pardon me Alina, but it seems our Nikolas here has been keeping secrets."

"It's no secret," Nik said holding out his empty goblet for anyone to fill. Carissa obliged.

"Well then, do tell all." Lucas insisted. Irene giggled, Alina and Carissa followed her lead.

Nikolas readjusted himself on the bench. "You should know, young lady that this man is nothing but trouble."

Alina covered her mouth and laughed. She held out her goblet and Lucas quickly filled it.

"The horses are in the stable and can wait until morning for the journey to the country." Nikolas said.

"Excellent point," Lucas agreed. "The day grows too late. And I must make my rounds tonight. He levelled his gaze at Nikolas who lifted his shoulders in agreement. Ikarus shoved food into his mouth, ignoring the conversation. "But don't try to distract us! What is the nature of your relationship with Madam Trous . . . excuse me, Brigit?"

"Use your imagination old friend," Now it was Nik's chance to laugh. "But I'm sure not even you can imagine . . ."

Blushing, Irene set bowls in front of Nik and Ik. "It's romantic. We understand." She glared at Lucas. "No more need be said."

The two men regarded each other. "Well, I must say, you took me by surprise, Nik."

"You have been distracted."

"I have." He nestled his cheek against Alina's hair.

"The aroma of that plum pie is distracting me right now," Nik said pointing to the sideboard.

"Finish your stew first!" Carissa got up to serve.

Once they finished their pie, Lucas rose and helped Alina to her feet. "Let's go up and prepare for the trip tomorrow."

They entered Lucas' room where a welcoming fire burned. The bathtub was full. "Would you like to bathe?"

"I already have," she murmured.

"You have, here?"

"Yes," she bit her lip. "I hope you don't mind."

"Not at all! I am delighted. I usually wait until after work, but I will enjoy this water that is still warm from your body."

She blushed. "Tis the fire that's kept it warm."

He cupped her chin in his hand. "Perhaps, you would enjoy going through my mother's trunk. Maybe there is something you would like to bring along on the trip."

Wide-eyed, she smiled at the trunk. "That will be all right with you?"

"Yes, absolutely. There is no one better to go through it than you."

She went to the corner where the trunk sat next to a rose-colored needlepoint chair.

"I'll just slip into the bath then" he said.

When she didn't answer but perched on the edge of the chair and opened the lid of the trunk, Lucas unbuttoned his white shirt and tossed it onto the bed. The black lace veil fluttered into his hand. The movement caught her attention. Turning toward him, her dark green eyes sparkled with playful delight. Their eyes held in deep awareness of each other. Wind rattled the window, logs tumbled. Lucas and Alina held each other's breath, locked in a heart burning trance. Long moments passed before he crossed the room, pulled her up into his arms, felt her soft hair and warm breath on his chest. Her head rose and fell to the beat of his thundering heart. She spread her palm over his scar, where he carried the veil. "Now you can remember my touch here," she whispered.

He closed his eyes and buried his face in her hair. If Madam Trousdale's hour glass was in the room, it would be absolutely still. He lost all sense of his surroundings, the room, the house, sounds from the street went mute, his body so calm he knew not whether they were standing or lying down. By the time, the window light shifted, her hand had grown cold and he clutched her in fear that this moment had lapsed into a dream, but she was real, peering up at him. He rubbed her hands between his. "The fire," he murmured.

"Yes," she hugged him close running her hands along his spine before taking a step to the chair where she sat and leaned over the trunk, her hair falling across her face. He stoked the fire, added three more logs.

Lucas loosened his belt and let his trousers fall to the floor. The tub was steamy. He leaned back in delight and watched Alina carefully lift his mother's red and black gown from the trunk. She looked over at him, her eyes alight.

"That suits you."

She rose and held it against herself. "It's magnificent! When did your mother wear it?"

"I don't even know." Lucas leaned forward and splashed water over his head, "Why don't you try it on?"

She bit her lower lip. "I don't know. It's so pristine and special . . ."

"And that is why it's perfect for you." He leaned back and closed his eyes. "Go ahead, let me know when you're ready." He heard the rustling as she removed the dress Carissa had lent her and pictured Alina gathering herself into his mother's dress. "May I assist?"

"No! I can manage."

After several minutes, she sighed. "I cannot lace the back, but it fits me."

His eyes flew open. She stood between the chair and the tub close enough that if he wanted to, he could leap up, grab her and pull her into the tub. But the dress stopped any thought of that. It held her form as if tailored for her body. The red satin panels fell in shimmering shades to the floor. The black trim enhancement was stunning, adding alluring curves to the dress. Her pale skin shimmered in the firelight and the ruby pendant perfectly matched the red in the dress. Lucas braced his hands on the edge of the tub and pushed himself up and stepped out. Alina exhaled and turned away revealing the back, left open all the way down to her spine. His wet hand found her warm skin and she shivered at his touch. He leaned close to her ear and whispered, "I would offer to lace you up, but I prefer it this way." His fingers reached around to her throat and he gently turned her toward him. A linen towel around his waist protected the dress. He leaned forward to place a deep kiss upon her lips. She grasped his shoulders returning the kiss. "Let's remove it now," he said, gazing into her eyes. She did not protest. Leaning over to the trunk he pulled out the lace shift. "How about this?" Draping it over his arm, he slid the dress off her shoulders, over her hips, down to her thin ankles, he lifted each of her legs, so she could step out of it. Keeping one arm encircled around her waist, he laid the dress across the trunk, then lifted the shift. She raised her arms up to pull it over her head. The fire crackled. "There is some time before my rounds, but not enough. Still, let us rest for a moment."

He led her to the bed and pulled back the quilts. They lay down pressing themselves against each other. Lucas threw his leg over hers and pulled her closer. She nestled in the crook between his shoulder and neck. He felt her warm breath on his throat. His heart pounded in a rolling fever that filled his body with such an intense heat that the fire sparked and flared. He planted one arm on her back under her hair and slid the other inside the shift. This is just the beginning he told himself. From now on every night we will lie down together. Feeling her fingers on the small of his back, he groaned and lifted her chin to gaze into those dazzling green eyes and kiss her full moist lips. She returned his affections with docile fervor. His hair tangled with hers. Her cheeks were damp. He licked her tears away, then added his own. So, strong their love, it poured from them. "We will be like this forever."

"I think we will," she whispered. "We will."

Lucas awoke in the gloaming. He had slept for a little more than an hour and although Alina still lay motionless, breathing easily at his side he must dislodge himself from their warm nest and go to work. How he dreaded letting go of her for even a few hours. The moment he moved away, holding her arm aloft so as not to awaken her, he felt a cold shiver where her body had rested against his.

Slowly, silently he pulled on his trousers, his boot socks, and his thick muslin work shirt. He stoked the fire, then standing with his back to it, warming himself, he observed the beautiful girl dreaming in his bed. If it weren't for the utter safety of the boarding house, even more so since they'd rid themselves of Dugald, he would never leave her alone. He wondered how soon, when, and where, they could marry. Arcana would be lovely. But would Irene be up for the journey again? No, it no longer felt like home there. A once upon a time home, but not now. Now, there was no other home than the City of Dreams. The river was his favorite place, the copse of trees set back from the bank where he often went to restore himself. That would be utterly suitable. They must discuss it as soon as possible. As soon as he felt she was ready, hopefully in a few days' time. He placed the water pitcher within her reach should she awaken with thirst. He stroked a strand of hair from her forehead barely touching her with his fingertips. "I'll be right back," he whispered.

Downstairs, Carissa clattered in the kitchen as she served the boarders their evening meal. Ikarus waited by the front door with the lantern lighting tools ready. Lucas gripped his forearm, "I thought you would have gone home by now."

Ikarus lifted his shoulders. "I know I'm not the bravest lamp boy ever to light the streets, but I have to work. And . . ."

"And?"

"Well I'd like to be more of a man." Ikarus reddened and pulled open the door. A blast of cool night air greeted them. "We're running late. I can help." He pointed to the adjacent streets. "I know you like to light this street, so I'll start over that way and meet you in the square, if that's all right."

Lucas clapped him on the back. "It is . . . yes, a good plan, Ik. Thank you."

As they parted, Ikarus called over his shoulder. "Nikolas has things to tend to at the harbour, he said he will see you in the morning before your departure."

He lit the lanterns outside the house and then all the way down the street. Good for Nikolas, probably checking on the warehouse and Trousdale's guards. Perhaps a ship was in. Nikolas always had a way to make the arrival of a ship in port work to their advantage. And then of course, Trousdale . . . what was her name again? . . . Brigit. He never considered that she had a given name, was once somebody's child, sister . . . mother. He shuddered at the thought and chuckled to himself. This city, always another surprise around the corner. He swung his supply bag over his shoulder. Tomorrow he was taking Alina to Arcana, an adventure he couldn't have imagined a week ago. With absent-minded diligence, he went about his work lighting the candle lanterns and the hand lamps finally turning into the square where Ikarus was just finishing with the lamps. He appeared relaxed and confident. Lucas greeted him with a handshake. He didn't want to worry that the City of Dreams would go dark while he was in the country. "Well done, Ik."

Ikarus grinned. "I can finish up if you want to get back."

"Let's go together to the house of Alina's uncle. The city officials have boarded it up. But I want to make sure there have been no intrusions."

They found the house dark and deserted. No signs of intrusion. A boarded house was a warning to others in the city, and to many a sign of bad luck. "Only a fool would enter here now," Ikarus said with a shudder.

Lucas made his way around the entire exterior, checking the planked windows, and sweeping the inside of the root cellar with his lantern. "It's good. Let's go. I have yet to light the oil lamps on the Boulevard."

"Shall I accompany you there?"

"No need, I enjoy the fresh air. Why don't you head over to the boarding house? The women will be in the parlour. Irene will feed you again. Rest up for tomorrow when you'll be on your own again. Practice staying alert, keeping an eye on things that matter. I'll be along shortly."

A gust of wind swirled through the square and heavy air settled down on them. Lucas raised his face to the sky. "Rain," he smiled at Ikarus, "Get along. I'll be fine."

* * *

When Alina awoke, she didn't know where she was until she rolled over and saw Lucas' clothes hanging in the armoire. She pulled the covers around her and sat up. The fire blazed a friendly greeting. She could hardly believe herself. Here she was in the bedroom of a man she barely knew! A few days earlier she would have shuddered at the very idea. But now, it felt like the most natural thing. She felt no fear of him as she did her uncle and that horrible Campbell Barrington, and the numerous other lascivious men she had encountered since the death of her father. Lucas was warm-hearted and gentle. Her father had chosen her guardian well. But where did they go from here? She flopped over onto her side, where did she want to go? Now, in so few days, she couldn't imagine her life without the presence of Lucas, the thrilling and consuming presence of him. Her grief over the loss of her father fell far back to the edges of her mind when Lucas was near. All of it, their estate in Ingleena, her studies, shopping with Daria, attending dinners and parties with her father, everything about her old life melted away when Lucas stood beside her. Someone she barely recognized as herself had emerged lately. She had never experienced such disparate emotions as she did now. Perhaps the trip to the country would settle her. With that thought in mind, she slipped from the comfort of Lucas' bed. Taking up Carissa's borrowed dress, she stepped into it, although the girl had told her to keep it—having never borrowed anything before in her life—Alina didn't know if that was the proper thing to do. She gathered the clothes he had given her from his mother's trunk—these were gifts, most definitely—and crossed over to her own cozy little room. The fire was warm, and either, Irene or Carissa had set out a valise. Also, there was parchment to place between her dresses, so they would not wrinkle overmuch. The women of the house took as loving care of her as Daria had. A sadness filled her at the thought of Daria, but she pushed the feelings away. She didn't want to think about her now. One day she would find Daria again, but for now she wanted to focus on the adventure in Arcana. With rising anticipation, she packed her belongings for the journey.

* * *

Lucas still had several more lamps to light along the opulent avenues lined with trees and three-story houses. He loved walking under the canopy of trees. The houses amazed and intrigued him with their steps leading up from the street to tall, beveled glass front doors, and dormer windows lit by dozens of candles in crystal chandeliers.

He let some oil slip onto the spare candles which caused one to ignite fully inside an old lantern shattering the glass. Slivers fell into the waves of his hair. As he brushed them out, he slit his thumb. The drizzle became a downpour. Lucas looked up into the heavy sky and watched the raindrops hit his face until they began to sting his eyes. Since this was his last stop for the evening, he took refuge under an awning covering the stairs up to a grand house. He set his equipment on the ground and sucked the blood from his thumb for a moment until it healed. The second story hall glimmered with a row of five crystal chandeliers flickering with expensive yellow candles. The kind Lucas didn't carry.

An elegant black and gold coach clattered down the street, the horses snorting and rearing against the reins, halting so suddenly that the carriage skidded sideways in front of him. The door flew open with a bang. From within the plush red velvet interior, a delicate female leg emerged followed by another and then the most stunningly dressed woman Lucas had ever seen. She tumbled from the coach. Lucas rushed forward and caught her just before her knees hit the cobblestones. The woman turned her head away but accepted his hand. She wore a silver and gold dress with cuffed sleeves, and on the placard a double row of burgundy, velvet covered buttons. The neckline so low that Lucas couldn't help but stare. Her shoulders barely held a sheer black shawl with long silken fringe that reached to her delicate ankles. A man as tall as Lucas loped from the far side of the coach. "Footman!" he shouted.

Glancing about Lucas noticed there was no footman in sight. Then a stumbling oaf came around the corner bearing a torch that was near out from the rain, his pants torn and blood splatters on his knees. Lucas turned away, feeling sorry for the poor old fool who had stumbled, unable to mind his own light. The gentleman, in his perfectly tailored suit, nodded at Lucas.

From inside his overcoat he withdrew a silver flask and handed it to Lucas. "For your trouble," he said with a flourish.

Lucas grabbed the flask with his free hand but kept a firm grip on the woman's arm. He could not fathom how she could stand in her unusually tall shoes. The woman glared at him as if he were a snake about to strike, yanked her hand away and reached for her escort. The two of them dashed up the stairs to join the glorious party. The gentleman, a well-known nobleman, guided the woman through the open door, handed her over to the doorman, then bounded back down the steps to press a satchel of coins into Lucas' hand. "This is a private gathering. Others are coming. I would appreciate your assistance and silence."

Lucas bowed slightly, looked up and down the Boulevard. These superior citizens possessed more wealth than prudence. Under the presumed cover of night, they went out in the company of citizens they would never converse with during the day. Nobles and merchants so rich they could not count all their money in this lifetime! He had learned long ago how to endear himself. He showed them discretion, and gladly accepted huge bribes. Like an observer in someone else's dream, Lucas stepped back into the shadows and waited only a few moments for more coaches to arrive. Each one held a bevy of intoxicated, porcelain figurines. He offered his arm to the made-up, perfumed women, assisted the unsteady up the grand staircase and deposited them among the festal revelers. The evening grew chilly and on the way down the stairs he opened the flask, taking several swigs. A fine cognac soothed his scratchy throat, worn thin from complimenting those who held his arm as if he were nothing more than a handrail. He hoped for an end to the boisterous nonsense. He wanted to get home to Alina and the warmth of the boarding house. But the money was abundant, and these nobles offered a rare entertainment. Of course, he had his own coffer full of valuables, but there was always room for more. After the trip to the country, he would take Alina to the house of Le Cameé for a celebration dinner. Her trunks would be back in her lovely hands. He could hardly wait to see her reunited with her possessions. In between coaches, he relaxed into his protected place under the awning. Another long swig encouraged him to murmur even more elaborate compliments, which increased the gratuity. Some women clasped his hand for longer than necessary. He realized the more cognac he drank, the more they noticed him. One young lady smiled shyly and squeezed Lucas' hand after he deposited her in the vestibule. As he watched her disappear into the grand ballroom, he imagined what it must feel like to enter through those illustrious doors. One day, I will give Alina a home such as this he mused from the top of the stairs where he now stood for the warmth. Perhaps it was time to revisit his stash in the cellar. It had been quite some time since he'd examined the treasure chests he'd acquired. The night grew colder. The carriages ceased. The lilting sounds of the orchestra emanated through the doors and wide, wood-framed windows. The dancing had begun. He'd passed many evenings like this, standing in shadow, and observing others. Suddenly it bored him. He hurled himself down the stairs. Before meeting Alina, Lucas never wondered where life might lead. Now, a purpose had found him. He retrieved his tools and turned toward home. Feeling a shadow cross behind him he turned back and there was the gray cat bounding up the stairs. It turned for a brief instant to cast its haughty, yellow eyes in his direction, then it leaped up and slipped through a slightly open window.

   * * *

By the time, Lucas returned home, the fire was low and only Irene sat by its orange glow. She brought a bowl of warm stew from the kitchen and poured him a cup of water. Lucas asked, "Did Alina come down for late supper?"

Irene shook her head. "When I went up to check on her, she was so sleepy I suggested that she not bother to dress and come down. Carissa brought a small plate up. We're spoiling her for you."

They laughed sitting side by side on the dark green velvet settee while he told her about his evening. She wanted every detail of whom he recognized, what the ladies and even the gentlemen wore. Lucas graciously relayed every aspect for her enjoyment.

"I have decided that we shall have a house such as that, Irene. All of us, you and I and Alina and Carissa, and another maid or two."

Her eyes sparkled in the firelight. "Will we now, and how can that be?"

Lucas leaned back, stretched out his legs. "I have many resources. And if that's not enough, it should not take over long to acquire the necessary wealth to purchase such a home." He licked his lips and gazed into the flickering flames.

"What do you have of such excellent value?" She knitted her brows.

"Information," he said. "Well," he cleared his throat, "rather I should say, silence."

Irene shook her head. "That is a dangerous road to travel, Lucas!"

"I know. Well, do I know. Don't worry. It won't be necessary, I'm sure." He wiggled his brow.

She shook her head. "Sometimes you frighten me, Lucas."

He placed his hand on her arm. "Fear not, Irene. I will always protect you."

"And yourself, and of course Alina now."

He pressed his lips together and closed his eyes.

"It's late and your trip back to Arcana is in the morning. Get off to bed."

"Yes," Lucas said rising, offering his hand. "Will you be all right here?"

"Of course, I will." She stood by as he banked the fire.

"Ikarus will stay here. It's best since he is covering the lantern rounds. I hope you don't mind that we are going?" He examined her face.

"How could I mind when I am the reason you have to go! If I hadn't lost that key, had only told you about it . . ."

"Don't fret," Lucas wrapped his arms around her shoulders and kissed the top of her head. "I will take care of everything."

Lucas stood still when he saw the empty bed. Even though he hadn't expected Alina to be there, he hoped it wouldn't be long before the shyness, as endearing at it was, had gone and he could expect to find her waiting for him. To his great delight, she had taken the things from his mother's trunk. He knelt beside it, reached deep inside for the arrow tip, unwrapped it and ran his finger along its edge. He'd like to toss it in the blacksmith's forge, but he couldn't dismiss the truth of it, nor the fact that it had found its way into his hands. He hated it. Wrapping it in the cloth, and adding a linen towel, it became nothing more than a misshapen bundle stuffed in the corner of her trunk. He retrieved the picture of the woman, disappointed that it wasn't his mother. She was fuzzy. If only he knew who was missing, torn from the picture, and why. A man most likely. A man she no longer wanted to be seen with when she tore it in half.

Glancing blankly around his room, he ran his fingers over the image. He would probably never know who the woman in the painting was and it didn't matter now. He and Alina had both lost much, but together they would leave the pain of the past behind them as they planned their future together. Grateful that he knew more about his mother at least, and that the headaches were gone, he decided it was not so bad, or unusual, to not know who his father was. The world was full of orphans and unanswered questions. Too tired to think, he returned the little painting to the trunk, closed the lid, and locked it. Slipping out of his damp clothes, he rolled onto the linen sheets that still smelled of Alina.

Chapter 14

After a hearty morning meal of warm bread, butter, honey, fruit and cheese, Lucas headed for the stables to retrieve their horses. He was startled to find Nikolas pacing out front.

"At last!" He rushed forward pulling Lucas inside where three horses stood saddled and ready to go.

"Why three?" Lucas questioned his friend. "Surprised to see you so early, Nik. Thought you may have reasons to stay abed."

Nikolas suppressed a snigger and shook his head. "Believe me I would prefer it. This morning I brought water to Dugald, he cried and clutched my arm, begged me to free him . . ."

"Ach," Lucas shook his head. "That creature. I've had enough of him, but you didn't release him, did you?"

"No, of course not. But I prodded him to talk some more."

"Good work, my friend. What did Dugald have to say this morning?"

"He said Vasil and Barrington are possibly on their way to Arcana."

"Arcana? What on earth would they go there for?"

"Apparently, when they first met, Dugald had spouted off his drunken mouth to them about a farm he will acquire there, and they thought it would be a good place to hide outside the city.

And, since they know he's not dead on the floor of Vasil's house, Dugald believes if they can't find him here, they will go looking for him there, in Arcana. They want those trunks and are willing to kill for them." Nik lowered his voice. "Again. They will kill again."

Lucas rubbed his temples. "This is distressing, Nik. Dugald is a liar. How can we believe anything he says?"

"I don't know if we can, but it seems, in a way, we've saved Dugald's life from those two."

"His life means nothing to me."

Nik inclined his head, "But yours means much to Marion. She sent Dugald here to snatch you!"

"Ha," Lucas clapped his hands together. "I suppose he intended to wrap me up in his cloak and carry me through the streets like a babe in arms." And when Nik didn't laugh also, he exclaimed, "You aren't serious."

"Bringing you back to Marion is the reason Dugald showed up in the City of Dreams. And he didn't say it, but I'm sure when he found you, he lost control of his bowels. He didn't come here to find a wife or his father. He came here to throw a net over you and haul you back to the country in a wagon."

"Is that what he said? A net and a wagon?"

Nik nodded. "I'm sure that plan was formed after he saw you and realized his glorious cloak wouldn't do the job."

"Ha Nik, I've always appreciated your humor, especially now when the city is teeming with lunatics. And Arcana as well! That woman must be daft. Bernard was right it seems. She wanted me for her own. Did she forget I would be grown after all these years?"

"Maybe she thought you would stay forever young."

Lucas slowly rubbed his hands together, "Hmmph. If I chose an age to stop growing older it wouldn't be ten. No wonder she was so shocked to see me at the Grande Inn. She sent Dugald here to fetch me and I showed up and walked right through the front door." He went to one of the horses that was stomping and straining against its tether. He stroked its brow and shushed it with a faint hum, then leaned his forehead against the horse's nose, forcing back the onset of a headache. "Why did Dugald reveal all this today?"

Nikolas rubbed his palms together. "He wants to go home and get his land from Marion. That's all, he claims."

Lucas brushed his fingers through his hair several times. "She won't give it to him, never intended to, I'm sure."

Nik clasped his hands together. "He's full of hate and rage, but he says he just wants to go home now."

"I don't want Dugald in Arcana and I doubt Marion does either. Her wicked head must be spinning in confusion now that she's met me again. I must inform Bernard of all this."

Nik nodded. "I can't wait to meet this Marion." placing his hand on Lucas' shoulder, "don't worry I'll protect you from her."

Lucas sputtered and burst out laughing, grabbed Nik in an embrace. "I can always count on you, comrogue. Who's with Dugald right now?"

"Brigit has her horde at the hut."

"Ha-ha, good. Well, Dugald is secure. But Vasil and Barrington are running loose all over the damn place." Lucas slapped Nikolas on the back. "All right then. You are joining us on the trip."

"Right."

"Not a word to Irene or Alina."

"No."

Gathering the reins, they led the horses out of the stable and clomped along the cobbled street to the boarding house. "Only we know that Irene took Dugald's key, correct?"

"Correct. Well . . . all of us."

"So, therefore," Lucas counted off his fingers, "As well as Irene, Ikarus, probably Carissa . . . and Alina . . . and of course the stalwart Madam Brigit Trousdale."

"Precisely."

Lucas released his breath. "So, we grab the key, and obliterate anyone who stands in our path."

Nikolas gazed at Lucas with the same excited sparkle in his eyes.

The ladies waited on the steps of the boarding house. Alina resplendent, even in a simple blue dress, now ready for riding. Immediately, Lucas noticed that she wasn't wearing her ruby pendant, and silently commended her insight. A strong hug from Irene assured Lucas she would be fine, most likely welcome the quiet for a few days. They mounted and turned to ride off when Madam Trousdale came running down the street, her bangles bouncing against her, hair flying behind and across her face. The hourglass, completely empty, gave Lucas a start. His heart raced. Not now, he thought, what are you doing here? He put his hand over his heart as he had become in the habit of doing ever since he began wearing Alina's black lace veil there. Trousdale rushed past him up to Alina and handed her a bundle. "Open it now," she demanded.

Alina tore at the paper and hastily opened it. A sheepskin vest with five loop buttons down the front. She ran her hand over it in wonderment before holding it out to Lucas. Was it for her or him? He raised one shoulder and looked at Trousdale. "Put it on" she said to Alina while visually warning Lucas not to interfere. He let his horse trot in a circle around the group but said nothing. For a moment, his mind turned to the gold-jewelled box, as it always did when he saw her. But now its whereabouts unknown. Alina slipped the vest on under her riding cloak and buttoned it up.

"It's warm" she said patting herself.

That was enough for Lucas, he nodded his approval and noticed the hour glass was now full. "Thank you, Brigit," he said. For what exactly, he did not know, but somewhere inside himself he understood that Madam Trousdale knew what she was doing.

They turned and trotted out of the city, an unsettling feeling for Lucas. The last time he left, he had feared he wouldn't be able to return for some reason. And now he had the same feeling. Although, he wanted to share his home with her and enjoy an adventure together, it occurred to him to leave Alina safely ensconced in the house. But he couldn't bear being away from her for more than a few hours. Besides, how did he know if Dugald's story was accurate? Vasil and Barrington could be hiding in the city waiting to pounce on her when the opportunity arose. She was much safer with him. He was excited to show her Arcana, but also hoped she loved the City of Dreams as much as he did because they were going to spend the rest of their lives in it.

The sun shone down upon them. Lucas watched Alina, pleased to see that she rode with ease and agility. She galloped and jumped for the fun of it. The three of them raced each other, laughing, and shouting over the rolling hills. Lucas remarked how much faster horse travel was than the carriage. Before they knew it, they were riding up to the *No Horses Tavern*. And there was Bernard. He was atop his horse in front of the tavern; his back turned. Lucas rode up, let out a whoop and circled him. Bernard's face lit with surprise. "Lucas! My God, where did you come from?"

Lucas laughed, reined in his mount, and waved his arm toward Alina and Nikolas. "I'm back on a mission and I've brought my friend and my betrothed." Alina blushed and murmured hello. Nik walked his horse up and offered his hand.

"Are you coming or going?" Lucas asked.

"I was going, but I can be convinced to buy you one if you're thirsty from your ride."

"We are," Lucas glanced at his companions, "And as I recall, it's my turn to buy the pint. But, also, we are anxious to get to the Grande Inn. We have pressing business there and will enjoy our libations more once this matter is resolved."

"Sounds serious," Bernard fell in alongside Lucas who kept an eye on Alina, reading her expression until he perceived acknowledgement in her eyes. Nikolas nudged his horse over toward Alina, so they could ride two by two.

Lucas explained the situation with Alina's trunks, Dugald, and the missing key. "Have you heard of Dugald Tendrick?"

"A puny sickly fellow?"

"Why, yes he is. At least now he is."

Bernard scratched his stubble. "Always has been. Claims he's Marion's kin. Her brother's offspring, I suppose. Sometimes she acknowledges him, sometimes not. Worthless lout in my opinion."

"He told me that Marion sent him to the City of Dreams to fetch me back here," Lucas frowned and rolled his eyes.

"Ach, that old scheme. I haven't heard that one in a while. Tsk. Stupid."

With a peek back at Alina, Lucas lowered his voice, "It was a plan then?"

"Once upon a time, yes." Bernard pursed his lips to spit but stopped himself. "Even for Marion, I can't believe this. A bit late now isn't it?"

"It is. But there he is in the City of Dreams."

"Lunacy runs in the family. I hope I can avoid it!"

"Awareness is the first step." He turned around to check on Alina who was gazing in the direction Nikolas was pointing. Leaning closer to Bernard he said, "Speaking of lunatics, have you seen any strangers about? Two older men? I can't call them gentlemen."

"You are the first strangers I've seen since your last visit." Bernard grinned as he reached over to grip Lucas' shoulder. "I didn't expect you to return so soon."

"Neither did I. Please accompany us to the Inn and then, if you will, let all the locals know that there are two vile assassins on the loose. They pose as innocent merchants." Lucas turned a pale face toward Bernard. "As for the lady, she should enjoy the lack of fear while we are here."

Bernard gave a slight bow. "Consider it done."

Lucas spurred his mount and they galloped over smooth ground. Soon, the beamed roof line, the row of windows–Lucas recognized his room–and then the large, arched timber doors of the Grande Inn appeared through the trees.

They all dismounted at the front steps. The stable boy took everyone but Bernard's horse. He was telling Alina about the wonderful Grande Inn garden, the delicious food, and the cozy rooms. "You will have the place nearly to yourselves. Most of the regular guests aren't in residence now."

Lucas nodded, understanding the message from Bernard. Alina thanked Bernard and offered her hand which he graciously kissed. She turned to Lucas with expectant eyes. He knew she was anxious to freshen up and relax after the ride. "You'll check back," he said.

"I will." Bernard nudged his horse and rode away.

Lucas took his same room and Alina was in Irene's room, Nikolas across the hall. He could hardly believe all that happened since his previous visit to the Inn. Now Alina was with him! He tossed himself on the bed like a man on holiday before he abruptly remembered the reason for their journey. The key. Waiting an appropriate three quarters of an hour, he knocked on Alina's door. She had changed into a dressing robe; his mother's red and black gown and lace shift lay across the bed. He hesitated until she opened the door wider. Stepping through he went to the bed, lifted the skirt of the gown feeling the fine silk and wondered again where his mother had acquired such a beautiful dress. He may never know, but now these treasures had new life in the graceful hands of Alina. "Thank you for accepting these clothes. It means much to me."

"And to me," she said offering her hands. Taking her hands in his, he bent and placed a kiss on her warm neck. She sighed. "It's lovely here."

"And more so with you. If you like, we will walk in the garden before dinner."

"I would." She went to a chair beside the fire. Shall we sit and talk for a while?"

"Yes." Lucas thought for a moment, brushed his hair away from his face with both hands. "But we should probably have a look for the key. I'd rather try to find it on our own before engaging the innkeeper in the search."

"Of course," she stood up and her robe gapped open. "Where shall we start? In the chest of drawers, I imagine."

Lucas folded his arms across his chest. "Certainly," he murmured. "You start there, and I'll try the wardrobe."

Alina pulled out the top drawer, leaned over reaching around inside it and Lucas stood motionless watching. After she went through all six drawers in this manner, she turned to him and said, "I think we should remove these drawers and see what is behind, that is unless you found anything in the wardrobe?"

"Ah . . . no." he let his arms fall to his sides. He approached the untouched wardrobe. "Let me just see to it now."

She flashed him a mischievous smile and he felt himself blush. He stumbled over to the wardrobe, his movements heavy and slow. What had happened to his normal, lithe confidence? Pretending that she wasn't standing there watching him, he opened the wardrobe and completely examined it with both his fingers and eyes. Getting down on his hands and knees he felt around under it and then turned around to search under the bed. Finally, pulling himself up he sat down next to the lace shift, running his hand across it, he decided Alina's veil and his mother's shift perfectly suited both women. Their bones as delicate as the lace itself. "Come here," he whispered.

And when she did, he wrapped his arms around her waist, pulled her toward him and turned his cheek to rest against her tummy. "We will have children together. Boys and girls!" She trembled, and he looked up to see her eyes shining. "Yes?"

"Yes . . . but not too soon. Not while I still feel like a child myself." she said.

"Of course, you are not yet more than a child. We should behave like children together."

"We should," laughing she gave him a gentle shove, so he toppled over, pulling her down on top of him. They rolled in a playful embrace while he kissed her neck and shoulders.

"I'd like to get started on that now," he said standing, returning her laughter, "but first your possessions must be restored to you, dear Alina."

Together they pulled out the top drawer of the bureau, it slid out reluctantly and was heavy, so Lucas held it while she looked behind and ran her hands along the edges. Then the second drawer came out and then the third.

"Ah!" she shouted, pulled out her hand and there it was, a shiny fat cylinder with several ridges and indentations tied to a braided gold-fringed cord. Eyes shining, she beamed at Lucas.

"There! You found it. What an amazing woman you are Alina! The mystery of your trunks is all but solved. We can move forward with our plans for the future."

Alina clutched the key to her chest. "We are not making babies right now, Lucas!"

"Ah . . . oh, no my darling, of course we are not. That is if you don't want to. It is quite romantic here, but we shall marry first. As soon as possible in the cathedral, Saint Siempre in the City of Dreams." He laughed at his own boyish enthusiasm, and to make a point, gave her a gentle kiss on top of her head. "I have a place for it," he said, reaching inside the front of his trousers to a secret pocket, he held it open and Alina dropped the key in.

"Now, I will go down and order wine before our stroll in the garden. Nikolas will join us later for dinner. But for now, we will celebrate just the two of us."

Her eyes sparkled. Holding up the red and gold dress she asked, "Is it appropriate?"

"It is absolutely perfect. This Inn truly is Grande. Especially at night, you will see. But please my darling, do not dress too quickly. I will return with the wine."

* * *

Alina sat on the edge of the bed her heart racing. How quickly life had changed. Her dreams had died with her father. But despite her wish to follow him to his grave, the ensuing days had consisted of struggling to survive. A disturbing comfort, the possibility that someday, if the need arose, she may have to take the dagger strapped to her thigh and plunge it into her own heart. But soon she would have her trunks and a piece of her former life restored. Lucas is keeping his promises. It seems that he always will. Still, what an audacious man he is. Marriage and babies. These are things I have not yet considered. We barely know each other! But in this brief time, it's apparent that he will always do as he promises. I believe he will protect me forever and never let any harm come to me. All the way out to Arcana, he always had me in his sights, made sure Nikolas kept watch as well, and even the burly Bernard. Lucas is a thief, he has stolen my heart. His countenance takes my breath away. But a husband, what a frightening thought.

She slid off the bed and went to the window to gaze out across the hills. She imagined Lucas running alongside his mother with fistfuls of flowers. It made her sad that they would never know each other's parents. What of Lucas' father? There was still so much to learn about each other. At least Lucas had met her father—ever so briefly—and father had approved, even recommended Lucas. Yet still, her stomach churned. She hardly knew him and the people of his world, kind as they seemed so far. Could the world change from horrible and mean to loving and beautiful in a single day? She must mind herself. Since the death of her father she felt always ready to run. It's best to remain on guard, she thought even though she wanted only to relax into the alluring ease this new life offered. And right now, she could hardly wait to find out what was in her trunks that Uncle Vasil so desperately desired. For herself, a letter would be welcome, but nonetheless her father had worked hard to leave an inheritance for her, and she intended to have what was rightfully hers.

* * *

When Lucas returned, carrying a tray with two pewter goblets of red wine, a plate of bread and cheese, he was disappointed to see that Alina had already put on her shift and underbodice. His mission had taken longer than he expected since the kitchen prepared the small repast while he washed and changed into his blue velvet suit. He placed the tray on the table beside the fire and helped her on with his mother's dress. As Alina stepped through the skirts and turned her head toward her shoulder, holding up her hair so he could fasten the buttons, his heart ached to know if a man had ever adored his lovely mother the way he did, Alina. He could only hope this dress was an indication that there had been someone with whom she shared a fervid love.

Lucas stood back and admired how the folds and panels of the dress shimmered in the firelight. He took her in his arms and embraced her with fierce passion, kissing her neck, her cheeks, her warm mouth, and her earlobes. Daylight disappeared as they stood pressed together in the glow of the fire, the heat of which eventually overwhelmed them enough to pull apart. Lucas lit the candles and they relaxed into the high-backed, upholstered burgundy chairs. Toasting the easy retrieval of the key, they sipped the robust wine and nibbled the hearty cheese. The goblets were large and round, so they took their time, he asked questions about her life in Ingleena, and she about his journey from Arcana to the City of Dreams. Lucas recalled what he could but left out some of the details. They had many things in common. The appreciation of beautiful things and the comfort of a well-kept home. Kindness to others, at least those who merited it, was a necessary and rewarding aspect of life. They steadfastly agreed that it was preferable to spend most of their day in the out of doors. Confinement to rooms was a bore. The world offered so much to see and discover. When Nikolas knocked on the door, their faces were flushed from the wine, the fire, and the excitement of each other's company.

Lucas held the door wide, but Nikolas didn't step over the threshold. He took in the scene and grinned at his friend. "I have examined the guest list and walked the gardens, all is well it seems." He remarked, "I must say Alina you are a princess in that gown! It's absolutely dazzling on you." Then to Lucas, "Bernard has returned."

"Excellent." Lucas clasped Nik's shoulder. "And we have good news as well." He patted his pant leg where he'd hid the key. "We have already recovered the key."

"This is excellent news!" A bow for Alina, "Well done my friends. It's amazing you had the time to search. I shall join Bernard in the parlour for libations. I believe you will have the garden to yourselves. There is a large group visiting from abroad, friends of Mr. Hartwinn. They are already seated on the east side of the dining room. So, we will enjoy fine foreign cuisine and wine tonight. Enjoy the garden, the candles are lit."

As Nikolas said, the garden glowed in the flickering light of dozens of white candles along the path, atop the stone benches, and in the nooks of the garden walls. "It's as if we are walking in the sky among the stars," Alina said.

The candles flickered like the twinkling stars above them. "You are the brightest star," Lucas replied as he kissed her hand and bowed. She laughed as he swept her up in his arms and carried her to the bench. Resting his hand gently along the nape of her neck he entwined her silken hair through his fingers. "If not for fear of ruining the gown, I would rather like to lie down here together in this rich earth and begin our life together."

Alina inhaled. Her cheeks turned crimson.

"Forgive me, my darling. I've frightened you again." He cupped her chin in his hand, then went to his knee and said, "You will be my wife."

She giggled and shoved him. "That is a statement, not a question."

"That is correct." Lucas took his seat beside her again. She rested her head on his shoulder. They held hands lacing their fingers. "I'm so incredibly happy we found each other. I never expected to find someone like you . . . we match each other . . . don't you agree? There is a quietness to you and a wild rebellious side as well."

Alina lifted her head to gaze into Lucas' eyes. "It seems you have spent much time observing me."

"I have. As much as I could since we met." He knitted his brows. "This doesn't upset you, does it?"

"No, of course not. I've watched you as well." Her lip quivered as she gazed into the middle distance. "My life is changing so rapidly . . . please remember, we've agreed to remain as children."

Lucas frown smiled, "Yes, we did just say that. I understand it must be overwhelming. And you are in mourning for your father. I'm sorry Alina if you feel rushed by my ardor." He held her hand and ran his fingers up inside the sleeve of her gown.

"I've spent much time alone with my books, my maid, or my father. Sheltered, I suppose you could say." She tossed her hair over her shoulder, casting her gaze toward the dining room from which Nikolas emerged.

"Ah, the love birds nestled in the garden," he exclaimed.

"Nik," Lucas indicated a seat on the bench opposite. "Join us."

"Dinner is about to be served."

"Good then. I'm quite hungry." Lucas rose and turned to assist Alina. "Are you ready, little girl?"

As they entered the dining room Lucas took notice of the group that sat around a table set for twelve in front of the fireplace. Two tall silver candelabra adorned their table. The guests were of varied ages, a family he realized, at least three generations. Vintners, he pondered. Bernard entered from the reception room. A quick dip of his head for Lucas indicated that all was well outside the Inn. This reassured Lucas, he did not want an encounter with Alina's uncle, nor his henchman, Barrington before dinner, or anytime actually, but he knew the moment would come. He would like to know when.

Bernard stated that his parents were not in attendance at the Grande Inn since they were preparing to travel abroad.

"For how long will they travel?" Lucas asked.

"Permanently."

"How delightful!" Alina exclaimed.

"A delightful escape," Nik said.

"Indeed," Lucas agreed. "Marion, the schemer, embarking on a journey with Wentworth, a good soul married to a battle ax."

Bernard clenched his fists, "I won't miss her."

After the dinner of coq au vin and a creamy, sweet pudding, they retired to the parlour. The family remained in the dining room, giving Lucas the opportunity to relax his guard, although they didn't concern him. He and Alina sat on the divan where he and Irene had sat. The fire blazed warm and low as the nights stayed comfortable longer now in the heart of spring. As much as he enjoyed sitting thus with her, it was not quite the feeling he wanted for them. All three men were aware that the two murderers were afoot. And, with the key recovered, there was nothing left to do but return to the City of Dreams, yet how could they go home knowing that Vasil and Barrington were out there somewhere? Lucas didn't enjoy keeping his concerns from Alina and he could see his companions were on edge as well, but they waited with loyalty to help him defend her and avenge the murder of her father.

Nikolas got up and paced in front of the windows, then went over to appreciate the massive tapestries. "What is our plan for the morning, Lucas?"

"Yes, I was just thinking about that as well. I'd like to show Alina the flower fields and the barn, what's left of it. Then we should get back to the City of Dreams with the key and open the locker. Would you like to accompany us there, Bernard?"

Bernard rose to stand by the fire. "Why, yes, I certainly would. The City of Dreams is like a dream to me. I've never left Arcana."

"It's time then. You are most welcome."

"Perhaps after we show Alina where you came from, she can return for a rest before the journey back. The three of us could take a quick ride out to the farm and I will take leave of my parents."

"Excellent idea. That's settled then. Shall we my dear." Lucas rose and took Alina by the hand. He clapped Bernard on the back and nodded to Nikolas. "Good night, friends."

Upstairs, he walked Alina to her room and accompanied her inside. Without speaking he opened her wardrobe, lifted the bed skirts, then pulled aside the heavy drape to peer behind it, check the window latch and peek outside where nothing stirred. Crossing the room, he stoked the fire. She sat at the edge of her bed watching, the flames reflected in her eyes. "Are you sure there aren't any monsters lurking?"

He took her hand in his. "One can never be too cautious. I can stay and sleep in the chair if it makes you feel better."

"It won't make me feel better, nor you! I feel safe here at the Grande Inn."

"As do I," Lucas agreed noticing her stifle a yawn. "I'll leave you to rest. I am close if you need me." He kissed the top of her head. "Good night lovely, Alina."

"Good night bold, Lucas."

In the hallway, Nik waited for Lucas. They moved away from Alina's door. "Bernard has ridden around the acres and says all is quiet and clear. He is staying in the room downstairs across from the garden door."

"Good, good. And nobody is coming through that massive front door with its three iron bolts. All right, Nik."

"See you in the morning." Nikolas retired to his room and Lucas did the same. He liked this bedchamber and had come to feel as if it was his own. As soon as possible, once back in the City of Dreams, he and Alina must discuss their living arrangements. Wedding plans first of course. But he needed to know if she would be comfortable living in the boarding house with Irene for some time, or if she wanted a home of her own right away.

In the morning, Lucas awoke to the sound of birdsong and opened his eyes to see the tree in full abundant bloom and the spotted brown bird watching him. It cocked its tiny head to the left then the right, keeping an eye on him as it hopped from branch to branch. Lucas slid from under the covers and tiptoed to the window, "Good morning little friend," he whispered. He wanted to show Alina, but he didn't know if she was awake. The bird flitted among the leafy branches while Lucas splashed water on his face and stepped into his trousers. For a while he sat by the open window and the spotted bird sat still on its branch. Grateful for the quiet company, he watched the sky turn from dawn to day illuminating the brilliant green leaves. With a generous flutter of tiny wings, the bird flew away. Lucas put on a white, billow-sleeved shirt. The warmth coming through the window indicated that was enough. He organized his satchel of belongings giving Alina an adequate amount of time to wake and dress before he went to knock on her door. She was radiant in a light blue walking dress that would serve well for the ride home as well. Their eyes met in greeting. He took her hands and kissed them. "As warm as it is, I think you should bring the vest Madam Trousdale gave you."

"Oh yes!" She grabbed it from the wardrobe and handed it to Lucas who offered his arm.

The dining room was busy with the foreign family, laughing and talking in their lyrical language. The children excitedly changed seats with each other. Nik and Bernard seated at a round table were stuffing pastry into their mouths like schoolboys, and soon Lucas and Alina did the same.

Afterward they took their time riding out to the old barn in the warm sun, under a deep blue sky, through lush green meadow grass that swayed in the breeze. The dirt road, now familiar to Lucas, wound down in its snaky curve before crossing the little stone bridge where they stopped. Wrapping his arm around Alina's waist, he inquired if she was faring well in the saddle for the second day. She assured him with a bright smile and patted the neck of her horse before leaning over to brush her moist lips across his cheek. He felt like sweeping her into his arms and carrying her to the row of ancient mortar and stone houses. But this was more than a horseback ride on a beautiful morning, it was a journey through the past, and forward into the future. "One last climb," he said as the road wound up the hill. The sight of the farm and the flower fields took his breath away.

They dismounted and walked the horses along the rutted dirt road that led to the old barn. This time it didn't seem so sad or sagging. Someone had removed and stacked the dangling rafters. The old wood should burn well.

"We lived here," Lucas said pointing to the southwest corner. "Over there was the bunkhouse," he and Bernard said at the same time. And Bernard added, "it was a grand farm in those days."

Lucas placed his hands on his hips. "It's different than when we were just here. I feel like someone else right now. Well, we may as well have a look at the pond." Alina followed him while Nik and Bernard stood around pretending to examine what remained of the structure.

They walked toward the woods and entered the grove of maple, and linden trees from the path. "It's magical!" Alina exclaimed. Lucas turned to gaze at her, delighted that she thought so, although he felt that she was the one who brought magic back to the place.

"My mother and I bathed in this pool. Would you like to feel the water? It's as smooth as your delicate skin."

She smiled. "I'd like to, yes," she pulled up her skirt and knelt in the dirt, reaching forward to dip her hands in the water. Lucas knelt beside her. They dangled their hands in the water and splashed each other. "It feels like silk," she said.

"It does. Someday we will swim here, when there's more time." The lonely ache for his mother swirled to the bottom of the pond. They walked back to the barn where Nik and Bernard were chatting. "Off to the flower fields, then," Lucas said, anxious to end the tour and return home. He wanted Alina to have her trunks and he'd had enough of Arcana for now. The wind had picked up and gray clouds raced across the sky.

At the field, hundreds of small pink flowers had replaced the sparse grass and mud puddles. They grew low to the ground, five pink lobes atop shamrock-shaped leaves. Lucas reined up his horse at the edge of the field and leapt off. "Oh, this is how it used to be!" He turned to Alina in time to assist her from her mount. "This is the beginning. Soon tall flowers will pop up everywhere among these. It's incredible Alina. The field has blossomed for you!"

"It certainly has," Bernard said coming up to stand beside them. I have not seen this field bloom in years."

Nikolas tied up all the horses and joined them. "I have never seen anything like this," he said. They gazed across the field in pure delight, then walked along the outer edge careful not to tread upon any of the delicate flowers. Lucas ran up and down dragging Alina along with him, soaking in all the splendor. "This field, it blooms now as I remember it. And like the painting in my mother's trunk. There is a woman standing in this field wearing a flowing dress like you are now." He furrowed his brow.

"What woman?" Alina asked.

He perused the field remembering, then turned back to Alina. He clutched her hand. "I don't know." His voice wavered, and his eyes turned dark. "And someone is torn away."

"Ach," Alina pressed her palm against her chest, and peered at Lucas. "I'm sorry Lucas." The breeze swept her hair back. "You wish to know who you are."

"I do." He raised his hands and let them drop to his sides. A cloud of dust swirled on the horizon. "Someone is coming." Lucas stood in front of Alina. Two men were galloping toward them. "Hail! Men!" he shouted to Nik and Bernard who were already running out in front toward the men.

"Oh no!" Alina turned and ran.

Lucas sprinted after her, stunned that she could run so fast. "Stay close to me!"

She nodded and kept running as fast as she could toward the copse of trees gathering her skirt up above her knees. Lucas, close behind, lunged for her just as she turned shouting something incomprehensible, tears streaming down her cheeks. She put her arms out defensively, still backing away. Lucas leapt for her again. He clasped her hand, but it slipped from his as she staggered and fell to the ground.

"No. Alina! Bloody hell!" he screamed. His heart stopped, and his breath caught in his throat. As he slumped to his knees, his breath gushed out. He scrambled toward Alina who was face down and not moving. Beyond the pink flowers, men were running and shouting. He swore, hoping Nik and Bernard could manage whatever was happening. Creeping up alongside Alina, he noticed bees and butterflies buzzing as if nothing were afoot. Slipping his arm around her waist, he placed his head against her back to listen for the beat of her heart. "I'm here sweetheart," he panted.

More shouts and a pistol explosion. Thudding hooves and whinnying shrieks, one horse bolting through the field. Then the distinct sound of Nikolas swearing like only a wharf man can. Lucas raised himself up and saw Vasil wielding a weapon just yards away. Lucas pulled out his dagger and lay down across Alina completely covering her with his body. The din of fighting men and frightened horses filled the dusty air. Lucas felt under Alina's skirt for the dagger he knew she had hidden there. He got hold of it and was about to leap up with both daggers in hand when she cried out, "It's Uncle Vasil. Here to kill me!" She shook and sobbed underneath Lucas.

"He will not touch you, Alina. I will rip him to ribbons," Lucas snarled.

"He'll kill us all . . . he will," she moaned burying her head beneath her arms

"No Alina. Nikolas and Bernard are still on their feet." Another pistol shot filled the air with the sharp smell of gunpowder. Lucas clutched Alina and rolled towards the bushes. Footsteps pounded toward them. Lucas turned and lifted his head to see Vasil standing above them raising a bent cudgel.

"Get off her lantern man. She is my property!"

Lucas lunged upward wielding both daggers and slammed Vasil in the chest with his shoulder. Vasil's knees crumbled, he cried out and swung the club, it grazed the side of Lucas' face tossing him over, the daggers flying out of his hands. He hit the ground, landing on his back. Peering up into the sun, he could see the short dark figure of Vasil bending over and grabbing one of the daggers. Alina was on her feet, a rock in each hand. Lucas on all fours dove toward Vasil. The dagger flew from Vasil's hand straight toward Alina. It plunged into her. She fell. Lucas darted toward her. Vasil had hold of the cudgel still, he swung at Lucas' head. Lucas reached out with both hands and yanked the cudgel from Vasil pulling him forward. He tripped and fell on top of Lucas. A shadow covered them. Everything went dark.

It was Bernard who shoved Vasil out of the way and offered a hand to Lucas. Nikolas was helping Alina up, Lucas rushed to them. "Are you all right, Alina?"

She gazed at Lucas as if she didn't recognize him. "Uh."

Protruding from her chest was Alina's own small dagger. He grabbed it and realized that the vest held it firmly away from her skin. "This saved you," he muttered incomprehensibly as he brushed her off. "And what is this?" He started tugging thorns from her back. "These are as sharp as arrows!" Lucas ran his hands up and down her body and through her hair.

Nik held the pistols. "Why carry pistols if you can't aim?"

Bernard held the cudgel. "You won't be needing this," he muttered to Vasil who lay motionless. The group stared. There was no way to shield Alina from the mess of her uncle crumpled in a bloody heap at their feet.

For several moments no one spoke, then Alina finally said. "He appears to be dead."

Nikolas stifled a chuckle. "Seems so," he said.

Lucas pulled Alina close. "You are safe. That's all that matters."

She gazed up at him, cupped his cheek in her palm. "You're hurt Lucas. Your face is bleeding!"

"Oh," he felt his cheek. "It seems so. Don't worry. I'll be fine." He held his hand against his cheek.

"You nearly lost your head," Nik remarked.

"But it's still here," Lucas said patting the top of his head.

"They attacked us." Bernard said turning to Alina. "I hope you can forgive me for clubbing your uncle, but the bastard had it coming!"

"He did indeed," she said. "What must we do now? I'd like to go home please."

"Well, Barrington got away," Nikolas said with a frown directed toward Lucas.

"How did they know where to find us?" Lucas removed his hand from his cheek and glanced at it to make sure there was no more blood.

"Huh," Nikolas narrowed his eyes at Lucas.

"I wouldn't be surprised if Marion is involved. I'm sure she has spies roaming the countryside. I'll go to the *No Horses* and get some men," Bernard said. He peered at Lucas' cheek and knitted his brows. "It's still true I see."

"What's still true?" Alina asked, tearing her eyes from her dead uncle. "I'm glad he's gone, but I can hardly believe it. Thank you for avenging my father, all of you."

Our pleasure, Lucas thought. But everyone was staring at him.

"Your face! It's healed!" Alina exclaimed. She took his cheeks between her palms. "What happened? There were lacerations!" She looked from one man to the other. "Who tended him just now?"

"He tended himself," Bernard said.

Nikolas stepped aside and whistled for the horses.

"We must remain alert. Campbell Barrington is still out there," Lucas said.

"He will flee to Ingleena," Alina said.

"Not from my harbour," Nikolas said as the horses rallied around them snorting and kicking up dust.

"Your uncle was paying him. He won't get far on his own now. . ... try not to keep looking, you don't want that image in your mind." Lucas took her hand and led her away.

Her eyes were watery but her chin firm. "That man, my father's brother . . . how can such a thing be? Why is he so evil when my father was such a true man?" A sob escaped her, and she turned, pulling away from Lucas. Running back to the body of her dead uncle she kicked dirt in his colorless face. "Burn in hell!" she shouted and spat.

The men exchanged wide-eyed glances, then Lucas let his face relax into a bemused grin. Standing nearby, but out of the way with his hands loosely on his hips, he watched Alina voice her anger and disgust. It made him love her even more. The men waited, and the horses settled as well, nickering, and nudging each other.

Brown birds like the one outside Lucas' window hopped about grabbing seeds, and the bees buzzed among the dainty petals. For Lucas, everything felt right with the world. And to prove it, Alina came over and rested her cheek against his chest. "I feel no sadness for him, only relief that he is dead," she said.

"As you should," Lucas said as he wrapped his arms around her. She gazed up at him and let him wipe the tears from her cheeks with his thumbs. He planted a kiss on her damp mouth.

"I know your cheek was badly cut. I saw it," she said, "what just happened to you?"

Lucas brushed his palms over his face, they came away clean. "Nothing happened, see? Somewhere, there are answers for everything. I'm ready. Let's get out of here."

They all mounted up and Lucas led them away from the body of Uncle Vasil. No one looked back. Bernard and his companions would deal with it in their own way. From beyond the ridge rose a cloud of dust. "What now?" Nikolas groaned.

Along came a wagon hurtling behind two galloping horses with the clapboard sides rattling and the man atop the bench shouting, "Whoa! Whoa!" Bernard kicked the flanks of his horse and dashed forward. Lucas grabbed the reins of Alina's mount and held fast as he pulled her off the road. Nikolas followed on the dusty heels of Bernard. The two-horse-team reared and swung left, launching the wagon onto two wheels. The man toppled sideways, landing on his face in a shallow ditch while the horse team neighed their panic. Bernard and Nikolas were off their horses at the same time. Bernard reached the man first and began to laugh. He waved at Lucas who recognized Wentworth as Bernard pulled him to his feet.

"It's all right," he said for the benefit of Alina, and Nikolas who had a dagger and a pistol clenched in his raised hands. Wentworth snorted like his horses who now stood awkwardly strained in the disheveled harness. Nikolas stowed the pistol in his waistband and used his dagger to free the horses. Lucas dismounted and helped Alina down. "He's from the Grande Inn. The man who knew my mother."

"What are you doing, Wentworth?" Bernard asked as he swatted at the grime on his step-father's face with a dirty handkerchief.

Wentworth shook his head. Beads of perspiration dotted his forehead. His hair matted. "I, well . . . I wonder the same. What are all of you doing here?" He gazed at Lucas with wild frightened eyes.

"Enjoying the scenery. Where is your wife, Wentworth?" As Lucas took a step toward Wentworth, Nikolas came over to stand beside Alina.

"She." He puffed, hung his head, then buried his face in his palms and mumbled.

Bernard flinched, "What's going on? Where's Marion?"

Lucas gazed nervously over his shoulder and beyond, across the flower field and up and down the road. He stepped closer to Wentworth and spoke softly. "Are you part of what just happened here? I will kill you if you are. Someone knew we were here. Don't pretend you didn't."

Bernard had a firm grip on Wentworth's arm now, although the old man was surely not going anywhere. "She's gone." Bernard released his grip but continued to breathe down upon Wentworth's head.

"Damn it! Where?" Lucas spun in a circle. "She was in on this plot to kill us!" Then thinking for a second, Lucas realized that Marion knew she couldn't kill him, so what did she have to do with it all. Or was that what Trousdale warned when she said, *don't lose your head*. He grabbed Wentworth by the front of his shirt and shook him. "Where is Marion? Is she still after me? What about Dugald, do you know him?"

"Please let go, Lucas." Wentworth brushed dust from his shirt and trousers. "I know of Dugald, haven't thought of him until just lately. Why? How do you know him? I can't handle a team of horses anymore."

Lucas gripped Wentworth's shoulders. "Never mind. Have you seen Campbell Barrington, is he with Marion?"

Wentworth wheezed. His voice high pitched. "Campbell Barrington? He's a bit too young for her wouldn't you say?"

Bernard broke into laughter, as did Nik and Alina but their faces displayed confusion.

"All right," Lucas chuckled. "Where were you going, Wentworth?"

"The Grande Inn." Wentworth rubbed his face with his dirty palms. "Marion is dead. She fell off the wagon." Wentworth snorted and covered his eyes with trembling hands.

Bernard's mouth fell open. Lucas glanced between the two men. An eerie sensation of complicity passed between Bernard and Wentworth. Lucas stared for a moment. "She fell?"

Alina gaped. Nik narrowed his eyes at Bernard who shrugged.

"Yes, she fell." Wentworth sighed. "My first wife was run over by a wagon."

"I remember you mentioned that," Lucas said. "And Marion?"

"Marion was at the farm paying us a visit that day. Interesting don't you think?" Wentworth said.

Lucas scratched his chin, "Hmmm . . . yes, it is. But what I was actually asking is, Wentworth, when did Marion fall from the wagon?"

"Ah, yes of course, Lucas. She . . .uh . . .ah hem . . . she fell this morning."

"Where is she now?" Bernard blurted.

"Buried."

"Ah ha! I cannot believe this," Nikolas said. "I have never been so entertained by a story. What fun these country folks are!"

Wentworth kept talking as if he hadn't heard Nikolas. "Well, I'm finished with the farm. She ruined it for me. He kicked the ground with his boot tip. So . . . I decided . . . best to leave her there."

"I can think of better places to put her," Bernard said.

Wentworth shook his head. "It is not the first time she's tried to use the land, my land to get others to do her dirty deeds. Two men, Vasil Sutcliffe and Campbell Barrington showed up last night. They asked about Dugald, her nephew, and demanded a place to stay. Said he stole something from them in the City of Dreams. Have you encountered Dugald, Lucas? Those two rude men slept in the hay last night, but this morning I chased them away with my flintlock, took a while to find it. After they left, Marion admitted she had promised Dugald a reward for some errand in the City of Dreams. Find a relative or spawn of hers, I don't know. She lies all the time. Gave him my deed in exchange for. . .this person she sought," he raked his hand through his hair. "I don't know what she was actually after this time, other people's things. She always wants other people's things. That Dugald is as useless as a dry cow. But I guess he took it. My property deed is missing. It's not in the box under the floor. I don't know what that means for the farm." He cast a watery-eyed pout toward Bernard.

"She wanted Lucas. Even after all this time," Bernard said and spat in the dirt.

"Really?" Wentworth asked mystified.

"The Grande Inn is in the other direction, Wentworth," Lucas said.

"It's been a confusing morning."

Lucas smirked, "Sounds like it. And you say, Marion simply fell off the wagon?"

"Simple as that."

"Sounds like it was simple as that," Bernard echoed.

"Well that was simple," Nik quipped.

"All right then, that's solved." Lucas said.

"Vasil fell off the wagon too," Alina said.

"Yes, he did," Lucas agreed. "So now, Dugald, he claimed he received papers and money from Vasil and Barrington, remember, Nik?"

"Yes, papers to dupe the harbour master, Mr. Merson to claim the trunks. And he also claimed he was to acquire land here in Arcana." Nik said.

Wentworth wobbled over to the broken wagon and leaned against it. Bernard turned the opposite way and walked off into the flower field. The clouds had blown through and the sun beat down on their heads. Alina removed her vest and Lucas held out his hand to relieve her of it. The dagger and thorns had pierced it through. Lucas paled, he must thank Brigit. Then he remembered that at Brigit's hut Dugald had said he hurt his hand rummaging in the bookshelf. He whispered to Nik, "If there are papers, they are hidden in the bookshelf at the boarding house."

"Right!" Nik agreed. Bernard circled back.

Marion was willing to give her own land to get her hands on him, Lucas realized. He shook off a shiver. At least he never had to see her again. And Dugald didn't matter now, he realized. If his hand healed, he could go free. The farm rightly belongs to Wentworth. So, whose name was on the land deed, and is it real or forged? Perhaps Dugald would get his land after all. Lucas would examine the bookshelf upon his return. "Are you planning to move into the Grande Inn permanently, Wentworth?"

Wentworth gazed off into the distance. "I don't know. This morning, I felt like a good fast ride out, you know. Didn't know where exactly, but I suppose I was in a big hurry to get there. As far as the wagon would take me. Then a ship . . . perhaps the south of somewhere."

Alina gasped. Lucas put his arm around her. "I'm sorry darling. You must be feeling terribly fatigued. Let's get you back to the Inn. Bernard, can you right this wagon and haul away the rest of the rubbish from this field?"

But Bernard ignored him, whispered to Wentworth. "You're just going to walk away from the land?"

"It's not the land I'm running from."

"Don't give up now." Bernard gripped Wentworth's shoulder.

Turning to Lucas, Bernard said, "I'll clean everything up and take Wentworth back to the farm for now."

Nikolas uncrossed his arms and pushed up his sleeves. "I'll help. Then we'll all meet back at the Inn."

Lucas inclined his head graciously. Alina turned and mounted her horse. Leaving the men to their task, they rode in silence back to the Grande Inn, although all the while Lucas expected Alina to rage against Uncle Vasil or lament her father. But she kept her jaw clenched tight and her sights on the road ahead, only once glancing at him with bright eyes and a resolute smile.

Lucas instructed Mr. Hartwinn to have the chamber maid prepare a bath for Alina. He accompanied her up to her room and assured her that now she truly was safe. Her dress was not too badly soiled. But he helped her out of it, put her shawl around her shoulders and wiped her dress with a linen cloth while explaining more of the details of Dugald and his warning that Vasil and Barrington had fled to Arcana. He was glad as he spoke that she didn't ask any further questions about his spontaneous healing. How could he explain what he himself couldn't understand? When the chamber maid and lobby boy brought the last of the buckets of hot water to fill her tub, he felt tempted to offer to join her, but her weariness dissuaded him from pursuing the notion. "We will retrieve your trunks right away." He patted his pocket that held the key.

"Thank you, Lucas. Thank you." She slipped out of her shift and into the tub, leaning her head back, the water danced at the nape of her neck. "No scars on me," she murmured.

"I can clearly see that," he said.

She smiled and closed her eyes.

"I'll leave you to it then." She didn't respond so he went out. In his own room, he washed his face and changed his shirt to a similar one with a heavier weave. Downstairs there was a tall glass of whisky waiting for him at the chair beside the fire. Mr. Hartwinn certainly knew how to care for his guests. Lucas relaxed into the chair, took a long swig of the whisky, leaned his head back and closed his eyes as Alina had done in the bath. After some time, the front door opened, and Nikolas, Bernard and Wentworth came in. Wentworth looked considerably better. Everyone took a glass of whisky except Wentworth who carried his valise up to his usual room.

"How did it all go?"

"Quite well," Nikolas said. "Wentworth showed us where he buried . . . um . . ." with a glimpse at Bernard. "Where he laid Marion to rest. We said a few words."

"Nikolas said a few words," Bernard pointed out.

"Right. I didn't know her but suggested she go in peace."

"If you had known her like Wentworth and I did, you wouldn't have said anything."

"I'm awfully sorry about all this Bernard. After all she was your mother," Lucas twisted his mouth.

Bernard took a gulp of his whisky and stared into the crackling fire. "We buried Alina's uncle right next to her. Let's see how they like that."

Lucas rubbed his hands over his face, "What about poor old Wentworth? Can we leave him out of it? I think he's harmless."

"Sure," Bernard agreed. "I believe Wentworth has more than paid his fair share to Marion. He should be allowed to travel like a free man."

"I suppose we will never know how involved Marion was with Alcott and Barrington."

"Wentworth said she only just met them last night. They were searching for Dugald out here," Nik answered.

"Does he know if she was responsible for my mother's death?" Lucas pressed his fists into his eyes as if to ward off the spectre of darkness. "What kind of devious woman was she?"

"One who hates her own child," Bernard stated. "She was horrible in many ways, murderer . . . maybe," he sighed. "Wentworth's first wife quite likely. But not actually your dear mother, Lucas."

"What do you mean?" Lucas leaned forward. "Do you know more than what you've told me?"

The lobby boy passed through the room and refilled all the glasses. Bernard waited for him to leave before speaking. "Your mother's death wasn't meant to happen, Lucas."

Lucas went white, "Well it did. Did it not, Bernard?"

Bernard chewed his bottom lip. "She was shot by an errant arrow. One intended for a rabbit."

Lucas grimaced and shook his head as he pushed out of the chair going to the sideboard to retrieve the bottle. "That can't be what happened. Someone would have come forward. It doesn't make sense."

"It does," Bernard said, "take it from the boy who shot her."

The bottle slipped from Lucas' grasp, shattering at his feet. Nik leapt up and rushed to Lucas' side. The two men faced

Bernard. The lobby boy entered but turned on his heel and withdrew.

Bernard flung his glass into the fire. "I'm sorry, Lucas. Please forgive me." He kicked the logs sending a shower of smoke and sparks into the room.

"What in flaming hell happened, Bernard?"

Bernard flinched as beads of perspiration appeared on his forehead. He closed his eyes, leaned his head back.

"What did you do?" Lucas snarled.

"A boy. Learning how to hunt. I was crouched in the grass. I noticed a hare. It jumped. I did too. Marion was beside me. She shouted shoot. The arrow released and the two of you fell." He gazed at Lucas through puddled eyes.

Lucas swallowed. He felt what Bernard said. The shadows of himself and his mother collapsing together.

Bernard braced both of his huge hands against the mantle and spoke to the licking flames. "As I told you before, you were both dead. I ran. We ran. Marion dragged me away. She said it was my fault. That I was a stupid useless boy, that only Linnea should have fallen. She said you should have been her child. She slapped me all the way home. But I could not stay away. I returned throughout the night to check on you. Every time, you were both still dead." He blubbered and wiped spittle from the corners of his mouth with his forearm. "I hid for a while thinking I should run away, but I was scared and hungry." He placed a meaty paw upon his stomach and dry-retched. "So... I don't know. But when I did return to the farm, you were sitting there at the table in a teary pallor. You had made it back on your own."

"So, I've heard," Lucas grumbled. "Did you shoot my mother with that arrow, Bernard? Or did Marion do it?"

Bernard stared at the floor. "She may have pushed my arm."

Lucas glared at Bernard's back, turned to Nik who stood planted in the center of the room, his gaze darting from Lucas to Bernard. Lucas slumped into his chair and Nik handed him his own glass of whisky which Lucas downed.

"I don't know if it was an accident. That's why I became so adept with the bow. I could never let something like that happen again." He crossed his arms over his face and began to moan, long, low and bereft with sorrow. Lucas and Nikolas sat silently watching him until the moaning turned into a deep keening wail. Nikolas went over and handed the weeping giant a handkerchief. Bernard blew his nose. His wailing took on the tone of a dying boar.

Lucas jumped up "Aaargh! Bernard shut up!" Crossing the room and grabbing Bernard by the shoulders he shook him, then knocked him on the top of the head with his fist. "Stop howling. At least I know now. Why didn't you tell me before?"

"Maybe Marion pushed his arm. Seems probable," Nik said.

Lucas shook his head, brushed his hair back with trembling hands. He paced. Bernard's keening filled the room like an out of tune orchestra. The tall pendulum clock ticked louder every second.

Lucas covered his face with his hands. "Shut . . . uuppp! My mother is dead. So why am I standing here? Where . . . is . . . the . . .damn . . . whisky."

The lobby boy rushed in with a fresh bottle and Nikolas grabbed it. Bernard turned to Lucas who puckered his forehead and opened his arms. Bernard wrapped his arms around Lucas, rested his soggy face on his shoulder and continued sniveling. A new group of guests scurried through the parlour. Red-faced, Lucas shot an exasperated look at Nik who came over and placed a glass of whisky in Lucas' hand. "Upon my soul," Lucas said. "If you will shut up, I and my mother will forgive you. Marion had her hand in it. You are not to blame."

Bernard hiccupped. Lucas unwrapped himself from the swathe of his burly arms. "Tell me now how the arrow tip got inside my mother's trunk."

"I wasn't truthful with you in the flower field last time you were here. After they carried your mother away from there, as I said before, I could see that the arrow tip had gone right through the two of you. I had to keep it. I kept the arrow tip, not just the bloody cloth." He grimaced and thought for a second. "I carried it all these years."

"Confound it, Bernard. What the hell? Be honest now."

Bernard shook his head. "I had it with me when you walked into the *No Horses*. I thought you had finally returned to kill me. The morning that you were downstairs getting the instrument to pick the lock I got into your room. I wrapped the arrow tip in a clean cloth and placed it inside your mother's trunk. Marion may have seen me in my hooded cloak that morning. Forgive me, I could not be completely honest at first, Lucas. I feared you would hate me, curse me." He pressed his lips together.

"She saw each of us then. Did she know that you were trying to tell me what happened?"

"She suspected."

"How did you open the lock on my mother's trunk?"

"It was my lock. I had the key. When I buried the trunk after you left Arcana all those years ago, there was only a meager lock on it. I broke it and put my own lock on. I wanted her . . . your possessions to remain safe."

Lucas stared at Bernard for a long moment. It wasn't even his mother's lock on the trunk now. So, *the lock is the key* meant nothing.

"It wasn't possible for me to admit all this at first. Having just found you again, I couldn't bear to disappoint you. As young as we were back then, I admired you so." His eyes cast down, his lips trembled, and his forehead beaded with sweat.

Lucas, feeling warm himself, went to the sideboard and poured two glasses of water. "Take a drink my brother. You have carried this burden too long. Holding so much guilt in your heart distorts the truth. You were too young to even know what happened. All is well now."

"I don't know how you can forgive me," Bernard swallowed the water in one gulp.

"We cannot regain what is lost."

"We can't, can we?"

"No."

"What is one to do then?"

Lucas patted him on the back. "Turn into the wind, Bernard. Eventually it will dry your tears."

Bernard slumped into a chair.

"It wasn't your intention to hurt my mother."

"No, but maybe it was Marion's."

"Well I took revenge on Marion, more or less. I took her necklace. So, if she had a hand in it, I got back at her in a way."

"How can I make amends to you, Lucas?"

"Please just refrain from crying anymore. You're much too large for me to rock in my arms like a baby." Lucas exhaled. "The past is gone. All is well now."

"It is?"

"Yes," Nik, quipped.

"That part of your life is over. Walk away," Lucas said.
Bernard lifted one shoulder in a half-hearted shrug.
* * *

Alina soaked in her bath for less time than usual; she couldn't wait to get back to the boarding house and tell the women what happened. Uncle Vasil was gone! She could hardly believe it. Now that he was officially dead, she allowed herself to admit that it was her wish all along. Her hope when she first met Lucas, was that he would avenge her father for her. And he had, with the help of his friends. And thankfully there was no actual blood on his graceful hands. Soon they would find her trunks. She couldn't begin to imagine what uncle wanted so desperately from those trunks. Her heart raced with the joy of freedom and relief. As she placed her belongings in her travelling case, she thought about Lucas' eagerness to marry. It flattered her that he was so enamored. But the idea frightened her. Having never known her own mother, she had little knowledge of the role of a wife. And it was a situation she hadn't bothered to think about. There was much to do first. She wanted to experience the City of Dreams with fresh eyes and decide if she wanted to stay. Since her arrival, it had been a place of isolation and confinement. She had not been to the book shop or the dress shops. Now, she could explore all that the city had to offer. How exciting her sad life had suddenly become again. And someday, not too far away, she would try to find Daria. She couldn't bear the thought of enjoying life without her devoted handmaid. Daria would help her decide what to do next. She knitted her brow trying to imagine all of them living at the boarding house.
* * *

When Alina entered the grand parlour all three men were laughing. She was wearing the light blue dress and a dark blue ribbon in her braided hair. "Alina!" Lucas rushed to her "You are a stunning sight."

She gazed up at him, "As are you!" Then turning her attention to Bernard and Nikolas she said, "It appears you men have sufficiently entertained yourselves."

"Ah, that we have," Nik said clapping Bernard on the back. Bernard bowed to Alina. "I'm ready to go to the City of Dreams."

"Aren't we all," Lucas agreed and called for the lobby boy to retrieve their luggage.

Climbing the stairs, Nik said. "I'll alert Wentworth."

"Can he ride?" Lucas asked Bernard.

Bernard shook his head, "Best to send a carriage for him in a few days."

"Yes," Lucas agreed. "We must ride fast to arrive home before nightfall." He squeezed Alina's hand and she squeezed back.

Nikolas came down with his satchel flung over his shoulder. The lobby boy came next with the rest of their luggage. Wentworth followed empty-handed. "I'm going to stay here." Wentworth announced clasping his hands in front of him.

"Right." Bernard said. "There's no reason to flee now."

They mounted up and waved goodbye to Wentworth who stood atop the stairs of the Grande Inn as relaxed as if he owned the place and had just arrived home after a long journey.

As drunk as he had felt for a few moments, the blubbering tears of Bernard completely sobered Lucas. The revelation concerning his mother's death didn't cause a headache or nausea. He rode alongside Alina, with Bernard in front and Nik following behind. Each of them taking advantage of the distance riding offered. There was no longer a need to fear an attack. Campbell Barrington was running without his puppeteer. He posed no threat. Bernard, the giant, had turned out to be a lamb with a lamentable secret. His brave admission resolved him of his burden. Lucas felt no anger toward him. The affliction of unanswered questions had fallen away.

Bernard veered left into the woods. Coming from this direction the *No Horses* could easily go unnoticed. "Shall we go in?" Alina asked with an expression Lucas couldn't read.

He scratched at the stubble on his face. "Would you like to? This is the best view of the place, but if you want an ale . . ."

Bernard had already dismounted, and Nik followed remarking he needed an ale to wash the whisky through his bloodstream. Lucas held the reins loose in his hands. "It won't be a moment, Bernard will give word to his countrymen to watch out for Barrington should he stagger in this direction. Although, there is an interesting chandelier held together by cobwebs."

She wrinkled her nose. "No, let's not. I'm anxious to get home."

"Me too," Lucas agreed.

"Will Irene be expecting us?"

"She will," Lucas reached over and took her hand.

Alina beamed, "I'm hungry now. I hope she serves one of her wonderful stews, and wine by the fire."

Lucas leaned closer and pulled her toward him, planting an errant kiss on her eyelashes.

"Let's go," Nik shouted trotting up beside them with Bernard on his flanks, "before you fall off your horses!"

They rode on without stopping. Lucas smelled home before the city came into view, the salt air, wood smoke, baked bread, simmering meats, the aromas of his life. The lights caused him to rein up. Pausing on the high road, adjacent to the cathedral dotted with work lamps, down into the city they could see that Ikarus had more than done his job. Lantern light from dark orange to pale yellow lit the City of Dreams like the king's palace. All the streets glowed like boulevards; the alleys transformed into tunnels of gold.

Lucas stood up in the stirrups and shouted, "Magnificent! I love this place!" Alina's face was alight as well, her eyes shining in the reflection of warm, welcoming light. Bernard sat atop his tall horse transfixed. His long black hair picking up shimmers of light, his mouth open, eyes sweeping the skyline in awe. He had never wandered from the woods of Arcana. The most lights he had ever seen, Lucas realized were at the Grande Inn. When he turned to Lucas his face was a mask of childlike wonder.

"Welcome to my city Bernard!" The four galloped through the brilliant streets, hooves clattering thunder over the cobblestones.

Chapter 15

Everyone was sitting in the front room. Irene, Brigit, Carissa and Ikarus, who wore a proud smile when he saw the appreciation written across Lucas' face. Lucas introduced Bernard to Ikarus first. "This is Ikarus who has so diligently performed my duties while I was away. And Irene, as you know. This is Carissa, our most helpful maid. And here is the illustrious Madam Brigit Trousdale, her talents unmeasurable." And her hourglass full, he noticed. The sideboard held the pewter goblets of red wine. "We have found the key," Lucas announced holding his cup high.

Irene dabbed her eyes. "I knew you would."

Madam Trousdale held Lucas' gaze for a long moment then tilted her cup a second time. After the toast, Lucas suggested to Alina that she take her cup up with her since he knew she wished to change her gown before dinner. He took his also and followed her up the stairs, looking back to see Bernard settle onto the settee next to Nikolas. Ikarus took a chair beside them and the women gathered at the side sofa.

Lucas opened Alina's door, the oil lamp burned as well as two candles shimmering inside glass globes. The fire sparked a merry greeting. He placed her luggage at the foot of her bed, taking care not to disturb her freshly cleaned coverlet. "Is this bed comfortable enough?"

"It is, yes! Thank you for my coverlet and the fine sheets. I am pleased with this little corner of the world."

"It's not the Grande Inn . . ."

"Or Ingleena," she bit her lip as a fleeting sorrow crossed her face. "But there is friendship and grace in this house, Lucas. Thanks to you and Irene."

He pulled her to him. They embraced and kissed until the warmth of the small room made him uncomfortable. He checked the window that was open, allowing in just the right amount of evening air. She already had her dress off and was changing into a clean shift. She crossed to the wash basin. Opening the wardrobe, he asked, "The green one this evening?"

"Yes, of course." her eyes sparked the color of the dress.

He shook his head. "I can't imagine Carissa wearing this dress, where would she get it?"

Alina fluttered her eyelashes, "May I tell you a secret?"

"Of course, you can." Lucas narrowed his eyes and smiled tenderly.

"Carissa said Madam Trousdale gave her this dress to give to me."

"Ah ha, now I understand. I'm sure she stole it then. Just for you of course. Perhaps, she and Nikolas helped themselves to some unguarded cargo at the harbour. She, herself would not wear such finery."

"When she was a young maiden, I suppose Brigit would wear a dress like this. Now though, Madam Trousdale wears the clothes of many layers."

"Like her personality."

"And her hair."

"You are clever and entertaining, Alina." He lifted her hair and did the clasp on her ruby pendant. "I will leave you for now, but will you think about resting with me in my room this night?"

She cast him an auspicious glance as they left her room and Lucas opened the door to his. The candles sent halos to the ceiling and the tub steamed in front of the fire. "It's a shame you're dressed already. We could bathe together."

"I had my bath this afternoon at the Grande Inn!"

Stepping back into her room, she retrieved her wine goblet. "I will wait for you downstairs. But don't take too long, I may have to devour your portion of dinner."

Lucas laughed, "It's roast lamb. I'd like to see you do that!"

When Lucas came downstairs dressed in loose gray trousers and a beige batiste shirt, he noticed that the silk merchant sat among the group engaged in conversation with Alina. But she held up a hand to interrupt the man and came over to Lucas.

"This gentleman, Julian, is leaving for Ingleena at dawn. I thought he may have known my father, but . . ." her mouth turned down, "he doesn't."

"I have heard of Louis Sutcliffe," Julian said as he came over and extended a hand to Lucas. "I am disappointed that there was not time for us to become acquainted during my stay. I've already had my supper, but I'm leaving several fine bolts of cloth as a gift for the ladies. This is a delightful house you and Mrs. Kempel run here. I also trade in wines. I will bring some upon my return."

Lucas shook his hand. Alina was cheerful. Lucas wanted to see what gifts the man presented, his interest in lady's garments and gowns having grown lately. Once Julian retired, accompanied by a satchel of fresh bread and provisions from Irene, and herbs for seasickness from Brigit, Lucas assisted Irene and Carissa in serving the platters of food. He inquired about other boarders, if anyone new had arrived other than the merchant and felt pleased to learn that only the usual masons were in residence. They kept earlier hours than Lucas and his clan and for that he was grateful. They all sat down for dinner together. Lucas and Alina sat side by side as did Nikolas and Brigit. Ikarus seemed satisfied to find himself seated across from Carissa. And Irene sat at the head of the table with Bernard at the opposite end, mostly due to his size. Everyone passed platters to each other, around and back and forth. Irene made a toast to her assorted family. They ate heartily emptying the platters and several wine bottles.

Once everyone finished, Lucas turned to Brigit. "What is the condition of Dugald?"

"He is restrained and resolute in his innocence. His hand doesn't ooze as much. Now he has a cough and yellowing of the skin. He claims he was bitten by a rat."

Lucas cocked his head, "A rat, not a spider?"

"As he says," Brigit nodded.

Lucas grimaced. "Well, so be it. Whatever it was. As long as he is not a concern for us now."

"He is well-guarded."

"Good. And Bernard. What did your companions from the *No Horses* tell you about Campbell Barrington?"

Bernard leaned forward resting his elbows on the table. "Wonderful supper, Mrs. Kempel. Thank you very much."

"Irene," she said. "You may call me Irene."

"Ah yes, very well. They said Barrington came in sobbing and blubbering, begging for a horse. He had no money to buy one. Ha! Can you imagine?" Bernard laughed and held up his goblet, draining it. "He stumbled off into the forest on foot with not so much as a sip of ale in him."

"What will happen to him?" Alina asked.

"They will make a sport of finding him."

"Who will?"

Bernard shrugged his big shouldered shrug. "The local villagers or wolves, whichever comes upon him first."

Lucas stiffened, grabbed Alina's hand under the table. She lifted her chin, and said, "He will get what he deserves then."

Nikolas, Lucas, and Bernard nodded at each other. Turning to Irene, Lucas said. "I know you have been frequenting the apothecary for your and Brigit's remedies, have you noticed any activity at Vasil's house?"

"It's still boarded up. How do you know I have been going to the apothecary?" She narrowed her eyes at him.

"I know things," Lucas said reaching over to squeeze her arm. "All is well it seems." Pushing himself up from the table, he said, "Very well then. I believe there are papers hidden in the bookshelf. Dugald's papers. Shall we all retire to the parlour?"

They made themselves comfortable with their wine goblets full, the fire burned low casting flickering shadows on the stone hearth. The windows opened half-wide to allow some of the pleasant evening air inside. Lucas noticed plants outside in the courtyard: that would be at the hand of Trousdale. Was she planning on moving in, he wondered? As he scratched his cheek and looked at her, the hourglass did one of its flips. She noticed his gaze but ignored him and took her place on the divan alongside Nikolas.

Lucas stood back perusing the bookshelves then stepped upon the hearth and reached up to the highest shelf. The bronze pot, the most obvious location. He lifted it down and peered inside.

Carefully, wary of a spider, he dipped his index and middle finger inside and pulled out a sack of coins. Smacking his lips together he shook it then tossed it to Irene. He peered into the pot, put his hand in and pulled out a roll of papers. "Voila`!"

Replacing the pot, he stepped down and slowly unfolded the papers. "I hope these papers don't bring any unwelcome news." Realizing he was stalling, he cleared his throat and began to read: *This document states that the cargo marked Sutcliffe, from aboard the ship Le Peresi, out of Ingleena shall be stored and delivered to none other than: Vasil Sutcliffe.* Turning the paper sideways he continued, "Then, scribbled here on the side it says *or Dugald Tendrick.*"

Lucas looked up at the group. "Campbell Barrington isn't mentioned here, ha!"

"Neither am I," sniffed Alina, her face had gone white.

Lucas gazed reassuringly at her, "Don't worry my darling the harbour master didn't accept these orders from Dugald. Nik and I will retrieve your belongings. We need nobody's permission to do so."

He went to her, squeezed her shoulder, and kissed the top of her head. The wind banged the window sash and Irene leapt up to fasten it. Brigit helped her close all the windows as a cool wind had blown into the room. Bernard drained his cup and rose to refill it. Carissa jumped up to help him.

"Now as for this other parchment." Lucas unrolled it and read: "*Title to Land, in the village of Arcana, located on the south west section. . .*" he paused, read, "there's details of the land, information on official officialness," he read more, mumbling to himself and making faces. "Here it says: *owner in full right, the gentleman, former yeoman, Wentworth Bodden of Bodden Fields.*" He held up the paper. "It is sealed with the mark of *Cyrano* . . . I can't read this part." Squinting and holding the paper closer to the candle, "I think it says, yes, *Cyrano– Abbot of Arcana.*"

Bernard held his cup to his lips, then stopped as if taking a drink would change his fate. Lucas continued, "And this second page, official description of the land with a map, signed and sealed as well by the same hand. *Upon the demise of Wentworth Bodden, the described land shall pass by the will of Wentworth Bodden to one Bernard Bodden, only, and none other. If Bernard Bodden should precede Wentworth Bodden in death, the land shall be granted to the proprietor of the Grande Inn, Mr. Hartwinn and his heirs.*"

Lucas went up to Bernard slapped him on the back and murmured in his ear, "It seems Marion had no ability to take the land from Wentworth or you. These official papers and the land that goes with them belong to you and Wentworth. Marion had nothing to give to anyone. It appears, Dugald told the truth when he said he couldn't read."

Bernard caught a sob in his throat, washed it down with the wine. They all clapped and lifted their cups to Bernard.

"Now, if you will wait just a moment, we have one more thing to do." Lucas said as he ran upstairs. He returned in a few moments carrying a packet of cloth. Sitting on the edge of the hearth he placed it in his lap and unraveled it to reveal the deadly arrow tip. Everyone gasped. Bernard stared into his wine goblet.

"Take this Bernard, and if you will please toss it into the fire."

Bernard flinched. "That won't burn," he mumbled.

"Come forward. Take it. It's yours to destroy. Do it for both of us, and for my mother."

He stood, walking as if his legs were stuck in deep mud, he approached Lucas. With shaking hands, Bernard snatched the arrow tip and flung it so hard it hit the back of the stone firebox with a ping then fell into the flames. He stood watching with his hands on his hips until Lucas led him back to his chair and handed him his goblet. "Tomorrow, anything that remains goes out with the ashes."

Brigit got up and smoothed her skirts. "I need to go back to my cottage and check on things." Lucas knew she referred to Dugald but hoped the gold-jewelled box was secure somewhere as well. He hadn't forgotten about it.

Nikolas bid everyone good night and avoided the smirk he received from Lucas as he followed Brigit out the front door. Ikarus retreated to his downstairs room where he had permanently moved. Irene and Carissa went upstairs with Alina while Lucas made sure Bernard was comfortable in his room.

"I can't believe it," Bernard said. "Marion never had anything, and she knew it. I wonder what she thought would happen if Dugald had succeeded in kidnapping you."

Lucas crossed his arms across his chest. "We can only wonder about her malice."

"She must have thought you would bring her power or prestige. I'm angry that I'll never know. I don't care that she is dead. Shouldn't I feel something?" Bernard gazed imploringly at Lucas.

"I think she should have been a true mother to you and not fought so hard for what she couldn't have."

Bernard dragged his hands across his face and through his hair knitting them on the back of his neck. "Once I was grown, there were days upon days when she wanted to spend time—*shall we share an ale*—she used to say. Perhaps I could have helped her be a real mother, a better person. Those days . . . those lost days, I cannot get them back."

Standing in the middle of Bernard's room, Lucas stared off into the middle distance, expelling a breath. "Tis true, my brother." None of his stolen treasures could replace the ones he loved. And for the first time in his life, he felt a twinge deep in his belly. He thought about Marion's silver pendant. It could not avenge the death of his mother. He wondered if she'd missed it during her final days on earth. If she searched for it among her possessions with hope and anticipation that could never achieve satisfaction, but still thinking it merely misplaced. It was just an item, he reminded himself. And yes, she was ruthless, evil even as well, but a part of her loved whom she loved. Apparently, that was him. A heart that feels love must also feel sorrow. She was dead now, and he genuinely believed she deserved to be. Best to let the sting of her actions die with her. "Our mothers are gone and our father's unknown." Unable to think of anything more to say to Bernard. He pointed at the pitcher and basin, "There's the water."

"Thank you for everything, Lucas. You are truly my brother. Marion has at least given us that. I would like to stay, but I must let Wentworth know. I will see myself off in the morning. And when things settle down here, you will all return to Arcana for a feast at my home on the farm." They shook hands, then clasped hands to elbows.

Before knocking on Alina's door, Lucas headed toward his own room to clear his head. Many good things had occurred over the past few days, finding Alina completely changed his life as well as his thoughts and desires for the future. He enjoyed the closeness of Irene, Brigit and everyone milling around him. He realized he didn't miss his nights wandering the city alone. He used to believe that standing on the outside looking in, observing life from a safe distance created a barrier of protection from the heartache of mankind. Now he knew it only widened the chasm. The past few years, he walked the streets lighting lanterns for his own sake, certainly not for the meager wages. It had begun with the ambition of a young boy to earn a coin, walking as a lamp boy, guiding the frightened and timid home, and from there the abundance of opportunity had filled his cellar treasure trove. Once Alina's trunks came home, he would make time to rediscover and assess the collection.

One hand unlacing his shirt, the other lifted the latch and there was Alina laying languid under his coverlet. "Ah!" his hand went to his heart and caught the black lace veil. She giggled. He tossed the lace as he went to her. It landed on the bed in the empty space beside her. She stretched out a leg. She was wearing her shift, the one he and Nik had saved from her old room at Vasil's house.

"It's warm," she murmured running her hand along the white linen sheet. Five candles burned in the iron floor stand and one in the lamp on the night table. As he entered the room, the fire sparked and sizzled. She had shut the window and drawn the curtain. Lucas tore off his shirt, tugged his trousers down, then hesitated and crossed behind the bed to his wardrobe where he retrieved loose-fitting trousers that he wore to bed on chilly winter nights. He slipped them on and turned to see her eyes wide as she watched him. Wetting his fingers, he extinguished the candles, so the only glow came from firelight. He lifted the coverlet and slid in beside Alina. She curled catlike into his arms. They entwined their legs, his arms around her shoulders, he pulled her closer with his hands upon her firm tummy, her breasts brushing his wrists. He lowered his head, buried his face in her hair that smelled of rosewood. His heart drummed from the depths of his chest; he wondered if she could feel the percussion against her back. His mind raced even as his body relaxed into hers. When she flipped her hair away from her face, it landed on his cheek with a soft tickle making him shudder. The joy of holding her in his arms barred words. He wished to say something eloquent and brilliant, but his mind was full of the sight and scent of her. Gently pulling her hair up from the nape of her neck he nuzzled and kissed her—soft, dancing butterfly kisses—his hand stroked her arm and down along her side. He longed to lift the soft shift, but vowed, at that moment, that, he would never take anything not freely given him again. Quickly adjusting his vow, he decided apart from the gold-jewelled box, should it come around his way. Stretching her legs with a dreamy moan, she stroked the back of his hand. He knew she felt safe in his arms. She turned over and wrapped herself around him and returned kisses on his cheeks and neck. He cupped her face in his hand and kissed each eyelid. She opened her sparkling green eyes. He traced his finger along her cheek. His hands slid down her back, over her hips and along her thigh. He could feel her hand pressed warm against his back. A log fell, sparked into a blue plume then vanished. All of these days when he walked up and down the narrow streets, and the dark quiet nights, comforted only by emptiness, a sense of vast unimportance beneath the vast sky, and days in the market, among the clusters–talking, bargaining, arguing, he'd never considered that one unexpected morning the answer to a prayer, he had no words or wisdom to form, would bump into him in the unobstructed light of day. Every pulse of his blood felt hot and alive, raging like rampant fire wherever their bodies touched. He intended to never move. Their breath matched, the rise and fall of her chest against his. His eyelids fluttered and he succumbed to sleep.

Much later, when the fire glowed only a thin orange line under a row of tiny, gray ash houses, he murmured, "Are you warm enough?" She didn't answer. Her lissome body pressed around him like a blanket, her breath soft and steady against his chest.

* * *

Alina heard pounding footfalls on the stairs. Lucas' place beside her in bed felt cold. She bolted upright, clutching the sheet. Sunlight streamed through the tiny window indicating mid-morning. The door flew open and bounced against the wall, Lucas backed through the door. "Good, excellent, that's it. Leave them there. Thanks, Nik and Ik!" Closing the door and turning to Alina, he bowed. "Mademoiselle, your trunks have arrived!"

She bounded from the bed, caught her foot in the sheet and tumbled into his arms. "Lucas! You got them already. Why did you not wake me? I would have gone with you." Her hair was wild around her face. She jumped up and down, clapping her hands. He grabbed her, hugging her tightly he planted a kiss on her cheek and ran his fingers through her hair.

"I'll bring them in now. There is good lighting for you to go through them. Are you ready, my darling?"

"Yes," she swallowed, shook her head, and hopped up onto the bed, tucking her feet under the blanket while he opened the door and shoved the trunks inside. They were identical. Wood framed, rounded at the top with leather and iron strapping and a large ring handle at each end. There was rust and the wood itself had a musty smell.

Examining her face, Lucas relaxed his jaw as recognition and delight gleamed in her eyes. "They were here at the harbour for these past few weeks, inside that huge locker but sitting in a puddle of water. I hope nothing is ruined."

She slid off the bed and placed her hand atop one of the trunks. "They are quite old, they were my grandfather's. How can I ever thank you for rescuing them?"

Lucas went to her side and wrapped his arms around her waist. "There are many ways, Alina. For now, let's open them up for you. Do you recognize these padlocks?"

"They've always been on these trunks. At home we stored winter clothes in them."

"You have keys then?"

"No, we never actually locked them. The locks just hung on there."

"There's nothing special about the padlocks?

"No, they're old. That's all. Why?"

"Nothing, just something I heard in a dream."

Alina rubbed her palms together. "Can't you just break the locks?"

"Certainly can," he nodded. The lock sprang easily when he hit it with the fire poker. "I'm getting good at this." He stood back to allow her to lift the lid.

Carefully she lifted the hasp, then with a deep breath she placed a hand on each side and pushed up the heavy top. A thick burgundy cloth covered the contents. When she pulled it back, she exclaimed, "Oh my!"

A silver candelabra with eight candle positions, stood to one side, with cloths tucked around it. On the other side, a stack of silver plates and tucked along the side, wedged here and there assorted bound books. She knelt beside the trunk and began to lift the items from it and hand them to Lucas. Along with the candelabra, wrapped in paper, were sixteen white wax candles. He had to set it on the floor as there was no stand or table large enough in her tiny room. "This silver is dazzling Alina, certainly explains the weight of this trunk. Is this what you expected?"

"I suppose so," she said with a faraway gaze. These are some of our books and our household silver. A wedding gift from my father to my mother. She averted her eyes, "As you know, I never met my mother. These pieces are most precious to me. I had only dreamed to find them in here. I think I can thank Daria for packing them." Tears rimmed her eyes, but she continued to unpack the trunk. An embroidered leather coin pouch, that was her father's, made Alina cry out and press it to her heart. A robe and dressing gown, a silver-handled mirror and comb. "These were my mother's as well," she murmured. There were linen handkerchiefs, and a tattered shawl. Lucas sat silently on the edge of the bed knowing full well how it felt to rediscover the past.

When the time came, he struck the lock on the second trunk. This one was full of dresses and gowns. Alina leaned over the trunk and sniffed, tears ran down her pink cheeks. She lay her face upon a gossamer rose gown. Lucas knelt beside her and silently stroked her hair. Finally, she sat up and he handed her one of her own linen handkerchiefs. She dabbed the corners of her eyes and tittered nervously.

"This is not easy, I know," he said as he rubbed her back in gentle circular swirls.

"But you made it seem easy. I woke up and here they are, my belongings that I have worried for and wanted all these weeks."

He brushed strands of hair off her damp cheeks.

"Was it difficult to open the locker? I had wanted to see that massive door. The key we found fit then?"

"Yes, it fit quite easily. The locker is in an ugly, frightening area of the harbour. It's better that you didn't see where the trunks landed. I couldn't bring you to such a filthy place. The stench is horrid. We rubbed your trunks with thyme and lavender before bringing them inside the house."

She tilted her head. "You did?"

"No, not I, of course, I didn't think of that, but Irene did. And she is relieved now that your trunks are here. Perhaps, she will not need so many visits to the apothecary."

"Perhaps she enjoys the trips to the apothecary for other reasons," Alina said.

"Ha! Is that so?" Lucas leaned back against the bed frame and stretched his legs out in front of him on the floor. "I will have to inquire about that."

"Well, don't let on that I said so." Alina said with a mischievous curl of her upper lip.

Lucas chuckled as he cupped her chin in his palm and planted a kiss on her warm cheek. He stared blankly for a moment. "It makes me wonder what they were after. Will you let me know if you find anything in these trunks that Vasil would want so desperately that he would kill for it?"

She nodded. "Horrible things have happened," her eyes closed for several moments, "to both of us."

"Not anymore. Wonderful things lie ahead for us. We are on the edge of a new beginning. The City of Dreams will never be as vibrant and promising as it is right now. And we are here to enjoy it." Lucas stroked her forearm, "Some areas of the city you may not have seen yet, fine homes on the Boulevard. We shall walk there and plan our future. You would like that, wouldn't you?"

"Yes, very much." Her eyes sparkled. "I've had enough of fear-filled days."

He turned her hand over to examine her palm. "Shall we have Madam Trousdale read your palm?" She laughed, as he had hoped she would. Draping his arm around her shoulders he gazed deep into her shining eyes, "You are safe now. I promise." She snuggled against him and they sat in comfortable silence watching the sun move across the floor until it settled on the colorful contents of her trunk. "I shall leave you now to enjoy your dresses and personal possessions. And, so that the gowns don't slip right off your beautiful body, I will bring your bread up on a tray."

* * *

Alina lifted each of her dresses from the trunk and laid them out on the bed, smoothing the folds and pleats with her palms. The trunk smelled of their home in Ingleena mixed with a hint of lavender and thyme. She imagined herself wearing each dress with Lucas, sometimes she had to correct her thoughts remembering she was no longer in Ingleena. But surely, as he said, there were many lovely places to wear her clothes and she felt satisfied that her wardrobe was suitable for the City of Dreams. The high-waisted, ivory, gossamer dress embroidered with little blue flowers and three-quarter sleeves was perfect for the coming summer, a beige gown in crushed velvet with brocade panels in chestnut brown, a matching cloak that was perfect for walking about the city to market. A blue-green gown with purple sash, corded sleeves, and a low neckline for perhaps the dining house, that Lucas had mentioned. A billowy burgundy with puffed sleeves, gold cuffs, and covered buttons. She had a V-neck ruffled blouse in white and a berry skirt; she loved how it swished from one side to the other when she walked. She also had three fur collars and another pair of boots, gloves, a dressing gown and two more white shifts.

After admiring her wardrobe with a happy heart, she reached into the corner of the trunk and pulled up the false bottom and set it on the floor beside the trunk. Only she, her father, and her grandfather knew about the secret compartment. There she found four neatly stacked paper piles. The first three stacks were banknotes. Alina's father always assured her of a respectable life, and before he went to his grave, he had kept his promise. Now, in the presence of her possessions that her father so carefully packed for her, she could still barely believe Vasil had killed him. Her blood ran hot, rushed into her head, screeching in her ears, blinding her in a flood of tears that sent shivers and convulsions through her. Her breath stopped, then burst out in a painful expulsion. She dove for the chamber door to turn the latch with a hand as cold as steel.

Kneeling over the trunk, she reached in and counted the banknotes—issued by the Bank of Ingleena. She held them against her heart knowing that her father's hands were the last to touch them. It was as if she could hear his thoughts as he placed them there. He must have known Vasil would chase her to the City of Dreams, but Vasil was no match to her father, nor to Lucas. And he had not succeeded in destroying her. Now, her heart settled to a soft rhythm. She unfolded the handwritten document that contained a stamp and seal. Closely examining it she found an address, what appeared to be a property description, but couldn't understand its full meaning. A letter from her father waited in the bottom of the trunk. Taking it in hand, she realized it was the final thread to her father. Once she read it, she would understand his thoughts in the days before he died. She would read it many times, but now, this time would be the only time she could read it for the first time. These, if he could have spoken them to her, were her father's last words.

Dearest Alina,

Even as I write this, I hope you will never have to read it. But if you are, then now you know that your Uncle, my brother Vasil, is an evil man. It is late, past midnight as I write this in haste. Unforeseen developments have occurred that cause me to regret not dealing with Vasil long ago.

In this trunk, you will find all the money I have left to give you. As was his custom as a child, Vasil has impersonated me and this time to his great advantage and to our loss. He has commandeered my trade accounts and drained the bank of assets. Upon your return from school, I intend to explain matters to you in person. But for now, I want to be sure that if that day doesn't arrive, these are your possessions. Our most valuable possessions.

If you are unable to remain in Ingleena, as I fear may happen, I have packed your clothing and made arrangements for the trunks to be shipped to the City of Dreams. I pray that you receive this letter before reaching the city. Vasil has compromised my old merchant house, but there is another home for you, Alina. An exceptionally fine home.

Herein, I place the deed to your house on the Boulevard in the City of Dreams. I have kept this house for myself while travelling for trade and as a security. I intended to bring you there in person this coming spring. The house is yours. It is your estate home. Vasil knows nothing about it. Bring the deed to the solicitor in the City of Dreams and he will provide you with the keys.

Lucas, the Lantern Lighter of the City of Dreams, is an inscrutable man of pensive demeanor and wise disregard for authority. These attributes, I can see now, are the substance of truth and honor. A man who makes his own rules abides with what he creates. And there is more, you will see. I have only briefly met him, but this man is legend. I see you and he as well-suited to each other.

But dearest, Alina, this is a matter for your choosing. Whichever way you choose, he will protect you, and help you take possession of your home.

Forgive me, my darling daughter. I have made mistakes. I wish I knew, when I was as young as you are now, that very few in this world are trustworthy. Those who most proclaim so, are full of deception. As was Vasil. Rid yourself of him in all possible manner. I wish you Godspeed.

Your loving, Papa

She read the letter twice, through streaming tears that finally subsided when she examined the deed to the house right here in the City of Dreams. The prospect of it thrilled her. Leave it to Father to divert my pain with such a marvelous surprise! This is a gift of refuge and freedom. Her tears dried on her cheeks as frayed filaments of acceptance entwined her heart. She witnessed Uncle Vasil's death. Her father's last wish was accomplished.

* * *

In the kitchen, Lucas helped Irene move the large pot from the fireplace hook and replace it with the smaller one. The masons and laborers had just left for their afternoon shift, some had retired to their beds to wake at dusk and trade places with their workfellows.

"How are things with you Irene? For several days, we've had no chance to spend time in the ease of each other's company."

She placed a cup of tea in front of him. "We must let the bread cool a bit longer. You have been busy young man."

Lucas chuckled. "I have, and I hope you do not feel slighted."

"Don't worry yourself, Lucas, you are a young man. I can take care of myself."

He placed his palm over the back of her hand. "Are the visits to the apothecary making you feel better?"

She slapped his hand away, "You are a shrewd devil!"

"Have you a story for me, then?"

Irene smoothed her hair back into its bun and smirked at Lucas.

"My god woman!" He slapped the table. "I have been so caught up in my own romance, I failed to notice yours."

"Humph . . . Lucas. You make me shy."

"All right," he rose to slice the bread which he placed on the table in front of them, along with a dish of quince jelly. "I can ask Brigit."

"Lucas!"

"I may be preoccupied, but things are changing around here. I have noticed." He slid onto the bench beside her. "Would you like to tell me what you've been up to or shall I wait for the gossip to reach me?"

She laughed and shook her head. "Very well then. I first went to the apothecary to inquire about Dugald . . . after the spider bite and all that. I wanted to discover from whence he came. Mr. Padgett is a kind man. He offered a chair and served me tea."

Lucas tilted his head. "I worried about plague, but he still has shown no pustules. That concern is past us now. What we will do with him I don't know. But tell me about Mr. Padgett."

"The next time I went to market, I stopped in to inquire of the refreshing tea . . . of which he served more, and eventually I told Brigit about it and she asked that I find out what it was, because even she could see how revived I felt after this tea he served me. So now we are planting spearmint and lemon in the courtyard. It's just the beginning, we will plant more. I will add candles, so we can enjoy sitting there in the evenings like at the Grande Inn, though much smaller."

"I noticed those plants. It's an excellent idea, but isn't that a lot more work for you, Irene?"

"It's pleasant work for me. Any day now, Carissa's sister will come to work alongside her in the kitchen and cleaning the rooms. I can devote more time to the garden. I am tired of the same old chores."

"You grow weary."

"I do. But now things are changing, aren't they Lucas? We go for so long, the same thing every day, and then finally something different happens." She wiped her hands on her apron.

"That's true," Lucas said taking her hand.

"Mister Padgett has promised to buy herbs from us."

"I can help with money, Irene. I have much saved."

"I know you do," she said. "You haven't fooled me. That what you have securely hidden, it's for you and Alina. In fact, don't you think it's time to let Ikarus light the lanterns?"

Lucas nodded. "He is showing earnest effort. Indeed, it could be time for him, and another as the city grows. I too grow weary and I'm no longer intrigued by the lonely streets at night. It's due time for Nikolas and me to further implement our legitimate trade plans."

"Yes, now you two men have found suitable women for yourselves."

Lucas gazed out the window, "Apparently we both have." He hesitated, shook his head. "Nikolas. That outlandish woman. She's bewitched him."

Irene chortled. "She's incredibly special. She is indeed."

"And Mr. Padgett, are these visits restricted to his shop or will we see him at supper soon?"

"Ach . . . I don't know if I want to cook for the man!"

"Pfttt…. Why not Irene? You cook for lots of men."

"That's the point, I guess." She pursed her lips. "I don't want to be a wife."

"Um hmmm, a mistress then." Lucas narrowed his eyes, scratched his chin, "He shall lavish you with gifts."

"That's right. I won't cook for him otherwise." Irene cocked her head and fluttered her eyelids, giving Lucas a glimpse of the maiden, she had once been.

"Have fun. I promise not to spy on the two of you!"

She shoved him so hard he nearly toppled from the bench. "Get out of here. Bring your lady some food."

* * *

When Lucas knocked on the door, Alina had already secured most of the bank notes and the deed in their hiding place inside the trunk, hung her dresses in the wardrobe, washed the tears from her cheeks and dressed in the berry skirt and white V-neck blouse with a charcoal sash. The ruby pendant sparkled against her gleaming skin. Her hair hung loose around her neck. Since she would be walking out with Lucas, she gathered up only the front sides and left the rest cascading down her back. She loved the wind in her hair and the warmth of the sun on her shoulders. Feeling the heaviness lifted from her heart, now that both she and Lucas were safe from Vasil, she threw open the door and jumped into Lucas' arms.

"My exquisite lass," he exclaimed spinning them in a circle. "I have food for you." Retrieving the tray from the hall table they stepped inside and shut the door. "It appears all has gone well with your trunks? Although I must say, I am disappointed that you have managed to get dressed without my assistance."

Alina flashed a captivating smile as she seated herself at the tiny table beside the window. "I hope you have already eaten because this won't be enough for both of us."

"Yes, sweetheart, I have eaten with Irene."

She took a big bite of bread and jam. "How is Irene this morning?"

"She's well. We talked about Mr. Padgett, and it appears that your instincts are correct." He winked as she wiped her lips with a linen napkin. "Also, the herb garden, that I assume you are already aware of." She nodded and sipped her tea. "Also, we talked about the possibility of my giving over the lanterns to Ikarus and helping him find another assistant." He turned his gaze toward the fire, near out now, the breeze coming in through the window warm and inviting. "It's a lad's occupation. I have no desire to wander the streets unless you are by my side."

Alina chewed her last bite, then went to the wash basin and washed her hands. "This is wonderful news Lucas. You and Nikolas have plans for trade. That is a respectable life."

Lucas reached his hand out to her. She came to him and sat upon his lap. He peered deep into her eyes. "Tell me sweet Alina, what treasures have you discovered in your trunks other than this beautiful blouse?"

Alina told him that there were some bank notes, but she didn't mention how many, or the secret compartment, nor the house on the Boulevard.

"Then Vasil, that snake, was after the money your father left for you. Let's secure your valuables in the secret cellar where I hide my jewels and valuable goods." Making sure that nobody was around, they carried one trunk down together and left the other in her room for her belongings.

Lucas held her and kissed her in the dark behind the cellar door. "Now, I will show you my treasures." He lit the nook lanterns and revealed the goods he had been collecting for ten years. "Someday we can purchase a home for ourselves with all of this. Maybe even on the Boulevard."

"I'm sure we can! It's wonderful, Lucas. This and your trade business. You will be very wealthy."

"We will be."

"I have many years of education. I can help with your business. And we'll have time to spend together," she added blushing.

Upstairs, they bid Irene good day and stepped out hand in hand to enjoy the day. Strolling up and down the streets they found themselves on the Boulevard in front of the house that was teaming with light and life the evening of the ball but today sat silent and dark. They don't celebrate every day, Lucas thought. He told Alina about his adventure that evening. Her eyes grew large and watery. "I've upset you sweetheart. Someday soon we will have a fine house. I promise we will."

"No . . . I enjoy my room. So much has happened, and I feel comfortable at the boarding house. The women . . .the garden . . . people coming and going."

"I'm happy to hear that, Alina. We will take our time and stay at the boarding house as long as you wish."

She inclined her head as they turned and walked on, but her face froze as the address emblazoned on her memory came into view. Her home was as grand as the one Lucas had pointed out. Hers too had an impressive staircase, beveled windows and double wood and steel doors but the curtains were drawn tight. Her heart raced. Why didn't she tell Lucas about this gift from her father? She faltered and stumbled.

"Perhaps you're tired. Shall we continue walking?"

"Yes," she flushed and squeezed his hand.

"We haven't talked about your house."

"My house!" Alina's hand flew to her heart.

"Vasil's house. It was your father's house, so it's yours now."

"Oh yes, I'd forgotten all about it."

"You don't want to live there?"

"No, certainly not. I don't know what to do about it. Someone could live there. Someone who needs a home. I saw a woman in the street last week, she had two children. A poor woman I believe. Someone like that should have the house. It should be filled with joy and hope instead of fear and despair. Can I do that?"

Lucas drew in his breath, "Of course you can, Alina. That is a noble gesture indeed."

"How do I get rid of it then?"

"We would speak to the solicitor to draw up papers."

"Yes, of course. All right then, I will ask Brigit to find someone who deserves a home." She linked her arm in his.

"I admire you so, Alina. You have a kind and generous heart. And you're brilliant as well." Lucas kept a protective arm around her shoulders as they strolled toward the river. The streets were busy with shoppers going to market and enjoying the warmth of the summer sun. The city felt bright and clean with overflowing flower baskets in the windows. He took a deep breath enjoying the significance of that.

Seated in the dry grass along the riverbank, Alina leaned against him. "I am excited to begin our adventures together, show me your City of Dreams. I believe we both have much from which to recover."

Lucas brushed her hair away from her cheeks to plant kisses. "As you wish, my darling. We will explore the city together and enjoy the pleasure of each other's company without the burden of plans or commitments."

She rested her head on his chest and gazed up into his eyes with her shimmering green orbs. "Can we commit to dining at Le Cameé this evening?"

"We can," Lucas chortled. "And someday very soon we can commit to buying the perfect wedding dress for you." He stroked her hair, fanning it between his fingers and across the scar on his chest where the arrow had killed him. He had worn her veil over it like a shield but now the veil was somewhere in one of their beds "We need a wedding bed," he blurted. "Both of our beds are too small for our wedding night."

Alina sat up. "What?" she pressed her palm on her throat. "What are you thinking about Lucas!"

He pulled her around him. "No secrets here, you know my thoughts. But first, we will shop for the dress." He narrowed his eyes. "Unless, would you prefer to shop with the ladies? We can gather, Irene, Brigit and Carissa to accompany you, and afterward Nikolas and I will join up for lunch."

"That's a lovely idea, Lucas. You startle me with your thoughtfulness." She gave him a little shove and he fell onto his back pulling her on top of him.

"I'm not completely unaware of social graces."

"I am beginning to see more of the gentleman that you are." She kissed each of his cheeks and Lucas felt his heart shudder. Her shyness was diminishing.

"And once we order the dress, we will go to the bedmaker." He rolled to his side and sat up, pulling her with him. "Let's walk and enjoy this beautiful day."

"Let's explore everything! When I was first here, walking to the market and visiting the widows near to uncle's house my vision was clouded with sorrow and anger."

"All of that is over now. We found each other. I believe your father invoked fate and it has worked on our behalf." Looking up, he raised his right arm and punched the blue sky. "The world is for us now."

They strolled through the city amusing themselves like children, making plans that felt as easy to attain as an apple from the vendor's cart. They stopped in front of the Cathedral Saint Siempre.

"I wish the addition could be finished in time for you to become my wife here. But the old cathedral in the back by the moat and the monastery is beautiful as well." Lucas led her through a massive wood door inside the new structure crawling with carvers and craftsmen. "This cathedral will stand, long after we, and our children's, children are gone."

They walked around inside and out observing the craftsmen at their work, some glanced up and waved; Lucas and Alina recognized them from the boarding house. From there they followed a slim path through tall grass that led around to the far back of the old cathedral. The moat gleamed green between the cathedral and the columned arches covered in vines that hid the monastery.

"I haven't been here since I was a boy. Legend was that the monks still live in solitude behind those walls."

"Do they?"

Lucas rubbed the back of his neck. "I don't see how. No one ever dares cross the moat."

They ambled along a crumbling, weather stained wall until they could look across and see a small wooden door carved out of the side of the monastery wall. "I can see why they wouldn't cross. The water is dreadful." She cupped her hand over her mouth and nose.

"I agree. Only a fool would attempt it. And if successful in crossing, who knows what treads within? Sometimes in the late evening, I have thought I noticed light coming from inside, but of course it is merely the glow of city lights in this eerie water."

"Or the steely eyes of snakes!"

"Ha! You are most amusing Alina." He grabbed her hand and they ran back along the path and back toward the city.

They meandered along the winding streets and stopped at the Blue Gate. The proprietor had set chairs out front along the wall in the sun. "This is the best time of year in the City of Dreams," Lucas toasted, "We have all of the summer stretched out in front of us." Lucas asked Alina questions about growing up in Ingleena. They had such different childhoods, her stories made him feel like he was watching a play. He told her stories of roaming the city streets as a boy, pulling tricks to survive, and then the miracle of meeting Irene who took him in without a moment of hesitation. Over a lunch of cheeses, grapes, and wine, cooled by river water in a pewter wine vessel, he told Alina that Mrs. Kempel took a hold of him as if she had been waiting for him all her life. "And she changed mine for the better. I would not be here with you, or perhaps anywhere at all if not for that blessed woman. She swept the demons from my life."

"As you have done for me," Alina offered.

The gray cat leapt down from a windowsill. It paused and stared at Lucas, as if it was as startled to see him as he was to see it in the light of day. He had wondered if the cat had been a manifestation of his lonely mind. It slinked forward, hesitated, then leapt into Alina's lap. After much kneading and purring, it curled up and went to sleep.

Lucas moved to shoo the cat, but she was caressing its head and ears.

"He used to sit outside my window at Uncle's house," she murmured. I rested easier then."

Lucas gently stroked her arm so as not to disturb the cat. He remembered the night that it first followed him, kept him company, when he was searching for her and ended up at Trousdale's house. He peered into her eyes, "Were there nightmares?"

"Some," she swallowed. "But now when I awaken in the morning and see where I am, I am grateful and hopeful that the fear and dread will not return as life goes forward. Now that I know how terrible people can be, I don't know how I will ever forget it."

Lucas leaned back in his chair. "My nightmares have subsided, but like you, now I know too much. A pebble is unscathed sitting alone on the sand, but once tossed into the pond the ripples distort destiny. We must always hold sure together Alina, now that we have found each other." He cupped her cheek in his hands. "Together we will keep our place in this world. Nothing will take our dreams from us! We will create a force of love, stronger than the fates."

The cat opened its eyes, yawned, stretched, and leapt from her lap to the spot where the serving girl had set out a bowl.

They strolled to the dress makers shop where they shopped for material for Alina's wedding dress. Together they ran their hands over the various fabrics. Lucas realized with a start that he had not presented Alina with a ring. He couldn't ask her father for her hand, but he should have thought of a ring. Across the courtyard from there was the apothecary shop. They loitered near the well for a while in hopes of seeing Irene walk past, but she did not appear. "Shall we visit the flower vendor before going back? Let's fill both of our rooms with flowers, and the parlour also. This is a time of celebration. You can choose as many as you like." Lucas winked, and Alina blushed, but she took his arm and skipped alongside as he weaved through the warm and colorful streets. The aroma of flowers was everywhere.

With arms full of flowers, they showed up at the house at the same time as Brigit. They left several bundles with her and Irene before going upstairs and decorating their rooms. They had blue bells, baby's breath, Queen Anne's Lace, and greenery. Lucas convinced Alina to lie down and rest before their night out. He wanted to perform the lantern lighting rounds and make notes for Ikarus and the city council. Now that Ikarus had lit the entire city, the widows' path and the road to the cathedral should become part of the permanent route. And possibly the cottages where Madam Trousdale lived could do with some lanterns. He was aware that she, and her neighbors, preferred darkness to better view the stars and to keep their night business secret. But Dugald was there and others like him found their way into the City of Dreams more often of late. They must learn that the city was not a place for thieves and vandals to hide. Those days were over.

Before gathering his tools, he joined Irene and Brigit in the courtyard garden. They had filled vases with flowers in the parlour and now they relaxed in the afternoon sun among their herbs. Carissa and her sister, Perina brought tea for everyone.

"It's delightful to see new life in the boarding house. Will you move over here, Brigit? Or to the harbour perhaps?"

"Ahh, no! I enjoy living where I am."

Lucas smirked and sipped his tea.

"I think you will agree," she continued, "that Nikolas isn't the kind of man who requires doting and attention. We are both of the sort that comes and goes as we please. But I understand those ways are changing for you, Lucas."

"They are indeed," he agreed.

"For the better," Brigit said as Irene dabbed her eyes.

Lucas set his teacup down and went over to sit next to Irene on the stone bench. He took her hand in his. "For now, Alina and I will remain here. There are lighthearted days ahead for all of us."

"Lots of them," she agreed.

"And now, on a more serious note," Brigit began, "What about Dugald? Shall we hand him over to the constable? What do you want me to do with him, Lucas?"

"Ugh, I agree, we must decide. I have found pleasant distraction of late, but his presence looms like a rat chewing in the corner. Have you discussed this with Nik? I suppose he believes Dugald knows too much."

"That's exactly what he thinks," Brigit agreed.

"All right then, I will gather my tools and go speak to Nik before dusk. We will think of something. Alina and I will dine at the dinner house of Le Cameé, why don't you and Nik meet us afterward for dessert and wine?"

"We will." Trousdale flashed her wild eyes at Lucas. The hourglass paused, flipped twice then trickled again. Her hair, he realized, hadn't changed color today, it shimmered its majestic blue-black. He pursed his lips, met her gaze, trying to discern if she used that thing to toy with him. Nonetheless, he felt they had become friends. It had happened suddenly as if they had both tumbled over the same hay bale. He glanced at Irene.

"I will be fast asleep by then," she said contentedly.

"You're certain you want us to join your romantic dinner?" Brigit twisted one of the rings on her finger.

"I'm certain. It will be the first of many nights like this for Alina and me. We are planning our wedding. But for tonight and the next few weeks, I don't want her to feel any obligation. It is for festivities. And by the way, I need a ring."

"I can help with that," Brigit said.

"It must be a new ring made especially for Alina. Not something stolen."

Brigit clasped her hands in her lap. "Lucas, you offend me."

"I doubt that."

"A new ring it is. You must decide on the design and inscription."

"I will. Thank you." He placed his palm against his abdomen, bowed and made his exit.

It was early, but he lit the lanterns all the way to the harbour. He found Nikolas lolling among the wharf workers, kicking his legs against the bulwark, and gazing out to sea. Dropping his tools with a clatter, Lucas edged in next to his friend. "Who's in?"

A shrill whistle jerked the harbour men from their stupor. They rose and ambled away like sheep.

"An interesting vessel arrives tomorrow from Port of Waterfeld. Wool and silk, these are profitable goods for us to trade in."

Lucas nodded.

"Brigit sent you."

"She did, but I was coming anyway, I've invited the two of you to join Alina and I for desserts at Le Cameé later."

"You are a gentleman."

"And a scholar," Lucas added with a kick to Nik's calf. "Do you know of any ship that will haul Dugald away?"

"Stowaway." Nik slowly shook his head. "Good thinking. Easy enough."

Lucas slapped his friend on the knee, bent to gather his tools. "See you tonight."

In the spring-scented air, evening birds angled from balconies to arched doorways. He could almost hear them laughing. Many citizens were out front of their homes and Lucas chatted with them, telling of his plans to pass the torch to Ikarus. I will still advise and monitor the lighting, he assured everyone, even himself. He strode up and down, working with ease, lighting the lanterns, and the small hand lanterns and even candles he came across in front of businesses or homes, and he did so with a sense of pride and gratitude. When he first came to the City of Dreams, only the Boulevard had lanterns. Lamp boys roamed the side streets and he was one of them. This long walk was not in vain, he thought. By the time, he reached the last lantern on his route, his mind filled with nothing more than images of he and Alina strolling out in the light he had created.

She waited for him in the parlour dressed in a blue and green gown—that reminded Lucas of the sea today—with purple sash, corded sleeves, and a low neckline. The ruby pendant graced her smooth décolletage. Her hair swept up at the sides and piled on top of her head with long amber waves cascading down her back. Irene sat in the chair opposite her in front of the doors that were open to the courtyard. Lucas handed his tools to Carissa and went forward to kiss Alina's hand. "I dare not touch more until I have bathed." He took Irene's hand and kissed it as well, before taking the stairs two at a time.

Exactly as he had imagined, they strolled along the cobblestones that gleamed in the lantern light. They returned greetings from shopkeepers and citizens along the way. "This is our debut, my darling."

The gold specks in Alina's hair sparkled in the light. Lucas opened the iron gate that led to the courtyard of the dining house, Le Cameé. The large entry door was open. Passing the fountain and flower boxes, they stepped inside. Gold drapes, wheat colored walls, gray tablecloths with Venetian vases of red roses, gold gilt chairs, a soaring wine wardrobe with beveled glass doors. Sublime candlelight cast a globe of privacy around each table, separated by carved wooden partitions. The owner, whom Lucas knew well, seated them. The man addressed him as Monsieur, and Alina, Mademoiselle. The corner table away from the window, Lucas had requested. From this table, they could view all the room, but others could barely see them. The chairs were plush and welcoming. The finest red wine available in the City of Dreams brought on a tray to the table and poured into cut crystal glasses.

"To the first evening of our new life together," Lucas toasted. He reached for Alina's hand across the small round table, her pulse pumped in his hand.

"I have asked Carissa to make our appointment with the dressmaker." Her face flushed, and her eyes sparkled. "In three-weeks' time."

"Ah . . . Alina, I am incredibly pleased to hear that. You will go with Irene and Brigit to the dressmaker?"

"Yes, Carissa will come also, now that her sister is here. I'm excited, I never thought I would be planning my wedding with friends now as well." Her eyes filled, but she wet her lashes before any tears spilled. "Irene suggested the courtyard. She said we will make it like the Grande Inn. And Brigit is bringing plants for the garden. Plants for us."

"You and me?" Lucas leaned forward. "We need more flowers."

"Yes but," she gushed. "For the wedding. The plants will grow and bloom. Jasmine for sweet love, Heliotrope for eternal love, and Myrtle, the emblem of marriage and true love!" She beamed, light dancing in her eyes, an exuberance Lucas rarely observed in a young lady, or anyone for that matter, and still, she gracefully contained herself in that beautiful composure that so overwhelmed him.

They dined on roast duck with orange sauce, stirred greens, boiled potatoes, and a capon pastry pie. Lucas requested a second bottle of wine and when it arrived so did Nikolas and Brigit. The four of them squeezed around the table, indulged in the wine and warm custard cups. When they finished with that, Nikolas bought another bottle of wine which they sipped while discussing the flowers and herbs that the new garden at the boarding house would produce. Lucas noticed that Brigit's hour glass remained full the entire time. He thought about the gold-jewelled box and realized he didn't care if he ever saw it again. But if he did, he would ask Brigit where it came from. When they finally left Le Cameé, the square was vacant, but the lanterns continued to glow and guide their way home. Lucas savored the walk through the oldest section of the city with tight streets that arched over the narrow glittering canals. The face of his beloved and their friends showed the same reverence.

At the boarding house, the low fire welcomed them in the deserted front room. Nik and Brigit went to the room they often used instead of making the long walk home to the cottages or the harbour. Lucas escorted Alina to her room, full of sweet-scented flowers, and made sure all was in good order there. Her bed lamp glowed, the fire banked and there was fresh water in the pitcher. He understood this night she wanted to sleep in her cozy bed and dream of her wedding gown and the celebrations to come.

"Tomorrow, I will leave early to meet with the councilors and then with Ikarus and another lad. I'll stop into the dress shop and make payment arrangements for you to have the most beautiful wedding gown you desire. I long for the day when I see you descend the stairs as my bride." He kissed each cheek, then unpinned her hair and ran his fingers through it. She stepped up on tiptoes and kissed him with deep passion. Finally pulling away, they gazed at each other and giggled. "I must make my departure before this becomes our wedding night."

He closed the door and waited to hear her slide the bolt in place.

Chapter 16

Madam Trousdale was a witch of the highest caliber. She had terrified him at the boarding house, but here in her lean-to she cared for him. Keeping him alive for the ultimate slaughter. Lucas and his brutes had led him to believe he could go home if he told the location of those trunks. Certainly, they had retrieved them by now. His hand had healed well enough, though it ached when he got angry which was most of the time. Last night he pretended to be asleep when the witch stepped in to check his restraints. If he was awake, she would have tugged them to be sure, but his still face and even breath presented a harmless facade. The waif changed his bandage at the same time. Perhaps the guards feared the pungent incense that the witch burned day and night, or he quite disgusted them, he didn't know, but although the guards varied, none ventured inside the tight enclosure. How he longed for a bath and a fresh suit of clothes. Wary and watchful, he noted it would be possible to slip away when his keepers changed over. That is if he could break free of the tight ropes. He had made some progress in that. Although fed regularly, he had lost weight from chronic nausea, so when Madam Trousdale did tug the ropes, he flexed to keep them tight. Now, there was some leeway. During the day, he had learned to spit out the tea and drink only the water from the ladle beside the bed. Only at night he welcomed the sleep-inducing tea.

After the gruel, delivered by a rumpled youth who set his bowl just inside the door and pushed it toward him with a stick, he lay back under the covers and worked the ropes. Encouraged by what he saw as two choices, he continued to work tirelessly on the ropes. All he had left to do was choose. He didn't know where to find Vasil and Barrington, after so much time certainly they had fled to Arcana or Ingleena, but he knew where to find Lucas and Marion. He could not suppress the burning desire to kill somebody. Perhaps two people, he chuckled to himself. Marion, of course had to have known all along it was impossible for him to abscond with Lucas. Tired of him begging for his share of land, she sent him to die, or suffer torture, as he did. The old Dugald, the naive man he was before coming to the City of Dreams, would simply steal clothes and money to take passage on a ship out of here. He was no longer that man, he thought as he rolled silently to the dirt floor and crawled out the back of the hut into the cool black night.

* * *

Lucas dreamed of he and Alina walking hand in hand along the river bank. The sky was a warm blue, a breeze swept through their hair. *What are your thoughts?* she asked. He answered, *my thoughts are of you, and all we will share together. . .* the wind scattered petals from the Linden tree around them. Lucas reached to brush them from her hair and awoke to his own petal filled room. Tossing the coverlet aside, he swung his legs around and planted his feet on the floor. In a few days, the dressmaker would be busy sewing Alina's wedding gown. And then they would choose which day for the ceremony. Today he would talk to Brigit about the ring.

He dressed and left his room feeling excited to go to the council and give up his occupation. He hoped Ikarus and other lads would find it as rewarding. Using his key, he unlocked Alina's door, opened it without a creak and stepped inside. Her hair fanned across the sheets and she sighed contentedly in her sleep. He trusted her dreams were as lovely as his. A brush of his lips crossed her forehead, "Rest well, my love." In the kitchen crowded with the workers and masons, Lucas grabbed a chunk of bread and stepped out the back door.

* * *

Alina stretched and opened her eyes before remembering the exciting plan she had for today. She dressed and hurried down to the kitchen. Perina told her she had already missed Lucas, but Irene had not come downstairs yet. "I'm going to the market, Perina. I wish to buy a gift for Lucas. You may tell Irene this, but please don't mention it to Lucas if you see him."

Perina, a chubby cheerful girl, held a finger to her lips. "I will keep your secret."

Alina rushed out the front door without her cloak but quickly realized she didn't need it. She wore the berry skirt with the ruffled blouse that perfectly suited the warm morning and her light mood. Over her shoulder she carried a satchel with the deed and her money purse. She would buy a pocket watch for Lucas. She wanted to present him with it tonight. She had noticed him watching the merchants and businessmen checking their watches as they made their way through the city. The watch would make him feel as one of them, especially since Lucas was a man who had kept time by the light, or lack thereof, in the sky. And with all the new opportunities coming into their life, it would be useful. Soon she would tell him about her father's gift. The house on the Boulevard. Not yet though. Her stomach churned a little. She shook her head, brushed a curl from her forehead. Why give him a watch when she could give him a home? She held her head high and continued to the office of the solicitor. For now, she had to keep this secret, her father's secret. It was all she had left of him.

The large wooden door was heavy and creaked as if it hadn't been opened in a long time. She peeked in. What if she was in the wrong place? She took a step back when a voice called out. "How may I help you Miss?"

"I . . . I'm . . . are you the solicitor?" Alina kept one foot outside the door.

"Yes, I am, Miss. Edison Reaves, Esquire at your service."

She expected him to bow, but he didn't. "I have a deed here. My father sent me."

"Ah, you must be Alina Sutcliffe, please come in."

"How do you know my name?"

"My dear, you resemble your father. I've been expecting you." She gaped.

"Come in." He took her hand and led her into his office of carved wood walls. The desk filled most of the room. Large round candles burned in sconces behind the desk. "I have a locker for you to keep your valuables in. It's where your father kept things in between his trips here. It's horrible what happened to your father. Please accept my sincere sympathies. At least you have the house. He's provided well for you. So now follow me." He led her down a polished hallway to a row of tall thin cabinets and handed her a key. "This one is yours. I recommend you leave the deed in there and take the key with you." He went back down the hall and left her alone.

When she opened the cabinet, she found a shirt that belonged to her father and a pair of boots. She buried her face in his shirt that miraculously still smelled of him. The small space had contained his scent. There was a leather pouch stuffed with more bank notes. She placed the deed on the shelf and held the sleeve of her father's shirt for several long moments. She started to close the cabinet but opened the pouch and counted the money. Tears filled her eyes, but she couldn't help but giggle. All that time that she scrounged for food at Vasil's house, money and refuge were waiting for her. She took only one of the notes and left the rest, deciding that she would buy Lucas the most exceptional pocket watch in the city. She secured the key to her house and the key to the cabinet in her hiding place inside her shift, and bid Edison Reaves, Esquire goodbye for now. He promised that someday soon, they would have a long talk about her father.

Just past the flower vendors stand was *Hands of Time*, a shoppe that made timepieces and pendulum clocks. She selected a gold pocket watch with hunter case and chain. The merchant presented it to her in a purple velvet pouch. She slipped it into her own money pouch that she tucked inside her shift. On the way home, she transcribed a note in her mind, *we will hold time in our hands*, or some such thing. She loved to read the poets and used to fancy herself one. When her father died, her musings had ceased; they were returning now. Perhaps the ladies could help her with the words, rekindle her imagination. Irene always seemed to know the right thing to say. The market stalls bustled with customers on this warm spring day. Alina had forgotten to bring a basket, so she bought one and filled it with everything that intrigued her. She stopped by the vegetable stall and the baker's shop. Today, Irene and Carissa could take a day off from the shopping. She made a stop at the flower vendor, having remembered it had been a long time since she had visited her widow friend, Madam Van Dessen. It won't take a moment to give her these and tell her to expect an invitation to our impending wedding.

A ragged figure broke from the market crowd and fell in step behind her.

Alina walked away from the square and turned down the narrow street that led to Vasil's end of town and the widow's home. She quickened her step and clenched her jaw. But Uncle Vasil was dead now. She had nothing to fear. The last time she had seen Madam Van Dessen, was the very day Lucas found her. Her heart fluttered remembering how boldly he had caressed her. She swung the basket, gliding past the houses, pretending not to notice Uncle's house, but her feet remembered the walk and she began to feel the panic that had always accompanied her when this place served as her home. She turned her face to the breeze, allowing it to blow back her hair. The jewelled hair pin she wore yesterday, the one Lucas had loosened from her hair last night, slid to the side and she fixed it back in place with her free hand. A snarl and hiss from behind knocked her nearly off her feet. She spun around. There, with its haunches up, fur on end, mouth wide with tiny pointed, bared teeth was the gray cat. She dropped the basket. Her hand flew to her heart as someone grabbed a fistful of her hair. The last thing she heard was the hair pin hit the cobblestones.

* * *

It was past midday, so Lucas didn't expect to see, Irene, Carissa, Brigit, and Nikolas gathered in the parlour when he returned to the boarding house. "If this is a ladies meeting, you're out of place, Nik. Where's Alina?"

"She's not with you," Nikolas stated.

"No," he said cautiously glancing upstairs. "I'm glad you're all here. I've been thinking about the design for her ring and would like your opinions. The ladies, mostly, no offense Nik, but I doubt you'd have any idea . . ."

Nikolas crossed the room and grabbed Lucas by the arm. "She's not with you."

Brigit leapt up.

He glared at the ladies who displayed collective pale-faced alarm. A statement not a question. "What!?"

"Dugald escaped!" Irene blurted and burst into tears. Carissa's eyes filled as well. Brigit gawped, and shook her iridescent head.

Lucas noticed the hourglass—empty—just before she shoved it inside her blouse. He glared, extended his hand. She took a step back. He went to the stairs grabbed the banister. Brigit came over placing a cold hand on his arm. He grabbed her shoulder. "That hourglass what does it mean?" he demanded.

Nik stepped between them, pushed Lucas' hand away. "He got away in the night. It's my fault."

Perina shuffled in from the kitchen, "She left hours ago. She wanted to buy a gift for you."

Lucas paced the room, looking at them, but not seeing them, raking his hands through his hair. Finally, he shouted, "No!!!" ran to the door, flung it open with a bang and dashed out. Nikolas turned back to the others with a stone-faced gasp of despair before he followed Lucas out into the street.

Low hanging, buttery clouds cast shadows along the street that led to the square. How quickly the world turns dreadful again, Lucas thought. He was aware of Nik sprinting behind him. They leapt and dodged their way between strolling shoppers and wagons laden with goods. They split up in the square, Lucas to the left, Nik to the right. The tower clock chimed three times when they met again in the middle. "This of all things, cannot be true," Lucas growled.

"I should have gone back and checked on him last night," Nik said as the two of them scanned every face in the crowd. "How can I be so senseless?"

"Alina! Where are you?" Lucas shouted and turned his back on Nikolas. He marched down the narrow side street. Approaching the flower vendor, he placed his hand on his chest where he had worn the black lace veil. He'd stopped wearing it. Why did he do such an ill-advised thing? They hadn't spoken their vows yet. "Have you seen my woman? Er, the young lady, Alina?"

"Ah yes," the cherry-faced woman said. "Just this morning. She bought daisies and irises."

"How long ago?"

"It was early this morning."

Lucas turned to Nik who loitered at his shoulder. "She was here. Why would she buy flowers? We have already filled our rooms." Before Nik could muster an answer, Lucas was striding into the *Hands of Time*.

"Have you seen a young lady with amber hair today?"

The shopkeeper set down the timepiece he was tinkering with and peered over his spectacles. "Good afternoon, Lucas. You've always been the suspicious sort. But, why not allow your young lady to have some fun and present her surprise?"

"She's gone missing!" Lucas barked.

The small man trembled, pointed a crooked finger. "From here she crossed over to the flower stall."

"Aggh . . ..!"

Nikolas grabbed his arm and pushed him from the shoppe.

"How could Dugald make it over here? I thought he was taking a potion."

"He was served a potion. He must not have taken it all."

"Are the cottage dwellers searching over there?"

"Everyone is searching, including Ikarus, Igmus and Ragbone. I have alerted Mr. Merson and all the lads at the harbour. Brigit and I put out the alert as soon as we realized he escaped."

"But they are not looking for Alina," Lucas groaned.

"No . . .well by now they are . . . Brigit will have sent word to tell them."

"I know what you're thinking." Lucas swallowed. "If we find Dugald, we will find Alina." He punched a fist into his hand. "Let's go. We'll double back to the cottages and then to the harbour, as well as all the tavern gutters along the way. Dugald will want whisky. And the storehouse. He may think he can still get to the trunks. He could come to the boarding house for the deed." He stopped. "We need to send a guard to the boarding house!"

"Brigit—Madam Trousdale—is there," Nik said.

"Ah, yes. That's good."

They searched Vasil's house, Lucas nearly ripping the boards from the windows, but it was immediately apparent nobody had been inside. They walked through every crooked alley on the way to the squat dwellings. At Trousdale's cottage, Lucas realized that the gold-jewelled box had truly vanished. Just like Alina. At the hut, the broken sticks in the back where Dugald had pushed through lay strewn on the ground. For a few paces, they were able to follow them, but the trail soon ended. Sometimes they walked in silence, sometimes shouting her name.

At the harbour, Mr. Merson met them with a grave face. "There is no sign of him." He pointed, "That ship is due to depart in the morning. I have men posted all over it."

Lucas felt his knees give way and steadied himself long enough to slump onto the wharf. His eyes stung, and his head ached. He hadn't thought of Dugald taking Alina on a ship. That couldn't happen, but Mr. Merson thought it possible, so why not. How did he find her? Did he even have her? Anyone could have stolen a beautiful lady like Alina. These things didn't occur in the City of Dreams, never had. All the stealing and underhanded dealings had left out women. The woman was sacred. Everyone knew and respected that. One of the wharf lads came forward carrying two torches. Lucas tried to spit but failed, his stomach churned, guts gurgling. From somewhere Nik produced a flask. Lucas gulped, ignoring the burning and stabbing. Taking the torches, Lucas and Nik set off again. When they strayed from each other, Nik waited to catch Lucas' eye. When he did, they exchanged brief desperate expressions. Nik turned one way and Lucas the other. They would meet again back at the boarding house.

As he walked the streets of the city, he had loved for so many years, Lucas tried to think of reasons to hate it. Its inescapable emptiness wrapped him in a pervasive cloak of loneliness. He scoured every inch of the riverbank. Ikarus had accompanied him for a time, lighting lanterns as they went, but Lucas didn't know when the lad melted away into the night. He walked until his legs were numb and he'd burned through three torches. He returned to the place on the street where he had first seen Alina. He pulled a candle from his pocket, igniting it with his dying torch and placed it at his feet. He waited, willing her to appear again as she had in the sunlight, her eyes shooting sparks, her hair flowing like a wind-blown mane and the black veil floating between them. His hand grasped the empty air. *Alina, through the veil of time and space I beseech you: return to me. I see you; I feel you. I hear the whisper of your voice, yet I ache with the inability to touch you. Return to me. Come back my love. Find me here, where we met before. This place in the world, where a door creaked open, a moment in time that lives within us still. I am here. Where are you? I will not go without you. Come to me. I speed you.*

The candle flickered and went out. Then the wick ignited itself again and the glow was taller and brighter than any candle flame that Lucas had ever lit. It filled the space where Alina had stood that day. Reaching for her, his fingertips brushed the warm skin where the ruby rested against her chest. He smelled her sweet scent. But Lucas was still alone. Alina was not really there, though her essence lingered in the spot where he stood surrounded by a sphere of amber light. He hung his head and waited until the sun forced its dawn face between the layers of silver clouds that framed the sea. The candle sputtered and went out.

He stumbled toward the boarding house. Dirty and disheveled, shivering from a place of horror hidden in the depths of his soul, he pushed open the front door. Irene was slumped sideways in her chair, mouth open, eyes squeezed shut as if she couldn't bear to see the truth. Brigit lay sprawled on the floor in front of the fire. Nikolas stood statuesque in the center of the room, clutching his flask in a white knuckled fist. His eyes rimmed in red.

"Lie down before you fall down," Nik said.

"Same to you." Lucas dragged his feet up the stairs. Alina's door was open. Someone had sprinkled sage over the floor and bed, ghost medicine—prevents night terrors. His stomach clenched. He went in, fell face down upon her bed and sunk into a strangled sleep.

Lucas was awakened by the scent of Alina's hair. He stretched and rolled over on his back. Reaching to pull the coverlet back his hand brushed something familiar. Her veil. He pulled it out and sat upright in the small bed. They'd taken to playfully tossing it at each other. Holding it to his face, he released a sob and stuffed it inside his dirty shirt. His boots were still in place. In a moment, he was running down the stairs. Nik crumpled in a corner chair with legs and arms askew jerked awake. He scrambled to his feet. "What is it?"

"Hours of daylight. Let's go!"

They scoured the streets again but this time they inspected inside every cart, under the skirts of vendor stalls, knocked on doors of private homes and stopped and questioned passersby. In the square they met Igmus and Ragbone and three cottage dwellers who Lucas thanked with coins for their help. They came to the Blue Gate just as it opened, and Lucas told Nikolas about his afternoon with Alina and how the gray cat had sat in her lap. They stepped inside long enough to drain two tankards of ale. The barkeep and patrons promised to look out for Alina, but Lucas knew by their expressions that none of them expected to come forth with any good news for him. Nik slung an arm around Lucas' shoulder, "Next time we come in here we will have Alina with us, and it will be an occasion of joy."

"It will." Lucas glared with defiant hope, although his heart shuddered with doubt. They walked in sober silence up and down every street and out to the cottages again. They found Madam Trousdale roaming those roads, questioning everyone. She handed Lucas and Nik bread from a satchel tied around her waist. Lucas wavered, but took a bite anyway and found the bread warm and fresh. How does she do it, he wondered. The hourglass apparently still sat tucked inside her blouse. He knew why she was hiding it. She had no control over it like he had thought. It kept time, his time—and it had run out. Lucas was sure of it. They returned to Vasil's house; nothing had changed there. No one dare enter and curse themselves with the anguish of the damned. The root cellar sheltered a decrepit dog sleeping fitfully, paws twitching. A hazy dusk descended upon the city.

"Best to go home and eat, sleep a little. Come back out in the night when thieves travel," Nik said.

Lucas, white-faced and black-eyed walked on. Nik trudged behind, offering reasons to go home for a short while. They came to the Boulevard and Lucas went up the stairs of the house that had held the grand party. A maid answered the door and told Lucas she would watch out for Alina but doubted her masters would give a missing girl a care. "Then they should not abide in my city," Lucas stated through tight lips."

Nikolas took Lucas by the hand and led him back down the stairs. "If she had roamed this way someone would notice her. Of course, they would. Don't listen to the griping of a bitter servant."

"We'll search the riverbank again," Lucas stated.

"I can do that, Lucas. Why don't you go back to the boarding house?"

"No."

"Don't you want to check on Irene? She's frantic with worry for Alina and you."

"She has Carissa and Perina." He strode away from Nik in the direction of the river. Suddenly Lucas spun around, "The widow! She bought flowers again. Our rooms are already full of flowers. She must have bought some for her friend!" Relief spread across his face. "That's it. That sweet old woman has distracted Alina with her gossip!" He ran with Nikolas close on his heels. The widow Van Dessen refused to open her door. Lucas had to speak to her through the little window.

"You've lost the lass! I should have never let you take her! Worthless men, the lot of you! Git away and don't return until you find her."

"Did she bring you flowers yesterday morning?"

"No. Go away!"

Nik placed a firm hand on Lucas' back and pushed him toward home. Irene paced in front of the fire. Carissa and Perina offered bread, cheese, and wine, none of which Lucas accepted. He climbed the stairs and once again collapsed on Alina's bed.

Every day the search continued. Days stretched into weeks. The dressmaker appointment forgotten. Lucas and Nikolas discovered parts of the city they had not explored in years. Clean and empty alleys between the Boulevard homes. Cottages hidden behind cottages in the dark zone and offices with cellars in the back of shops. The citizens began to scurry out of the way when Lucas and Nikolas approached wearing hollow-eyed masks of misery and gloom.

"Perhaps we should travel out to the country," Nik suggested one damp night when the harbour fog curled around their ankles.

"Brigit sent a messenger to Arcana. She is not there. Bernard keeps watch."

"I know, Lucas, but you need rest. You may have to . . ." Nik stopped himself, squeezed Lucas' shoulder.

"Give up. I know. Dugald may have dragged her to the bottom of the sea." He raked a shaky hand through his tangled hair.

"You are thin and pale. You are a spectre of death." Nik clutched his friend's forearm and pulled him through the glowing streets toward the boarding house. Even in his suffering, Lucas wondered where Ikarus got all the supplies to light so many extra hand lanterns and candles. A lack of light was not preventing her return.

The two men walked in their new-found silence until Nik asked, "Whisky?'

"No Nik. No whisky. I can't feel better, don't want to feel better until I find Alina."

"You are drawn out, exhausted, my friend."

"I am Nik. My eyes are tired from seeing everyone except her. My ears are tired from not hearing her voice. My hands hurt from reaching for my love who is not here. My legs are tired from running along streets that won't reveal her path. My head aches from thinking, and not knowing what has happened. My heart aches with emptiness. I am worn to the brittle fragments of my bones."

Nikolas put his arm around Lucas' waist. Lucas leaned against him and Nikolas walked them slowly home. "Let's go to Ingleena. Leave tomorrow," he said to Nik before dragging himself up the stairs.

Nik stayed every night at the boarding house in case the women needed help with Lucas. Brigit remained scarce, out searching on her own, but she brought calendula and other calming herbs to the house that Irene baked into Lucas' bread. The only thing that Lucas noticed is that despite Alina's absence, the plants Mr. Padgett had brought for the garden flourished. He liked to think it meant she was still alive.

* * *

In the alley behind the Duck Tavern, Dugald cowered among the crates of rubbish. He chewed furiously hoping to finish before the rats came around, but scraps of crust came back up in his throat. He gathered his spit to get rid of it, but a paste of the misbegotten bread filled his mouth. The offending mess slid back down his gullet. When it hit his stomach, he lurched forward gagging and choking. Again, he spewed the globby substance. The swirling motion of his tongue worked against him and the mass of undigested food slid backward once again. He heaved, breaking out in a hot sweat that felt as if his own body gouged him with swords from the inside. His heart jerked in his chest and he fell onto his back. Boiling blood skidded in all directions, he choked and clutched his throat and keeled sideways onto the cool cobbles as the spew firmly lodged in his throat shot out. When he opened his eyes, Dugald saw a familiar beady-eyed creature crawl forward. The rat come to finish him off as he deserved. He regretted taking Lucas' girl. Like himself, she had done nothing wrong. The moat was deeper than he guessed. She could swim! At least, in the dark, it looked like she was swimming to the bank when he went under. Blood oozed from the wound where her dagger had slashed his thigh. All that green chunky water he swallowed was still trying to come out. He'd sprawled on the bank for nearly half a day in his rank and sodden clothes, never seeing any sign of the girl, so she must have gotten out and made her way home. If the rat didn't finish him off, Lucas surely would.

Chapter 17

Lucas tossed in fever. He saw farmers coming through the flower fields, igniting them with torches. Candles melted inside their pockets. Wagons ran over citizens fleeing the brightly lit streets of the City of Dreams. Pitchforks rose from hay carts, their prongs stained in blood. He moaned, threw an arm over his face.

The door banged open; Nikolas came in. "Lucas wake up! The entire house can hear your shouts."

Lucas lurched upright. "What is . . . who is . . . someone downstairs?"

"Your nightmares shake the timbers. Wash up. Change your clothes. A ship leaves for Ingleena in two bell chimes. Do you still want to go?"

"Oh." Lucas sat on the edge of the bed cradling his head in his hands. "Yes, let's go. I guess so. I don't know what we'll do when we get there. But what else is left?" He got up and splashed water on his face, pulled on his trousers and shirt.

"Grab some things," Nik said.

"I don't want any things."

"A change of clothes to look presentable in Ingleena."

"Can't be bothered. Let's go before anyone notices. I don't want Irene trying to stop me. You haven't told anyone."

Nikolas tilted his head, "Well just . . ."

"Trousdale."

"She can keep a secret."

"I don't doubt that," Lucas uttered between clenched teeth as he watched Nik shove some clothes into a satchel. They skulked from the boarding house without having taken bread or tea. Lucas ignored the growling in his stomach. Once on the ship, he was startled to see the city from that vantage point. He searched for Alina even as the crew cast off. Nik sat beside him on the long board bench and pulled from his pocket a clod of parchment wrapped fish. He held it out to Lucas who covered his mouth and turned away. "I wish I had some of Brigit's bread right now."

"You do," Nik dug into the deep pocket of his long coat and pulled out a loaf of bread wrapped in warm cloth.

Lucas grabbed it and ripped off a chunk. "How does she keep it warm for so long?"

Nik raised one eyebrow. "It's a secret, she says."

Lucas pursed his lips, then muttered. "I refuse to laugh ever again, Nikolas."

Nik stuffed the last of the fish in his mouth and mumbled. "I understand, Lucas, but for just a second there showed color in your face. You resemble the belly of that fish I just ate. Your face has gone ashen. More so now than even of late."

Lucas clutched his chest. "I'm all right. When we get to Ingleena we will find a solicitor and inquire of Louis Sutcliffe. That will lead us to conversation about Alina."

Nik nodded. "It's windy out here. Let's get inside, you need a lie down."

"No, it's fine, Nik. I need fresh air. I can't see the city anymore. The land is gone."

"It's still there just beyond the horizon."

Lucas wrapped the remainder of the bread in the cloth and handed it back to Nikolas. "Tell her thanks."

"You'll tell her."

"Maybe I won't."

Nik stared at him, pressed the back of his hand to Lucas' forehead. "You're on fire!"

"I'm cold. I feel cold." He put his hand over his heart. "It feels cold."

Nik stood in front of him and reached inside Lucas' shirt. "Open it, let me see."

"Are you a witch now too?"

"Damn all, let's see, Lucas."

Lucas leaned back and let Nikolas open his shirt and run his hand across his chest. "What's this?"

"Alina's veil."

"No, this."

"What?"

"This red gouge?"

"It's my scar. Remember. I survived death by an arrow. It pierced my heart and I lived even after I died. But now this . . ." he pushed Nik's hand away, "if Alina is gone, my heart goes with her."

Nik braced his hands upon Lucas' shoulders. "You're wound is opening up. We must get you back to the City of Dreams. Don't move!" He rushed across the bow toward the stern, waving his arms and shouting.

Lucas got up and staggered to the rail. His head ached so badly that his vision was patchy. He felt his way toward the lower deck. He craved darkness. Gripping the ladder, he swung in and placed a foot on the rung but missed.

When he opened his eyes, scraggly sailors stared down at him. One grabbed him and began to run his hands over his stomach and chest. Lucas slapped his hands away. "Nik, get your mob away from me."

They carried him to a bunk. Nik covered Lucas in blankets and mopped his brow with a wet cloth. Eventually Lucas felt Nikolas lie down beside him and wrap his arms around him to quell the shivering. He fell into a fitful sleep with Nikolas' warm breath on his neck.

At dawn, Nikolas threw Lucas over his shoulder and hauled him up on deck. The bell clanged and the lads raised the red and yellow flag. They luffed the sails. Nikolas forced water down Lucas' throat.

"You're choking me. I need to sit up."

The sun was inching up from the dark line of the open sea on one side, and a hazy image of land was just coming into view when a small fishing vessel appeared alongside them. Somewhere in the depths of his fever, Lucas heard Nikolas and the crewmen shouting to the vessel. They were arguing. And the next thing he knew he was wrapped in flour sacks and lowered down onto the rocking boat into the waiting arms of Nikolas.

The next time he awoke he was inside Nik's room at the harbour. He sat up. Trousdale was standing in the corner murmuring to Nikolas. "What's going on?" Lucas swung himself off the bunk and stood up.

Trousdale ordered," Sit down. Your heart is bleeding!"

Lucas scratched his head with both hands. "Bloody hell, I dreamed I was on a ship to Ingleena."

"We were," Nik said. "You got sick. And your wound opened. The one on your leg also. I was sure you were dying."

Lucas opened his shirt. The black veil was stuck to his chest.

Brigit rushed over. "Don't touch it!"

But the veil fell off into his hand. He ran his hand over the pale scar. He lifted his leg but found no scar. "Which leg was that?"

Brigit's hair turned blue then melded into red before turning back to black. Her eyes blazed like stained glass windows. Nik staggered as if he were about to faint. "What in damnation happened to you?"

"I don't know what you mean. What about Ingleena?"

Nik and Brigit exchanged a glance. Nik placed his hand on her shoulder, and she went outside. He stood in front of Lucas with his hands on his hips. "Lucas trust me as the one who guards your back. You cannot leave the land. You will die."

Lucas slumped back down on the cot. "I've wondered about that." He buried his face in his palms. "Who will go then?"

"Bernard showed up at the boarding house. He offered to go."

"Bernard! What is he doing here? He can't board a ship, he's never been out of Arcana, but for one day."

"He has a better chance of surviving than you. And Wentworth is going with him."

"Ah, I see. That makes better sense then. When will they leave?"

"They left four days ago. You've been asleep for six days."

"Six days . . . here?"

"Yes, we kept you here. Irene doesn't know. We let her believe that you were thrashing about in a drunken torpor."

"Well done, Nik, thanks."

"My pleasure, friend. Come on, I'll take you home."

Brigit was gone when they stepped outside under an overcast sky. Lucas shielded his eyes. "What's the hour?"

"Around midday. I think we'll see sun today. It's been raining since we took you off the ship."

Lucas turned as if he wanted to go back inside. "I need a cloak."

"I have this for you." Nik handed him a hooded cloak. Nikolas donned one also and they walked unnoticed to the boarding house.

Nikolas stepped in front of Lucas and pushed open the door. "Don't forget, you've been drunk at the harbour all this time."

"I have."

Grateful to find the parlour empty, Lucas took the stairs two at a time. Alina's door was firmly shut. He pushed open his own and found his steaming bath waiting. Nik hovered in the doorway. "Take your time, Lucas. They're in the kitchen, Irene and Brigit."

It was dusk when Lucas, ignoring Alina's door again, forced himself to descend to the parlour. Brigit sat by the fire with crossed legs, swinging her foot as if she were waiting for something. He could see the chain for the hour glass, but it was still tucked inside her blouse. She was combing her hair with the claw but dropped it when he entered. "Welcome back to the living."

"Shut up. I was merely sleeping. Where's Irene?"

Brigit inclined her head toward the kitchen. When Lucas entered, she was seated at the table clutching a cup of tea. "I'm sorry," he blurted.

She pushed a cup across the table. "Nothing to be sorry for. Come and sit. We will start again. Stop searching and start living. Tomorrow we will go to the river and then you can walk with Ikarus and light lanterns. If anyone is about, you will know."

"You've been thinking a great deal."

"What else can I do? I am old, but you are still young and must go on."

"Irene . . ."

She got up went to the sideboard and sliced a large piece of pie that she placed in front of him. He shook his head but, in a moment, took a large bite and then another until it was gone.

"I'd offer wine, but you've been so drunk."

"It might help my head though."

"Were you drinking whisky?"

"I think so."

"All right, wine it is."

Lucas forced a smile as he took a large gulp from the pewter goblet. "Is there stew in the pot?"

"Of course. Are you ready?"

"I am." After two bowls were empty Brigit and Nikolas came into the kitchen and served themselves. "Where's Carissa and Perina?" Lucas asked.

"I gave them the evening off to go out and enjoy themselves."

The back door opened and Ikarus bounded in. "I found Dugald!"

Lucas jumped up tipping the bench over. "Where?"

"He's in the alley close, behind the Duck Tavern." Ik went to the table and poured a full goblet of wine.

"Dead?" Lucas asked as he headed for the door with Nikolas at his side.

He shook his head. "I don't know for sure. I didn't want to touch him."

"Aagh," Lucas checked his dagger and threw open the door.

Ik gulped his wine. "I'll show you where."

They followed Ikarus behind the Duck Tavern along an alley that led to an even narrower one. It was cluttered with crates and empty flour sacks. Dugald was a lump among the rags. Lucas squatted down and placed his palm on his back. "He breathes."

Nik opened a tiny glass bottle and tossed its contents over Dugald. "That will do for now." Lucas chuckled and Nik flashed him a look of surprised relief, "Brigit . . ."

"Is teaching you her trade." Lucas lifted Dugald from the sloppy cobbles.

Ikarus was as pale as the sliver of moon. "What kind of man can live through so much?"

Lucas gazed down at Dugald. "A man who has something to live for. This time, he's coming home with me."

"We can put him in the room Brigit and I use. It has a good lock and no window."

Brigit rolled her eyes and followed the men into the small room. Once they set him on the bed and tied his wrists and ankles to the wood frame, she lifted his head and poured a large cup of tea down his throat. "I'm tired of this man."

"We all are," Lucas agreed. "When will he wake up?"

"A few hours."

They locked the door and went out to the parlor to wait. When Carissa and Perina returned they were warned not to go near that door. Lucas avoided the garden and sat facing the fire. They passed the time by asking the young maids about every aspect of their evening out in the city. Lucas felt a twinge of regret for the loss of those carefree days of simply wandering from one tavern to another. Finally, Irene couldn't keep her eyelids from closing and bid them all goodnight.

Lucas periodically paced outside Dugald's door. Finally, sometime after dawn, hearing groaning and thrashing, he,

Nikolas, and Brigit went in. Lucas bent close to his face. "Tell us where Alina is, and we will tend you."

Dugald gagged when he tried to clear his throat. Madam Trousdale held a cup of water to his lips. He swallowed, glanced at Lucas. "I'm surprised you haven't killed me already. Is she all right?"

"She's gone! What have you done with her?!"

"I . . . I lost her at the moat. It was a mistake. I saw her walking. I don't know why I grabbed her. I only want to go home. Everything I did. None of it. I didn't mean to hurt anyone."

"Exactly what happened?"

"I grabbed her. She fainted. I took her to the old monastery. I thought I could cross the moat and hide her in there. I would make you pay me for her return. But the loch was flowing and the water deep. She can swim. I cannot."

"Of course, you can't. You are an idiot."

"She sliced my leg!"

"Good!" Lucas turned to Nik and Brigit. "Stay with him Brigit. Don't let him escape no matter what this time. Let's go, Nik."

Nikolas and Lucas ran like athletes, whizzing past people as if they were insects. They only slowed when the cathedral came into view. They followed the slim path through the tall grass that led around to the far back of the cathedral to the loch, the moat, and the monastery. "We have to cross the loch," Lucas spoke grimly. "There's footprints on the other side," he pointed.

Plunging through the murky water that came up to their armpits they scrambled onto the bank and followed the footprints to the small paneled door set in the otherwise blank stone wall. It opened with a solid shove. They emerged in a slim dark passageway. Neither had thought to bring a candle and soon the light from the door was gone as they turned many corners in the labyrinthine hall. Feeling their way in total blackness Nikolas twice ran into the back of Lucas. They kept silent, listening for the sound of human life. In some time, up ahead, bathed in the circular glow of a single candle, a cloaked figure stood before them. With Nik's hands clutching his shoulder, Lucas crept toward the figure. When they stood an arm's length apart, a bony white hand crept out from a long oval sleeve and grabbed Lucas' wrist. Lucas gasped and pulled his hand back, but the long cold fingers held fast.

"Who are you? Are you alone here?"

The cloaked figure raised its head. The hood fell away from a pale, sunken-eyed face. The man slowly lifted his eyelids. Lucas stared. He felt like he was gazing into his own eyes.

"No one of us is alone here." The voice echoed along the chamber walls.

"What are you doing here in the dark?"

"We keep the monastery. We are monks."

"I thought all the monks were dead or gone." Lucas could feel Nikolas shuddering behind him.

"We are three here."

"You never leave?" Lucas reached behind himself and grabbed Nik's hand.

"Sometimes we go into the city for supplies."

"Tsk, I've never seen anyone like you in my city."

"We wear hooded cloaks when we don't want to be recognized. Don't we, Lucas?"

"How do you know my name?" Lucas asked in a breathless voice.

"I know who comes into my monastery."

Lucas stumbled back, stepping on the foot of Nikolas who screeched, then yanked Lucas by the arm. "Let's get out of here," he hissed.

"What in hell are you doing in here?"

"Hell is not here. We keep the candles burning. Before one burns out, we light another."

The man still clutched Lucas' wrist. "Your girl is no longer here. She stayed for a time. But she is gone now."

The figure raised a crooked finger and pointed down the snaking corridor. Before Lucas or Nik could utter another word, the man was gone, but the narrow passage glowed in full illumination.

They found themselves back outside. "Ohhh . . . not even Brigit will believe this." Nik scrubbed his face with his hands, "Is that what I think I saw?"

"I don't know what it is." The door had closed with a click behind them. Lucas shoved against it. This time it held fast. He peered at Nik and shook his head. "Did I die again?"

"Maybe we both did. Let's get out of here. If Alina was here as that creature said, at least she had the sense to get out of here."

Lucas reluctantly followed Nikolas as they retraced their steps. "I had a dream some time ago about my mother, in it, she said, *the lock is the key*. We got through this locked door just now. Recovered the trunks. Mine and Alina's, two trips to the country . . . Brigit was right about three trunks and two in water. But . . ."

"There are no other locks," Nik said.

"No other locks to open." He sighed, rubbing his hands over his eyes. "Did you know there were still monks in there? I can't believe I didn't discover that before."

"Nobody, not even you, comes to this eerie place."

"I can think of no more locks to open." Lucas stopped, gazed toward the sea and then around at the overgrown hay grass. "Nik, wait. Don't you see. This is a moat. It's fed by the loch. Right there. This loch that the monks built."

Nik kept trudging. "I know it's a loch. It doesn't mean anything."

"My mother said the loch is the key."

"Your dream said that. . . no Lucas . . ."

But Lucas was already running back to the monastery. They plunged into the murky water again. "We're going to have to throw away our clothes," Nik protested.

"This is for Alina, Nik."

"We try again, then," Nikolas stepped in front of Lucas and went ahead to shove on the door. It wouldn't budge. They took turns shoving, banging, and shouting.

The orange sun dropped below the arch of the new cathedral and gleamed along the monastery walls. The door creaked open. The bony hand appeared and once again clutched Lucas' wrist. It placed into Lucas' palm an object wrapped in gold cloth. Then the door slammed shut. Lucas rammed against it and either his shoulder or the door cracked, he couldn't be sure.

"We have to cross the moat before dark," Nikolas said.

Chapter 18

The monks never spoke to Alina, but they fed her and gave her water in the day and wine at night. When she said she was ready to leave, they led her through cellar passageways that eventually opened up on the other side of the river, a short distance from the bridge that led into the City of Dreams. She'd had much time to think. Alina, draped in one of the monk's cloaks, made her way to her father's house. She could not trust Lucas to keep her safe after all.

Her father's house, her new home was as grand as their home in Ingleena. It was clean and well kept. The solicitor had mentioned he sent a maid inside from time to time to be sure the cobwebs didn't accumulate. On the desk in the study she found a ledger that contained the name and address of Daria. She waited a week before writing to her long-lost maid. It wasn't possible that she remain in the City of Dreams now. But if she were to leave and never return, she would need assistance. And only Daria could help her get back to Ingleena. Knowing Lucas' schedule was easy enough, but she hadn't anticipated such a diligent search party. Those first weeks, as soon as the market opened, she donned the monk's cloak and slipped out to buy bread and vegetables. She avoided the flower stall and kept her head down only pointing to what she needed. Sick with heartache she needed little food and only ventured out twice. Now, that Daria had arrived, she had no need to leave the house.

"Why don't you hide in the storeroom, and I will bring in another maid to pack the house?" Daria suggested.

Alina glanced up from her book and nodded, "I will. But not today."

"What are you waiting for? Lucas is a lout. If you continue to tarry, he will discover you. Is that what you want?"

"Please Daria, I am so happy to have you with me. Can't we just read and talk as we used to? I will not be discovered. I haven't stepped outside in all these weeks since your arrival."

"You grow pale. And your eyes are swollen from crying. It's best to be done with this wretched city."

"My father left this house for me."

"It wouldn't be his first mistake, after all," Daria sniffed indignantly.

Alina set her book down. "My head aches. I'll have a nap. Go out if you like."

Daria peeked through the curtain. "Perhaps, I will."

"Did I see a gentleman walking you home a few nights ago?" Alina prodded.

"No! You didn't. It must have been someone else. I walked home alone."

As Alina climbed the stairs to her splendid bed chamber, she thought about Lucas descending the stairs after his bath in the evening. Would he ever stop searching for her? It wasn't fair not to speak with him and explain that she felt differently now. Dugald had frightened her so that her heart had gone empty. At first, she thought that Lucas would find her spilled basket on the street and come for her. But the basket was new, and urchins would have had her food and flowers in mere minutes. He may not even know it was Dugald who draped her over his shoulder like a lamb for slaughter. If she went to him and spoke to him, he would never let her go. It didn't take Daria to convince her of that. And not only that, she doubted her ability to resist him even though he had failed to keep her safe. But there was no house to go back to in Ingleena. The creditors had taken it, Daria assured her. She could do as Daria suggested and let the solicitor sell this home. There was enough money in the locker to return to Ingleena right away. She curled up on her bed. It's best to go before I become attached to this room and this house. I will become a prisoner here. In the morning I will tell Daria to book passage on the next ship.

* * *

While the women waited in the kitchen, Lucas and Nikolas removed their clothes in front of the fire in the parlour and tossed them in. The moment they came through the door dripping with slime, Irene and Brigit had scrambled to gather fresh clothes for them.

"Should we tell them about the monk?" Nik asked.

"I don't know. Let's see what's in this package first."

On the mantle waited the package from the cloaked monk at the monastery. Lucas sat down and placed the package in his lap.

"Careful," Nik warned.

Lucas took a deep breath. "It probably can't hurt me."

"Not here in the City of Dreams, or Arcana," Nikolas agreed.

Lucas slowly unwrapped the folds of cloth. There, sparkling in his hand sat the gold-jewelled box. It was warm and cool at the same time. The gems were more radiant than he remembered. "This is it!"

"That's magnificent!"

"It's more precious than I thought!"

"You've seen it before?"

"Yes, at Madam Trousdale's cottage. Surely, you've seen this Nik. Didn't Brigit show it to you?"

"I've never seen that stunning object before!"

The women streamed out of the kitchen. "What's all the commotion?" Irene asked.

"I have your golden box here," Lucas said to Brigit.

Her eyes spun through their color shifting and her hair flew straight up for a few seconds before spiraling down around her face. She brushed it aside before asking, "Are you presenting that to me?"

"No . . . well yes or no. Didn't I see this in your cottage that first day and then on that evening?"

"That is not my golden box. I've never seen it before. It is marvelous!" She reached for it and ran her fingers admiringly over the gemstones.

"It sat on top of the wardrobe in your cottage." Lucas scoffed.

"Believe me if that was in my cottage, I would know about it!"

He turned it over in his hand then opened the lid. Inside a miniature rolled painting. Slowly spreading it open on his thigh, he began to recognize it as the other half of the painting from his mother's trunk. Another woman stood in the flower field. The painting slipped from his hand and Brigit snatched it up. The color drained from her face. The hourglass popped out of her blouse. It was full. Lucas grabbed her wrist and took the painting from her.

"What's going on," Irene stumbled toward a chair.

Clutching the small painting in his hand Lucas headed toward the stairs. "I'll be right back."

He retrieved the other half of the painting from his mother's trunk. Back downstairs sitting on the hearth, he spread out the two pieces and put them together. It was several moments before he realized Brigit stood behind him, peering over his shoulder.

"This is my mother," he said. And this one from the trunk, that is you."

Her eyes and hair went completely black. "Where did you get this?"

"From the monastery," Nikolas cried.

Lucas shook his head. "A monk, they are still there. Three of them. But we only saw one. He said Alina was there but left on her own. He gave this box to me. This box was in your cottage, Brigit."

"If it was in my cottage, it was a sign for only you to see."

"No wonder I was drawn to this jewelled box, a piece of my heart rests here. I have never forgotten my mother's face. But long I have missed it. Now the portrait is complete. And now I see, I don't know why I didn't before, maybe because you kept changing. Now, I realize this other woman in the portrait is you."

"That is my sister and me, Lucas."

"Why didn't you tell me?"

"I didn't know. She ran away only a few days after this was painted. Our parents were gypsies. We roamed from place to place. We met travelers, traders, artists, scribes. Linny grew tired of it and ran away. I never saw her again."

Irene gulped repeatedly and fanned herself with a handkerchief. Nikolas called for Carissa to bring wine and bread.

Lucas gazed at Brigit. "Are we kin?" he smirked and shook his head.

She inhaled, her eyes brimmed with tears. "I have been drawn to you. But I don't know."

"You have the gift of seeing, why don't you know?"

"We all have gifts, don't we, Lucas? Sometimes they benefit us, but not always. Anyway, you hide yourself quite well."

Lucas flushed. She was right. Ever since that day in childhood when his soul was torn asunder, Lucas kept separate from the world in which he walked. He resolved himself to remain on the outside looking in, not only at others but at himself as well. After all, one step closer would surely send him spiraling into the dark abyss. And it had.

Perina came out of Dugald's room carrying an empty tray. "Lucas, sir, he says to thank you for not killing him."

Lucas laughed, "Why does he keep saying that? I intend to kill him if we don't find Alina." Only Nik caught his eye and nodded. The women gazed into the fire or at the floor. Lucas sat down, rolled up the little paintings and replaced them in the golden box that he set back on the mantle.

"Are you going to leave that there?" Nik asked with alarm in his voice.

Lucas shook his head. "I'll put it away. Don't worry."

The front door banged open. Brigit flew across the room, grabbed the golden box, and shoved it into the sideboard.

Bernard and Wentworth stepped inside. Lucas leapt up.

"Alina did not return to Ingleena," Wentworth said.

Lucas had his hands on his hips, but his shoulders slumped. "How many days did you spend searching?"

"Three full days," Bernard answered. "Many know of her and her father. Friends and business acquaintances that she would seek out if she returned. Everyone assured us, Alina did not arrive on any ship. She is not in Ingleena."

Fidgeting, Wentworth waited for Bernard to finish. "But just now, as we arrived, Mr. Merson warned us that Campbell Barrington was spotted on the Boulevard late last night by one of the cottage dwellers."

Lucas glanced at Trousdale. The hourglass drained. She slipped it back inside her blouse. "Damn that thing," he muttered.

"Is anyone hungry?" Irene pushed herself up from the chair and crossed the room to the kitchen. Bernard and Wentworth followed, as did Nikolas and Brigit.

"I'm not hungry," Lucas said to the empty room. He stood in the doorway of the kitchen and watched them assemble themselves around the table. "Did you give dresses to Alina?"

Brigit flicked her eyes. The others mumbled quietly among themselves. "Were they your dresses or my mother's?"

"As I recall, one was mine. And one or two belonged to Linny."

"Is that what you called her?"

"It is. Come and sit down, Lucas. You and I will find time to tell each other our stories about your mother."

"Where would the daughters of gypsies get gowns like that?"

"Stolen of course." She gestured for him to sit down.

Lucas grimaced and took his place at the end of the table. "I'm not hungry though," he told Irene when she set a bowl in front of him. He broke off a chunk of bread and dipped it in the stew. "So, Bernard and Wentworth, tell me about Ingleena. I fear I will never see the place."

After they ate, Lucas and Nikolas headed out to the harbour. They would talk to Mr. Merson and find out exactly which of the cottage dwellers had reported the sighting of Barrington. He was well known at the harbour after his drunken antics with Vasil.

After the harbour they planned to scour the Boulevard "We have to scrutinize every single person we see. Especially those in cloaks and hoods." Lucas said.

"Good thinking. Even the monks skulk around in them."

After getting a thorough description from a young cottage dweller with a severe limp, and paying him more coins than necessary, Lucas and Nik went to the Boulevard. They walked up and down the street and through the back lanes until both men began to stagger. Lucas hadn't slept since his six days in Nik's room. "I wish we could knock on every door and demand to be let inside." Lucas grumbled.

They walked home before dawn. Lucas noticed that Ikarus and his new helper were doing a respectable job with the lanterns. He wondered if he would ever feel that sense of freedom again. And what about Alina? If she was still alive, how different would she be, her precious innocence destroyed?

* * *

Alina spent the day packing the new trunks that Daria had brought her. She wondered what Lucas would do with her trunks. Would he someday find the secret compartment and the bank notes there? She hoped he would. Maybe she would send him a letter and tell him about that, but even as she thought it, she knew she wouldn't. Then she would have to admit her father had given her a house right on the Boulevard where Lucas hoped for them to live. No, once she left, she would never come back or send a letter. Daria would sell the house quickly and join her in Ingleena. The City of Dreams would vanish from her mind like a dream dissipates within minutes of awakening.

By evening, Daria returned and told her that the meeting with the solicitor had gone well. He accepted the letter Alina had written and secured with the family seal. And she had purchased passage for Alina to return to Ingleena the day after tomorrow. While Daria worked in the kitchen, Alina peeked from behind the curtains. She saw Ikarus come down the Boulevard whistling as he lit the lamps. He swaggered with confidence now. Her heart fluttered as her hand quivered. She nearly tapped on the window to get his attention. But she let the curtain drop, buried her face in her palms and wept.

Daria came in and rubbed her back until the tears subsided. She handed Alina a fat glass of whisky. "Come, let's get some food in your stomach." After a quiet dinner in the large dining room, Daria retired to her room leaving Alina to sit beside the fire alone with a book. She almost felt like she was at home with Father again. It was nearly midnight when she finally went up to bed. Daria had turned down the bed and tied the curtains closed. It didn't matter, Alina had no desire to look out the window again.

Sometime during the night, she thought she heard voices. She rolled over and pulled the coverlet over her head. In a little while her feet turned cold and she had to get up and use the chamber pot. She distinctly heard a door closing. Tiptoeing down the hall to Daria's room she tried the latch, but the door was locked. "Daria," she tapped on the door. There were sounds coming from behind the door. Even though she had never actually heard it before, she recognized the unmistakable sounds that come when a man lies with a woman. Alina turned and fled back to her own room, bolted the door, and covered her head.

After a night filled with twisted dreams, Alina awoke to the sound of birds chirping. She thought of Lucas, how he always noticed birds, flowers, buds on the trees and expressions on people's faces. He noticed things, that most people couldn't be bothered with. She donned her dressing robe and scurried down the hall to Daria's room. Her door was open. The bed in order. In the kitchen she found Daria preparing the morning meal. "Who was in your room last night, Daria? I have not given you permission to bring a man in to my home!"

Daria turned to her with an expression of disgust, "What are you saying? There was no man in my room, Alina! How can you say such a thing to me?"

Alina crossed her arms over her chest. "I heard you. The door was locked. I know what I heard, Daria."

"How could you know?" I, myself, cannot imagine the sound of what you accuse me of. It's just as well that you leave tomorrow. Your imagination is making you sick."

Alina bit her lip. "Are you saying I dreamed it?"

Daria smirked, "Well, this is the city of nightmares, isn't it? Sit down. Eat. It will be over soon."

Alina poked at her food. Daria tried to make conversation about Ingleena and all the wonderful times they would have there. "I will come to Ingleena in no more than a week or two and if you haven't' found a new home for us yet, we will find it together. It will be like old times, you'll see."

"Except for Father. He won't be there."

Daria handed her a cup of tea. "Take this to your room and rest. The voyage home will be tiring."

Alina was all packed and ready to go. She drank the tea and climbed back into her bed. She didn't hear the knock at the front door.

"I'm looking for a young lady," Nikolas said.

"You found one. And who are you?" she fluttered her lashes. "Come in then."

Daria opened the door and gestured that he step inside.

Nikolas stepped in and looked around. "There is a young lady missing."

"There is no missing young lady here. My master and mistress are out walking at the moment, but they will return soon. Would you like to wait by the fire?"

Nikolas glanced around the well-kept room. He'd never been inside any house on the Boulevard and today he'd been allowed inside three. "No, I don't have time to wait. But if you hear of a young lady in distress please send word to the Kempel Boarding House. Her name is Alina. And we are also seeking the villain, Campbell Barrington. He is medium height, dark hair swept back. Walks with a swagger. Wears fine clothes. He appears as a gentleman, but I warn you he is not. He is a criminal of the worst sort."

"Are you sure you wouldn't like a glass of wine? All this searching must be wearing."

Nikolas scowled and shook his head. "No. I have to continue."

Daria curtsied and thanked Nikolas for the warning.

Back out on the Boulevard he met up with Lucas who appeared more haggard every day. His face was pale as it had been ever since the incident on the ship. He shook his head when he saw Nikolas. "We will go back to the monastery in the morning. Alina must still be in there."

* * *

Just after dawn, Alina, and Daria, wearing their hooded cloaks, made their way to the harbour.

The city solicitor knocked on the door of the boarding house. Lucas dressed in old clothes for crossing the moat opened the door.

"Good morning, Lucas. I am bound to keep the counsel of my clients, but there is something I believe you should know. There is a young woman named Daria who has brought me a letter from Alina Sutcliffe stating that she has power of authority over her estate."

Lucas' eyes nearly burst from his head. "When? Where?"

"I have the address for the home on the Boulevard that Louis Sutcliffe left for his daughter."

"Let's go!" Lucas rushed out the door, followed by the solicitor and Nikolas who was coming downstairs, struggling to get his arm into his sleeve.

"I was just here yesterday," Nik said as they went up the steps. They knocked and knocked to no avail. Finally going around back, Lucas climbed up to the kitchen window and hammered on it with the handle of his dagger. The glass shattered and sliced his wrist as he reached in breaking more away before crawling through. He unlocked the door for Nikolas.

The solicitor had hurried off when he saw what Lucas was doing. They crept silently through the house, looking in wardrobes, behind curtains and under the bed in the master bedroom. At the end of the hallway they came to a locked door. The two men hammered against it. Lucas shoved his blade into the lock, twisting and prying until it sprang open. There, perched on the bed like a farm chicken was Campbell Barrington.

"Uh oh," he said.

Lucas pounced on him and began pummeling him with his fists.

"Wait, Lucas, wait. Don't kill him."

Lucas hesitated, "Where's Alina?"

"On a ship," Barrington croaked.

Lucas punched him again and he fell backward onto the bed. "Deal with him, Nik."

Lucas had never run so fast in his life, not even when he was being chased by authorities as a boy. He saw a flash of gray and nearly tripped over it. The gray cat was streaking along beside him. The blood from his wrist flew into the wind so that when he reached the harbour there was no sign of it. There was a crowd of wharf lads gathered by the gangway. Mr. Merson had a tight grip on the arms of two cloaked figures. If it's that monk, I'll choke him on the spot, Lucas thought. He pushed through the crowd. "Who are they?" Lucas yanked the cloak from the tallest one. Alina threw up her hands and burst into tears.

"Alina!" He grabbed her and wrapped his arms around her. She sobbed against his chest and crumpled in his arms. He lifted her like a baby and shoved his way through the crowd. Glancing back over his shoulder, he shouted to the harbour master. "Turn over that one to the constable."

"I'm sorry, Alina. I'm sorry."

"You can put me down. I can walk," she sniffled.

"No. I won't let you go again. You're hard to hold on to."

She buried her head in his chest sobbing and giggling at the same time. A crowd of citizens followed them all the way to the boarding house.

Just as he approached the door, Irene opened it. "Lucas, I could hear . . . oh my good lord. It's Alina."

Lucas expelled a breath as he carried her straight up the stairs to his room.

"Is she all right? I'll bring something," Irene called up after them.

He kicked open his door and set her on the bed, keeping one firm hand on her shoulder. "Alina forgive me."

"I was so scared," she sobbed.

Irene appeared in the doorway holding a quilt. "What happened to her, where's she been all this time?"

Lucas went to her, took the quilt, and whispered, "Make sure Dugald is tied up tightly."

He cradled Alina in his arms. Tears poured down their cheeks, mingling as they sat entwined, gazing into each other's eyes, ultimately lying down and stretching out side by side under the thick quilt. Soon, they slept.

* * *

As Nikolas marched Barrington with his wrists tied behind his back to the constable, Bernard found him. "The city is buzzing with joy. Lucas has her home."

"At last." Nikolas hung his head, then gazed up at Bernard. "I didn't think he would survive much longer."

"Me either. Nothing like love to drain the life from you."

Barrington ranted like a fool. "It was the girl's idea. Daria said we could take the house, that Alina was so wealthy that she wouldn't even notice."

"How did you make your way here from the country," Bernard demanded.

"I walked most of the way. Your henchmen are easy to evade. I paid a farmer to ride me in."

"Paid him with what?"

"A promise." Barrington derided. "Daria found me as she landed here in the city. I intended to go to Ingleena. I would have boarded the very ship she came in on. She talked me into staying. This plan was all hers."

"Shut up, fool," Nikolas commanded. "You're both going to prison."

After depositing Barrington with the constable, who already had Daria locked up and was questioning her, Bernard and

Nikolas went to the harbour and retrieved Alina's new trunks, just before they got loaded on the ship to Ingleena.

"We spend a lot of time hauling baggage around," Nikolas remarked. From there, they stopped off at the Blue Gate and sat outside atop the trunks for a meal and a couple of tankards.

* * *

When Lucas awoke, Alina was stroking his hair. He cupped her hand in his. "Did you run away from me, Alina?"

"Dugald snatched me."

"Yes, but you got away from him, my brave lass."

Her eyes filled. "I did."

"I didn't know that Dugald escaped."

"It's my own fault," she said half smiling. "I had to go shopping. And I wanted to bring flowers to Madam Van Dessen. I still have it."

"Have what?"

"Your gift, Lucas. Oh no! My trunks they are at the harbour." She pouted. "My new trunks."

"Don't worry. Nik will get them."

"How do you know? He won't know I have them there."

"Yes, he will." He brushed her hair away from her face and kissed her softly on the lips. "Silly little girl. I need no gifts. You are the most precious of all the treasures in the world."

"Lucas," she cooed as she threw her arms around his neck.

"Did Dugald hurt you?"

"Only by grabbing my hair. I lost my hair pin."

"I'll buy you a dozen hair pins."

She snuggled against him. "I don't need them. I enjoy these things, but they don't matter. Loved ones are what's important."

Lucas stroked her cheek. "Did you forget that I love you?"

"I was furious with you."

"I doubt you could have been as furious as I was with myself."

"I'm sorry I fled, Lucas. I didn't feel safe after Dugald grabbed me. And I did blame you. But it's not your fault. I have never experienced the frightening parts of life."

"It's up to me to protect you. Once I found you, I felt as if our love created a barrier against evil. I should have known better."

"You couldn't have known, Lucas. I think Daria tricked me. She has a suitor."

"She had Campbell Barrington in her room at your father's house."

"What? Oh no! How could she?" Her bottom lip trembled. "I have a house on the Boulevard."

"I know, the solicitor came to me this morning. When you are ready, you can show me your house. Well, I've seen it briefly. There's a window that needs repair."

"Were they conspiring against me, Lucas?"

"It seems so. We will sort it all out. They are locked up. No one can hurt you now. At least no one that I know of. I intend to keep trying to protect you."

She kissed his cheek.

"That is if you will let me. Please don't run away from me, Alina."

She snuggled into him. "Please don't doubt that I love you," she whispered.

When Alina fell asleep again, Lucas wrapped her in the comfort of his bed and went downstairs. Everyone waited in the parlour. They had already celebrated with wine. Bernard and Nikolas followed him to Dugald's room.

The only ship in port had just tossed its lines. When Lucas walked up and shouted to the Captain, the man turned away, but Nikolas grabbed the thick rope and swung it around the large cleat. The three of them pulled the ship back to the mooring.

Holding Dugald up, Lucas bargained, "He is not contagious. Take him and my pocketful of coins are yours." For several long moments nobody moved. Dugald stirred, lifted his head, and waved his good hand. The plank came down and three rats fell off into the water.

Gazing down at Dugald, Lucas whispered, "Shine your own light."

"What?"

"Go forth and walk your own path. Then the rats cannot devour you." He slipped three gold coins inside Dugald's bandage. "No one will steal from there."

Dugald stared up at Lucas through pale blue eyes round with surprise. "It's true, everything that they say about you. You found her? She is . . ."

"Safe. My lady is safe, as am I. There was never any land for you, Dugald."

"I'm a fool."

"Marion is dead."

Dugald blinked. "There's no reason to go back."

"No."

"What ship? Where bound?"

"It doesn't matter," Lucas murmured.

Two skinny young lads gingerly gathered Dugald between them. Lucas reached into his pocket for the satchel of coins. He tossed the sack to the Captain. "Treat him well."

The three friends turned and walked away without looking back.

Wentworth dozed by the fire. Brigit sat outside in the garden. Bernard and Nikolas went through to the kitchen to join Irene, Carissa and Perina.

Lucas stepped into the candle-lit garden and took a seat on the bench across from Brigit. "So, who is this mysterious being lurking around the monastery with a painting of my mother, and you, inside the gold-jewelled box?"

Brigit tilted her head and twisted her upper lip. "Your father?"

His eyes grew wide, the reflection of flame burning in them as he remembered the man's eyes. "How can that be? Is he who I saw in your crystal ball?"

She glowered. "Is he?"

"It's possible, I suppose. If my mother had the portrait when she ran away, she must have kept your half and given her half to the mysterious . . ."

"Monk, at the monastery."

"A monk would explain why he couldn't marry her. Bernard told me that there was a cloaked entity that roamed the fields at dusk when I was a child."

Brigit remained silent but her hair and eyes created their display of colors.

"I have much to understand. What more can you tell me Brigit?"

She stroked her chin, "Maybe this explains something about your gifts, Lucas. Content yourself to know that your mother lived a full and happy life, as short as it was." Her hair wisped in a spiral then fell.

"Why did she and I end up in Arcana alone?"

"Are you sure you were alone?"

The gray cat landed silently atop the garden wall. It sprang onto the edge of the fountain where it took a drink before settling itself among the plants.

"What is going on with you and that cat?"

"What is going on with *you* and that cat?" Brigit shook her head into a shimmering black waterfall. The cat flicked its tail and yawned.

"Answers can be more baffling than questions." He pressed his palms against his thighs and stood up. The hourglass hung in plain sight. He reached over and clasped it as it dangled from her neck. It was full. He turned it over and it remained full. "Someday soon I will return to the monastery and speak to the monk. I have questions for him."

He took the gold-jewelled box from the sideboard and climbed the stairs to his room. One of the women had left a basket outside his door with dried meat, cheese, bread, and wine. Alina was sitting up in bed gazing into the fire. He set the gold box above the fireplace and placed the basket on the bed. "Let's have a picnic."

She giggled and held up a cup for him to pour the wine. "Ikarus is lighting all the lanterns now, I noticed."

"Yes, he and another lad who I have yet to meet. They are managing it." Taking a seat beside her on the bed, "Tell me Alina, what do you remember about the monastery?"

"Oh yes, there are monks in there after all. They were truly kind. They didn't speak but they served me food and provided blankets. There's another way out as well. A tunnel leads out onto the road that goes to Arcana."

Lucas smiled and closed his eyes. "Extraordinary." He squeezed Alina's hand. "We have stories to tell each other and plenty of time to do so. I won't rush you. But one thing is most important now," he stroked her hair, curled it around his fingers. "I . . . before everything changed . . . I was designing a ring for you. Would you like it if we did this together, Alina?"

She reached over and wrapped her arms around his neck spilling her wine down his back. They tumbled off the bed onto the thick rug in front of the blazing fire.

The End

Glossary of Names

Alina: Graceful and Noble

Arcana, the Country Town: A deep secret, a mystery

Bernard: Bear

Bridgette: Celtic Goddess of Fire

Campbell: Twisted Mouth

Carissa: Grace

Daria: Trustworthy person

Dugald: Dark Stranger

Ikarus: To have come to be present

Igmus: Unlearned

Irene: Peace

Linnea: Flower

Lucas: Light Giving

Marion: Rebellious

Nikolas: People's Triumph

Ragbone: Rag gatherer, bone picker

Vasil: Imperial

Wentworth: From a farm near woods

About the Author

Suzanne Burkett lives in Incline Village, Nevada with her family. As well as writing, she enjoys skiing, hiking, and mountain biking.

Her books: *How to Get Along with Yourself and Others*, and *Life is a Piece of Pie in Your Eye* are available in print and on Kindle.

Love Poems, Journey of the Raindrop and *Still Waters* are available on Kindle.

City of Dreams is her first novel. *Hidden Beneath,* the sequel is available now.

Wearing an oversized hooded cloak, the locksmith strolled along the crowded street as if he had no place to go. A man of such desirable skills, he did his best to keep his identity secret when among the public. Stepping deftly sideways, he stopped in front of the door. Slipping one rust-stained hand from inside his cloak and clutching his heavy satchel with the other, he lifted the triangular rapper hanging below the lion head and then let if fall. Inclining his head, he bent and listened as the key engaged the gear, the cylinder turned, and the door opened.

"I didn't call for you," Irene declared.

Pushing the heavy door fully open, Lucas placed his hand on Irene's shoulder and said, "I did."

"Whatever for?" Irene protested.

Lucas briefly closed his eyes, leaned over, and whispered in Irene's ear. "I want even more security." Beckoning the locksmith, Gacheru, to come through, he led Irene back toward the kitchen.

She stood in front of the simmering iron pot with her hands planted firmly on her hips, a stern but amused scowl on her face. "When did you decide to lock her in?"

"I'm not locking her in." Lucas swung around to nod to Gacheru to get on with his work. "I'm locking them out."

"Who? Our boarders?"

"No, no of course not. They now come in from the back door anyway."

"They do?"

"Um hmm," Lucas glanced around the kitchen and grabbed a chunk of bread from the sideboard.

"Since when?" She tapped her foot and coughed to cover a chuckle.

"Well, as you know, Irene, at the present time, all of our boarders are laborers and masons and the like, those working on the cathedral. They come through the back door. That's what they prefer. None of them are parlour sitters."

"So, you're changing a perfectly good lock to . . .?"

"No, I'm adding another lock to the lock that is already in place."

Irene shook her head, unwound her morning shawl, tossed it onto a ladderback chair, and picked up the iron kettle. "On the back door as well?" she took a seat with her cup of tea.

He nodded.

"I thought we were safe from Barrington and Dugald and their kind now. They're all dead, jailed, or banished. Is that not correct?"

"It's correct." Lucas braced his arms in the doorway and kept his eye on the locksmith.

"Does Alina know you're locking her in?"

"I'm not!"

Irene burst out laughing and spit her tea across the table. "That lass will be climbing out the window or going through the courtyard and over the garden wall. You can't lock her in."

"I have new locks for the courtyard doors and windows as well." He nodded and left her at the table as he went to oversee the locksmith.

She called after him, "Make sure I have a key to all these locks. And Carissa and Perina too. And Madam Trousdale and Nikolas, of course. And Ikarus and all the boarders. Oh, and don't forget Alina. She should have a key too lest you lock her out."

Lucas raked his hands through his hair as he swaggered back into the parlour. Gacheru had strayed into the courtyard where he stood at the threshold aimlessly opening and closing the garden door, his eyes fixated on the assortment of herbs and plants that sat on shelves and ledges. Their fine tendrils dangling like emerald filigree swayed slightly by a phantom breeze.

"What are you doing?" Lucas demanded.

"Oh, uh . . . you mentioned the courtyard door. Wall is tall . . ." His gaze drifted from the garden wall to stare blankly at Lucas.

Lucas moved closer. "I instructed you to begin with the front door."

"Just me thinking, Gacheru shifted his gaze from Lucas to scan the parlour. He leaned left to peer into the kitchen before turning his attention back to the copious assortment of greenery.

"Have you never seen plants before?"

Gacheru shook his head while mumbling incoherently. He hobbled back to the front door and rummaged through his satchel, dropping implements on the floor as he searched.

"Never mind. Forget about it," Lucas growled. "Collect your junk and get out of here." He opened the door and shoved the fumbling buffoon and his tangle of tools outside. After closing and locking the door, he glanced up the stairs and then retreated to the garden bench that had become his refuge. Since her return to the boarding house a week ago, Alina had not yet come downstairs.